John Grant spent about a dozen years in publishing before, in 1980, becoming a full-time writer and free-lance editor. Since then he has written over twenty books under his own name and ghosted more; his articles, short stories and reviews have appeared in various magazines, anthologies and reference works.

Albion

John Grant

First published in 1991
by HEADLINE BOOK PUBLISHING PLC

First published in paperback in 1992
by HEADLINE BOOK PUBLISHING PLC

A HEADLINE FEATURE paperback

10 9 8 7 6 5 4 3 2

ISBN 0 7472 3593 7

Phototypeset by Intype, London

Printed and bound in Great Britain by
HarperCollins Manufacturing, Glasgow

HEADLINE BOOK PUBLISHING PLC
Headline House
79 Great Titchfield Street
London W1P 7FN

Catherine: this novel is definitely yours and yours alone, because you kept faith in it from the time when it was hardly more than a gleam in my eye.

It's nice, for the first time, to put this on the dedication page rather than tuck it away among the acknowledgements:

$$4\pi + 0 \to \infty$$

Acknowledgements

Countless people have, often without realising it, contributed to this novel: listing them would be virtually to reproduce all the names in my address book. Specific thanks, however, to Catherine Barnett, Jane Barnett, David Barrett, Paul Cockburn, Joe Dever, Mary Gentle, Howard Harrison (and Mina's nose-flute), Penelope Isaac, John Jarrold, Jane Judd, Linda Mallory, Val Maund, Caroline Oakley, Liz Sourbut, Rory Stewart (and Rehan's bodhran), Ron Tiner, Colin Wilson and especially Fay Sampson. In addition, my gratitude to all who have helped me at Milfords and Blots and to the members of the Exeter University SF Group and the Coaver Club CC. In addition I'm indebted to the various musicians – from Byrd to Meatloaf *via* Orff, The Incredible String Band, Enya and most notably Savourna Stevenson (and Alyss's clarsach) – who painted in the backgrounds.

Contents

It should be stressed right at the outset that there is by no means unanimous agreement among physicists, let alone philosophers, either on the nature or existence of reality, or even its very meaningfulness . . .

Paul Davies, *Other Worlds*, 1980

Prologue

. . . And they were *touching* her. There were people on either side, pressing in on her, shoving against her arms. The touch was more than she could bear. The intrusion seemed somehow a more grievous thing than the sight of her lover spreadeagled on the hard wooden cross that had been erected on the platform that reared high above the gossiping crowd. She wanted to be away from here – she had no wish to watch Lian suffer. And yet at the same time she knew she *had* to be here, that to leave him now would be the ultimate desertion.

His eyes would have tried to seek her out in the crowd, but he no longer had eyes. His mouth was curled into a soft smile – deliberately designed, she knew (she who knew him so well), to torment his tormentors. *The pain you are inflicting*, his smile was telling them, *is nothing to me. I've suffered pain before. It's like an old friend to me. Of course it hurts, but once you've accepted that fact there's no more it can do to you*.

Far away there was a snap as one of the flags caught the wind. She looked up and saw it whip against the sky again. She knew the emblem well: a dog skewered by a sword, the image executed in reds and greens. Blood flowed from the dog's mouth as it twisted on the blade. The sign of the Ellonia – the sign she detested. Lian – He Who Leads – was being killed because he had dared to doubt the eternal rule of the Ellonia. His father had come from who knew where, yet she had loved Lian as best she was able – better

1

than she had loved any other man. She pulled her grey-brown woollen hooded cardigan closer about her shoulders, thinking of the past. There was little enough time left to her to think of it.

Lian screamed briefly as a torturer castrated him and then held the sad, bleeding little sack forward from the platform, so that the crowd could see it. The sight affected her not at all.

She was in Ernestrad for the first time in her life. Two years ago, Lian had told her that one day they would come to Ernestrad in triumph, riding side by side on white mares, to accept from a loving people the right to govern Albion. Lying in his arms, the two of them warm under furs, she had shared his vision; she had kissed the tip of his nose and told him to get some sleep because the waking-period was not very far away. He had fumbled his way down beneath the furs until his beard was tickling the space between her breasts, and then he had fallen asleep. As he had snored peacefully, she had looked up at the brilliantly blue sky. She had felt then that her lover was doomed – that one day he would die on the scaffold. But at the same time she had wanted him to carry on, to raise his army so that he could battle with the Ellonia and, perhaps, bring mercy to Albion.

The mob moved around her. A man dressed in mud-green leather jacket and leggings bumped against her and apologised. He glanced at her for just a moment, and then turned his attention again to the mutilated figure of He Who Leads, splayed, bleeding now in many places. 'We love you, Lian,' yelled the man.

She acknowledged his courage. Some of the guards had heard him and frowned at the crowd, but they couldn't identify the person who had shouted and soon lost interest.

If you knew that I was here, she thought, *you would cut your way through all these living bodies . . .*

They were crammed in their thousands into the court-yard of Giorran, the palace of the Ellonia at Ernestrad. Behind them was the palace's great gate: set in walls a metre thick, it was ten metres high yet could be closed with crushing finality in a second. Its two doors were made of shining metal; they had been forged in an earlier time that no one, not even the Ellonia, could remember. On either side of her were tall white walls – so white that they hurt the eyes – punctuated by rectangular black windows. *The windows*, she thought, *are rather like the sockets where Lian's eyes used to be*. The walls seemed to stretch for an infinite distance up towards the sky. She knew that petty princes and princesses of the Ellonia were looking through the gaping windows at the torment of Lian, thrilling themselves at each new agony, and beneath her breath she cursed them. Behind the platform was a blank wall of silvery-white marble across which spread the brown stains left from previous executions.

Another spurt of blood from Lian as his left foot was chopped off with a sword. One of the torturers held the foot up to the mob, but his smirk was less certain now. His eyes, like those of his fellows, were masked to indicate that he showed neither favour nor malice towards those who suffered under his instruments of torment, but it was plain from his stance that he was being made restless by the restlessness of the crowd. Tentatively he threw the foot at the people – those people who had so often in the past howled their approval of such actions – and heard them shriek as they moved away, opening up a space to let the foot fall slappingly onto the marble paving of the courtyard. Blood still leaked from its severed ankle.

Lian's blind face was smiling still.

Another torturer smashed out Lian's front teeth with a hammer, so that the smile was covered with blood. The crowd in the courtyard became very still. The only sound was the cry of a curlew overhead as it wheeled and circled, perplexed by the activities of the people below. Eventually it flew off towards the purple-painted clouds, leaving behind it a hoarse cry of bewilderment.

Now, she thought, *now is the time that I* must *leave*.

She struggled to work her way back through the throng, doing her best to look anonymous. Some of these people might recognise her if they saw her face clearly under the

3

shadows cast by her woollen hood. She was curiously cold
about the death of Lian, her lover, He Who Leads – He
Who Has Led . . . It was as if someone had told her that
all of this was nothing but play-acting, that He Who Leads
would come out at the end of the performance to take a
bow and reassure his admiring audience that it had been
only a charade.

The mob howled its misery as one of the torturers peeled
away Lian's nose with a sharp knife.

I ought to be feeling *something*, she thought. *I ought to
be in misery, sharing his pain, wanting to be up there in his
place. But all I have is a coldness in me . . .*

Men, women and children looked resentfully at her as
she shouldered them aside. She was relieved: that meant
they didn't recognise her. Time and again she reached up
her sinewed hands to pull her hood closer about her face.
In the crowd there were hundreds of other women wearing
knitted hoods, so there was no reason why she should seem
in any way remarkable, yet it would take only a word from
one of these people to encourage the Ellonian Guard to
swoop down on her – perhaps to put her to the same torture
to which they were now putting He Who Leads.

The smell of the crowd was overwhelming, the mixed
odours of unwashed bodies and stale furs. Some of the
throng had brought their beasts with them – sheep and
goats and even a few cows – and those acerbic animal scents
too assaulted her nostrils. As she pushed her way among
the people and animals it seemed as if the brightness of the
sky were being turned muddy by the dun colours of the
clothes milling all around her.

And yet these men, women and children had *loved* Lian.
Some of them bore the scars of wounds they had received
fighting on the battlefield with him against the Ellonia. As
she brushed past a lean-faced hunter she felt the emptiness
of his jerkin sleeve; perhaps she had struggled alongside
him once, perhaps she had even seen the savage glint of
the weapon that had severed his arm at the shoulder . . .
So why was she so afraid of him now – of him and of all
the others around her?

4

Lian screamed again. A torturer had branded his stomach with the insignia of the Ellonia, and another was moving forward with a white-hot knife, about to disembowel him.

An officer, sitting aloofly on horseback, turned his steed and trotted around the periphery of the crowd. She looked her hatred at him briefly. He didn't see her. The horse was a grey. Its head was held proudly, and its long, flax-like tail was upright at the root. It obeyed its master's bidding.

Dressed in gloriously rich embroidered reds and greens to signify his high rank, the officer tapped his horse on the shoulder, speaking softly but firmly into its ear, urging it to climb the wooden steps up to the platform where Lian was slowly, mercilessly, being put to death. The beast was obviously terrified of the climb, but the force of its rider's will pushed it upwards. Picking its way nervously, occasionally stumbling, its eyes moving in panic, it managed the ascent, so that soon the officer was high above the throng, looking one moment at the mutilated body of He Who Leads and the next out at the mass of upturned faces.

He threw off his iron helmet and tossed it behind him. It bounced a couple of times on the platform's blood-soaked boards and came to rest directly in front of Lian.

'See!' shouted the guard. Small white clouds speckled the shining sky behind him. His head was little more than a silhouette as she watched him speak. 'See what happens to those who attempt to defy the Ellonia!'

He gestured at the wreckage of Lian. The three torturers watched him, two of them grinning but the third beginning to look increasingly uneasy.

'You called him "He Who Leads"!' yelled the guard, reining in his horse, which was moving skittishly beneath him. 'Who can he lead now? If we were to let him leave here he would never be able to do anything more than hobble. And the only army he could lead would be an army of blind capons!'

The officer, alone, laughed at his joke. He drew out his sword and held it high above his head. The crowd was motionless.

She recognised him now: Nadar, the second most senior

5

officer in the Ellonian army. Once he had tried to rape her, but He Who Leads had beaten him viciously and then, with an ironic courtesy, ensured that he was returned safely to his home. No wonder the man was gloating over Lian's castration. Her face was completely concealed, but nevertheless she drew her hood still tighter about her.

A little boy near to her unbuttoned his shorts and began to urinate unconcernedly on the flagstones. The steaming water splashed the sandals of the people in front of him. She loved him briefly for it.

And yes, she loved – had loved – He Who Leads. Or Lian, as those close to him had called him. Lian, he of the golden mane. This mane had been shorn off earlier in the day, of course, as part of the ritual humiliation that had preceded the torture. Every sleeping-period for two years she had run her fingers through those curls, muttering drowsy endearments or growls of passion – sometimes both mixed together. She had fondled a thousand times that foolish little packet that the torturer had shown such glee in amputating: it meant nothing to her now, because it was no longer a part of Lian. Now it was just a grisly object that she would rather not look at.

'Shall he die or shall he live?' shouted Nadar, the wind whipping his cloak. A low mumble grew among the crowd. There were no real words, only muttered emotions.

Let him die, she thought. *He would never want to live the way he is now.*

She remembered running with him across a ploughed field, the two of them tripping and laughing, their feet being scratched by the sharp flints in the turned soil. That had been another blue-skied waking-period. The sentinels around their encampment had deliberately looked away. They had come to the soft green banks of a small river and plunged into its chilling waters. She had splashed him with a sweep of her hand, and he had retaliated. Later they had dragged each other up over the mud onto the grass, pulled away their soaked clothes, and made love as the sparrows watched.

And now I want him to die . . .

6

She pushed herself further and further back through the crowd. They were still, yet she could sense the energy building up inside them. Nadar's speech was almost enough to arouse them to revolt, but not quite. Had He Who Leads been among them, moving around, talking in his persuasive way, perhaps by now they would already have become another rough and ready army, yelling for the blood of the Ellonia, surging forwards to exact vengeance for the infinitely long time during which they had been trampled underfoot. But He Who Leads wasn't with them: instead, his tortured body was crucified as they looked on.

She could lead them, she knew, if she rallied them around her immediately, before all the life had ebbed from him. But she didn't know how to. Better to get away from here, to save her own life, to get back to her own home and look at her scribblings, to find something else she might do to destroy the Ellonia.

The writings would help her, if she ever found them again and if she were still able to read them.

The curlew had returned. Raucously crying, it circled the courtyard, looking for a good perch. Finally it found one on the cross, just above the left hand of He Who Leads. It trotted backwards and forwards, finding the ideal place to settle, and then eased down onto its belly.

She was right at the back of the stinking mass now. Behind her there was nothing but the open metal gates and a rumpled blanket of green slopes. All eyes were on Nadar as he swept his sword through the air, asking the mob what they wanted to see happen to Lian.

Then there was chaos.

She threw her back against one of the walls of the deep gateway as a troop of horsemen poured into the courtyard. They were dressed in all the colours she had ever dreamed of, their weaponry clattering and clashing; flecks of froth speckled back from the mouths of their steaming mounts. She felt as if she were being assaulted by sound as hoofs rattled across the cobbles; as the warriors shouted their defiance she let her head fall forwards so that her brown hair hung in front of her eyes. Tears obscured her vision, so that all the world was a blur.

She looked back into the courtyard. With difficulty she realised that the horsemen had slaughtered most of the attendant guards. One of the torturers – the one who had looked so uncertain earlier – had slit his own throat, his blood spurting over the edge of the platform and into the eyes of those of the crowd who had so eagerly fought to be at the front; clearly he had thought that this would be an easier death than any he might be granted by the mob. The other two raised their sharpened weapons.

Nadar continued his speech, despite the uproar.

'All who defy the Ellonia will come to this!' he shouted over the din. He gestured again towards He Who Leads, but his bright metal sword was rusting.

The intruders were now using their crossbows. One of the torturers took a bolt in the throat and collapsed in a fountain of blood; the crowd cheered as he died. The other attempted to plead with the attackers, claiming that he'd only been doing a job, and as his head spun off it seemed that he was still mouthing the words.

The guards at the far side of the gate didn't stop her. They were too busy watching what was happening and working out which side they ought to be on. Again she looked back through the gate into the courtyard, the scene in front of her looking as if it had been punctiliously framed up by some perfectionist artist. The mob was beginning to turn, looking for escape; the Despot's guards were dying, toppling from their horses as bolts took them.

She was delighted to see that Nadar was now on the ground and that his body looked like a pincushion. Even as she watched, more bolts stabbed into his corpse, throwing it about on the wooden planks, convulsing it wildly in a horrible mimicry of life.

Beyond Giorran's gate there was a gentle slope that ran down to a diseased-looking river. She propped her back up against the palace wall, and exalted at the way the cold water from the moss soaked up through her woollen skirt to scald her bottom with its iciness. She pulled her knees up almost to her breasts and clutched them with her arms, looking out over the valley, hearing the screams of the dying from the courtyard behind her: the muffling effect of the thick walls made the noise sound very distant. But she no longer cared about other people dying. The life of He Who Leads – Lian – was ebbing away. It wouldn't be long now before her memories of him would similarly fade . . . until such time as she could read the words she'd written down. She had only the next few minutes to spend revelling in the times she had had with him.

A little spider ran over her leg and onto the back of her right hand. She blew gently on it, and momentarily it pulled in its legs and stopped moving. The sky had become a complete translucent blue – all the clouds had vanished. She stopped looking at the spider and, after a short pause, it ran up her arm to seek sanctuary under the sleeve of her cardigan. She breathed out, feeling the roughness of the stones digging into her back.

It had all begun so very long ago, of course. Or, no, maybe it hadn't been that long. It was becoming so difficult to tell how long things had lasted.

She shook her head, trying to get rid of the dustiness in her mind.

She had first met He Who Leads two years ago – no, longer, it must have been three or more. Until then she'd lived hazily from one moment to the next – literally. She'd been a prostitute somewhere down near Qazor Harbour, touting around for any hirsute sailor that might take her. Yet it was all very odd, because she had a vague half-memory that, the waking-period before, she'd been an Ellonian princess, picking and choosing among the many admirably qualified suitors who came here to the palace. But that might have been a false memory, of course: maybe she'd been a prostitute for all her life. Yet she hadn't felt like a woman of broad experience . . . nor like a virgin, which the royal princesses were decreed to be.

Lian had discovered her on the docks. She'd been looking out over the river waters, watching the sunlight being scattered by the ripples and thinking about . . .

No, that wasn't the truth at all. Albion had no docks

where prostitutes could hang around, leaning against walls and taunting the passers-by with suggestions about their virility or lack of it. She'd been a princess. She'd been strolling in the forest one time when she'd . . .

But that memory seemed to belong to someone else. Was it not possible that she'd been the daughter of a merchant, a fat man who had traded furs and slaves around all of the known lands, himself remaining at home to watch the gold pour in?

And yet . . . And yet she had no clear remembrance of that, either. All she could really remember were the times she'd had with Lian, either just the two of them or riding beside him at the head of his army, the army that he'd raised among the peoples of Albion to challenge the ancient tyranny of the Ellonia. The sound of nervous horses and the slap of leather upon hide, the clashing of armour, much of it worn ill-fittingly by boys and girls too young to go to war but going to war nonetheless, and the gurgling wail of people dying at the end of her sword.

She shook her head, this time angrily. It was as if all she could see were images of blood. And yet she and Lian had shared many tender moments, times of tranquillity when the reality of Albion might have been a forever away.

The sun was a white-hot disc at the zenith. She veiled her eyes to look at it, ignoring the crescendo of sound from within the palace. A dark speck moving across the dazzling light was a high-flying bird, its destination unknown to her. She was too hot in her cardigan but she couldn't shuck it off because she was wearing too little underneath. Her grey canvas dress was riding up above her knees as she sat, but there was no one around to see, so she let it do what it wanted to.

Her knees . . .

Perhaps she had been the daughter of one of the Despot's concubines, a bastard child whom he declined to acknowledge? Or maybe . . . maybe somebody's wife?

Ah, yes, her knees . . .

She didn't know. That was the worst of it – the not knowing. The first thing that she felt she knew for certain

10

was the time when Lian picked her up as she stood on the docks . . . no, it had been the other way around: she'd picked him up. She'd been standing there, propped against the slated wall of a warehouse, smelling the spices stored inside, her skirt hitched up to show her knees – commercially her most significant asset – when his voice had spoken out of the shadows to her.

But that hadn't been the reality of it; surely not. She just couldn't imagine herself in the role of a common harlot.

She settled down so that she was almost lying, only her head supported by the stones, those knees exposed to the air just as they had been that long-ago time – she must have been exercising one of the privileges of her regality by exploring the dockland area of Qazor Harbour, her merchant father having given her his smiling approval.

And a voice had spoken: 'Tell me that you are not evil.'

She had said: 'I touch nothing, so I cannot be evil.'

She was a princess. She was of the Ellonia.

The voice had hissed at her again. 'There's no evil in touching.'

'Of course there is. But a nice evil.'

She was a whore . . .

'Forget this.'

'There's nothing to be forgotten,' she had said. And there wasn't – because until now she hadn't been able to remember anything.

'Oh, there's certainly a lot to be forgotten,' the voice sighed out of the silvery shade. 'There's more to be forgotten than you could believe . . .'

'Who *are* you?'

Was it the yell of a pestered harlot, or of an imperious aristocrat, or of a merchant's daughter, or of someone else entirely?

Had there never been any docks?

'Syor,' she said into the darkness. She had given away her name, and she didn't know to whom she had given it.

'My name is Lian,' he had said. 'You and I will have great joy before we die.'

One of the drunks coming out of the tavern near which

she'd been standing fell into the water and began to splash around. His friends watched him. They whooped their approval of his predicament. Eventually, when he must surely have been close to drowning, they scooped him up out of the river.

'What kind of a name is "Lian"?' she had said.

'The name I was given by my mother.'

There had seemed to be little answer to that, so she had kept her silence.

Now, with the warmth of the sun on her, she picked idly at an old scab on her calf.

She'd been in a village whose name she could no longer remember.

'It's because of my hair,' he had said.

Then he had come out into the light in front of her, so that she could see him properly. He was of no more than average height, but he was very stocky; standing there in the docks that had never existed except in the reality of her imaginings, a distance away from him, she could feel his weight. His blond hair rattled down over his shoulders. He was wearing a leather vest, short leather trousers and very little else except for a scabbard at his belt; the hilt of the sword was covered in fake jewels.

He had smiled at her.

'Syor,' he had said, 'you and I, between us, we'll conquer all of Albion.'

Only . . .

Only that hadn't been the way it had happened at all. She recalled having been at a curtained ball, watching detachedly as the merry young women had, one by one, peeled off into the gardens with the merry young men. There had been hustle and bustle all around her, and the flickering hot lights from the candelabra had glinted into her eyes, so that she had had to half-close them, as if – but only as if – she had been squinting at the shattered reflection of the sun on the choppy water of a river in spate . . .

He had approached her then. He was dressed in the most exquisite satin from slim shoulders to elegantly pointed shoes. His beard had been neatly trimmed; its hair finely

12

spun bronze. The jewels on his black velvet scabbard and on the hilt of his sword had shone like stars, twinkling in the candlelight. His froth of fair hair had seemed to fill all of her vision as he bowed, dropping onto one knee in front of her, removing a brown cap that held an impossibly long feather.

And his voice had said, 'Tell me that you are not evil.'

She had said, 'I touch nothing, so I cannot be evil.'

She was a whore.

Her father had nudged her, hiccuping at the same time so that the mouthful of red wine he had just taken spurted out from his lips, spraying down over his white robes, and her white robes, and the face of the man in front of her. The stains looked like blood.

'I touch nothing,' she had repeated.

'Touch me.'

Ignoring the splattered wine – ignoring the suddenly angry glare of her father – he had reached out his hand towards her, the rings on his fingers glowing in soft, fiery colours, like dying embers. She had reached out her own thin hand, her arm so white that it silenced the din of the musicians and merrymakers, and their fingers had interlaced . . .

And that wasn't it, either.

They'd met some other way.

She was neither princess nor harlot: she knew this for a fact.

She had been . . .

And *there* was an interesting conundrum. Who *had* she been? Her memories of the time before Lian were better than most people's, but . . .

No, she hadn't been a princess. If she'd been a princess she'd have been able to remember things more clearly.

A scream came from behind her, penetrating all of the others to which she had long ago inured herself. She let her green eyes scan the landscape in front of her, seeing the soft, feminine curves of the hills and the scrubby patches of forest. Giorran, the palace-fortress of the Ellonia, had been built on a high point, so that it could look out over the surrounding land, save for the plateau that reared even higher above it. Ditches had been dug around Giorran, longer ago than even the Ellonia could remember, so that attacking armies would be fatally slowed. Unless the Ellonia had warred with some forgotten ancient foe at the dawn of eternity, there had only ever been the one attacking army, of course: the one led by her mate and herself.

Lian.

Lian was dying.

She was alive.

The surviving Ellonian Guard were being put to the sword by her lover's followers; in due course, she knew, they themselves would be put to death as the House of Ellon exacted its revenge for this impertinence.

Lian was dying . . .

The worst of it was that she didn't really care. Couldn't care.

The sun seemed to have become a swollen orange bag. The sky was filled with an unhappy mixture of reds and blues and greens. Peace was emanating towards her from all the land of Albion.

Another of those very loud screams.

She sent her own peace out into Albion, letting the fingers of her right hand move in a dance in the air.

He Who Leads died then . . . Lian died.

For a fraction of a second she felt each shred of the pain of his going, and then there was just an emptiness. She was a collection of flesh, lazing on a grass bank by the wall of a castle – she was nothing more than that. She had had no yesterday, and for all she knew there would be no tomorrow; she had no real idea of the meaning of the word 'tomorrow'. All that she was aware of was *now*.

She folded herself up until she was as small as she could possibly be and felt the tears beginning to come from her eyes. She didn't know what the tears were for, because now there didn't seem to be anything she should be unhappy about, but she let herself cry for a while anyway.

Then, dull-eyed, she joined the queue of peasants who made their slow way down the hillside, up and down over the ditches, back to the plains where they would till the fields for the rest of eternity.

She looked behind her just once at the tall white walls of the palace, then she turned away. This palace-fortress had been important to her, she knew, but right now she couldn't recall exactly why.

She followed the crowd.

PART ONE
He Who Leads

Chapter One
Names

Here is one of the songs that Barra 'ap Rteniadoli Me'gli'minter Rehan used to sing in the days when he walked the land.

The wave burst all over Terman, throwing him down onto the greasy boards of the deck. He spat out the bitter-tasting water, trying to dig his nails into the gaps between the planks. His back felt as if someone were beating it with a mallet, his legs as if someone were trying to pull them off. All he could see was the darkness of the night, and of the water that was sucking away his life, dragging him inexorably across the deck towards the churning sea.

There was water in his nostrils, his mouth and his ears; he tried to scream to his shipmates for help, but the only sound carrying through the lashing water was an ineffectual bubbling which he himself could hardly hear above the vindictive shriek of the wind. Another wave crashed down, tormenting his body. He yelled again, but even as he did so he realised that there was little possibility of his friends aiding him. He swallowed a large gulp of salt water and was almost immediately sick, the vomit instantly washed from the planking by the furious sea as he slid across the deck. Three of his fingernails were torn away as he grabbed desperately at anything that might save him.

From the other side of the vessel came a surge of water, washing its irresistible way across the deck at him, filling his mouth yet again with brine. He gagged on the stuff and then was able to spit it back out. He turned over, hoping to snare a capstan between his legs, whatever the pain, and failing by a couple of metres. He skidded over the ship's side and into the tempest-torn sea; the sea itself seemed, strangely, a little warmer than the spray that had been beating him.

He basked in the brine, rolling easily onto his back. Was the apparent warmth just an illusion – his body's misleading response to the shock of the cold? He pondered the question philosophically, his mind curiously placid.

The ship was sinking: one of its masts had already been lost to the waters, the other was now thumping down along the length of the deck. He lay in the turbulent seas, thrown up and down and from side to side, watching all this. He saw as the second mast shattered through the forecastle and the layers beneath, so that the ship began very speedily to founder. He supposed that he ought to feel some kind of regret for his comrades, but he wasn't able to. He felt so comfortable, lying here in the waters.

There was a full moon high in the sky. It stared at him, frequently seeming to blink as thin-shaped clouds fled rapidly across it. Through the blasting din of the wind and the waves he heard the screams of his friends as the ship settled sternwards into the water. He turned his head disinterestedly, watching the cabin lights as they were extinguished one by one. A woman had climbed up the frothing deck as far as the bow, where she clung desperately, yelling her terror at the night. From this distance he didn't recognise her.

Then, very suddenly, the ship glided down between the waves. The woman leapt from the bow and swam rapidly away from the vessel, obviously anxious not to be pulled down with it. He watched all this dispassionately, as if the whole episode had been merely a series of illustrations in a book. Then he saw, in the moonlight, that she was swimming towards him, her arms and legs flailing.

She might drown! a part of his mind insisted ludicrously – of course they were both going to drown – but almost at once the thought took him over completely. The idea that his own death was inevitable had scarcely concerned him, but the realisation that this woman – whoever she was – might likewise die sparked him out of his lethargy. At once the water was freezing. Twisting himself over onto his stomach, he made hurried strokes towards her, losing sight of her frequently as he plunged into the troughs of the great dark waves which seemed determined to drag him in the opposite direction. As he swam, he was reciting to himself the names of all the gods he could think of: the list was desperately short for, like his parents, he had always believed that the teachings of the Holies were rubbish. When he got to the end he began all over again. He knew the exercise was meaningless but he didn't let his will choke off the repetition of the names, right now even the remotest possibility was worth pursuing. His inner mind swore allegiance to each and every one of the divinities, recognising even as he did so that the promises were vacuous. He'd seen a human sacrifice once as a youth and been sick; he'd never seen another, and his disbelief in the existence of the cruel gods had hardened, because no all-wise and benevolent deity could have permitted human beings to perform such an act of barbarism.

'Help me!'

Her voice was a tiny pinprick of sound in the thunder of the elements.

At last he reached her, stretching out his hand to her until their fingers intertwined. Her hair was flattened against her head, so that it looked as if she were wearing a shawl of seaweed. It was with difficulty that he recognised her: Bella, one of the stokers – the red-headed one. He'd occasionally looked at her with vaguely lustful thoughts, but had never approached her. She was sobbing, he could see, and she drew herself along his arm to clutch him in a tight embrace, pressing her body against his.

He felt her weight pulling him down.

'We'll never reach home!' he shouted, hoping that she could hear him. 'We're days away! We can't swim that far!'

She stopped weeping, let go of him, and began to pull herself through the water again.

'Not . . . so . . . far!' he heard her shout.

21

He looked in the direction in which she was swimming. There was a sort of silver mist on the water, but it was a long way away. Then the crest of a wave briefly separated them.

The next time he saw her he yelled, 'It's a nothing, a delusion! It's just a fog!' Immediately thinking, *Yes, but wouldn't it be better for her to drown feeling hopeful, straining to reach her mirage, than to lose herself willingly to the ocean?*

She ignored his cry and kept swimming. If anything there was now more power to her strokes. Again a wave-crest intervened, so that she was out of his sight, but he continued to pull himself in her direction. The icy cold of the water was making his genitals shrivel and his leather clothing feel like lead.

Now he was over the top of the wave; she seemed to be far beneath him. He was thrown down almost beside her.

'It's a chimera! A trick of nature!'

He accidentally swallowed some water and was unable to speak for a few moments as he choked.

Again they were hand in hand, swimming as if they were a single creature joined loosely at the centre by a long limb.

'Undress!' Bella yelled. 'Clothing . . . drowning . . . us!'

He let go of her hand and used his feet to shove off his flat slippers. He had to double up to get rid of his trousers and then turn over briefly onto his back to strip away his jerkin. He was naked now and the cold felt even more intense than before. He retched, but nothing came up. Bella was lost somewhere in the night. He tried to listen in case she was calling out for him, but all he could hear were the shrieks of the wind and the crashing of the waves.

'Bella!' he shouted.

'I'm behind you,' said a voice, quite calmly.

He turned about.

'We're heading for the shore,' said Bella. A dimly seen paleness beneath the surface of the water told him that, like himself, she was now naked.

'What shore? We're in the middle of the bloody ocean.'

'The shore ahead of us.'

The wind was dropping but the waves seemed just as

huge as they had been earlier. It was hard to hear each other.

'There *is* no shore.'

'Of course there is, you idiot!' Her right breast rose above the water. In the moonlight it looked as if it had been cast in metal by a master smith. She stretched out her hand, pointing ahead of them.

Again all he could see was the mist, although now it seemed that they were closer to it.

'Albion!' she cried.

He tried to reply, but just then another gush of water hit his face. He spat and gurgled weakly, and felt her arm under his chest, supporting him. His head slipped beneath the water and he resolved to meet death gracefully, as his father – if he had ever had a father – might have done. Bella pulled her other hand around under his chin, forcing his face up. Now she herself was totally submerged. He began to swim again, weakly, so that she could release herself.

'Albion, dammit! Albion!'

'Don't be so – urrgh! – stupid! That's a sailor's myth! There's no such bloody place!' But nevertheless he began to swim a little more firmly, his cynicism tempered by an urge to get out of the clutching waters.

The end of a floating log caught Bella between the eyes. He saw black blood on her forehead. Grabbing her to him with one arm, he swam fiercely towards the distant mist. Now the waves seemed to be helping him on his way. Beneath her small breasts he could feel Bella's heart pumping. To save her, to save her – that was his only thought. It gave strength to his right arm as it hauled them both through the water.

The edges of the mist rose high above them, curtaining the rim of the World. His toes touched gravel and then finer, sludgy sand – although his feet were so cold that he felt these surfaces only as obstacles of differing textures. He heaved himself up through shallower and shallower water, his back no longer thrashed by the waves, the burden of Bella almost forgotten. His breath came in great painful wheezes, as loud as a shout. The beach ahead of them was as different as could be from the maelstrom they had left behind: it was dry and sweet and lit by a golden light.

He pulled Bella twenty or thirty paces up from the shore and laid her down on the pale yellow sand. Standing next to her, he felt warmth bathe his naked back. Surely this was far enough away from the water? Exhaustion over-powered his body, flowing through his limbs inexorably. He tumbled down beside her and put his hands to her breast, hoping muzzily to confirm the fact that she was breathing, that the two of them had somehow survived, but before she could respond he was asleep.

The light stabbed through his eyelids, and he turned over on the softly abrasive surface. There was coolness lapping at his feet. He was half-snoring, half-moaning. His bunk had never seemed so uncomfortable to him before, and the reassuring swell of the sea beneath him was missing.

'What's the matter?'

The voice was soft, but its noise caused him physical pain. His hands went to his ears.

'What's the *matter*?'

'Nothing,' he mumbled. 'Go 'way. Sleepy.'

'The tide's coming in.'

It was a woman's voice. Had Bella woken before him? But why should he be sleeping beside Bella? She was simply one of his shipmates; they'd never . . .

And then the memories came back. They didn't play in his mind as any kind of accurate record; they were just remembrances of mood – resignation, terror, coldness and misery. He moved over onto his stomach and opened his eyes to an uninterrupted vista of pale, sparkling yellow.

Sand.

Yes, he and Bella had reached a beach. They'd done so in silence. The wail of the wind had left them. He'd pulled her up here, far above the waterline. The ship . . . the ship had been lost. They must have been the only members of the crew to survive. The night. The cold. The hammering waves.

'Terman,' he said, and was sick onto the smooth yellow-ness.

When his body had stopped jerking he instinctively wiped his hand across his mouth and brought himself up onto his hands and knees. The bright sunlight still pierced him, but he forced his eyes open. He saw a pair of knees, and above them the ragged hem of a knitted skirt.

'Bella?' he said.

'Bella?' the voice repeated, obviously confused.

'Bella – is that you?'

'No, I'm not a Bella.'

He slumped, catching himself just before his face fell into his own vomit. Working with difficulty on the yielding surface of the sand, he retreated a metre or two, then looked upwards.

His eyes met the steady grey gaze of a young woman.

'You're not Bella,' he said. He'd never seen her before. 'Where is she?'

'I don't know,' said the woman. Although she was obviously still very young, her hair had the same cool greyness as her eyes. She was wearing a rust-coloured woollen dress which had obviously been made years before and darned in different wools wherever it had worn thin. Her face seemed to him to radiate a sort of innocence – an ignorance of the concept of duplicity.

'Bella,' he said, his voice just a deep-pitched croak, 'she was with me . . . last night.'

'I wouldn't know,' said the woman. 'I've only just come to look at you and the thing.'

She gestured to her right and his eyes followed her hand. The thing . . .

Blood had oozed into the sand all around Bella's head; her hair was a knotted, stiff structure. He had always heard that the dead looked peaceful, but her face was twisted into a crumpled mask. Had she been screaming as she died – screaming as he lay unhearing beside her? Perhaps she had hit her hands against him, trying to make him wake up, hitting and hitting as the life ebbed from her and he just slept on, nuzzling his weary body more comfortably down into the softness? No, it couldn't have been that way: the sand around her body was hardly disturbed – there were only the two tracks leading up from the water's edge. She must have been dead already as he'd pulled her ashore.

Bella. As they'd struggled through the tapestry of mist to Albion he'd loved her, wanted to be with her forever as a recognition of what they'd been through. Now she was a 'thing'.

He muttered her name and began to cry, sitting up on his haunches and holding his hands clenched in front of his eyes. He forgot that the strange woman was watching as he let all his grief pour out. And there was more than just grief. The tears were a way of discarding the terror he'd felt in the cold waves, the hours when he'd resigned himself to death.

An arm came around his bare shoulders.

'Why are you crying, sea-beast?'

'Bella,' he said, bending forwards so that his chin was on his knees.

'I'm not a Bella, I told you,' said the woman. 'Oh, you mean the thing. Is it a favourite object of yours?'

'Can't you *see*?'

'See what?'

The coolness of her voice was like a blade in him.

'A friend. She was a friend. We saved each other's lives.' The words were coming more easily now, anger replacing his anguish.

'What friend? Where is your friend? There's only you . . . and me. We're alone.'

'She's there. Bella's *there*!' He threw out his left arm blindly, pointing at the pale corpse.

There was a long silence, and his body slowly came under his control. He rubbed his wet eyes with the heels of his palms, getting a few grains of sand into them but not caring.

'Can't you *see* her?' he shouted.

He opened his eyes and saw a bare foot idly kicking Bella's body. The dead head flipped over to the other side.

'No,' said the woman. He looked up and saw that she

26

was scratching perplexedly at her armpit. 'No one else but you. I said – we're alone.'

'Oh . . .'

He screamed at the sand and then, climbing to his feet, at the breakers. He turned around and screamed at the woman, who retreated, baffled, fearful. He threw himself down on Bella's corpse, kissing the dead lips, hoping that in some way he might be able to restore life to her.

'Why do you kiss that thing?' asked the woman politely.

'It's not a thing.'

'But it is. I can see that it is.'

Reluctantly he pulled himself free of Bella. The sky was far bluer than a sky should be. Far above him he could see a seagull floating, allowing itself to be carried along by the updraughts.

'Are you hungry?'

And suddenly he was: he was starving. He wanted to pick himself up off this sand, leave Bella behind and take himself to somewhere he could find a large, filling, ridiculously hot meal. Embarrassed, he began to crawl up the beach, trailing his feet behind him.

'Yes,' he said. 'I need food.'

'Then come to the home of the person who says he is my father. He's a very good father – better than most. I love my mother too, because both of my parents have instructed me that I should do so. Don't be shy. Come on.' The sounds of her voice were clearer than they ought to have been.

But he was shy, self-conscious. He took one further look at Bella's body and then followed the woman up the beach, cupping a hand protectively around his genitals. He coughed uncontrollably, feeling his brine-shrunken balls bounce; his penis had retreated almost completely into his body, so that it was just a wrinkled, apologetic stub. But the woman didn't look back.

'I remember,' she said, as if to the air, 'the way that you came onto the sands. You and the thing. Just before I took my time for sleep.'

He muttered a word or two.

'Yes, it was pleasing to watch,' she said. 'As if two great creatures of the ocean had decided to crawl up onto the land. I felt for you both. And then almost at once I realised that there was only the one of you, pulling the object behind you.' He could hardly believe the way that her crisp words chilled him.

'If you say the thing was once a person I have to believe you, for it would be discourteous of me to disbelieve you. The person must have disappeared before you came ashore, I suppose. I can't really recall it. Are you sure you're not mistaken? Disappearance leaves no traces. This thing, are you sure it isn't . . .'

'She wasn't an "it",' he said determinedly.

'Well, whatever it – she – was, I saw you dragging it. Have you looked at this dandelion yet? Aren't the colours beautiful? All of the different yellows mingling together; welcoming you here. You *must* look at this dandelion . . .'

He flew at her back, throwing her to the ground. He beat with his fists at her puffy mouth, bloodying it. He wanted to destroy her, to hammer her into lifelessness, to see the soul flit away from her. He was shouting incoherently, trying to tell her of the love he'd so briefly had for Bella, hoping that he could somehow get through to her the fact that this wasn't just an interesting game. He hurt. He *hurt*.

And her calm grey eyes just looked at him as he beat her. 'You've made me drop my dandelion.'

'Bella's dead!' he shouted. 'Bella's *dead*!'

'What is "dead"?' she said quietly through split lips, as his fist rose to strike her yet again.

She really doesn't know, he thought, and he let his hand fall to his side. *But then I never really believed there was such a place as Albion. Whenever we sent navigators to search for it, they found nothing – just vast tracts of open sea. Maybe it only exists* sometimes. *So if it's like that, why should I be surprised if its natives don't see things the way that we do? The attention-span of a cat or a dog is supposed to be only a couple of minutes – after that it has no memory of events. Yet it can still learn things like how to get home at nights, and where its*

28

feeding bowl is, even though it doesn't really have a proper memory.

Ach, no – I'm being fanciful. She's a human being, not a bloody cat. She must just be simple-minded. But her eyes . . .

He stood up and brushed some of the sand out of the curly hairs on his thighs. He wasn't worried any longer about the fact that she could see his nakedness – after all, she'd seen him that way for some while before it had occurred to him to care. His thoughts were gradually becoming less sluggish.

'I'm sorry,' he said, pulling her to her feet. 'You may have saved my life. I should be on my knees thanking you, not shouting at you and hitting you. If you hadn't woken me I might have slept through the tide and drowned without ever waking. I could be dead. I had no right to . . .'

He was ashamed.

She looked at him and ridges appeared on her forehead. He was struck once again by the clarity of her eyes.

'Would it have been important to you, this . . . deadness?' she said.

For a moment he couldn't speak. Whether or not she was a simpleton, the question displayed an incredible naïvety. He was about to yell at her again when he remembered what he'd just said, that she'd saved his life. In a quieter tone he said: 'Yes, it does matter to me. And the death of my friend Bella matters to me, too.'

He turned back to where the waves were rolling onto the beach. It was difficult walking through the sand. The dead woman's face was all that showed above the edge of the froth. As he approached her he was walking through damp sand, wetted by the stronger of the breakers, and it was like trying to tread through mud. But he reached her, took her arms, and slowly, walking backwards, rescued her from the water. He kept going up the beach until he found himself in the soft dry sand, then leaned down to put her over his shoulder. Her limp head tapped against the base of his spine as he clambered clumsily back up the slope to where the grey-eyed woman was waiting for him.

'You require the thing?' she said as he came near. She was obviously perplexed.

'This was a friend of mine,' he said, still speaking gently. 'She died – I don't know exactly when. She died in the sea somewhere out there.' He was tottering under the weight of Bella's body, and so all he could manage was a backward toss of his head. 'I want to bury her – put her in the ground. It's a mark of respect among my people.'

A cloud went across the sun, changing the colours of the light on the beach; within moments it was gone.

The woman was trying not to smile.

'You're a very odd person, sea-beast,' she said. 'Perhaps you could plant the thing in one of our fields, so that it'd help the crops grow.'

Anger surged again, but he kept it in check. It was wrong to blame a retard for the things she might say – and, anyway, why not let Bella be reborn in the form of wheat or barley? Maybe that was more of a tribute than consigning her to a formal grave. Yes . . . maybe.

'If you like,' he said eventually.

'My father would be so pleased and grateful.'

After that they trudged up the beach in silence, Terman's breath growing harsher as he stumbled along under Bella's weight. The day was hot. He was sweating profusely when finally they reached a scrubby region of sharp-edged grass. Once through this, he was walking on softer turf. They came over a minor crest and he found himself looking down onto an area neatly demarcated by dry-stone dykes, a patchwork of different colours laid out across the gently sloping land. In the distance he could see a brown stone cottage with precarious-seeming walls. Further away were other cottages scattered sparsely across the landscape.

'It's the farm where we live,' said the woman. She smiled at him; he tried to smile back.

'Where would you like me to dig her grave?'

'Grave?'

'The hole in the ground where I want her to rest. Which field? Which crop would she most help?'

The woman began to walk down the hill. 'I don't know,'

30

she said. 'Put the thing wherever you like. The fields'll all be changed tomorrow.'

The flat statement astonished him, and he missed his step, almost tripping under the weight of Bella. Surely changing around all the crops in the fields would be incredibly difficult. He wasn't even sure it would be possible. Besides, what would be the point?

'Of course the fields will shift,' she said, turning to look at him. 'Where have you come from, sea-beast?'

He drew in a breath.

'From a country that's very far away – in more ways than one,' he said at last.

She took this as enough of an answer, sombrely nodding her head. Then she began once more to pick her way down over the springy moss and heather of the hill. He followed, hearing the softness of her padding feet and the humming of the insects as they tended the flowers of the heather. A fly made of metallic red skitted with a whirr of wings in front of his eyes: he'd never seen anything like it before. He reminded himself that he was in a strangers' land, that he couldn't expect things to be the same here as they were at home. As he plodded along behind the woman, the burden of Bella becoming heavier by the minute, he looked from side to side. Some of the plants he recognised – there were foxgloves and pansies and snowdrops – but surely they shouldn't all be flowering in the same season? And there were other things on the hillside that he'd never seen before: giant weeds, swivelling in the breeze, sprouting blue growths that seemed to watch him and the woman as they picked their way down the slope; little clumps of flowers that he walked around, the pink unfolding head of each one looking like the face of a waking baby; one or two tall trees whose violet leaves rustled together to produce a sound that was agonisingly like speech, yet in a language he had never heard before.

They came to the first of the low walls and he turned around to lean his bottom against it.

'Can I bury her now?' he said with difficulty. His breath was short and there was a tension in his chest.

31

'Plant her, you mean?' said the woman, pausing with one foot on the top of the dyke, preparing to leap over.

A small new rage, swiftly suppressed.

'Yes. Yes, plant her. I can't carry her much longer.'

'Here would be as good as anywhere.'

'Have you got a spade, back at your home?'

'We had one yesterday. It's probably still there today. Shall I go and look?'

He looked over his shoulder at the earth of the field. It seemed soft beneath the rape-seed. Perhaps he could dig deep enough with his hands to . . .

'Yes, please,' he said. 'I'd like a spade. And perhaps you could bring your father to do some of the digging. It's a lot to ask, I know, but it would help. And if he's got any clothes I could borrow . . .'

Leaving him, she jogged lithely towards the cottage. He realised that she'd been deliberately walking at an easy pace so as not to tire him. And yet, of course, he *was* tired – exhausted to the point that his limbs seemed to belong to somebody else. He fetched Bella's body down from his shoulder and pushed it over the wall, trying to keep it clear of the sharp stones at the top of the dyke; even so, a couple of deep gouges appeared on her belly. She collapsed with a gentle sound onto the uncultivated soil at the edge of the field. He forced himself over the wall to flop down beside her. Patterns of soap-bubble colours darted in front of his eyes as he regained his breath.

The woman wasn't gone for long – or so it seemed to him. She arrived carrying a purposeful-looking spade. Behind her came a middle-aged man with hair an even paler grey than hers; he too was holding a spade. She was smiling like a small child who has just impressed its parents by doing something very clever indeed.

'Here,' she said. 'Here we are.'

In the event it was the two natives who did most of the digging. Terman took out the first sod but then had to back off, waving them towards the spades, feeling his heart pounding threateningly against the inside of his ribs. He sat down, his legs crossed in front of him, and watched as they laboured. Soon they started to sing in time with the *swatch, swatch* of the spades chopping into the earth. The song didn't have any words and the music didn't acknowledge any of the rules he had ever learnt, but music it was, and far more than a mechanical working-song: the woman and her father clearly understood when each should sing or stay silent, and sometimes they sang in duet, weaving an incredible complexity of slurring notes. Watching them and listening to them, it was obvious to him that the song wasn't something they were consciously composing – not something new that they were making. Rather it was an inbuilt response, almost an instinctive one – a predetermined acknowledgement of the situation they were in: they were recognising the circumstance, and nor was there even the smallest thought in their minds that they might encounter something like it ever again. As a kitten might seize at a moving ball of wool, dancing with it in unremembered choreography, so they were singing a song whose echoes reflected the long ages of a past they seemed not to know existed.

And if he had been a professional musician he would have tried to memorise it all, knowing that his fame would stretch far and wide if ever he were able to reproduce the sound on his return to the World. As it was, he simply leaned back more firmly against the wall. The pressure of the sharp edges of the stones became pleasant reassurance rather than a source of pain.

Soon the two natives had dug a pit about a metre deep – deep enough, Terman decided. They moved to pick up Bella but he gestured them away. He had loved the woman for only a short time – the time they had been struggling together in the sea – but that had in its own way been forever. Maybe he and Bella would have hated each other had they both survived the storm. He had saved her life, true, but she had saved his as well. Although he was so drained of vitality that he had difficulty working his back up the uncomfortably rough surface of the dyke until he was standing, it was his duty to lay her in her grave.

Her body looked very pallid and grey as he squatted to

33

pick it up, pushing his arms under the cold flesh, taking her weight and forcing himself to his feet, lurching like a drunkard. He took the necessary couple of steps towards the pit the natives had dug and then tried to lay Bella gently into it.

The effort was too much for him. He let the corpse drop flatly down. Bella's right arm flailed away from the rest of her body so that her hand remained hooked over the cut edge of the grave; had it not been for the huge gash on her forehead it would have looked almost as if she were trying to heave herself out again. The father idly kicked the hand so that the arm dropped down onto Bella's stomach.

She might be asleep, thought Terman. *Except for the flaking blood, she looks almost comfortable, curled up there.* Then the first spadeful of red-brown earth landed on her breast.

He felt he ought to say something – a few stanzas of one of the religious verses in which he did not believe, perhaps, spoken as a token of respect. But then he realised how wrong that would be: to mouth insincerities would be to insult her. Instead, he bowed his head and closed his eyes, concentrating on wishing her well in the afterlife, if there were any such thing, and hoping that the gods who might or might not exist would hear his thoughts. He had had little knowledge of her before her death – ah, yet . . .

And the tears began again.

The woman and her father let him cry as they quickly filled in the earth. It didn't take them long, because they were strengthened by the new song that they were singing. Then they threw their spades against the base of the dyke – to be picked up another day, should the spade or the dyke still be there then – and put Terman's arms around their shoulders. Slowly, laboriously, they walked with him across the multicoloured fields towards their home.

'You're different, you know.'

He had spent most of the past few days in delirium, so that he hadn't at first recognised her when she'd come into the sun-filled room. He watched her as she pulled the rather thin, badly made curtain over the single window.

'How long have I been here?' he said.

'A while.'

'How long a while?'

'Several sleeping-periods.' She came over and straightened the furs around him, then forced him to lift his head so that she could puff up the cushions. The cushions were covered in some kind of coarse woven fabric that had been irritating his ears, so that whenever he'd turned over in his half-sleep he had found the new position even worse than the old. He tried to gesture to her that he would prefer to have no cushions at all but she ignored him.

'How do you mean, I'm "different"?' he said.

'Things have changed here. At the start of each waking-period the fields are the same as they were before. I can picture our bringing you here, and my father and I have pictures in our minds of the two of us digging the hole for the planting of the thing.'

She put a cup of water to his dry lips and he silently thanked her. Wispinesses of pale shadows chased each other across the whitewashed walls as the wind caught at the curtain. There was a cool breeze on his forehead, drying the sweat. He opened his eyes and saw her face, which looked infinitely beautiful to him: he imagined that he was in the afterlife the Holies believed in.

With difficulty he recalled the events she'd been describing. He said so, moving his tongue and lips as if he were unfamiliar with them.

'I remember,' she said, picking up the word he'd used, '*not* remembering.'

He took a sip of water down the wrong way and spluttered weakly against her wrist. When he'd finished he said, 'I don't know what you mean. You're talking in riddles.'

His voice was furrily indistinct.

She moved away from him, putting the cup down on the windowsill. Her hair was lit up by the sunshine, so that it became a corona of soft light caressing her shoulders. She was still dressed in the same darned woollen skirt in which he had first seen her. She turned abruptly and looked directly at him; the grey eyes that he remembered as so

35

still were now vital and angry, the pupils small.

'Sea-beast,' she said, 'you say that you've come from somewhere outside the curtain – from somewhere you call "the World". You've talked a lot in your wildness. All my life I've known that there's nothing beyond the curtain but, all right, I believe you – because, frankly, I don't *care* where you came from. You're here now, and that's all that matters. You're here in our land, and you could at least have the courtesy to *understand* us. My father, and my mother and me – we've tended you all through the times you were shouting obscenities at us and shitting your bed and talking offal about this "World" of yours. We fed gruel in between your lips. You've been sick twice on my mother's dress – it's lucky that she has two. You hit my father on the side of the head. You . . . you bruised my breast when you seized it, and my father could almost have killed you for the things you said then. He might have done, too, if it hadn't been for the gift you've brought us.'

Terman had dim memories of shameful acts. Somehow they were all mixed up among the images from the dreams he'd been having – it was impossible for him to separate reality from the unnaturally bright scenes that had been flitting in front of his eyes. Perhaps she was lying, trying in some obscure way to put him even more in her family's debt than he already was.

It seemed more likely that she was telling the truth.

'I'm sorry,' he mumbled.

'I accept your apology,' she said with a formality that divorced the meaning from the words. 'And I accept that you haven't been responsible for all these things, that you've been ill. And I thank you on behalf of my family – and other families who live around us – for the gift.'

'Gift?' He was beginning to drift back to sleep again. 'What gift? I was naked when I came here. I didn't bring any gifts.'

'I've told you.' Her anger was dying. She sat down on the side of the bed and ran her fingers soothingly across his forehead and through the sweat-wet hair of his head. 'You've brought us something we didn't have before.

36

You've brought us "remembering". I *know* how hellish you were when you were raving: I've got the knowledge right here inside me.' She pointed uncertainly first at her chest and then at her face. 'Before you were here that would have been something lost to me.'

She laughed unhappily. 'Before you were here I wouldn't have been able to think about there having been a time before you were here. You've given us all a sort of clarity of vision which is crystally sweet . . . *painfully* sweet, in some ways.'

Her voice fell away, floating in the shadows like a feather to the ground.

He remembered his conjecture when they'd been down at the beach. Cats . . . dogs . . . the people of Albion. Her eyes so far-seeing and yet her perplexity so great. She'd told him then that she had no idea what Bella's body was, that the shapes of the fields on her family's farm changed daily. He looked at her face, and was glad to see that her lips had healed; somehow it made him feel less guilty.

'I need some more water, please,' he said. As she turned away towards the badly fitting wooden door he added, 'When you come back, tell me more about this place. I never wished to cause you pain – it just happened. I'm glad I've given you something in return.'

She turned at the door and looked at him. 'If you hadn't given me this gift,' she said, smiling, 'I wouldn't remember now how much you hurt me.'

'What's your name?' he asked her when she returned with more water in a roughly hammered pewter jug.

'I don't know,' she said, speaking more lightly now, as if they were playing games. 'It's up to you to give me a name. To name all of us.'

So he called her Mina, and her father Lantz, and her mother Gred: the names themselves had no meanings, but he chose them because the sound of them on his tongue somehow seemed to describe these people.

Mina kissed him gently on the forehead as he sank back into half-sleep.

37

'Tell me of this place,' he said at last, watching the light on the back of her hand as she pushed her hair away from her face.

In the next few weeks he would name many other people, and over the years he would give his gift to many hundreds. But he would never forget the giving of that first name.

Chapter Two
Trumpet

Mina told him much about Albion, and Terman discovered more as time went on.

There were no days and nights in the land Mina agreed was called Albion. There were simply times of sleep and times of work. The sun seldom moved more than thirty degrees from the zenith, evenly warming the land beneath it but not to the extent that the land ever became baking. Most of the natives obeyed an internal clock that dictated their 'nights', being undisturbed by the permanent brightness of the sky. He himself had to draw the curtain firmly across the window in his little room in the house of Lantz and Gred every time he wanted to sleep. The curtain was just a little too long, so that he was able to use heavy shells lent to him by Mina to hold down its bottom edge and keep most of the sunlight out. Even so, however firmly he clasped the window, draughts still came into the house and, when the wind was strong enough, the curtain would be shifted, dragging the shells with it, so that a blaze of light shone onto his eyes until he was forced awake. He grew accustomed to controlling his level of consciousness, so that he could climb out of bed, haul himself uncertainly across to adjust the shells and the curtain, and then somehow get back under the warm furs without ever really waking up. The worst bit was climbing into bed.

During the times when he was not asleep he received a constant string of visitors, eager to be given names. The men were farmers, stock-breeders and river-fishers. The women and all but the youngest children toiled in the fields, sowing, tending and gathering in the crops. This was a never-ending labour, he learnt: at the times when Mina seated him at his window he could often see one field being sown while the field adjacent to it was being harvested. To the elderly were reserved the menial jobs, like cleaning dishes, laundry and rooms – very badly, as he soon found.

He was horrified by the amount they all worked – and by the division of labour. Young children were accustomed to scything corn for periods he estimated to be longer than a day without any break for food, drink or rest – they barely paused for purposes of evacuation. The adults would often continue for as much as what would have been two of his days, ignoring the intervening sleeping-period. And none of them complained. Terman supposed that somehow, like the working-song Mina and Lantz had sung, it had been built into them, almost like an instinct, that this was to be their role throughout their lives. Which, he guessed, would not be long ones: he saw elderly people, but nobody who was too old to perform hard physical drudgery for hours on end. He was something of a wonder among them, because he was capable of merely resting in his bed, not feeling compelled to totter out into the fields.

Yet there was no resentment. He was embarrassed by the way they almost worshipped him because of his power to give them names.

Mina was sitting in his room one day, alternately playing on a nose-flute and singing to him. From time to time she paused and used stone scissors to trim his curling black beard. He had told the people of the region to stay away, that he was tired, that he wanted a little time to himself. Mina had been readying herself to go out and work when he had called her back, saying that on this day and all the subsequent days it was her duty to tend the namer rather than to reap corn or clean out the byre. Her grey eyes had smiled at him, her face rather less so; he had had to explain that he wanted her company and conversation, not that he wished to exercise any kind of *droit de seigneur*. The whole episode had been very embarrassing to him: her signalled willingness to make love with him just because he had a talent for giving names – and the strength of the temptation to take her to his bed just because she was available – had made him feel ashamed. Had she been one of the women in the port bars he'd once frequented, back in the World, he'd have fought to have bedded her. Now things were very different.

Her music caressed him, wandering all over his body. The tugging of the scissors around his chin and his cheeks hurt him, but he kept his whimperings to a minimum.

She put away the scissors and laid the nose-flute on the windowsill. He knew what she was about to do: there was a mingling of dread and pleasurable anticipation in him. She drew back the furs and sheets from his bed. There was nothing sexual in this, although there was a great deal of affection in the gentleness of her movements. Every few days she insisted on washing him like this, using the water she brought to his room in a coarsely whorled earthenware ewer. The water was hot when she arrived, but invariably lukewarm by the time she had ministered to him.

'Why do you – all of you – keep on working?' he said, cringing from the water. 'Why do you want to produce so much food? The people here in the village can't possibly eat that much!'

She turned him over onto his stomach, using a soft cloth to cleanse his back and the cleft of his backside. She retreated to the stool she'd been sitting on and played a short rill of notes on the nose-flute, watching him as he dried in the air. He lay, puffing into his cushions, wondering how long these indignities could go on.

'We work because we have to,' she said. Her voice had the same coolness as her eyes. 'There's no other way. Is there?'

'But where does all the food *go*?'

'Wait with us a little while and you'll see.'

'Oh, for the sake of bloody love, woman, obtuseness is the kind of thing that's attractive in adolescents! I'm way past that age and so are you – can't you simply tell me the truth?'

41

He beat the cushions until they satisfied him, then forced himself to sit up, his neck propped against the oak bedhead. He didn't want to hurt her in any way with his questions, but at the same time he needed to know why the people of this valley were prepared to be . . . slaves. Yes, that was the word. They were slaves, and they didn't know it.

'Slaves!' he said loudly.

'A word I do not know.' Said sombrely, with deliberation, after a long silence.

Terman lugged himself out of his bed. He crawled towards the curtained window and threw the thin cloth to one side. Shells rattled painfully around his shoulders. He pulled himself up and looked out onto the fields, where the women and children were slowly going about their work. There he could see a woman straightening herself slowly, a great stook of severed corn over her back; nearer to the house a smiling child was walking towards him, carrying a huge bale of hay.

The boy stumbled and fell, grazing his knees. He picked himself up. The smile was still locked on his face.

The sun hung at the centre of the sky, as if someone had nailed it there.

'You'll be well soon,' said Mina softly, 'well enough to be in the fields. After that you might perhaps become a river-fisher . . .'

'Is that what you want me to be?'

He stood at the window, feeling his knees beginning to melt beneath him. It wouldn't be long before he had to get back to his bed. Mina would help him.

He had come here from what was, to this world, a no-place. She'd helped him. He wanted to be beside her, to make love with her – not because he loved her or thought he was ever likely to, but because he wanted to be closer to her, as if through the exploration of each other's bodies they might discover all of the ways in which they could *be* together. The physical pleasures would be almost irrelevant. Yet how could he make love with her if all of the time he were conscious of the fact that she was simply repaying him for his 'gift'?

42

She was playing again on her nose-flute, while he still clung to the windowsill, the strength ebbing from his arms and legs. The boy had reached the cottage and was beating on the door. Terman heard Mina scrape her chair back as she stood, then heard her pad out of the room to let the boy in. *Another*, thought Terman, *another who wants to be named. Can't they all just let me have some peace?*

But, of course, he gave the boy a name.

It had taken a long time, but he was feeling stronger now, so that he could manipulate his own pot and every few hours walk as far as the kitchen to wash it out for himself. Mina had drawn back the curtain, so that yellow light splashed across the bare boards, mixing into purple where it met the woven rug that was laid by the side of his bed.

'Mina,' he said, his eyes half-closed against the brightness, 'why do you and your people *do* all this?'

'We are intended to,' she said. Today she was knitting an as yet unidentifiable garment, using badly made wooden needles. Long fingers moving with a rote precision; a little grime, startlingly grey-black, in the corners of the chewed nails. 'We have always been intended to, perhaps even since before the Ellonia came – if there ever was a time like that.'

'You've said that before, blast it!' he said, his voice thin and hard with frustration. He pulled himself up, feeling the slithery sweatiness of the sheets and furs clinging to him; light from the window was playing across her face and making little flickers of colour dance among the hairs of her eyebrows as she concentrated on her knitting. Her forehead was too broad and too square and yet, whenever he looked at it, he saw it as perfect.

'But it doesn't bloody mean anything,' he whined.

'Yes it does,' she said, so quietly that he could hardly hear her. Her needles clicked and spat, faster and faster. She raised her voice a little. 'Before you came, we'd never know for sure when the Ellonia might come among us until just before they did.'

'Who *are* these Ellonia?'

'The ones.'

'Tell me more, Mina.'

As soon as he'd said the words he was sorry for their evident sarcasm.

'You'll know who they are. This waking-period. We must keep you hidden while they're here. They'll kill you if they find you. They may kill any of us. They have created many disappearances – deaths – I think.' Her brow furrowed: she was trying to sort her new-found memories. 'They're allowed to, you know. It is given to them.'

'"Given"?'

'Yes, given. I don't want to talk about it, Oh, by the way, I love you.' Her needles missed a stitch. Her voice could have been announcing that it was time for him to eat his early-waking meal. She carried on knitting until she had finished her row; with an expansive sweep of her right arm she drew away the free end of wool, clearing the needles, then swapped them around in order to begin the next row.

'Mina,' he said. 'Mina . . .'

She looked at him briefly, then back at her work.

'Don't love me.'

She glanced at him again.

'Why not?'

Her grey eyes held him. He moved uneasily in his bed, the boards creaking under his weight.

'The woman I came ashore with – I loved her.'

'Yes, I recall her, now. At the time I thought she was just a something; now I know that she was a dead person. You told me so, and I believe the things you tell me.' Mina was knitting contentedly again now.

'I've loved a lot of women. Only some of them have loved me back.' He wondered how come it was that he was saying these things to her. Back in the World he'd never known anyone to whom he could have said them. He'd have been either laughed at or brutally rebuffed. Friends. He had called many people friend, but he'd learnt too often how superficial friendship could be. It was ridiculous that he was talking to this woman whom he hardly knew (although *she* knew *him*, physically, very well) with a frankness he had never conceded even to a lover. Perhaps he should reach out, knock away her knitting, drag her into his bed with him, move his body inside hers. But he didn't want to, very definitely didn't want to.

But why not? He liked her; she had just said that she loved him; he certainly found her attractive – in more than one dream he had watched the swathe of her grey hair spread across his belly.

'I very much want to hold your hand,' he said.

She linked her fingers through his, leaning forwards, allowing a needle to drop.

A knock came at the door of the cottage. Gred or Lantz shuffled across the red stone tiles of the kitchen to tell whoever it was, in muffled tones, that the giver of names was resting. All of them had had to become accustomed to frequent callers.

There was a butterfly in Terman's room. Both he and Mina watched it for a while. The insect fluttered around for a long time before it discovered the window and sang away into the air.

Mina came back and kissed his hand, very softly. She ran her tongue over his knuckles, darting its tip here and there.

It was time for the mid-waking meal.

Afterwards they made him use his pot and then they led him up a rickety makeshift ladder to the cottage's attic. It was dusty and dirty up there, the small space packed with the detritus accumulated over more than one lifetime – boxes and bales and barrels. The interior of the slanting roof was in immaculate condition and obviously was tended regularly, which for a few moments surprised him – why bother with a roof at all under the ever-present sun? Then he realised that, for the crops to grow, it must rain sometimes; if the weather was as well regulated as everything else in Albion seemed to be, the rains, when they came, might be torrential. It was presumably for this reason that the single skylight, unlike the other windows in the house, was filled with a corrugated stuff that looked like grey glass

45

but felt quite different – warmer, more yielding.

Mina stayed behind for a few moments after her parents had gone.

'I don't think it would be too dangerous to open the skylight,' she said, wrestling with the window. 'But the soldiers may come into the house, so keep yourself still – don't knock anything over. We'll make the hatch look invisible – or at least as if it hasn't been opened for a very long time.' She rubbed dirt away from the insides of her wrists. 'I don't think they'd be interested, anyway. They search some of our homes every time they come here, but they're not really looking for anything. I think they do it just to remind us that they'll be back again.'

'Mina, how do you know things like that?'

'Because all of us know. That is the way.'

And he suddenly realised what she meant . . . To the people of Albion there were two types of knowledge, each utterly distinct. First there was the knowledge which you simply *knew* – how to hoe a row in the fields, how to patch a roof. This category of knowledge must, essentially, be a sort of instinct, either instilled so deeply in childhood that it became virtually a part of the person or – Terman struggled with unfamiliar thoughts – inherited at birth, just like red hair or a long nose.

The second type of knowledge was quite different. It involved the things that the people learnt through the course of their daily lives. It was also very transient: if the boundaries of fields could change at random over the course of just one sleeping-period, and the whole of past reality be mutable, then memories would always be unreliable – as would the knowledge gained from them. In fact, the faculty of memory would be *unnecessary*. Perhaps people could change, as well as dry-stone dykes? A person whom you loved in one waking-period might, by the next, no longer exist – might *never* have existed. But if something had happened not once but several times before, then perhaps that could be picked out among all the false memories – identified as a reality rather than a possibility. Something as regular as the growing and ripening of grain would be imprinted on the mind. As would something as regular as the arrival of the Ellonia – or their soldiers – to take the food away. All the memories of any occasional lapse in the regularity would be erased – perceived as false memories and hence discarded. Dripping water in a cave can leave hard stalactites and stalagmites, but random drops of water that fall elsewhere and simply run away leave no trace behind them.

No wonder the peasants were so insistent that he give them names. A name was a *repeated* thing. In the World, Terman had often come across people he'd known he'd met before, yet had been unable to remember as a *person* until he'd been reminded of their name; only then had the memories of their likes and dislikes, their occupations and interests, come flooding back to him. It must be the same here in Albion – but a hundred times more so. By giving people names he was also giving each of them a personal identity – and, through that, concrete memories.

'I'll be as quiet as I can,' he said.

Mina smiled broadly at him.

'Be quieter than that,' she said, 'and you should be all right.'

He squatted on the attic's grimy wooden floor, and grinned back at her.

For a while they stared into each other's eyes, and then suddenly she stepped forwards, half-crouched because of the lowness of the roof, and kissed him firmly on the lips. Almost at once she retreated.

'I'm sorry,' she said. 'I shouldn't have done that.'

'It's all right. I enjoyed it.'

He drew the back of his sleeve across his mouth.

'But we're not lovers,' she said.

'Perhaps we will be.'

His voice was saying that 'perhaps' meant 'never'. Again the question: why didn't he want to become her lover? In a very profound way he *did* love her.

Motes of dust circled around her as she knelt in the curtains of yellow light.

Gods curse the mind, he thought. *It makes things that ought to be simple so very complicated*. Taking her as a lover would be like . . . like paedophilia, because in a very real sense she was only a few weeks old. Yet she had also been almost a mother to him, tending him and feeding him when he was an infant. Was that what frightened him – that she had known him when he was hardly more than a suckling baby, puling and incontinent?

She became suddenly brusque. Again she rubbed dirt from her wrists, concentrating her eyes fixedly on the task, which this time was unnecessary.

'If the Ellonian soldiers are late,' she said, 'we'll pass you up a meal and your pot. I'll let you know what's going on – not if they're in the house, of course, because they'd hear me.'

He wanted to ask for the thousandth time: *Why are you doing all this for me?* Before the words came to his lips, however, he knew the answer: more important to Mina than any feelings she might have for him was the fact that his presence had, as it were, brought the peasants of this little community out of the shadows and into reality. So instead of asking the question he just said, 'Don't worry too much about me.'

'It's not you I'm worried about,' she replied, looking out through the skylight at the fields. 'Well, at least, I am – a lot. But what really concerns me is *us*. We'll have to appear to the soldiers to be just like we've always been, and that isn't going to be easy. We'll have to pretend to forget our names for a while . . . and things.'

'What things?'

'They're men. We have women among us – don't pretend you haven't noticed.' Her sarcasm was heavy. 'The soldiers can do what they like with the women.' She turned back again to face him. Her words came in a rush: 'It doesn't take long and it doesn't hurt much, and afterwards it's hard to remember the experience in any detail.'

'But this time the victims will be able to remember.'

'Exactly. And whoever it happens to will have to pretend that it doesn't matter. Which will be very difficult.'

His hands became fists, the knuckles going white.

'Don't you ever – *ever* – want to kill the bastards?'

Her voice lost any trace of emotion. 'It has never occurred to us before that we could. Some of us have been saying, these past few weeks since you came to us, that we should fight against the soldiers, but there seems to me to be little sense in that: they would just kill us and burn down our houses.'

'But surely they need you to provide their food?'

'There are other villages.' She spoke simply, stating the obvious.

'Well . . . well, what if you killed *all* of the soldiers? And then went on to kill the Ellonia themselves? After that you'd need to grow only enough food to feed yourselves – and you could all have times to rest, to *enjoy* life.' He shifted. Now he was on his hands and knees.

'I don't like to talk about killing,' she said, leaning forward to place the cool fingertips of her right hand momentarily on his forehead. 'Killing is a thing the Ellonia and their soldiers do, because it is given to them to be able to do so.' She looked at her hand, now against her lap, pale on her skirt. 'I couldn't kill someone. Not myself. I couldn't. It would be . . . wrong. Most of us feel that way.'

'But sometimes people *have* to be killed.' He was whispering. 'Can't you see that?'

'No.'

He thought of all the revolutions and counter-revolutions that plagued the World. He had fought for some years as a mercenary, serving whichever warlord would pay him the highest price. For most of the time he'd thought nothing about the men and women who had died beneath his sword as he'd played his minor part in one pointless war after the next. Sickened at last by it all, he'd become a merchant seaman, but there was still a great part of him that was a warrior. Now at last he'd discovered a war that clearly *ought* to be waged, and the people whose war it was – if Mina was typical – didn't want to raise so much as a voice.

'How often have they raped you?' he said harshly.

'It's hard to remember. A few times, I suppose. It doesn't hurt too much, as I said – not after the first time. If they rape me today it'll be worse, of course.'

A fatalistic shrug of those rust-coloured shoulders. A toss of her grey hair. It was not for her to decree what would happen. If it happened, it happened.

'You could stay hidden here with me,' he said, again whispering.

'No. The soldiers count us – enumerate us.' She pronounced the word carefully. 'If there are too few of us they want to know where the people have gone to, and they search. Sometimes the old ones have disappeared – died. But I'm not old, and we have no plague.' Dusting her hands once more on her skirt. 'If they discovered that I wasn't there they'd look for me, and then they'd find both of us and destroy us – and my parents, and this house, and . . .' She began to cry. 'Everything. All of it burnt. Even the pig.'

He worked himself towards her and put his arms around her hips, drawing her to him. He nestled an ear between her thighs and held her very tightly, smelling the softness of her lap, trying to convey to her the misery he felt for the ordeal she might have to endure. He wished he knew some way that he could help her avoid it, but she was right: anything he might do would only make matters worse for her and the other peasants in this valley. Even if he were armed he'd be able to kill only a few of the Ellonian soldiers before being killed himself, and then the gleeful massacre would begin. All he could do was hope that the physical contact between Mina and himself would allow some of his frustrated strength to seep into her.

After a while she said, 'I must go now. My parents – they'll be expecting me. Don't make a fuss: even the worst of it can't be too bad.'

She pushed away his arm. He looked up and saw her face smiling down at him, although her eyes were moist.

'It'll be all right,' she said softly. 'Honestly, it'll be all right.'

'I don't believe you.'

'Please do believe me. Your life – all of our lives – they depend on it.'

50

She blinked, looked annoyed with herself and then brushed at her eyes with a sleeve. From where he knelt her face looked very different. Now she had a strong chin, a large nose and a tiny forehead. Impulsively he reached up to take one of her shoulders and pulled her down so that their faces were level.

'You tasted sweet when you kissed me. Kiss me again.'

She did – on his forehead. Then she stood up cautiously, bending her head to avoid the low roof. In a businesslike manner she took the few steps necessary to reach the open hatch. As she lowered herself down backwards onto the top rung of the ladder she said, not looking at him, 'Don't pretend that you love me. If you do you'll hurt not just me but yourself as well. But I'm glad of your friendship.' And she was gone.

All of a sudden he was alone. The hatch was beaten back into place, and he heard sounds from below as the ladder was taken away and dismantled – to make firewood, he supposed. A little later he heard a shuffling noise from the direction of the hatch: he guessed that Lantz, Gred or Mina was using a long-handled mop to wipe muck around the ceiling so that the edges of the hatch would be less obvious.

He found that he could half-stand, with knees bent, to look out through the skylight, locking his elbows into the lower corners of the frame so that they took most of his weight. He knew that the position would become painful in time, and that he'd have to use all of his willpower to avoid moving should the Ellonian soldiers come into the house at the wrong moment, but he didn't very much care. He had to see what was going on.

At first, that wasn't a lot. A curlew came plummeting down to land on the roof just below the window, looking at him with interest until he shooed it away. Otherwise he could see little apart from the perpetual tableau of women and children moving slowly up and down the fields. His own window was on the far side of the house, but the view from it was much the same except that, about a hundred metres away from him now, there stood a tall, cylindrical building, crudely built using the ubiquitous white stone;

he took this to be the community's granary. The edge of the valley – at least in this direction – was skirted by a fringe of conifers; from the darkness at their hem he guessed that it was the edge of a fairly deep forest, but his vantage point wasn't quite high enough for him to be certain. Above the trees he could see one of Albion's few clouds; it was a white, thinly woven thing, bearing no threat of rain. The breeze made it move very slowly across the sky. He felt the dirty cotton of his nightshirt – made even dirtier since he'd come up here into the attic – pressing greasily against his chest, stomach and buttocks. He knew that he stank, but couldn't smell himself.

What in all the worlds possesses Mina that she'd want to be anywhere near me? he thought. He remembered the sight of her under the blaze of light from the window; she'd looked lovely then. Back in the World, whatever her birth, she could have ended up as a rich man's wife or, if she'd preferred, a royal courtesan. Or she could have done something else. Bella had chosen to do something else. She'd become a respected member of a ship's crew, and then dead. She'd become a 'thing' stuck with little ceremony into a shallow grave. Wasn't Mina better off, just being alive? *No*, he thought, *she's not. For Bella it's all over, the pains are done; but for Mina the agonies will go on for the eternity that is the rest of her life.*

He rocked back a little, grabbing the lower edge of the splintery wooden sill with his hands to keep himself half-upright. *I can change the way things* are *here*, he thought. *I can help Mina and all the other Minas – and the Greds and the Lantzes – to discover how to live the lives of real people. But I can't start now. I've got to wait a bit – wait until I've more strength.* He looked at the thinness of his white arms stretched out in front of him. *But then I'll find or forge a sword, and then I'll lead these people to freedom, and then I'll . . . And then I'll what? Become their king? Me – the new Ellonia?*

Again he let himself muse for a while about Mina, and the way she had looked just a little while ago, when she'd been talking with him here up in the attic. No – it wasn't the way that she'd looked, although that had been a part of it. It was the way that she'd *been*. If she'd been a sister of his he'd have loved her like a brother loves a sister: the fact of her solemn grey eyes and her pointed chin would have been irrelevant. But she wasn't a sister. And, because of the way she felt about him, they could never have a relationship like that. He did love her, he recognised, but he wasn't *in love* with her.

And he didn't know why he wasn't.

I wish I were.

His thoughts were circling. Maybe he *was* in love with her. Maybe that was the reason his thoughts were circling. Because, whatever he told himself, he really was in love with her. And being in love with her made his thoughts circle. And the more they circled about her the more likely it was that he would become in love with her. And . . .

A little gust of wind came in through the skylight, cooling his face and bringing him back to full wakefulness. He pulled himself forward again until he could see as much as possible of the complex of farmsteads.

There was the squawk of a rather badly blown trumpet. Terman winced. He could play several musical instruments quite well.

Again a blare. Now his ears were picking up the regular thumping of horses' hoofs. Soon after, he heard the jingling of the bells of their harnesses.

Now was the time for caution. As quietly as possible he dragged one of the upright barrels from behind him so that he could seat himself upon it and watch comfortably from the skylight. The effort of lugging it across the greyed floor sucked at his strength, but he managed it. Seated, he could enjoy almost as full a view as before. He let his bearded chin drop onto the chest of his nightdress for a few moments, catnapping again. Then he jerked himself upright.

Please, please, he thought to the gods whom he knew only remotely, *please let Mina be unharmed. Let them* all *be unharmed.*

As far as he could see, the peasants were doing a superb job of acting their parts. The soldiers – perhaps twenty of them – came cantering on their horses into a natural clearing about fifty metres away, directly between him and the tower: presumably he'd been right and it was indeed a storehouse for grain. One man was carrying a banner showing a dog impaled on a sword. Six horses, following the warriors, were pulling empty wooden four-wheeled carts. The convoy came to a halt in the well trodden clearing.

But the soldiers weren't solely interested in grain: they wanted to record the people. The trumpet blared two or three times more, calling the peasants in from their fields. They moved slowly and seemingly aimlessly towards the granary. Once again Terman was amazed at how well the villagers were playing their roles: they looked exactly like the slow-brained creatures they were supposed to be. It seemed to take forever before they were all finally there, but at last one of the soldiers – the leading officer, to judge by the fact that his dress was largely composed of dazzling vermilion and cobalt green, while the others were uniformed in deep swamp-reds – leapt down from his horse and began to herd the peasants into some sort of order.

Terman heard the man's high voice as he shouted: 'Stay!' The peasants froze where they were.

The officer strutted among them, a metal helmet under his arm, tapping a hand to the top of each head, obviously counting. From here it was difficult for Terman to follow his progress – every time he thought he'd got the right number he began to wonder if he'd missed a row or if he'd counted the same row twice. Some of the faces he recognised, because they belonged to people he'd named; he was ashamed how rare it was for him to be able to remember the name which he'd ascribed to a particular person. The woman with the dewlaps that made her look like a turkey – yes, he'd met her and named her, but all he could recall about her was the way she'd smiled as he'd spoken to her. The small boy whose head was tapped next by the officer's gloved hand – he was . . . he was . . . By the gods, was the lack of memory infectious in Albion? No. Wait. It wasn't. That was young Redin, far too bright for his own good – now.

Now.

Terman knew that he had changed things here. Redin had been just *any* little boy until he had been given a name. The lad couldn't be more than about ten. Surely something in his demeanour would give away to the officer the fact that there had been a change . . .

The officer was tapping the head of the next peasant in line.

Terman breathed deeply.

Mina, in her woollen dress, was just another figure in the ranks of the peasants: Terman could distinguish her only because she was unusually tall and stood head and shoulders above all the other grey-haired people. He sent a mental message of friendship to her, at the same time knowing that she wouldn't receive it.

Oh shit, he thought. The officer had reached Mina, and his hand was poised above her head. The hand hovered, and then was withdrawn.

'This one – she may be a rebel!' shouted the officer, the words clear enough across the distance for Terman to understand them. *No*, he thought, *but she's pretty, and you think it would help you control your men if they were allowed to screw her. Have the guts to admit that to yourself and I'll spare your life. If you don't, then by all of the gods that may or may not exist I'll pursue you to the furthest shores of Albion.*

Then he thought: *He said she might be a rebel. But from all Mina has told me there can't possibly be such things as rebels among these poor forsaken people. Unless there have been others here before like me? Then again, maybe it's one of those vague insults that haven't got any real meaning in themselves, like 'bastard' . . .*

She is me and I am her . . .

Mina was dragged out from the ranks of the peasants. The officer seemed to have lost all interest in counting them, and was now issuing high-pitched orders that the cattle (for a moment Terman was confused and then realised that what the officer was talking about were the oxen) should be brought to the clearing. He paid no attention as a couple of his men pushed Mina onto the ground, pulling her skirt up over her thighs.

Terman threw up. He couldn't watch, and he couldn't not watch. He wanted a sword, one of those foolish little phallic symbols he'd always been so bad at using; he wanted his full strength back. But she'd told him that any foolhardy attack would just make things worse for the peasants – and he'd agreed with her. He still did, yet that didn't stop his fingernails scraping away greyish splinters of wood from the window-frame. There was a soldier on top of her now, trousers around his ankles; she lay on her back, face staring towards the sky, apparently registering no sensation at all. The other peasants didn't look at what was happening. A second soldier waited his turn.

The cattle were brought, then the sheep. They were loaded onto three of the supply carts, protesting loudly in their animal ways. A cow lifted its tail and let ordure splatter loudly over the side of its cart; Terman reckoned that the Ellonian soldiers would be unlucky over much of their journey home, because the beast was obviously suffering from some kind of enteric disease. At a further sharp command from the officer the peasants began to bring out sackloads of grain from the granary and load them into the other carts. A third soldier was now mounting Mina, who was still lying there like a corpse.

And that's her revenge, Terman suddenly realised. *They don't know it, but that's her revenge. Each of them wants to make her react in some way, but she's not going to. And they can't blame her, because as far as they know she's just a mindless peasant slave.*

The sight of her being raped hurt him. He could imagine nothing less erotic. More than ever, he wanted to kill – preferably her attackers but, failing that, anyone at all. Killing had once been his trade, and he'd been adequate at it. His emotions were mixed, though. Watching also made him want to make love with her, to show her what love-making really was – not a throwing to the ground and a taking, but a long slow process of giving.

Most of the grain had been loaded, now.

For a while, back in the World, he'd flirted with the

crossbow, an instrument of death that could strike people down a hundred metres away. He didn't have a crossbow here. He wished that he did. But he might mis-aim and hurt Mina. There was a wooden stock in his right hand and he lifted the weapon, squinting along its sights . . . and then there was no such thing, just himself, confined in this musty-smelling attic, watching as Mina was thoughtlessly defiled.

No, 'defiled' wasn't the word. The soldiers were defiling themselves. She would be unchanged, would remain the way she had always been.

After a long while the Ellonian soldiers left, announcing their departure by another cracked blast of the trumpet. They hadn't bothered to perform more than a perfunctory search of a couple of houses. Mina waited until the last sounds of hooves had disappeared, then stood up, her skirt falling easily back down over her hips. She smiled wanly at those peasants – including Gred and Lantz – who gathered around her, offering consolation and praising her for the way she'd acted out her part. She brushed them aside. She looked up to the skylight where Terman had been watching, and he caught her gaze.

Later Mina bathed for a very long time in front of the open fire. Afterwards, smelling of coarse soap, she crept up to Terman's bed. He was almost asleep, but he took her into his arms; then he pulled the nightshirt he hated up over his head and threw it away to a far corner of the room. Though the smoothness of her in his arms was something he now realised he'd been wanting for as long as he'd been telling himself he didn't, they just allowed their bodies to fall into sleep nestled against each other.

Waking was different.

When they awoke they made love to each other so peacefully and so tranquilly that it was almost as if there had been no such thing as time.

To her, he thought, *there really has never been such a thing as time*. He wondered at his callousness in thinking such things when, after all, it was his *duty* to be lost in the sensuality of her. *I feel that just for now I have no* understanding *of the fact that there was a time before we made love. In these sweaty shared moments my memories are only half-recognised miasmas. And yet for her that's the way time has always been. Whenever she's tried to look back in her mind, all she's been aware of is a kind of non-time: a vague idea of a yesterday about which she can remember almost nothing. Dammit! She knew in a hopelessly hazy way that things had happened in the past – just the same way that I sense them now, as if they were furry objects I could never quite touch – but to her that was natural, a thing that was elementary because it was accepted, not just by her but by her mother and father and all of those who went before them.*

I should have brought her clarity, but instead I've brought her the kind of non-time that I've always so enjoyed while lying beside my lovers.

The feel of her skin is a form of memory.

She has a past, even though she doesn't much like that notion (neither do I). I've created for myself a state of mind that to me is paradisiac, but to her it's a sad return to the haze of her previous existence . . .

He ran a fingertip all the way down the ridge of her spine and began to cry against her shoulder.

Chapter Three
Giorran

The young sub-lieutenant paused for breath. He'd been climbing for more than an hour now, struggling over slopes of scree that gave way beneath his feet so that he had to climb three metres to gain only one, and scrambling up near-vertical walls of flaky shale that crumbled away in his hands: several times he'd found himself swinging vertiginously out over empty space before he'd been able to grapple his way back to a more secure handhold. Now he'd found a ledge where he could rest for a while.

He looked upwards, towards the summit, currently obscured from his sight by the swell of the hillside. He knew that there wasn't far to go, but the last part would probably be the hardest.

He sat down, his arms around his knees, and gazed out over several hundred square kilometres of Albion. From here the countryside looked like a patchwork quilt that someone had carelessly thrown on the floor. He couldn't fully see the Ellonian palace-fortress of Giorran: instead, beyond the boundaries of Ernestrad there was laid out before him a many-coloured pattern of greens and yellows and golds and browns. The early-morning haze muted the tones into pastels. The pattern itself was constantly changing, as if a draught from beneath the door were blowing under the quilt and puffing it up here and there, wherever it wished. The tight grey lines of demarcating dykes moved slowly into different arrangements as he watched, like the gossamer strands of a spider's web in the breeze.

He nodded. All was well in Albion, then. As ever, all was flux.

So all was well?

He had led a convoy of soldiers on a tour of inspection around the villages in the southern part of the region, near to the fringes of the mist that, according to a few heretics, separated Albion from some unimaginable other world. The tour had lasted nearly fifty waking-times, and it was only towards the end of it that he had begun to experience concern.

In one of the villages which they had pillaged – no, taxed – for crops and livestock, there had been some kind of incongruity, but he still wasn't quite sure what it had been. The soldiers under his command had noticed nothing, and at the time neither had he. But later a twitching somewhere in his mind had become an itch: yes, there'd been *something wrong*. The trouble was that, since all of the villages they'd been through had been so very much alike, he couldn't remember which of them it had been that had made him sense this wrongness in the scheme of things. The system whereby the convoys worked in each village was always similar: the soldiers appropriated the provisions, he made a pretence of counting the peasants, and a select few of the men took turns in screwing the prettiest women on display. It had all been repeated so many times during the short course of his military career that the villages had become an inchoate blur to him – sunlight and animal smells and glum-faced serfs were much the same anywhere.

He looked down at his red and green uniform sadly. On the two previous occasions he'd climbed this hill he'd had the foresight to dress himself in tough furs; this time he'd acted on the spur of the moment, when suddenly his doubts had crossed an invisible threshold and forced him away from Giorran. He'd pushed his horse into a gallop away from the palace even though the beast had whinnied in terror and attempted to baulk as he forced it to traverse the protective ditches.

His palms and fingers were in worse condition than his uniform. They were covered in a multitude of cuts and slashes, most of them superficial but some of them deep and oozing dark blood. It was odd that he hadn't noticed his injuries while he'd been clambering up the sharp scales of the shale; now that he looked properly at the abrasions for the first time they began to sting and throb.

Well, his uniform was beyond salvage already, so he tore strips from his trousers and used them to bind up his hands, making the knots as tight as he could. He winced as the bandages made the pain, for a few seconds, even more intense; then he applied extra pressure to the knots.

His breathing was coming more easily now.

Again he looked up-slope. Was it worth it? Would it *really* be worth it to hazard the final stages of the ascent just so that he could test his undefined doubts?

He shrugged.

Yes, it's worth it.

He got wearily to his feet and reached up with his bandaged hands towards a sharp granitic shelf. He felt the inevitable pain even before he touched the stone edge.

The shelf was narrower than he'd hoped – no more than twenty centimetres wide – but from this new vantage point he could see that there was a stream-bed some thirty or forty metres to his right. Only an outswelling of rock and the perverse course of the stream had stopped him seeing this from the ledge where he'd been relaxing. Momentarily he thought about dropping back down to the ledge, but then the idea of going backwards repelled him: no, he couldn't allow himself the luxury of retreating, in any sense of the word.

He spread his arms wide on either side, knotting his fingers through stubbly tufts of coarse grass and leaning as far in towards the curve of the hillside as he could. The brown grass smelled spicy and warm, recalling the kitchen at home in his childhood. He hugged the mountain for fully a minute, as if it were his mother's soft thighs, and then he carefully took a step sideways.

A section of weathered, friable rock immediately gave way beneath his right foot, and he forced his weight back onto his left. Instinctively, he clutched even more tightly at the grass, although he knew that it would never support him if the shelf gave way beneath him now. He had a vision of himself tumbling away and away down the hillside, bouncing from rock to rock until, bleeding and tattered, his body lay brokenly in the midst of a final bed of scree.

He was not a man accustomed to fear of any sort, but for a little while he felt terror.

Don't look down! said an internal voice.

'Don't bloody worry,' he muttered to it. 'I won't.'

Once he felt that he was again in full control of his body, he shifted his left hand towards his right, gaining new purchase on the tough grass, and then his right hand further away from him, so that he was draped at an acute angle over the gap where the rock had given way.

Sweat ran down over his forehead, bringing the salt from his eyebrows into his right eye. He blinked furiously and painfully, his vision swimming. His natural reactions were urging him to pull a hand away from the hillside so that he could draw a sleeve across his stinging eye, but he knew that if he did so he'd topple outwards to his death. He tried to force himself to cry, to wash away the stabbing saltiness, but even in infancy he'd never been much good at crying.

He had to look down – had to if he wanted to be able to carry on along this shelf.

He saw a blurred shape which he interpreted as the gap in the rock with, below it, the cruelly toothed precipice of shale. He jabbed out tentatively with his right foot, tapping it against the crumbling rocky edge on the other side of the hiatus.

What are you doing here? said the internal voice.

I need counsel, he thought angrily, wondering if he had the courage to kick out harder.

Yes, the voice agreed, *I know that – and I know why you need counsel. But that doesn't really answer my question. What's it to you if you had a creepy feeling in some little anonymous dump of a village? Why risk your life over it?*

Because I'm a member of the House of Ellon. When I reached puberty I swore that I would die rather than betray it in even the smallest of ways.

How small is 'smallest'?

He landed a solid kick against the thin edge of the rock on the far side of the gulf. A few small fragments were dislodged, and they pitter-pattered swiftly away down the shale face beneath.

The smallest of all, he responded sharply.

Is loyalty your only motive? Isn't there something else?

'Shut up!' he said aloud.

But the voice persisted.

The real truth is that you're ambitious, isn't it? You're young for a sub-lieutenant, and your superiors, however much they may resent you, have nothing but good to say about you. You hope to reach the summit not just of this hill but of the whole Ellonian army, don't you? And from there it would be just a short step to the Despotism itself. Isn't that it?

Another hearty kick, and another heartening feeling of solidity against his toes.

A short step, said the voice.

'Yes, damn it, a short step! Right now I want to take a short step across this bloody gap, and you're distracting me! We can talk about all this later.'

The tuft of grass he'd been gripping with his right hand abruptly came out by its roots.

Reactively he let go with his left hand as well. He twisted his body towards the hillside as he fell.

A moment later his chin hit the shelf on the far side of the gap with such force that he came near to losing consciousness. He was now lying face-down on the shelf, his head, arms and shoulders secure on one side of the gulf and, on the other, his legs from just above the knee.

He waited for the creaking beneath him that would signal the end. It was several minutes later that he realised it wasn't coming.

Timorously he raised his head.

This seemed to serve as a cue for the internal voice to return to nag him again.

Is it worth it, though? Wouldn't it be better to spend the rest of your life as a minor scion of the House of Ellon than to kill yourself on this hillside?

63

'No!' he shouted at the top of his voice.

Don't cause an avalanche, said the voice smugly, like a tutor he'd once had who had taken great pleasure in pointing out the folly of his pupils.

'I'm – not – causing – an – *avalanche*,' he said furiously but quietly, much as he'd replied to the tutor on similar occasions.

So, you need to take counsel because you're worried about this rural slum whose name you can't even remember – right? And the only reason you want to do so is to advance your career – hmm? Be the village's crime ever so small, you – you clever young junior officer – will have been the one who discovered it. That'll go down well with the generals and the Army-Master, won't it?

'Be quiet. Please.'

And the generals and Army-Master Garndon will say to all the other officers: 'Look, here's a young man with promise. He spotted something a bit odd in a village somewhere, so he climbed up a hill to ask for counsel, and after he'd been given the counsel he came back down again and he led a patrol to put the village to the torch and the sword. Only he couldn't remember where the village was, precisely, because they all look the bloody same, same, same.'

If he could hump himself up like a caterpillar, he might just be able to spring with his legs hard enough to throw the whole of his body across the gap to safety. He looked over the edge of the shelf and then, very swiftly, stopped doing so. Using his elbows as a fulcrum, he scrabbled forwards with his feet until his stiffened legs forced his pelvis into the air. He was sickly aware that, in this position, his balance wasn't very good.

Why didn't you just go back and burn the village on suspicion? asked the voice.

Because I couldn't remember which one it was. And anyway I'm a just man, he thought with part of his mind, the rest of it concentrating his energies for the forward leap. It was unlikely that he'd have more than one chance: failure would almost certainly mean death or – worse – devastating injury. Few people came up this hill, so he might linger for days in agony before finally dying.

But that's not the real reason, is it?

He wished the voice would go away. He tucked his head down to look back between his elbows. He saw ragged trousers at the end of which were his boots, firmly secured against the edge of rock. Now came the tricky bit, getting himself from his elbows up onto his hands.

In fact, this proved easier than he'd expected, despite the fact that his hands were now hurting him so much that his arms throbbed in sympathy from wrist to shoulder. He pulled his elbows along the rough brown-silver rock until his bandaged hands were directly beneath his collarbone on either side.

His arms trembled like those of a person with fever as he strained his muscles to force himself up.

Now. If he could do it.

The real reason, said the voice, as usual carefully picking the wrong moment to intrude itself into his consciousness, *is that that wouldn't be enough. Who in Giorran would want to hear about the razing of a small outlying village and its pitiable populace? Why – no one! But if you come back to Giorran, all fine and fancy in your bright and dandyish uniform, your pennants flying high in the air and your carts groaning with grain and livestock and your soldiers telling good tales about the wenches they've raped – ah, then, it's a different thing if you tell your superiors that there's a strange place out there where things aren't exactly as they should be.*

'My hands can't take this much longer,' he half-wept to himself. 'Please – I've asked you before – please go away.'

But then you've got to seek counsel. Yes indeed you do, do. You've got to make sure, because otherwise you might make not so much sure but a fool of yourself.

Leave me!

The force of his thought was so great that it drove the voice away back into the part of his mind from which it had earlier emerged, unwelcomed.

It seemed to him that he was moving in slow motion as he tensed his legs and arms, and then lunged forwards to find himself in a precarious crouch on the far side of the cleft. He was on his hands and knees, his head slouched downwards as he struggled to control himself.

The shelf was only just wide enough to hold him in this position. With infinite care, he turned his torso towards the hillside, again grabbing at the sprouting grass. If he remembered not to put too much faith in it, he would be able to pull himself to his feet.

It was a long, slow operation, but at last he was successful.

As he crept around the mountainside towards the stream-bed, his breathing like a shout in his ears, he made a point of securing himself at every crablike pace before thumping his right foot down on the next section of the shelf.

He was lucky.

Soon he was at the stream-bed, down which danced a bubbling gush of ice-cold water. He propped himself against a tall rock and cupped one bloodily bandaged hand to drink. It seemed to him that he drank for a lifetime, and when he had finished there was a hard coldness in his belly; at first his hand had stung from the water, but then the coldness had taken the pain away. He splashed his face a few times, mopping at it with his sleeve before splashing it again.

He pissed into the water and then squinted up the stream-bed.

He could follow it for the next hundred metres or so, he reckoned, perhaps further, so long as he didn't mind being drenched in frosty spray the whole way; right now he could think of nothing that would give him more pleasure. The stones underfoot were rounded by the flow of the stream, and therefore treacherous, but if he straddled his hands and feet on the firmer ground to either side he could climb up it without too much difficulty.

Moments later he was working his way upwards, sometimes cricking his neck to look ahead of him but more often just watching the flow and bubble of the stream as it passed between his arms and legs, feeling its cooling splashes on his face.

* * *

Despite his forebodings, the route to the summit was comparatively easy once he had scrambled out of the streambed. He found himself under the brassily open sky once more, walking confidently – despite his exhaustion – towards the cairn that marked the peak of a slope so mild that it was almost a plateau. The grass beneath his feet was closely cropped; he remembered from the last time he'd been here that the hill was the haunt of various grazing creatures. Although there were none visible now, he could see their droppings, like perfectly formed raisins, littering the ground all around him.

The pain in his hands seemed to ebb away as he walked easily towards the cairn. He felt supremely confident. Those who conquered this hill were granted the blessing of counsel; those who failed to make the ascent were doomed to death or, even worse, a lifetime of enforced mediocrity.

The cairn was just as he had recalled it – a haphazard pile of loose grey-white stones, weathered by the millennia until it was as if, from whatever angle you looked at them, you could see sly faces peering back out at you. Of course, this was just an effect created by the patterns of cracks across them.

He knew this.

He told himself very firmly that he knew this.

From here he could see even more of the plains of Albion than before. He wandered past the cairn and gazed down on the shimmeringly white structure that was Giorran, near which he'd been brought up. From here it looked like a child's toy – but a toy carved and lovingly painted by a master-craftsman. The pennants that flew from its turrets were nothing more than spots of colour that he could see out of the corners of his eyes: as soon as he looked at them directly they disappeared. The dots seemed red, the green being subsumed into the stronger colour. There was a convoy of wagons forming up before the great gates – again he thought of a child's miniature toy. He could just about make out the moving figures of soldiers as they tended the horses – but those specks might have been only an optical

67

illusion, his brain telling his eyes to see what it knew must be there.

It's odd, he thought, *that when I'm in and around Giorran, or even when I'm touring the land collecting tributes from the villages, I regard that place as my home. Every time I think of it, it's as if it were a part of me and me a part of it. But when I stand up here on this hill I see the place differently: it has nothing to do with me at all. Standing here gives me freedom from Giorran. The trouble is*, his thought continued, *that I'm not sure that it's a freedom I really want.*

He let his gaze rove onwards.

In one place the shifting patterns of the coloured fields and their enclosing dykes were fixed. That must mean that there was a patrol at work there, with its Ellonian leader fixing reality by his presence, his unconscious, inherited magic stilling the landscape around him. He wondered who that leader might be – but there were so many of his own rank that it was unlikely that he knew the man.

He turned back towards the cairn, and saw the curlew perched at its peak.

His heart sank.

The breeze that had refreshed him was now beginning to whip at his curly red-orange hair, and he realised that his time of counsel was approaching.

But the curlew! he thought despairingly.

The curlew was never a bringer of good news; usually it was a harbinger of evil. He willed the bird to fly away but it refused to move, settling itself comfortably on its yellow claws and watching him through one bright blinkless eye. He'd faced swords in his time – what trainee soldier hadn't? – but he found himself terrified of the bird's long, viciously curved beak. *What if it goes for my face?*

He forced the fear away from him, almost as if he were using his hands physically to shove at it. Looking always at the curlew, he made himself adopt an easy stroll as he approached the cairn.

Once there – his cloth-covered, still-bleeding hands touching one of the warm stones – he looked up at the bird; it looked back at him, unconcerned and seemingly uninterested in his presence.

He let the air out of his lungs in a gust, and then turned deliberately away from the metallic stare. He settled himself down with his back against the side of the cairn, feeling the comfort of its stones caressing him. He closed his eyes and felt the choppy wind increasing in its intensity, so that now the rags of his uniform were lashing at his limbs.

Cautiously, he half-raised his eyelids.

All around him, there were seeds and leaves and insects and other small things being blown from left to right across his dimmed vision. The clouds were fast-flying feathers beyond. Beneath them he could see, away in the distance, a line of trees on the plains of Albion being tormented. He put his hands behind him to take a more secure grip on the rocks of the cairn. They had felt warm to him before. Now they were cold.

The gale grew ever more powerful. It was tearing at the remains of his clothes and trying to rip his body away from the security of the cairn, but he held on determinedly. Blood dribbled down his clean-shaven chin as he involuntarily bit his lower lip. The thundering noise was more than his ears could bear, and a trickle of impossibly red blood dripped down onto one shoulder. He screamed, but the sound was lost in the din of the elements. It seemed as if all of Albion was erupting, the ground being pushed up from beneath by some subterranean behemoth eager to escape into the open air. The whole hill was moving, rocked backwards and forwards by the ferocious blasts of the gale. His lips pulled back from his teeth as he swivelled his head from side to side, trying to ignore the pain in his hands and his ears, his spirit caught up in the power of the wind.

And all of a sudden it was gone.

He wasn't in the wind any longer.

He was in the presence of the Wind.

Although he knew that there was still a gale rampaging all around him, he was no longer affected by it; it was as if he had fought his way through a hurricane until he had reached the calm at its centre. He opened his eyes. He could see the plateau being thrashed by the wind, but he was in a place where there wasn't the slightest of breezes to disturb him.

He got to his feet and looked around.

The curlew was still there, on top of the cairn, looking unruffled. Everywhere else, though, there was chaos as far as his eyes could see. He wandered across to look down once more on the nursery model of Giorran he'd been looking at before. One of the flagpoles had come down, and miniature men were battling against the winds to keep the others erect. In the distance, he could see that the forest margins were being brought down. But he himself felt as if he were out walking in a balmy glade.

'I've brought myself to you, Wind,' he shouted.

The curlew turned its head to look at him sceptically with its other eye.

And I am with you.

At once he was thrown to his knees, the hurricane tugging him inexorably towards the edge of the summit. He dug his fingers into the hard ground and let himself be pulled down until he was prostrate, his face pressed against a mixture of short grass and animal droppings.

'Give me mercy, Wind,' he said softly and humbly into the grass.

You have my mercy.

This time the effect of the Wind's voice was like little more than a pat on the back. Reassured, he sat up, crossing his legs and putting his battered hands to his groin. The curlew was still watching him with interest. The whole of the plateau seemed to be encapsulated in a shining grey cylinder of serenity; now he could only dimly see through it the turmoil of the outside world. It was rather as if he were at the centre of the vortex that forms as water disappears down a drain.

'I bring you my respect,' he said quietly.

I accept your respect.

'I beg your counsel.'

Most people who come here do, remarked the Wind waspishly.

'I do not insult you by bringing any form of gift or

70

tribute to pay for your advice. I know that you have wealth beyond anything that a mere mortal could even dream of.'

The Wind was silent and, momentarily perplexed by this lack of response, the soldier found himself stumbling with his words.

'There's a village . . .' he said, 'a village – over there somewhere.' He gestured in a fashion that showed he was indicating no direction in particular. 'I was in the village a few weeks ago with my men, collecting its produce, and . . . well, it was a strange kind of feeling, but I didn't like it.'

Nadar, said the Wind, *if I had to rely on your words I would never discover your meaning.*

Nadar sighed.

'Well, let me put it – ' he began.

Child, said the Wind wearily, *I am as old as time itself, a thousand times older than the insignificant species of which you are an insignificant member. Do you think that I have not learned how to read the expressions on your faces and the movements of your limbs? I know what your doubt is.*

He leaned forward, his bloodied face alert.

You were right, Nadar, the Wind told him slowly, breathing each of its words directly into his mind. *In the village you talk of there has indeed been a change.*

'What? Tell me – what?'

In his eagerness Nadar had accidentally raised his voice again, so that the Wind's answer bruised his face and body, knocking him sideways until he lay at full length on the grass.

It is not within my power to tell you. I can only tell you things that you can understand. This change I talk of involves the World, which means that it cannot be comprehended by you.

'The World? The outer world? But that's a myth! This is all the world there is.'

Pulling himself back up to a sitting position he waved his arms to indicate the spread of Albion all around them.

You make my point for me, child, said the Wind.

'Then why do you talk of the World?'

71

That is not what I meant.

Nadar was puzzled. The Wind seemed to be teasing him, deliberately talking in riddles. First of all it talked about the World, and then it said that there was no such place. He shook his head briefly. It did not do to antagonise the Wind by asking too many questions: if it were to become exasperated with him it could easily, with all the colossal power at its command, destroy him utterly.

'Can you tell me more?' he asked humbly.

Yes, but only a little. The voice of the Wind in his mind sounded oddly reluctant.

'Then tell me. Please. I implore you.'

This change you sensed, Nadar: it affects all of the House of Ellon, but no one more than you.

Nadar's spirits surged. He had been right to come here after all. The Wind was as good as telling him that he would rise to a position of great authority among the Ellonia.

There will be war because of a man. You would hardly even notice that he was a man – you would dismiss him as just a peasant, barely seeing him for what he really was. The Wind paused, as if searching for words. After a few moments it continued. *There will be blood – far too much blood. And you – you will lead the army of the Ellonia across the face of Albion. Eventually you will triumph, but the moment when you feel that you have achieved paramount victory will be the moment that sees your own destruction.*

His mind filled with dreams of glory. To be victorious and to die in battle – what more could a warrior seek?

'Then I shall wage war against this . . . this peasant you talk of?' he said.

No, replied the Wind. It was aware that Nadar was frequently misinterpreting its words, but knew that it was useless to try to disillusion him: the man was hearing what he wanted to hear, and would continue to do so. *He will remain a peasant, nothing more, for the rest of his short life. And you will never meet him, or know who he is. But by his presence alone he has started a pattern of changes that will in due course transform all of Albion.*

Nadar thought for a few seconds, watching his hands as

the fingers laced and unlaced. Then he said, as much to himself as to the Wind: 'I can change that, can't I?' His voice was barely more than a mutter.

No.

The single syllable in his mind was flat, unyielding, final. 'Can't I?' Nadar whispered to himself.

You have my counsel, said the Wind. *Now it is for you to do with it what you wish. I can tell you no more than what I have already told you, and I can offer you no guidance.*

The shining grey cylinder of calm melted slowly into invisibility, and Nadar found himself once more in the teeth of the tempest. Precariously poised on his hands and knees, he made his way uncertainly towards the cairn, on top of which the curlew still perched; still its feathers were unruffled. The bird looked at him with a sort of beady interest which he interpreted as an expression of contempt.

'Go away, foul creature!' he yelled, huddling for shelter against the rocks of the cairn. 'Get away from me!'

The shriek of the gale drowned his words but, as if it had heard him, the curlew stretched its wings and flapped away from the hilltop in a leisurely fashion, apparently unaffected by the winds. Through watering eyes he watched it until it was just a distant black dot.

The storm lasted for several hours before Nadar, chilled through to the marrow of his bones, was able to pick his way back down the slopes to the place where he had tethered his horse.

That sleeping-time he had no wish for the feel of peasant-flesh against him, and so he bedded one of the minor aristocrats who littered Giorran with little purpose other than to be pampered, fed and, should it prove necessary in order to maintain their lifestyle, bedded by soldiers like himself. Nadar was young, sturdy and good-looking in his own harsh way, so he had little difficulty in obtaining the services of one of the prettiest. She proved to be one of the most agile and imaginative as well, and gave a brilliant impersonation of ecstasy. It was only after his second climax, his body stuck to hers from shoulders to loins, feeling her weight on top of him and her soft breasts squashed against his chest, that warmth finally returned to him.

The fortress of Giorran was, like the House of Ellon, as old as time itself. Of course, this wasn't strictly true – it must have had builders in some ancient era, but who they were and why they had built the great gleaming white palace was a historical mystery – although the theological explanation was clear enough. Ernestrad's mages had built up a complicated tapestry of legends about the earliest race of human beings with the express aim of being able to trace the direct patrilineal descent of whoever was currently Despot back to the most prominent ancients. This required rapid revision of previous interpretations of the legends whenever a Despot died childless and the title passed to a cousin, an even more distant relative or, quite commonly, to the person who had been his Army-Master. Lives were often lost in the interim period before such scholarly researches could be completed, so the mages spent a considerable amount of their energies in performing incantations to ensure that, on the death of each Despot, his eldest son and heir proved to be astonishingly fertile. The mages had also persuaded the ruling line to adopt extensive polygamy. The fact that on occasion the successor bore little physical resemblance to his deceased father concerned no one at all, least of all the mages, who were the only ones who had an inkling of why this might be. Sometimes the heir looked rather like one of the mages, who would nod his head sagely and announce that this merely proved the efficacy of the powerful magic he had used on behalf of his master.

Their practice in all things was as in the matter of the inheritance: they used enchantments and spells but, just in case, they also supplied a more mundane fall-back. This was sensible of them because, as most of them guiltily suspected, they possessed no magical abilities at all. Perversely, the land of Albion – a land in which magic ran riot in the shifting forms of every field and stream – had failed to grant the conscious use of magic to all but a few – the dreamers and the singers among them – who wisely stayed as far from Giorran as they could in order to avoid capture and enslavement. The haughty aristocrats of the House of Ellon and the officers of their army believed that they possessed small splinters of magic, but they were wrong: instead, they lacked the ability to experience magic at all, thereby positively repelling it from their vicinity.

In the beginning – the mages still told the rulers of the House of Ellon – there was nothing but the Sun. This all-powerful and benevolent being had existed on his own in perfect contentment for untold aeons until he detected within himself a sensation he had never experienced before: boredom. Another few aeons went by before he hit on a solution to this problem: he could make another sun, just like himself. He promptly did so. However, this proved unsatisfactory because almost immediately the two of them began to quarrel over who was more powerful than the other. The original Sun decided to exterminate his creation, and the two of them fought a long and painful struggle before one triumphed, consigning the other to oblivion. Small fragments remained after the destruction, and these coalesced and clumped together to form the multi-aspected entity that manifests itself as magic.

Which of the two was the victor? Ah, that became one of the great mysteries of the cosmos, the answer to the question being known only to the mages, who were sworn on pain of death never to reveal it. (In fact, millennia before, one of them had decided that the Sun himself could tell the mages through influencing a mundane action. This wise man had therefore taken a flat pebble and inscribed different patterns on either side of it. He had cast the pebble high into the air and watched eagerly to see which pattern would be uppermost when the stone landed. At this moment the Sun decided to punish him for his impertinence – the mage went blue in the face and dropped down dead – but his acolytes were able to determine which Sun it was who had triumphed.)

The Sun – whichever one he was – still faced the problem of boredom. He decided that he must bring into existence *something* which would help him pass the time because, even though a millennium was to him nothing more than the blink of an eye, there had been really rather a lot of millennia by now. This time, though, the creation would not be of anything that might rival himself in mightiness. He therefore brought Albion into existence, and that was the start of eternity.

At first Albion had been populated by vile slinking creatures who infested not just the land but also the rivers, including the greatest of them all: the river that ran right around the edge of the world. This river was, of course, alive: it breathed, and it relied upon the lesser rivers to give it sustenance. The primeval denizens of the Sun's creation were not at all to his liking, so he decided to change them into something a little more interesting to watch. He experimented countless times, and some of the results intrigued him enough that he allowed them to continue in existence; others were less pleasing, and were therefore discarded.

At last the Sun hit on what seemed to him to be a good template: a creature with two arms, two legs and a head. This was the first human being, and she was called Redfo. The Sun looked at her and made a second human being, who was more complete; he was called Casaub. Neither of them were quite up to the Sun's exacting standards, but he reasoned that, if he gave them the power of breeding together, then in due course, after many generations, perfection might result.

He blinked an eye, and when he opened it again, sure enough, Albion was populated by thousands upon thousands of human beings whom he found, in the main, visually appealing. Indeed, there were some among them whom he considered to be as near to perfection as he was ever likely to attain. To these fortunate ones he gave the powers of reason; it was their duty to organise and lead all of their mindless brethren. He called them the Ellonia in recognition of the fairest of them all, a man who stood two metres tall – perhaps even taller, according to the more fanciful of storytellers – and who had given to himself the name of Ellon.

Yet even the Ellonia were not yet *quite* perfect, so the

Sun did not give them the gift of immortality. Instead, he decided to blink his other eye, leaving them to breed ever closer to his ideal. That eye is still, as it were, blinked, but one day the Sun will open it again, and on that day he will discover that true perfection has been brought into existence in the form – of course – of the current Despot of all Albion. *We mages had thought that this would come in the time of your father, oh great one, but obviously we were wrong by a few decades. Who knows what the next waking-period may bring?*

There was still the matter of the repulsive primeval creatures to be dealt with, because the Sun had failed to eliminate them all, and the most perverted of them were showing their evil by breeding true. Furthermore, they resented the presence of the human beings, especially the Ellonia; the thing that infuriated them most of all was that the Ellonia were clearly much more favoured by the benevolent father (some say mother) in the skies than they themselves were. They declared war against the beautiful creatures whom the Sun had created, and for a time it looked as if they might prevail. However, Ellon himself, drawing upon all the reserves of his huge strength, single-handedly built the fortress of Giorran, chopping rocks into smooth blocks using nothing but the edges of his hands; the metal of the gates he made by pulling soil from the ground and breathing fire on it until it turned into rivers of brilliance which he stamped upon until they were flat and hard. With his bare hands he scraped out the ditches that still surround Giorran. All the surviving Ellonia gathered here around him, and the stone walls confounded the hordes of the accursed ones.

Then Ellon himself breathed fire down upon them from the highest of all the towers, and they were scorched to ashes where they were. New ranks of the creatures advanced, to be consumed in their turn. This went on until Ellon was an old man, nearing death; it was with his dying gasp that he slew the last of the accursed, a beast called Aliberi which had believed itself to be immortal. With his immediately preceding gasp Ellon had sired his only son – *of which you, oh Despot, are fortunate enough to be the direct*

77

descendant, as you can see from these charts.

The mages themselves believed very little of all this, although they accepted as obvious the fact that the Sun had brought Albion into existence as his sole companion. Still, it kept the Despots happy, something very important to their own continued survival. Behind locked doors, over a draught or two of some refreshing medicinal beverage, they would amuse each other by adding embellishments, frequently of a peculiarly obscene nature, and by telling ribald and not terribly funny jokes about the near-idiot stupidity of the ancient line of Despots.

After all, wasn't it obvious that the Sun considered the *mages* to be the beings closest to perfection?

The Sun always forgot about Alyss. She was rather older than he was and, she considered, very much prettier. But gods who are created by self-appointed mages are frequently forgetful about such matters. The mages, of course, had never heard of her at all.

The peasants had, but didn't know that they had. What could one expect from people so stupid that they worshipped no gods – not even the Sun?

It was some waking-times before Nadar was able to speak with Garndon, the highest officer in the army of the Ellonia and answerable only to the Despot himself. Nadar was merely a sub-lieutenant, and many of his seniors felt that he was too youthful for even this junior ranking. He had to wheedle and cajole each of them in turn before they would grant him an interview with the next officer up the line. However, he finally achieved his aim.

Army-Master Garndon was an old man and a disappointed one. There had been no great wars in Albion for as long as history had existed, yet he had had dreams of leading his troops into battle and emerging gorily victorious. Instead, like his predecessors, he had lived a life during which the fiercest foe he had faced was a momentarily rebellious peasant. But he was not without cunning. There was very little that he did not know about what was going on, wherever it might be. His crouched – almost hunchbacked – appearance and his wizened face betrayed nothing of the power he held.

Garndon received Nadar in his office. The room was precisely square and not large; the white walls were uninterrupted by pictures, flags or any of the other impedimenta which might have been expected. The floor was of bare boards whitewashed to match the walls. The only furniture consisted of a large empty table and several upright chairs. There were no papers littering the room because Garndon was capable of keeping everything pertinent in his head. A single window admitted bright sunlight.

He waved Nadar to one of the chairs and himself sat down in one of the others, so that they were both seated on the same side of the desk. Nadar had never seen the Army-Master before except from a distance, and had expected to feel intimidated; instead he found himself instantly warming to the man.

After a few relaxed greetings, Garndon clicked his fingers casually and immediately a corporal, dressed smartly in muddy reds and greens, appeared in the doorway.

'Wine, please,' said the Army-Master courteously.

The corporal disappeared.

'What is it?' said the old man, leaning forwards and tilting his head so that his sharp blue eyes were looking directly at Nadar's face. His grey eyebrows were bushy and domineering; they drew attention to the fact that he was almost bald. 'What is it that can be so important that such a junior officer as yourself should seek an audience with me?'

Nadar explained about the village where all had not seemed right, and about his consultation with the Wind. The only interruption to his speech was the arrival of the wine, which was strong and rich stuff, although a little too bitter for Nadar's own taste. He described how his doubts alone would not have been enough to have made him persevere in his efforts to speak directly with the Army-Master, but the Wind's confirmation that they were far from groundless had determined him.

Garndon heard him out in silence, contributing nothing

79

more than an occasional encouraging nod or a friendly smile, although his eyes were constantly locked on Nadar's face. The younger man found that he felt almost guilty whenever he turned his gaze away from that of the Army-Master and so, except when he turned to raise his goblet to his mouth, his eyes remained complementarily locked with Garndon's.

His account of what had happened dribbled away towards the end – something of which he was aware. He tried to disguise the fact by adding afterthoughts, recapitulations and vague speculations, and Garndon allowed him to do this for a short while before raising his hand for silence.

The old man raised himself from his chair with the stiffness of age and walked around to the other side of the naked wooden table.

'You bring me nothing but a collection of unproven suppositions,' he said, wearily sinking down into his chair.

'I beg your pardon, sir, if you feel that I've wasted your time. And your wine.'

'No, no, don't apologise.' A back-handed wave towards the flask. 'Help yourself to more, if you'd like. You've earned it, and far more besides.'

Nadar filled his goblet to the brim.

'You were quite right,' said Garndon, his voice like the dust in a long-abandoned room, 'to bring this news to me. To tell you the truth, I'd been rather expecting it.'

'You'd . . . why?'

'Things go in cycles,' said the Army-Master, kicking off his boots and putting his feet up on the table; his casualness astonished Nadar. The old man put his hands behind his head and his gaze wandered away to look through the window at the luminous sky. 'Every few generations there's an insurrection among the peasants – the Sun alone knows why, because they're incapable of doing anything more organised than making sure they don't put both legs into the same half of their trousers. Perhaps the Sun sends us these uprisings just to test us, and our fealty to the perfection he strives for. As I say, I don't know. Perhaps one of the mages might tell you the reason, but I very much doubt it: they're a secretive bunch and, just between you and me, I think their insight into the Sun's intentions is little greater than our own.'

Nadar was shocked. This verged on heresy.

The Army-Master gestured him to silence. 'That was just between you and me, Sub-lieutenant,' he said crisply.

The mention of his junior rank bore it home to Nadar that, if need be, the Army-Master would deny any aspect of this conversation.

After a few seconds, the old man continued. 'It's now been many a long while since the peasants rose. I thought they might do so when last we increased our demands upon them for food – that was when I was a young man and a sub-lieutenant, just like you are – but they were too stupid to organise themselves. They always are. Always . . .'

The Army-Master pulled his feet down and leant forward, one elbow resting on the table, pointing a finger at Nadar's face.

'They're always too stupid to rise against us except when there's some focus for them. It's been known for one of the House of Ellon to rebel and join up with the moronic hordes, so that they gather around their self-appointed folly-ridden leader, revelling in the memory he gives them, and try to do battle against us. We slaughter a few hundred of them, torture the turncoat to death, and there's an end of it. It's never happened in my lifetime, alas.'

'"Alas"?' echoed Nadar.

'Yes . . . alas. The only people I've ever sentenced to death by torture have been peasants so stupid that they've been unable to appreciate the exquisiteness of their own sufferings. Do help yourself to a little wine, if you'd like. I can always ask for more to be brought.'

Garndon stood up and took a few short steps to the window. The sunlight made his wrinkled face turn from grey to a curious muddy yellow.

'But every now and then,' he said, starting softly but ending in something little short of a shout, 'we suffer an invasion from the outer world.'

'The World's a children's story,' said Nadar, baffled.

The Army-Master whipped round, and for the first time Nadar realised the full extent of the old man's potential for cruelty. The blue eyes were like daggers striking at his face.

'You fool! Fool! Little jumped-up arsehole of a . . .'

Then Garndon's voice softened again.

'I forget. You're so young. The young must be forgiven. It's not your fault that you're ignorant. I was much the same when I was your age. Thank the Sun I no longer am.'

Nadar said nothing.

'Yes, yes,' said the Army-Master, once more looking out of the window into infinity. 'Ah, yes, young man, the World is there, beyond the walls of mist. It's lucky for us that *they* – the people who live in the outer world – don't really know that we're here, or otherwise they'd be among us, robbing us Ellonians of our rightful Sun-given heritage and taking the peasants for their own.'

Blasphemy again! said Nadar's internal voice.

Don't be silly, he thought back to it. *If I told anyone about this they'd refuse to believe me.*

The Army-Master was still talking.

'. . . but every now and then, by accident or sometimes even by design, one of them is able to find his or her way to the pristine shores of Albion. And then we have trouble, because they bring with them the loathsome barbarian ideas of the World.' He patted his thighs, obviously not realising that he was doing so. 'And in some way I don't understand – none of us understands – they can gather the peasants around them just as if they were Ellonia. That's the time of danger.'

Nadar found his voice at last.

'Do you think, sir, that this is what has happened now?' He felt uncomfortable, remaining seated while his ultimate commanding officer was standing, but he recognised that to get to his feet would be an even more severe breach of etiquette.

'Probably.'

The Army-Master turned to look at Nadar. He was smiling in such a way that he might have been someone's favourite uncle.

'You did well,' he added, 'to notice that there was something wrong in that village. You did even better in seeking counsel from the Wind – even though, through its normal perversity, it refused to give you more than the vaguest of advice. But the best thing that you've done is to insist on bringing all of this to my attention.'

He came back, moving silently across the whitewashed floorboards in his unshod feet, to sit behind the table.

'Do you know which village this was?' he said, his voice again sharp.

'No.'

Nadar, hands locked together, looked down at his feet through a diamond-shape formed by his thighs and his arms.

'No. I've no idea. I think it was near the great river. It was certainly to the south.'

'That's not good enough. Next waking-period, take a hundred of our men and destroy all of the southern villages. I will authorise the increase of the tributes to be taken from the others to make up the shortfall until such time as we can repopulate the south. Don't allow any of the peasants to survive – not even the children. The Wind may prophesy, but that isn't to say that its prophecies will come to fruition. Is it?'

The last two words were as hard as stone.

'No, sir.'

'Then go. This interview is over. If you fail me, your life will be at stake. If you are successful, all of the House of Ellon will be grateful to you and you will be promoted far beyond your wildest dreams.'

'Yes, sir.'

'You're still here? I thought I told you to go.'

'Yes, sir.'

Nadar left.

That sleeping-period not even the most ingenious antics of the young aristocrat could arouse him. She fell asleep contentedly in his arms, thinking, for a reason which would forever escape her, of marzipan.

Chapter Four
Children

His fingers a mist across the face of his bodhran, Rehan sings.

A forest, somewhere in Albion, the trees showing the coats of all the seasons in a blend of improbable hues that alternately clash and harmonise with the brush of the lethargic wind. Small animals dartingly obey the commands of their inscrutable instincts, their hasty paths linking the shadows to each other. Here there is the dismal scratch of naked branches against each other; over there the fresh yellow-green leaves rustle together. An eddy creates a brief dance of golden shapes, drifting across to fall on sullenly dark old moss or to glide onto the uneven surface of a narrow stream that plays with them childishly, pushing and pulling them along until it tires of them. Birds shout hoarsely incomprehensible expletives at each other.

Only the sunlight is silent: even the nervous creatures make small sounds as they scurry over the muffling moss.

Overhanging the stream is a silver birch that seems only three-quarters grown, its trunk no thicker than a thigh, its bark still flesh-smooth, the clefts between its shanky branches not yet grown mysterious. For some reason that cannot be understood the little animals avoid it – not out of fear or revulsion, nor even out of respect. Perhaps they recognise that it has become different, and their small brains have no other response to such a difference than avoidance. But the sunlight has no qualms: it runs its fingers across the strong suppleness of the youthfully stretching bole, imparting its warm life to the multiplying cells.

Look more closely now.

Run your fingers up the trunk, feeling its coolness where other trees cast their shadows across it. At about shoulder-height the first major branch diverges, the junction like a tensed small muscle under your touch. It seems that the branch quivers suddenly, as if it is startled by the incursion of your hand as you pass your palm along it, brushing aside green twigs no more rigid than grass.

You lean out over the stream, drawn by your hand into a precarious balance, until at last you can lean no further.

At your very fingertips there is a sharp-edged ripple in the bark, and you can just detect the faintest sensation of rapid, almost furtive movement from within the wood. Fascinated, you try to make your arm just a little longer, as if by touch alone you could comprehend the changes that are happening in the branch, but it's impossible without falling into the cold waters below you. Besides, your body is beginning to ache from the strained position you've adopted; your muscles have tired of your brain's orders, and are making their displeasure felt. And perhaps even your brain senses something of what the shy forest creatures sense, because it makes no argument.

So you haul yourself back, and spend a minute or two with your hands on your waist, staring along the branch's shiny length, hoping frustratedly that perhaps your eyes will be able to tell you what your fingers cannot.

But there's nothing to be seen. Not yet.

A bird with blue and yellow plumage skates along the length of the stream and your eyes are distracted, following the living colour until the flurry of wings is lost from view.

You wonder why you're here, why you've been standing so still, waiting for something – you're not sure what. For a little while it seemed as if you were so close to a rushing, turbulent understanding of yourself and the world surrounding you, but now even that is a forgotten sensation, lost in the dusty parts of your mind that you never dare intrude upon.

Shaking your head, you urinate where you stand, spattering the moss and the base of the birch's trunk. Then you turn away, taking a few irregular paces through the snatching undergrowth until your feet stumble across a path etched out over the forgotten years by untold thousands of travellers who've followed that way because somehow it felt . . . downhill. That's how you feel about it, too, as your body carries you along in the direction of your home.

Behind you, unseen except by a finch that has paused in its song out of sheer tiredness, the bark is splitting open along the line of the wrinkle your fingers were touching just a little while ago. A bud is pushing its way incongruously out of the wood, and as it does so the rest of the birch is beginning to draw in upon itself, its silveriness tarnishing and crumpling, its youthful vivacity being drawn from it towards the site of this new growth. The other leaves on the tree slowly fade from existence, their flesh vanishing first to leave the veins as deltas of gossamer that, in their turn, collapse into tiny dust-storms that are swiftly dispersed by the impertinent breeze. Curling bark peels downwards, disintegrating as it falls; the wood of the exposed trunk is dead with an ancient grey-white darkness.

The birch can no longer support its sole healthy branch. There is a tired-sounding crack, like the noise of a carious tooth resignedly permitting itself to be drawn from its socket, and then almost immediately a splash as the bough drops into the stream. Sluggishly, too heavy with resin to float easily, it drifts erratically with the current for a few metres, catching its ends on the larger boulders, until at last it is snagged immovably against the bank by the arching roots of a semi-aquatic shrub.

The developing bud protrudes upwards, clear of the water's surface. Now even the bough that is giving birth to it is crumbling in on itself although its outer bark remains whole, the pink-green spots turning abruptly silver to match the rest. The emerging tip of the bud is russet-coloured and smooth, furry like the coat of a fieldmouse, yet sleekly moist like the head of a new-born baby.

The finch eyes the rapid flowering with taut interest. There is the chance that this might be food.

A blink of the bird's bottomless eye and the growing bud is gone. Now, poised delicately on the tapering empty cylinder of bark, there is a small shrew-like creature, its nose sensing the air with fine whiskers above its in-slanting teeth, its tail a flattened metal rope on the bark behind it. The little animal holds its position for only a second before its strong hindlegs propel it in a jumping, skittering run along the length of the bark and up to clutch frantically at the overhanging roots. An instant later and it's losing itself in the reeds.

The finch feels and then immediately forgets disappointment. It darts away from temporary perch to temporary perch until it reaches the further end of its territory, where its mate waits for raucous news of its travels.

Soon there is a commotion among the reeds, their browned tips waving in protest as the stalks are pushed away from a common centre. The shrew-like beast is growing ever more rapidly, its shape transmuting in a series of flurries as it does so. The creature is the size of a coypu before its hindlegs dramatically increase in length and strength, so that the rest of the body is pushed into a vertical stance, the stubby paws of the forelegs extending and refining themselves to form lean-fingered hands. From the smooth wrists a swift-moving front line of pale flesh runs up the arms, subsuming the reddish-brown fur, as if the creature were stripping on long thin gloves. Soon the forelegs have become fully formed arms. The hindlegs are straight by now and, as with the arms, they lose their fur to show calves and thighs separated by narrow knees.

More and more of the trunk becomes denuded, leaving a spark of russet pubic hair beneath a perfectly coiled navel that is set in a flat abdomen, framed to either side by prominent pelvic bones. The pinkness of the arms has invaded the shoulders and upper torso, revealing small, widely separated, brown-tipped breasts and sharp shoulder-blades. The arms reach up together high above the head to touch the warm air with sensitive outstretched fingers.

The head is the last part of the body to change. The blunt, pugnacious features of the rodent pull themselves inwards to reveal an inquisitive cleft chin, a small mouth with narrow lips that pull back in a lazily hedonistic smile to reveal twin rows of pointy white teeth. The eyes above the clearly delineated cheekbones lose their roundness and their slight bulbousness, elongating and narrowing, changing their colour to a pale feline green. The thin eyebrows and the long eyelashes are the same forest red-brown as the perfectly equilateral pubic triangle and the hair of the rest of the head.

Lowering her arms slowly, the creature – the woman – looks down approvingly over the planes and contours of the body she has grown, and her smile broadens a trifle as she nods her head. Taking swift but smoothly graceful movements, she treads the few necessary paces through the reeds to reach the edge of the stream and, her features sobering, passes the palm of one hand over the surface of the water, stilling it so that its music dies and for as far as the eye can follow its passage the stream has a flawlessly even reflective surface.

She gazes at her face, thinks for a moment, and adjusts her nose so that it is a little less snub. She runs her hand over her hair, but elects to leave it the length it is: its shortness, she decides, excellently accentuates the trimness of the rest of her face.

Then, with an airy wave of her hand, she frees the stream so that it may pursue its course, and droplets of water dance around her arm as if to express their gratitude. She stoops to retrieve the cylinder of bark, which is in danger of being tugged free of its mooring by the rejuvenated current, and holds it high above her head, turning it with her quick fingers so that it seems to dry – impossibly swiftly – in the warmth of the sun. Satisfied, she holds it vertically beside her, its narrower end resting on the ground, and casually draws the fingernails of her left hand down its length, so that the branch tumbles downwards as a cascade of countless coiling silver threads. Once more her fingers move with invisible speed as she weaves for herself a vest, a jerkin and a pair of ragged-edged breeches. Clad, she spends a few moments flexing herself, becoming accustomed to the feel of the garments against her new skin, and then, as an afterthought, bends down once again and seizes a handful of the long reeds, throwing them into the sky above her; they swirl slowly downwards, intertwining with each other, to drape themselves as a cloak around her shoulders.

Satisfied, she looks around her, and then squints up at the sky, smiling cheerfully at the Sun. An Ellonian would deem it more than coincidence that a small, petulant-looking cloud should choose that moment to start moving across the face of the golden disc. For Alyss is older than not just the Sun but also this universe – older, indeed, than all the universes that she selects as her playgrounds.

And there are so many of them for her to choose from, each dependent on its own particular and infinitely long series of quirks of fate, accidental ripples in the substrate of spacetime, randomnesses that were individually meaningless but, when placed with each other in just the right order, came together – and are still coming together – to form the infinitude of discrete probable or, more accurately, possible universes through which it is Alyss's joy to flit. She can remember the spark that set off the reaction that has created the incomprehensible multitudes of shadow universes; to her it seems as if it were only yesterday that a tiny shift of logic concentrated the existing probabilities of the void called God in a certain locus, and thereby started time on its inexorable path.

For before the shadow-universes blossomed there was no time – not even a 'before'. Instead there was just a nothingness composed of the twelve dimensions, which were impotent to effect change but uncaring about that fact, for there was nothing for them to exert their influence upon – and, besides, in timelessness there is no tedium, and hence no ambition. And so the twelve-dimensional void, the state of no-time, might never have ended had not an accidental trace of probability, like a mischievous imp, given an infinitesimally tiny touch of texture to the nothingness, contaminating it and, incidentally, giving birth to time.

The contamination spread with almost instantaneous swiftness, now that there was time through which it *could* spread and against which its swiftness could be measured.

Creation necessitates destruction. In the microseconds of the birthing of the multiverse, the twelve-dimensional void devoured itself, invaginating to create a forest of spacetime structures. Eight of the dimensions were destroyed, springing back in on themselves to disappear entirely except for the infinite echoes that they left, which spread themselves throughout the multiverse as an unbounded and ever-expanding pattern of invisibly small cosmoses. The four remaining dimensions – including time – threw chains across the flanks of the multiverse, controlling its savagery, tethering it as well as they were able so that it couldn't respond to *all* the whims of rampant and playful probability.

Their control of the multiverse was only partial, of course, so that probability was still able to tease the edges of reality, fraying them as time passed. In fact, the infinitude of realised possibilities would soon have nullified each other, recreating the twelve-dimensional void commonly known as God, had it not been that, in the self-immolation that had immediately followed the spark that instigated the evolution of the multiverse, a tiny portion of the void somehow escaped – a scrap left over from the moment of creation.

That scrap travels among the shadow-universes, reifying any one of them in which it chooses to tarry for a while. Here, visiting the universe containing Albion for as long as its caprice encourages it to stay, it has chosen to take the form of a young woman – Alyss – the woman whose emergence from the straits between the universes you might have witnessed had you had the ability to be patient long enough to wait beside the silver birch near the stream's edge. As it is, you become aware of her arrival as you trudge along the worn path, even though you don't realise quite what it is that you've become aware of. Everything is suddenly there with more clarity, and soon you begin to recognise elements of your surroundings – a sensation that you have never experienced before. This path is no stranger to you any longer.

91

The torrent of liberation from the stifling embrace of your amnesia makes your mind wild. Delirious with an emotion that is fresh to you, you almost turn and retrace your steps – simply because that is something you've never done before and which is therefore tacitly taboo. But no: you're hungry and your deep unconscious as well as, now, your intellect is telling you that food awaits you if you keep on going in your original direction. So you don't go back, but still your soul is dancing in the awareness that you're going this way because you *choose* to.

Alyss, undisturbed by the changes she has wrought in you, calls a small white butterfly to her shoulder and cranes her neck to stare at it solemnly.

Her eyes almost cross, and she giggles.

Then, her green cloak liquid about her, she sets off with a floating step to explore her new universe.

'Mother! Mother!'

The little boy was running along a street of the village which Terman had, after many months of thought, whimsically named Lianhome in honour of his son, whom he had called Lian. The giver of names was not ashamed of his vanity in this: as far as he was concerned, Lian was the single most important person in the world, not excepting himself and even Mina.

'Mother, I've found a shell.'

He caught up with her, his feet pittering on the baked mud and his breath sounding like a hydraulic engine. His face was red from exertion under his curling yellow hair. He was tall for his age – according to the calendar that his father had introduced, he was nearly six – and very sturdy, but Mina was still capable of scooping him up from the ground with one arm.

When first he'd been born, she and Terman had speculated that he might have been the son of one of the soldiers who had raped her one day, rather than the product of the loving they had since shared. Terman, to a great extent, didn't care: he was proud to accept the lad as his own. But Mina had worried until she had seen, in her son's eyes, the same singlemindedness that characterised his father.

Yes, this was Terman's son.

Laughing now, she looked at the 'shell' he proffered.

'What have we here?' she said, feeling the firm warmth of his bottom weighing down on the inside of her arm. 'That's no shell, little man.'

'Not so little.'

'All right, medium-sized man.'

She turned the thing over and over in her free hand. Her husband had taught her and the other villagers many things about the knowledge that was current in the World, but she was still rather nervous about pronouncing judgement on the various artefacts and specimens that Lian brought to her. Their house was a new one, much larger than the hovel in which her parents had reared her – Lantz had died, the first dead person whom the villagers could remember – yet it seemed to be filled to bursting point with the 'discoveries' that Lian made. Terman groaned each time the child arrived home with a new consignment; she suspected that, from time to time when there was no one else around, he took a few armfuls of 'interesting rocks' and the like and buried them.

'Looks like a shell,' Lian said, his arms wrapped around Mina's neck.

'But I don't think it is,' murmured Mina. 'You'll have to check with your father, but this looks to me like a fossil.'

The stone showed the imprint of part of a segmented, insectile creature. As far as she could recall from what Terman had told them all, this was an early marine being that had existed before Albion had been sealed off from the outer world. There was some resemblance to the appearance of a crab – especially the size of the main body and the prominence of the imprint of the single pincer claw.

It's only a while ago, she thought, *that we thought things like this were jokes of chance – or, as the Ellonia might think of it, sports thrown at us mockingly by the Sun.*

Very carefully, she tossed Lian away from her, so that he landed safely on the hardened mud. He looked up at her accusingly: mothers weren't supposed to do that, were they?

She laughed at him, which made things worse.

'Shit!' he shouted, obviously hoping to impress her with his profanity.

'No, not now . . . I had one this morning,' she replied dispassionately.

'A good shell, isn't it?'

He was suddenly contrite, nestling up to her.

'It's not a shell, darling.'

There were people all around them. Now that Terman was an accepted part of the community, Mina and her child were widely honoured for their relationship to him. In the earliest days there had been public discussion concerning the baby's paternity; like Mina, the villagers had been concerned that she might have been impregnated by one of the soldiers, and tongues had wagged eagerly in the fields. This fear had been dispelled as soon as Lian had grown old enough to display his independence. Wherever he went, even as a baby, the villagers found that their memories of past events were further fixed.

'It's a fossil,' said Mina. 'Not a shell.'

'I hate you,' he screamed, breaking away from her and pushing his way through the crowd of spectators, who parted to let him escape.

He'd be home that sleeping-period, she knew. She'd witnessed his tantrums many times before, and they'd always ended at mealtimes.

She wondered, as she strolled home, where Terman was.

Terman was dying.

He'd been out on a foraging expedition, looking for berries and roots, when he'd run across a troop of the Ellonia. He'd heard of the atrocities committed by the Despot's cohorts on neighbouring villages over the past few years, and so he had retreated into the forest's shadow, hoping to be able to cut across country in order to warn his friends in Lianhome. Unfortunately, his rapid dart of movement had been observed by a sharp-eyed subaltern, and a section

94

of the military column had split off from the others in order to hunt for him. Like a chased fox, he had used every possible subterfuge to deceive them, but finally they'd tracked him down.

He was resting under the cover of a bush when the first arrow hit him from behind, piercing his left shoulder. He looked astonishedly at its point, protruding bloodily through the front of his jerkin, before he felt the pain. He spun around, his hand instinctively groping for the sword that would have been at his belt had he still been in the World, but it wasn't there.

The second arrow took him full in the chest.

Again there was initially no great sensation of pain. He was half smiling as he pulled the shaft out of his body; the feeling as the smooth wood came away from his flesh was almost pleasurable.

After it, though, came a gush of blood, and for the first time he realised that he was about to die.

He sent a thought in the direction of Mina and Lian, wishing for their safety. He knew he was being killed not because he was who he was but simply because he was a peasant: the army of the Ellonia had been sent out to slaughter people like himself and his wife and his son, whoever they might happen to be. These past years, he knew, Lianhome had escaped the carnage only because his own presence had somehow affected the Ellonia so that they had difficulty focusing their minds on the fact that the village was actually there: it was as if, every time they had approached Lianhome, their minds had been diverted so that they automatically skirted the hamlet and went else-where. He wasn't sure how this had come to pass; perhaps he had the unconscious ability to give the peasants their grasp of reality through partially robbing the Ellonia of theirs.

He fell forwards onto the bath of brown leaves surround-ing the bush. He heard the laughter of the soldiers as they watched him die. He coughed up blood and sniggered, admiring the colour of it; a little bile and he could produce a grotesque parody of the red and green Ellonian colours, but to his chagrin he couldn't manage it.

He counted the hooves circling around him and reckoned that there were seven horsemen.

Seven horsemen to kill a single peasant? He placed a mental bet on the future chances of the peasants.

Then he died.

Nadar had become a captain in the army of the Ellonia. His exploits in destroying most of the villages of the south were well known throughout the court at Giorran, and so his successive promotions had come swiftly. Once in a while – more to keep his hand in than for any other reason – he led a troop of hardened soldiers out into the southern lands to slay the innocent.

Yet he knew in his own heart that he had yet to find *the* village, the one that had so disconcerted him.

As the middle-aged peasant in the forest died under the arrows of his bowmen, he pulled his horse away, deliberately distancing himself from the killing. He pretended that his eyes were scanning the trees, looking for any signs of ambush, but in fact he was remembering what the Wind had now told him several times. This rebellion wasn't just a rush of blood to the collective heads of a bunch of illiterate peasants: there was a lot more to it than that. He could sense it. And hadn't Garndon told him to treat the matter seriously? The old Army-Master – who had surprised everybody, most notably himself, by staying alive all this time – still earned Nadar's abject respect.

Hence his sense of guilt. Nadar knew that Garndon would have required of him that he watch the peasant's death, gloating over every agony as if it were a contribution to the continued survival of the Ellonia. He had little taste for the voyeuristic witnessing of other people's pain, however; he placed little value on peasants' lives, and was best pleased when they ended swiftly – as this one seemed to be doing.

He said a few words of gratitude to the Sun, and asked that the peasant's soul – if peasants had souls, which was doubtful – be treated kindly in the next life.

With maturity Nadar was becoming increasingly concerned about his vocation. 'Raze villages!' 'Slaughter peasants!' 'Torture children!' All of these had seemed, in the abstract, so many waking-periods ago, like soldierly commands, appeals to his virility. Now that he had smelled the scent of cooking human flesh on the breeze while seeing the blueness of the sky beyond the dark and swirling pyre, now that he had heard a man laugh at the antics of a screaming spitted baby, he didn't want his memories to belong to him any longer. Thank the Sun that this peasant was already nearly dead, his going apparently a comparatively peaceful one.

Are all the deaths worth it? said his internal voice.

'Yes,' he growled to himself.

And they were. They had to be.

Nadar was the youngest captain his senior officers could remember, but he was determined to climb higher up the ladder of rank – if possible to the very top. He wanted to be poised to accept the post of Army-Master when Garndon finally gave up his dispute with life – an event which, surely, couldn't long be delayed. The deaths of a few hundred peasants were as nothing compared with the thrust of his ambition. He just wished that the mindless creatures wouldn't scream so much as they died, and that their bodies held less blood.

Good. The man was dead.

That was over, then. Now he and his handful of men could rejoin the main party.

One of the soldiers was down on the forest floor, preparing to hack Terman's corpse to pieces, but Nadar snapped an order and the man rather sheepishly clambered back up onto the saddle of his horse.

A shallow mercy, said the voice.

Mercy? thought Nadar. *The man's dead. He can't suffer any more.*

Yes, said the voice, *that's what I meant. It makes you feel better to stop a lifeless body being chopped up – not because you feel any empathy for the person but because now you can pretend to yourself that his death was unreal.*

You lie! lied Nadar to himself.

He banished the inner voice and called his men to him.

A few minutes later they had joined the rest of the patrol, and Nadar was riding once more at its head. His deputy, a lieutenant called Riba, kept his proud black horse a tactful metre to the rear.

'Riba,' said Nadar after a while, 'this time we're going to find the village. I can feel it.'

'Yes, sir.'

'Once we've destroyed it, we can stop all this.'

'Stop all what?'

'The killing. The destruction.'

'Why should we stop?'

'These peasants – they don't deserve to die. Not the way we've been killing them.'

'Sir?'

Nadar said nothing. The Ellonia had always killed peasants. That was what they – Ellonia and peasants – were *for*. He was watching the trees on either side of the long avenue down which they were riding. He envied them. Trees felt no pain, and never had difficult decisions to make.

He put one hand under his armpit and scratched.

'Sir?'

Riba was almost up with him. Nadar waved him back: for the man to draw level would have been a breach of protocol.

'We say the peasants are nothing more than vegetables,' he said quietly, his voice barely audible over the sound of the horses' hooves. 'I've never heard a vegetable scream the way that some of the peasants do.'

'That's why we don't put cabbages to the torch, sir.'

'Yes, we can all come out with cheap jokes.'

'Sir.'

'We're facing a time of change. In the old days it was all right to regard the peasants as rather less important than the cattle they reared. I think that soon we'll have to reckon with them.'

Harnesses jingling. The lieutenant wondering if he should kill his heretical officer right here and now or wait until later. The horses' hooves making a slow form of thunder along the beaten road.

Riba put away all thoughts of assassination. Instead, he asked, 'Why are you so certain that we'll find the village this time, sir?'

'I don't know,' said Nadar slowly, leaning forward reflexively to pat his horse's neck, muttering a few meaningless sounds of encouragement to the animal. 'I wasn't so confident when we left Giorran, but just in the past hour or two I've become convinced about it.'

Riba looked pointedly at the shoulders of his commanding officer, and Nadar obliged him by turning his head briefly to look him straight in the eyes.

'That peasant,' said Riba.

Nadar turned away again, looking at the track in front of him. Strangely, he hadn't made the connection earlier. But Riba was right: his lieutenant must be a more observant man than he seemed on the surface. Yes, it was as the peasant had died that Nadar had first begun to feel certain that this time they would be successful, whatever the Wind had told him all those years ago on the hilltop above Giorran.

This time, surely . . .

And then his confidence suddenly wilted.

Riba sensed the change in his captain.

'What's the matter?' he said cautiously.

'It's gone again,' snapped Nadar, angrily hitting the scabbard of his sword, as if he were blaming the weapon for the abrupt shift of his mental state.

'Gone?'

'Yes, gone. The feeling I had that we were going to find the village today. Oh shit. Let's find somewhere to stop for a meal. I want to go for a walk and think about all this.'

Minutes later they came to an unploughed field where the men could spread themselves out for an hour's relaxation. Riba shouted the necessary orders, and the small convoy came to a halt. Soon after, the provisions were broken out – salted meat, hard biscuits, ghee, cheeses and strong wine. The soldiers lounged on the lush grass. In the distance there was a herd of cattle, but the beasts showed little interest in the men who had intruded into their pasture, and so the men in return showed little interest in the cattle.

Nadar had a couple of bites of food, not because he was hungry but because he felt that it was somehow expected of him to lead the way. Then, leaving his men eating, he crossed the track and entered a small copse.

The shade of the trees cooled him. They were conifers, growing close together, so that their interlocking branches formed an almost complete parasol over him. From time to time, as he picked his way slowly across the mush of decaying needles and cones, he had to duck to avoid low branches. In the end he threw himself down on a yielding bank, putting his hands behind his head and staring up at the glimmers of brilliant blue sky he could see through the prickly foliage. He half-closed his eyes, so that the blue became a pinkish grey. In a curious way, although he sensed that the mission would end in his frustration, he felt peaceful, contented.

You don't want to find the village, the voice said accusingly. *That's what it is, isn't it?*

'Don't be so stupid,' Nadar mumbled. He was beginning to roam towards sleep, and the last thing he wanted was to be kept awake by misgivings.

Yet he had to recognise the truth of what that hated little voice was saying. The quest to find the village where the invader from the outer world (if indeed, he thought sadly, there was such a place as the outer world) had established himself (or *her*self?) had guided his career for a long time now. If he finally managed to destroy the interloper, might it not be that the primary motivation of his life would disappear? It wasn't a thought he particularly wanted to face. He wanted to leave it a while and then see what happened.

But earlier today he'd been exhilarated by the conviction that he would at last destroy the village that had avoided him for so long. Now he was certain that it would continue to evade him forever. At a moment of self-doubt like this, he shouldn't be feeling so complacent – should he?

He fell asleep. The men had an extended mealtime before Riba came to wake him up.

Lian felt his father die.

The boy forgot all of his rage against his mother for having contradicted him: now he started running back, as fast as his short, immature legs could carry him, to the family home, shrieking uncontrollably. Domestic animals bolted from him as he sprinted across the fields: he needed the softness of his mother's body against him.

She looked up from the stove where she was preparing the sleeping-period meal.

'What's the matter, Lian?' she asked coldly. 'Decided your mother might have been right after all about the fossil?'

'No – no,' he said, finding difficulty drawing breath. 'It's father. He's dead.'

'No.'

Nevertheless, she believed him immediately, implicitly.

Her eyes filled with tears, but she very carefully rearranged the pots on the stove before seating herself at the table and putting her forehead in her hands. She looked at the wood of the table, vaguely hoping that its knots and whorls would tell her that everything was all right, just as it had been for so long now. Terman: he had been a good and loving husband, and he had meant so much to the village, protecting it from the mayhem that had been visited on its neighbours. They had made love last night, and she could still smell the touch of his sweat on her body. The thought of facing the world without him seemed impossible to her, yet she knew that, for the sake of her son if for nothing else, this was exactly what she must do. Her mind was so full of logistics – what to do, when to do it, how to do it – that it was some little while before she began to feel any real grief.

When it came, the emotion was overwhelming.

She gathered the weeping child onto her broad lap and held him very tight, rubbing his back as if to provide him with a reassurance that she could not give. His streaming eyes and nose soon painted a silvery sheen on the rough wool of her blouse. Her own weeping dampened his yellow hair.

She was aware of the fact that her memory was fading, to the point where she was uncertain why she was sobbing like this. She had her child next to her, hadn't she? Surely that was all a mother could wish for? She had a recollection that there had been someone else important in her life, but all she could remember right now was a myriad echoing of shared laughter and loving.

Her eyes fastened on an object lying on the table nèar to her. It had a leather covering and seemed to be composed of a large number of thin, flexible sheets, across which someone had draped scratchy patterns. Settling Lian, who had briefly fallen asleep, more securely against her shoulder, she reached out for the object. As soon as she touched it, her memory began to return, like an old friend.

This was her book.

Terman had taught her the art of writing, and so she had made herself a book, in which she had written down at the start of each sleeping-period everything that had happened to her, in case of a moment like this. Awkwardly, using her single free hand, she opened it to the most recent entry.

The scrawls meant nothing to her.

Lian stirred in his sleep, tears drying crustily around his eyes.

She knew there was a message there, somewhere. Her son's half-awakening had brought the meaning of the squiggles tantalisingly close to her understanding, but not quite close enough: before she could snatch at them they had receded back into the great mist of incomprehension that filled much of her mind.

She turned backwards and forwards through the pages. What was so infuriating was that it was obvious that these scribbles did indeed *mean* something: their positioning on each page was careful, rather than haphazard, and she could see that there were repeated symbols which, she assumed, shared similar meanings. There was a whorl of curves that reappeared ten or twelve times on each page; and there was a smaller, less complicated sign that she'd written even more frequently.

Lian woke, his earnest eyes watching her fingers as she leafed perplexedly through the book.

And now the images on the page were no longer meaningless scrawls. They were speaking to her, in her own voice.

'Lian is growing so tall, now. He'll be taller than his father, before he's fully grown.'

'The pig died, so we ate some of it fresh and salted the rest. Lian was sick afterwards. Terman went to the granary and named five people (two men and three women) from the next village. Of course, as soon as they've crossed the hill they'll have forgotten their names again, but Terman expects they'll be back.'

'The second child I thought would be mine is not to be. I was straddling the latrine when I felt a great burst of pain. I looked down and there was a mess of blood beneath me; as I watched, the skimpy little afterbirth followed the same route out of me. I think I'd have been more upset if the child had appeared more like a human being. At the time all I could think about was how glad I was that I hadn't told Terman there was another baby on the way. Even better that I hadn't told Lian – he'd have blamed the sky itself for having robbed him of his much wanted younger sibling . . .'

She read for a short while longer until she realised that Lian's eyes, too, were combing the pages, his lips moving as he apparently drank in everything that she'd written.

She shut the book firmly, pushing away his small hand as he reached out for it. There was too much in her book that was too personal for her son's eyes to see. She'd never before known that he could read. Terman must have taught him during their periodic trips away from home together.

Mina patted him and kissed him on the forehead.

'I think you're right,' she said. 'You're going to have to

face up to it, li . . . medium-sized man.'

'I know. Father's dead. I'll have to look after you now, mother, but don't worry: I can protect you from the wild animals.'

Despite her misery, she found herself smiling.

'I don't think that'll be necessary. We don't see too many wild animals around here.'

'The Ellonia?'

'Yes, there are the Ellonia. But your father's kept them away for so long now that they may have forgotten that we're here.'

She pulled him tightly to her breast, crossing her fingers behind his back.

He clung to her for a moment, and then pushed himself away.

'I can keep the Ellonia away, the same way that father did,' he said forcefully.

Again she smiled despite the pain of loss inside her. He was still such a small fellow, but he was trying earnestly to look like a full-grown man.

'Can you?' she asked wistfully, patronising the vanities of childhood.

'Of course I can,' he said, looking at her in bewilderment. 'Didn't you know that?'

This time it was her turn to be surprised.

'No,' she said. 'Are you sure?'

'Naturally I'm sure. I watched father when he was doing it. I don't think he knew quite how he managed it, but it was easy enough to see if you looked at him.'

She was ashamed. She'd been closer to Terman than anyone else had ever been, and yet the child had seen something that had escaped her entirely.

'How?' she said, pretending that she was bantering. In fact, her grey eyes were very sombre and sorrowful.

'Like this.'

He climbed down from her lap. Lines of concentration formed on his smooth forehead as he focused all his attention on his hands, outstretched before him. Time seemed to stand still as she watched him; the humdrum sounds of the village and the chirpings of the birds ebbed away from her, so that it was as if she and Lian were locked away for an eternity of solitude in this humble, dusty room.

Then the boy made a complicated twitching movement with his fingers – too fast for her to see – and relaxed, visibly exhausted.

'We're safe now,' he said, 'and I'm thirsty.'

She poured a mugful of cool water from the ewer kept in the cold-room, asking him over her shoulder: 'How can you be so sure we're safe?'

He took the mug from her with murmured thanks. It was clear the drink was more important to him now than her questions.

'Can't you feel it?' Lian said. 'There was a time, for a little while just then, when I could feel that Lianhome was defenceless. That was how I knew father had died.'

'I never saw your father do anything like . . . like what you've just done.' She made a palaver of chopping up some green vegetables to stew for their supper, trying to keep any trace of seriousness out of her voice. *How wonderful it is how quickly children can recover in adversity*, she thought. *Just a short while ago the death of his father spelt the end of the world for him, and now he's almost forgotten it. I wish I could do the same. The bed'll feel cold and lonely this sleeping-time – and for many sleeping-times to come, I think. Ah, Terman, Terman: I hope they at least buried you.*

'Father didn't know all the things he did,' said Lian brightly, wiping the back of his sleeve across his mouth and putting the coarse mug down beside her. 'He just sort of did them without thinking. But I watched him a lot of the time when he thought I wasn't looking.'

'What else did he do?' Again she was doing her best to sound casual and superficial, as if this was merely merry mealtime prattle between mother and son.

'He named people.'

'I know that,' she said, exasperated. 'I'm sorry, Lian,' she added immediately, trying to excuse the sharpness of her voice. 'I almost cut my thumb just then.'

'But you can't just tell people they've got names – other-

105

wise they soon forget all about it. It's true. Father always did something with his hand when he gave people names – or places for that matter – except he didn't know he was doing it.'

'You're an observant young man, aren't you?'

'Am I?' Lian looked surprised, but then dismissed the matter as of little consequence. 'He used to turn his thumb away from his palm, just – like – *that*.' He demonstrated, and Mina watched carefully. 'That made the name per . . . per . . . forever. You could tell it was so by the way that afterwards the air hugged the person he'd named, so that the name couldn't escape.'

'And you can do this as well?'

'Of course.' He was now sitting on a stool at the kitchen table, watching his mother with interest. For supper they'd have the stewed vegetables she was preparing, but he was rather more concerned about what they might be having for the mid-waking-time meal. The early part of the waking-time had been energetic and tiring – it wasn't all that often a child threw a tantrum with his mother and then sensed his father had been killed, all in a single waking-period – and he was ravenously hungry.

'Show me,' she said lightly.

He slithered down from the stool.

'If you feed me,' he muttered.

She found herself laughing, but then the laughter turned into tears. She propped herself against the surface where she'd been cutting up the vegetables and allowed herself to descend into a dark trough of misery.

'I'm sorry, Lian,' she said, forcing the words out with difficulty, 'but I loved your father, for all his faults.'

'I loved him too,' said Lian, 'but that doesn't stop me being hungry. Anyway, he's not really dead.'

It was rare for Mina's placid grey eyes to flare with rage, but now they did. She turned to him, her face furious.

'I think you'd better go out and play, Lian,' she said carefully.

'But I don't want to.'

'Get out. Quickly.'

106

'I'm hungry.'

'Go.'

Bemused by the perverse ways of adults, Lian left the house; the rough wood of the front door was reassuring against his palm as he opened it and then, sensing that quiet was the best option, closed it softly behind him. There was no particular place he wanted to go. The fact that his father was dead seemed to have retreated a long way from him. He was hot, and so he stripped off his leather jerkin. For a few moments he thought about going down into the centre of the village to play with the other urchins who romped around there, but he wasn't in the mood. Already he was tired of the fact that his father would no longer be with them in body: he'd enjoyed mock-punching that hard chest, or holding that strong hand as the two of them had trekked for long and pointless walks over the surrounding hillsides, but all of these experiences were now behind him. He played the memories across his mind, watching them and sensing them as if they were happening right now.

Lian dropped himself down a few metres to the side of the front door. The white-painted boards of the house were hot against his naked back. He stretched his arms out as far as they would go and then folded them on his lap. He was still hungry, but it would be a while before his mother would calm down.

Why was she so blind?

The body-bit of Terman might be dead – in fact, an awful lot of him was dead – but there was still much of him that remained alive.

Father, Lian thought towards the glare of the sky.

Yes, Lian, said Terman.

Father, thought Lian, *I deceived my mother. I pretended to her that there was a way of moving hands to give people names. But that's not right, is it? It's something inside you, not just an arbitrary waggling of the fingers. Something inside* me.

Yes, Lian, said Terman again, *but there are some people within Albion who can use their fingers to give names, and bring about alterations of reality that are – and almost certainly*

107

will always be – beyond your comprehension.

Father . . .

There's someone called Alyss, but I don't know who she really is because she refuses to tell me. You'll know her when you see her, if she allows you to.

Lian's father's voice faded away from his mind. Looking up at the sky, Lian wondered if he could hear the smallest of echoes from its brightness.

Time passed. Lian became a tall young man. His best friend was Redin, whom Mina remembered as a small boy whom Terman had named in the earliest waking-times after he had come to Lianhome. The two youths met daily and challenged each other to mock duels using wooden swords. Redin was by far the bigger of the two of them, yet Lian regularly won their pretend fights because of his quickness on his feet and his inventiveness as he countered his 'enemy's' blows. Afterwards Lian and Redin, laughing and boasting about their untutored military skills, arms about each other's shoulders, usually went back to Mina's house, where she fed them with whatever she had to hand.

Later she rebelled. The group of returning boys had become not just the pair she loved – her son and Redin – but now also included a bunch of hangers-on, some of whom she liked not at all. Besides, she had little wish to get into a situation where this band of voracious young men relied upon her to act as their skivvy. Lian took her point fairly when she explained this to him towards the end of one waking period.

'Yes, you're quite right, Mother,' he said quietly. He put his palms together and ducked his head towards her in apology for the sins of the past. Redin, a little drunk, followed suit.

'You're a fool,' she said fondly, looking at Lian as he sat there in the firelight, his mane of hair glowing as if it had been cast in yellow bronze.

'You're right, Mother,' he said, taking her words at face value, 'and I've been using you too much. It's just that I think the time has passed when I can carry on doing nothing more than make the Ellonia avoid us. I think I've got to rally people around me – strong men, like Redin here' – a gesture at the now half-slumbering figure – 'so that we can take the war into their camp.'

'What does your father say?' Mina had long ago accepted that Lian believed that Terman's spirit was still able to talk to him.

'He says I should do this.'

'He does? You promise me you're not lying?'

Her voice was sad.

Since Terman had been killed she had taken only a few lovers, and none of them for very long. She had sensed the approval of her husband: he would never have wished her to lead a stunted life just because of her memories of him. Nevertheless, she envied the way that Lian seemed to be able to talk directly with Terman whenever the two of them wanted that to happen.

'I would never lie to you, Mother.'

'Hmmm.'

'Not about something as important as this,' Lian added hurriedly.

She had a sudden and horrible vision of the future. Her son – her only child – was going to be killed brutally by the Ellonia. She could feel his pain in all of her limbs. Yet there was no way that she could stop him if that was the course he wanted to follow. Terman was dead; soon Lian would die as well. She looked at the snoring form of Redin: was it worth the lives of good men like her husband and her son to protect sots like this?

Yes, she acknowledged to herself glumly, unfortunately it was.

'It's something of a tinpot army you have,' she said out loud. They were sitting around the kitchen table – now spotted with age – and she pressed her fist against the mellowed wood.

'There are twelve of us now, Mother,' he said.

'Twelve against the Ellonia. May they quiver and quake in their boots all sleeping-period long!'

Her sarcasm was wasted.

'I think we should travel in a great circle to the north,' he said reflectively, 'passing through as many villages as possible. When I bring awareness to the people there, I'm sure they'll join us, the same way the young men from Lianhome are so keen to be a part of my army.'

He picked up a lump of the cheese she'd left on the table and swallowed it in a single mouthful.

'Some enthusiasm,' she said acerbically. 'There are a dozen of you so far. The Ellonia may not tremble at the sight of an army that size.'

Redin snuffled in his sleep.

'A dozen from this village, and a dozen each from the next, and the next . . . and the next after that,' said Lian. The cheese had been good. He looked around for more but the table was bare except for a litter of empty plates, mugs and goblets. Mina took the hint and went to fetch some from the cold-room.

'There must be thousands in the army of the Ellonia,' she called to him. He watched her bending over in the doorway to pick up the cheese; her hips had broadened, he thought, but she was still an attractive woman – no wonder she could find lovers whenever she needed them. He felt proud of her for it, at the same time wishing that some of the girls with whom he'd slept had had a tenth of the grace of his mother. 'And,' she continued, 'they're armed with axes and swords and pikes. At the moment all you can conjure up are cross-staffs and the occasional knife. I've heard of fools before, but never one as foolish as you are.'

'My father says that this is the thing I've got to do.'

She dumped a heavy plateful of cheese in front of him.

'And is your father right in everything?'

He avoided her gaze.

'Yes. Usually.'

'You could strengthen your silly little army twice over, you know.' She made a great play of sweeping away crumbs from the table, using the side of her hand.

'How?'

He was interested, at last, in what she was saying.

'Women can fight.'

He looked at her in horror. She'd spoken the words so casually that he hardly believed he'd heard them.

'Not very well,' he stammered.

'Try me?'

'Why should I bother?'

He picked up another handful of cheese and raised it to his mouth.

A while later Lian woke up in a corner of the room and raised a hand to the swollen puffiness of his right eye; simply touching the affected area was extremely painful. He pulled himself to his hands and knees and crawled across to the table, at which Redin was still snoring.

Mina had long since gone up the stairs to bed, but she'd left some more bread and cheese for him. He ate it hungrily, ignoring the crumbs that caught in the long curls that draped around his chin and his shoulders.

Yes, his mother had a point. If he recruited women into his army as well as men he might have a better chance of ousting the Ellonia.

Upstairs, lying in her soft bed, Mina was trying to fall asleep despite the chimeras that passed before her eyes. She knew – *knew* – that her only son would fail in his venture and be put to death by the Ellonia. At the same time, she was honest enough to recognise that keeping him here for the rest of his life in the village that had been named for him would be an even more cruel punishment. She was willing to fight and if necessary die alongside him – and she thought it probably *would* be necessary for her to die in battle. It seemed to her that it might be worth it.

She moved her head on the pillow, so that now it was her left ear that lay on the rough cotton. She turned the rest of her body over to follow her head. The knuckles of her right hand stung like the very blazes, but that wasn't what was keeping her awake; it was the unshakeable thought that the death of her son couldn't be too far in the future.

She heard him now, downstairs, escorting Redin to the door. The process was rather noisy, as Redin hadn't really

111

woken up properly and so bumped into anything that was there to be bumped into. Then there was the racket of Lian throwing himself onto his own bed, near to the door, and fumbling around as he dragged furs over himself. His eye must be hurting, and she felt very sorry to have given him this pain. Nevertheless . . . well, it had been worth it.

She was smiling as she fell asleep.

Lian was smiling as well.

His pitiful army would be twice the size he'd thought it could possibly be – and that might make all the difference.

Time had passed for Nadar as well, and the memories he'd had of that village about which there had been something distinctly unusual slowly left him – although, even now, some sleeping-periods he would suddenly start up in bed, thinking of the *wrongness* he had sensed. Usually this was greeted by a resentful grumble from his bed-partner: although he was just a senior officer in the army – he was now Deputy Army-Master, serving alongside Garndon – he had established for himself a harem in the style of the Despot's. If need be, Garndon, who had clung on to life for so many years longer than he should have, would have to fall down a flight of stairs or, perhaps, out of an oubliette.

Nadar was putting on weight. His orange hair was now turning grey. There were red lines criss-crossing his brown eyes. All of these things were the price of success.

He had once told Garndon about all of this, and then demonstrated his superiority by pushing the old man back into his chair and walking across to look out of the window.

'You failed,' said Garndon. 'You should be killed.'

'Things have changed,' said Nadar. 'Now you're the one who runs the risk of being killed.'

Garndon had smiled.

Nadar hadn't liked the look of that smile.

Chapter Five
Singer

To Lian's disappointment, recruitment in the village did not go nearly as well as expected, and a few of those who had volunteered at first had had second thoughts when they'd realised the dangers that would be involved. Some of the villagers were obviously either too old or too young to enlist, and others had familial commitments that made the whole venture impossible for them. Lian was surprised, too, to find that there was, within Lianhome, a substantial minority of people who rejected the whole idea of combating the Ellonia. Things might not be ideal, they reasoned, but at least everyone knew where they were – so why try to change the situation? The other side of the coin was that Mina's presence at her son's elbow swelled the numbers of women volunteers from one – herself – to seven. Eventually, men and women together, his 'army' numbered a mere fifteen – hardly a force likely to conquer a nation.

Mina tossed her head, the long grey hair flying, as the small party rested for a few moments at the top of one of the hills surrounding Lianhome, saying farewell to the village where they had lived for all of their lives. Three of them rode horses, the rest were astride oxen. Progress was going to be slow until they found a hamlet willing to contribute not just people but also more horses.

There were tears in Mina's eyes as she looked down on Lianhome. She and her mother had buried Lantz many years ago; some while later, she and Terman had buried Gred. Terman himself hadn't, so far as she knew, been buried; they had never found his body, and it was unlikely that his Ellonian murderers would have taken the time and trouble to dig a grave. She shuddered for the thousandth time since her mate's death, hoping they hadn't put his head on a pike or inflicted some other mutilatory humiliations on his body. She had hoped that her own last resting-place would be somewhere near the village, but she was honest enough with herself to realise that this was improbable: she was strong and agile for her age, but she was unskilled; she knew that she was unlikely to survive her first encounter with a fully trained Ellonian soldier.

The peasant warriors' body armour was made of leather. The wives of some of the men who had most resisted the whole concept of Lian's makeshift army had covertly helped sew it – as had, oddly enough, some of those men themselves. Swords had been crudely crafted from iron that had once been cooking-pots and ploughs. The villagers had made bows and arrows, Terman having shown Mina how to do this years ago in case she ever needed to pass the knowledge on. They already had felling axes.

Mina was one of those who had been allocated a horse, as had Lian; her justification was her age, whereas his was that if they were to recruit supporters in the other villages they were more likely to do so if he arrived at their head on the great white stallion than if he dragged along behind on a dysenteric cow. In fact, since the troop's oxen moved with such painful slowness, he planned to spend most of the time walking, leading Anan by the reins.

Mina turned to look at her son and smiled with approval. He'd grown up into a handsome giant of a man. His hair was a flowing flourish of gold that wrapped around his shoulders; oddly, he'd never before been able to grow a beard successfully, however hard he'd tried, so that his face was always in the state where it looked as if he'd simply forgotten to shave that morning. In Mina's mind there suddenly appeared a mental image of the aggressive black brush Lian's father's face had sported. In all of her memory there had been no lover who had affected her as much as Terman had. She remembered his beard tickling her breasts or thighs, and her free laughter as it did so. She shook her head again, tossing away the remembrance. Lian had wide-set blue eyes in a broad face; fine lines around his mouth betrayed the fact that he smiled easily. His forehead was high, and his hairline was already beginning to recede.

The villagers were now calling him 'He Who Leads'. The epithet had come into existence as one of mockery, but had swiftly been adopted by his adherents, who recognised the truth inherent in the name. Terman had been the one who had initially named them and kept them from the attentions of the Ellonian patrols, but Lian was the first person to have shown that he could lead; there was no other 'he' who could have led them. The fourteen amateur soldiers who followed him well-nigh worshipped him – even Mina, rather to her own annoyance, found herself caught up in this feeling. *I remember when he couldn't control his own bladder or bowels*, she thought, *yet I accept him as my leader. Each time I look at him I see the little boy who fell flat on his face one day and smashed both of his front milk-teeth. It's as if the child had put on just the costume of a leader, yet I see him as my master for all that. I obey his commands.*

Lian had trained them as best he could in the art of combat. First he had taught himself the skills of the sword and axe by challenging trees and bushes and, sometimes, Redin to duels. The techniques he had learnt through this he passed on to the others, hoping that this would be enough to equip them for battle. Later, in real combat, he would discover that some of the movements he'd devised were so unorthodox that they were of brutal effectiveness against soldiers trained in a more conventional way.

Mina lay down, feeling the heather pushing against her shoulder-blades. She wished they could stay here forever, soaking in the warmth of the sky, rather than having to venture through Albion until – as must happen – they found themselves waging war with the Ellonia. Her own guess was that this war would be lost: however many other peasants they persuaded to join them, they would still be outnumbered by the Ellonia, whose army was well drilled and equipped with weapons far better than the rustic

115

approximations Lian's troops carried. But she was quite willing to lose her life, even so. Even if this war failed, there would be another and another and another, until finally the Ellonia were laid low.

'Mother.'

He Who Leads was standing above her. She opened her eyes and smiled drowsily at him.

'Yes?'

'I saw a curlew just now.'

'What of it?'

'They say the curlew's a bird of ill-omen.'

'No,' she said, 'that's not the whole of it. The Ellonia say the curlew's a bird of ill-omen to them.'

'Oh.'

'Which means it's a good omen to us. You should have thanked the curlew for having given us its blessing.'

She closed her eyes again. The matter was closed, as far as she was outwardly concerned. In her mind, however, she admitted to herself her own sophistry and accepted the verdict of the curlew: they were, as she'd been thinking, doomed.

He walked off to mix with his other warriors. The atmosphere among them was a mixture of forced light-heartedness and gloom. He felt for them: he, too, recognised that theirs was likely to be a futile venture, but at the same time he knew that destiny was pulling him – and them – along this way. None of them had any choice in the matter. At some time, not too long in the future, whatever army he'd managed to put together would do battle with the Ellonia: that was as certain a part of the future as if it had been cast in iron.

Yet so many of his people had so little idea of the meaning of the word 'future'! Terman had brought them the concept of the passage of time; it was too much to expect them to grasp intuitively the more complex concept of the future. As they lazed in the heather and bracken, he could see that they had resigned themselves to the fact that life might not always be as pleasurable as this – that their own agonised deaths might be a price they had to pay for freedom – but few of them were more than dimly aware that, through their own actions, they could *change* the course of the future.

He pushed these concerns away to the back of his mind, and grinned like the leader he was supposed to be.

'Triumph soon, comrades,' he said, trying to raise his own spirits as much as theirs.

A great cheer rose from his company.

They waved their fists in the air.

He looked around at them as they sprawled. They seemed an unimposing body of warriors. The average age of the women was – if he ignored his mother – somewhere in the mid-twenties, if not younger, but aside from himself and Redin the men were all the far side of thirty, Jonn, at fifty, being the oldest. All of the ages were guesses, of course, because until Terman had come to the village no one had known how to keep track of time. But it was very obvious that Jonn was no youth; a tall and almost cadaverous man, he had thinning hair which seemed to cling to his skull more out of sheer willpower than for any other reason.

Daif was tall and strong, but partially deaf. Coll was so small as to be almost a dwarf. Bruiss was the kind of person who could make faint the heart of an enemy just by opening his mouth, but Lian had little hope that he'd prove equally effective in battle. Then there were Marc and Fil. The former was skeletally thin and seemed somehow remote from reality. The latter was a rounded man who had once tried to seduce Lian: it was possible that Fil had joined the venture solely in order to be able to be close to He Who Leads.

The women were perhaps more promising, if only because of their relative youth. The tallest – and the laziest – was the red-headed Lanyor. The youngest of them all, and the most unreliable, was Sinede. The chillingly blonde Andia was slow-moving but ruthlessly efficient in everything she did; it was no surprise that she had ensured that she was riding a horse rather than an ox. Marja and Reen could have been twins, although in fact they weren't related, so far as they knew: both had long black hair and quick tempers, Reen especially. Wand, with her curling dark-blonde hair, was exceptionally beautiful but somehow not attractive to Lian, for reasons which he had never been able to understand.

'We're doing well so far,' he said to them all, smiling.

'Not so very far, as yet,' said Reen. She spoke the words bitterly.

'It'll take us some time,' He Who Leads agreed. 'It may be a long while before we reach Ernestrad and then Giorran.'

'So the sooner . . .' began Jonn, putting a hand through his sparse hair.

'Yes,' said Lian, 'but I think we can afford to rest a while. There's no point in us wandering around looking like a bunch of shagged-out crazies. We'll gather more people to us if we look fresh and relaxed. It may take us a little longer, but I think it's worth it.'

'Some of us look pretty shagged-out and crazy anyway,' remarked Reen pointedly. She was cleaning her fingernails with a twig, but glanced up to give Jonn a frosty smile.

Lian squatted down beside her.

'You can go home right now, if you'd like, Reen,' he said, struggling to keep his voice casual.

For a moment she looked startled, and then she brought her face under control.

'You can't do without me.' She was a study in disinterest. Still picking at her fingernails, her hair covering her cheek so that he could see only half of her face. 'I'm the best warrior you have, Lian, and you know it.'

'On the contrary, right now you're the most useless,' he said, uncrossing his legs to sit down next to her. 'I'd rather have a blind, one-armed person on my side than someone who tries to put down her comrades the whole time.'

'Oh yeah?'

'"Yeah", as you put it. Can we keep your cow, though?'

It was the mention of the cow that convinced her that He Who Leads was really serious. She threw away the twig and looked frankly at him, her dark eyes wide.

'You mean that?'

'I'm sorry, but I do. If you want to be part of this . . .

118

this army . . . then that's fine by me. But if you're going to disrupt it by making bitchy comments about the rest of us, I'd rather do without you.'

Marja chipped in. 'If Reen goes back, I go back with her.'

Lian shrugged.

'All right.'

'Shut up!' Reen snapped at Marja. 'This is between him and me. Stay out of it.'

She turned back to Lian.

'Can we,' she said with exaggerated politeness, 'go off together for a while and discuss all this?'

'If. you like.' Lian wondered momentarily if she was trying to proposition him, and very much hoped not. The last thing his 'army' needed right now was a sexual relationship between its leader and one of the troops.

She read his eyes and laughed.

'You should be so lucky,' she said. 'Come on.'

Reen got to her feet in a single supple movement; Lian felt large and clumsy as he attempted to copy her. She took his hand and led him through the heather until they were well out of earshot of the others. A gust of wind eased the oppressive heat as they seated themselves.

'You want to win this war?' she said abruptly.

'Of course. That's what we're all here for, isn't it?'

She kicked off her boots. She'd found another twig and now set to work on her toenails. Her feet were small and clawlike.

'Lian,' she said, 'you're very young in a lot of ways.'

'Thanks.'

'Sorry,' she said, smiling at him. 'You're quite right: I'm being a bitch. Blame it on nervousness. I'll keep it all in control in future. I'm still the best soldier you've got, of course, but I'll stop talking about it.'

'Is that a promise?' He was watching her toes because he couldn't think of anything better to watch. *This bloody woman* . . .

'I don't say things I don't mean.' She was bored with the excavation of the undersides of her toenails, so she pulled her boots back on again. 'Mind you,' she added, 'I'd think twice before I picked a fight with your mother.'

'What about the others?'

From their initial position of antagonism they'd quickly slipped into one of easy cooperation.

'Marja's likely to be useful,' Reen said. 'She's another I wouldn't be keen to pick a fight with. Wand's more ruthless than you or I could imagine: she's a bit lumbering when it comes to using her sword but she's a killer. It's sort of built into her. Apart from yourself and Redin, the men are a waste of space – except, perhaps, Marc. He seems useless on the outside, but there's something about him I can't *read*. I'd be wary of underestimating him.'

'Well,' he said, 'you don't exactly mince your words, do you?' He linked his two little fingers together and tugged at them and, as he did so, remembered a conversation he'd had with his dead father, long ago.

'Would you prefer I did?' she asked.

'No. You're quite right. Only . . . you can say these things to me, but if you start saying them to the rest of the people you'll destroy them. So keep your opinions to yourself or – and I mean it – I'll send you back to Lianhome. I'd rather lose my best soldier than have a dozen people who reckon that their sole purpose in life is to lose a battle.'

'Understood,' she said.

'Good.'

'Shall we go back and join the others? They'll be starting to talk.'

'We could give them something to talk about.' Lian was only half-joking, despite his earlier resolution.

'Don't be so bloody silly.'

They made much slower progress than they had expected. The oxen were soon discovered to be more trouble than they were worth. Lian had ridden back to the village to fetch a herdsman to take charge of them and returned looking rather concerned. Even though he had been away for only a short time and had travelled no further than a few dozen kilometres, already the villagers were betraying signs of his absence. One or two of the older people had difficulty remembering his name, and even their own. Sinede cheered him up by pointing out that this might well be a good thing: the more naturally people behaved should an Ellonian requisitioning party happen by, the safer they were likely to be.

Another reason they were making such sluggish progress was the matter of navigation. The villagers knew the line of north and south, because Terman had worked it out approximately using the direction from which he had arrived on Albion's shore. However, despite frequent efforts, he had been unable to make a compass, so as soon as the village had dropped out of sight behind them they had had to make use of the relative positions of landmarks – trees, hilltops, and so on – to help them follow their planned direction as accurately as possible. They were thus unable to take the easiest routes. Lian was constructing a strip map of their progress by scratching lines onto the inside of a large sheet of bark with a sharp stone, which might help future parties, and he frequently called the party to a halt.

Two waking-times after Reen and Lian came to their understanding, the troop were crashing their way down through a belt of green, thorny bushes towards a large, swift-flowing stream when they encountered a platoon of Ellonian soldiery on the old track near the waterside.

Sinede and Wand were the first to reach the road, and stumbled out of the bushes into the direct view of a party of soldiers about a hundred metres away.

'Get back!' the two women said forcefully to the others, trying not to raise their voices loud enough that the soldiers might hear them. Instantly the people on foot melted back into the greenery. The horses, however, could not be concealed. Mina and Andia had no choice but to carry on down to the track, leading their animals. Lian was about to do the same when Reen snatched Anan's reins from him.

'Give me!' she spat. 'I'm expendable – you're not.'

'I can't let a . . .'

'Shut up, you fool!'

Before he could stop her, she was gone.

He crouched down in the bushes, cursing her for her impetuosity and blessing her for her courage. Through the interlocking branches he could see a cameo of the five women standing on the rough brown track, their hands at the hilts of their swords, the three horses grazing contentedly in the lush grass beside the stream beyond. From his left he could hear the shouts of the soldiers as they approached.

He slithered carefully forwards, easing the longbow from his back. Again reaching behind him, he found an arrow and silently nocked it, although as yet putting no tension on the bow.

Hushed whispering around him revealed that someone else in his band had seen what he was doing and was passing the word along the line that the rest should follow suit.

The Ellonian soldiers surrounded the five women like an incoming wave surrounding a rock. Immediately He Who Leads could see nothing of Reen and the others; instead there was a haphazardly shifting pattern of reds and greens.

The last to approach was an officer on horseback, his long shining sword sparkling in the sunlight as he held it ahead of him. Its chilly gleam was in stark contrast, He Who Leads mused glumly, to the dull metal of the home-made weapons the villagers carried.

'Who are you?' shouted the officer, forcing his men to create a space.

'Loyal servants of the House of Ellon,' said Reen, taking a step forward and bowing gracefully.

'Rubbish!'

He looked disdainfully at their clumsy leather armour and their crudely fashioned weapons.

'Aye, sir,' said Mina, aping Reen with a show of respect. 'We have been commanded to comb the countryside in peasant garb. There is concern among your superior officers over reports of a renegade village' – this was a lucky guess, and she was pleased to see from the rider's start of surprise that it had hit home – 'and we have been sent to seek it out.'

He looked at her consideringly. Clearly he was halfway persuaded, but still full of doubts.

Lian started to put tension on his bowstring.

'And which of your commanders sent you on this mission?' he eventually asked, watching her face.

Mina looked confused. *Shit!* thought Lian. His mother should have thought beforehand that this might be one of the officer's first questions.

Reen stepped adroitly into the breach.

'We have orders to reveal his name to no one,' she said swiftly.

Gripping the saddle with his knees, the officer looked at her sceptically.

Slowly he said: 'I don't believe you. I think your story is a fabrication.'

Andia, fighting with considerable success to conceal her terror, said in her clear, cold voice: 'She speaks the truth, sir. Those were our orders, and we dare not disobey them. For all we know, you and your men may yourselves be rebellious peasants in captured uniforms.'

'Then at least you can tell me your rank.'

A mistake had been inevitable. All the women could have hoped to do was delay it.

'I am Lieutenant Reen. My companions are . . .'

'Seize them!'

The guards moved in instantly, grabbing the women by their shoulders and forcing them to their knees, foreheads close to the hot stony metal of the track.

'You poor ignoramuses,' said the officer quietly, almost sympathetically. 'Our army has no women.' To the soldiers he said, rather more loudly, 'Enjoy them as you will, and then kill them.'

He turned the head of his ebony-black horse away and continued slowly down the track, sheathing his sword.

Lian released his bowstring.

With a small truncated scream the officer toppled from the saddle, Lian's arrow sprouting from his neck.

The soldiers stopped in the act of ripping at the women's leather armour with their swords. For a moment they were completely motionless as their memories fled, and then two fell forwards, arrows between their shoulder-blades. The others threw the women from them, searching desperately for cover and drawing their swords.

Once more the arrows took their toll. Blood spurted out over the road as a man staggered backwards, clutching at his throat, and fell heavily into the stream. He floundered for a few moments and then stilled.

Reen took the opportunity of the remaining men's consternation to lunge upwards with her sword into a soft underbelly, raking the coarse blade backwards and forwards, the muscles of her forearm straining. She was immediately covered in a mess of gore, and shuffled rapidly away on her knees, wiping at her eyes with her free hand.

Soon all but one of the Ellonian patrol was motionless and it was clear that the injured man hadn't long to live. Reen picked up his heavy sword and coldly dispatched him with a fierce slash across the throat.

But the archers had done their work too well.

Among the twisted bodies in red and green there were two crumpled heaps in brown leather.

He Who Leads pushed his way through the bushes to reach the road.

Reen put her reeking arm firmly on his elbow and tried to restrain him.

'Every army suffers casualties, Lian,' she said. 'There's no need for you to look at this. She and Wand died in the knowledge that they were helping bring the reign of the House of Ellon to its end.'

He pushed her away and strode forwards, knelt down.

An arrow had struck Mina in the back of the neck and passed up into her skull. There was surprisingly little blood in her mop of grey hair. He turned her gently over sideways and saw the grey eyes he had loved for all of his life wide open in the instantaneous agony she must have felt as she died.

Andia put her hand lightly on his shoulder. He turned his head and looked up at her pale face. The unfamiliar tears in her usually ice-like eyes matched his own.

124

'We all loved her, Lian,' she said, her voice rough-edged. 'We all loved her.'

'Well,' said Reen, 'now at least we've got some decent weapons.' She waved an inquisitive insect impatiently away from her face.

'And,' agreed Marja with relish, patting a half-empty earthenware bottle at her side, 'some decent wine.'

They were all, except Lian, sitting, lying or squatting in a glade about two kilometres from the scene of their first skirmish. He Who Leads himself had been ruthlessly dosed with the rich red wine they had discovered in the Ellonian wagon, and was now snoring gently among the trees a little way off. Birds were twittering or squawling in the branches above them.

Everyone was exhausted. Clearing up the evidence of the skirmish had been an arduous and often repulsive business. Reen and Marja had cheerfully taken on the task of stripping the soldiers of their uniforms, salvaging any garment that was not too badly torn or bloodstained and burying the remainder under a pile of stones in the stream. Bruiss, although his brashness had been muted, had been determined not to be outdone in callousness by the two women, and so had helped them drag the corpses out of sight among the bushes, where they were unceremoniously left to the mercies of clouds of flies. Fil and Jonn, having first caught and tethered the officer's huge black mare, had used a leather bucket they'd discovered in the provisions wagon to sluice the worst of the blood away from the road-surface. The remainder of the depleted band had comforted He Who Leads and helped dig shallow graves for his mother and for Wand.

Lian had broken down weeping as Daif pushed the brown earth over the object that had been Mina. Redin embraced him as if they were brothers, and led him away.

At Reen's insistence they had, without further delay, forded the stream and, moving as quickly as they could, crossed open grassland to find refuge in this small outcrop of forest.

'We'll have to make good progress the next few waking-periods,' Reen was saying, 'and just hope that another bloody bunch of Ellonian scum doesn't come that way before then. With any luck it'll rain soon and wash away the evidence.' Her thin face looked doubtful as she looked up at the sky above them, her eyes narrowing against the brightness.

'It'll be hard to get Lian to move very quickly,' said Redin morosely. The huge man was obviously still deeply grieved by his friend's bereavement. 'He may not be much of a horseman for a while yet.'

'You could always carry him,' drawled Sinede loosely, pouting at him with studied overtness.

There were a few uneasy smiles among the others but, to everyone's astonishment, Redin suddenly grinned broadly at her.

'By my right hand but you're an impertinent young trollop!' he said, slapping the hand on the soft forest floor beside him.

'"Trollop"? Why, sir, a maiden like myself? Say it not that my character is besmirched, I pray you. Do you wish to contest the issue with all of those who've had a significant struggle with my maidenhead?'

She fluttered her eyelashes at him.

'Have some respect for the dead,' hissed Jonn furiously.

'Don't you see?' said Redin loudly, turning to face the elderly man. 'That's exactly what Sinede's trying to show us we shouldn't be doing. No, that's not quite it; she's showing us how we *should* be doing it. They're dead – gone. We can't do anything to help them. Each time we lose some of our comrades, we can't just sit around moping like a man on the closet. If we do that, the House of Ellon'll finish us off in no time. And d'you think Mina and Wand would think it any sign of respect to their sacrifice if we let that happen? No – they'd think they'd thrown away their lives in vain for the sake of a ragtag collection of spineless thickwits.'

'I can be *totally* spineless on occasion,' muttered Sinede, making herself as buxom as possible.

This time several of them laughed.

'I remember it all too well,' said Redin. 'In fact, I expect most of us can.'

'I can't,' said Lanyor's slow voice, entering into the spirit of things.

'No,' Redin said more seriously, 'Sinede's right: we should remember our dead not with tears but with tales of what fine and courageous people they were in life, reminders of how lucky we were to have been their companions, jokes about their failings and mistakes. And Reen and Marja are right, too, in their different way. We've got good weapons, now, and an extra horse, and some Ellonian uniforms – rather tattered ones, to be true, but uniforms nevertheless. And this *is* damn good wine, so let's appreciate it while we can – by drinking toasts to Mina and Wand until we're all sleeping as soundly as Lian.'

'Don't drink *too* much, Redin,' purred Sinede, and there was more laughter.

The big man leaned forward, raising his finger and pointing at each one of their circle.

'So celebrate, blast you all. The most important thing we can all do is have a bloody good time!'

'May I help you in that?' said a light voice.

Immediately they were on their feet, their crudely made swords drawn, eyes searching the darkness of the trees for any flicker of movement.

'You're all looking in the wrong direction,' said the voice, with a touch of exasperation.

They spun back with various degrees of clumsiness to face the centre of the clearing.

Standing there was a slight figure, little more than a metre and a half tall, dressed in a silver jerkin and breeches that finished in ragged ends halfway up her calves. Though her shape was boyish and her red hair was close-cropped around her high-cheeked face, it was instantly obvious to them that she was a young girl. She was carrying a zither made of walnut, with ebony pegs and fretwork. Her eyes were yellow-green, almost catlike, as she surveyed them calmly.

Reen was – as ever – first to recover herself.

'Who are you?' she whispered intensely, her outstretched sword wavering not at all.

'I,' said the young woman with a little bow, 'am Alyss, at your service. I seek only to entertain wayfarers like yourselves as they ply their weary travels across the breadth of fair Albion.'

Her smile was courteous enough, but to Reen it seemed that the girl was mocking them.

Jonn sheathed his sword and sat down.

'A singer once came to Lianhome, soon after Terman arrived,' he explained to the others, giving a small gesture of acknowledgement towards Alyss. He was a little startled when she turned and mimicked his acknowledgement precisely, because he was sitting behind her, but he continued: 'We've nothing to fear from a singer.'

The rest seemed to take his word for it; only Reen and Marja remained suspicious. Bruiss half-sheathed his sword and then drew it again, still determined to match the steeliness of the two women.

'How do we know we can trust you?' said Marja.

'You might as well,' replied Alyss with a sort of airy impatience. 'There's nothing you could do to harm me, and if I'd wanted to I could have killed you all several times over by now. We singers have great powers, you know, even though we hardly ever need to use them.'

She squatted down unconcernedly and twiddled with the ebony pegs, tuning her zither.

'How many of you are there?' growled Bruiss.

'Oh, one of me and lots of me, scattered throughout millions of worlds that are further from Albion than you could ever imagine.'

Most of them felt instinctively that Alyss was lying about there being millions of worlds beyond Albion; Terman had told them that there was only one. Marc, however, who seemed always to be thinking on a different plane from the rest of them, looked gravely at the girl: some element in her voice or attitude told him that she was lying about something else entirely.

'You shouldn't laugh behind your hand at us, you know,' he said quietly.

She glanced up, her eyes showing him a sudden respect.

'My apologies,' she said. 'You're quite right.'

'Thank you.' He moved his head in acceptance of this apology, and she gave him a genuine smile.

Reen had been becoming more and more infuriated by this exchange, which seemed to her to be a meaningless fencing with words.

'Don't play with me, you little tart!' she snarled. 'You know what I wanted to know: how many of you singers are there?'

'I'm not a tart, Reen!' said Alyss her eyes flashing. 'On occasion I've – but let's leave that behind us for now. In answer to your question, there are at the moment,' she cocked her head to one side, 'forty-seven singers in the whole of Albion, but one of them's just had his tongue cut out on the orders of the Despot, so he hardly reckons in the total. He was a lousy singer anyway. On the other hand, my friends, I've decided for this sleeping-period to be a singer, easily the best of them all – as you might expect of me. So that makes the number back up to forty-seven again.'

'You're sure you're the best?' said Marja sarcastically.

'Oh, quite sure,' Alyss replied easily. 'Please put those silly skewers away and sit down, for I've got a long song to sing you – and a very good one, if I may say so. And why shouldn't I, come to that? I wrote it, after all; I know it better than anyone else, so I'm the best judge of quite how excellent it is.'

The zither strings were proving recalcitrant, the ebony pegs apparently not moving smoothly in their holes, so that the chords she was stroking out of the instrument were abysmal dissonances. Alyss addressed it with a terse imprecation and it instantly tuned itself perfectly, seeming almost to quiver in her lap.

'That's better,' she said mildly, patting its walnut case encouragingly.

Reen found that she was sitting cross-legged on the grass,

her sword sheathed. *That's funny*, she thought. *I don't remember how I got to be down here like this. And how did she know my name?*

She started to move her hand to the hilt of her sword again but, for a reason she couldn't quite define, found that she'd changed her mind. Instead she leaned forwards, her elbows on her knees and her firm chin cupped in her hands, looking at the singer and waiting for the entertainment to begin.

Alyss had been right – it *was* a good song. What she failed to mention was that it was not just a long one, but an extremely long one. Whenever she performed a part of it that she thought was particularly good, she repeated that section so that her listeners could have a second chance to appreciate how exquisite it was.

The song told the tale of a man who had been brought to Albion and who had fathered a son called Lian. Lian had led a small band forth to raise troops to conquer the Ellonia; all of the band were named, and extended compliments were paid to their virtue, courageousness in adversity, amiability, chivalry and other characteristics – each of the listeners recognised themselves in these descriptions, while finding less accuracy in the depiction of their comrades.

But then the song changed, the chords shifting into predominantly minor keys, and the whole ambience became rather more sinister. This alteration of mood came at the point in their travels when they had spent much of one sleeping-period listening to Alyss the singer entertain them. Although she was singing as of past events, they soon realised that she was now telling them in detail of their future exploits. The trouble was that, although the words were crystal-clear in their minds as they heard them, they seemed to seep away into the mistiness of forgetfulness almost immediately afterwards. Fil's face was a mask of gloom as his demise was recounted, but within minutes he was smiling cheerfully again, although wondering why it was that his name never seemed to be mentioned any more. Marja and Sinede looked at each other with a sudden flush of embarrassment which swiftly disappeared. And so it went on around the circle.

Finally Alyss slapped the palm of her hand against the strings to silence them.

'I haven't finished writing the song yet,' she said brightly, after the applause had died away so that the only sounds were of the birds and the insects and Lian's muted snores. 'Perhaps some other sleeping-period I'll come and visit you again and sing you the rest.'

She looked a little disconcerted as several of her audience made hasty excuses and blundered off among the trees to relieve their bladders. But she welcomed each of them with an ingratiating smile of welcome as they rather sheepishly returned.

'You were telling us of the future,' said Coll, awestruck. The small man looked at her face intently. 'That was what you were doing, wasn't it?'

'There's no such thing as *the* future,' she replied. It looked as if she were absently folding up her zither, but of course that would have been impossible. She popped it into one of the pockets of her breeches, where it twanged a few melancholy notes before she gave it a smart admonitory slap. 'I sang to you about *a* future. That's why you can remember only that you heard about it, but cannot recall any of the things that I told you happened in it.'

Marc knew exactly what she meant. He'd thought of such matters for a long time now. As far as he could imagine, there was only one past – although he accepted that he might be wrong even in this – but it seemed likely that there could be an infinite number of futures, each branching away from the other during every moment of each of their existences. The singer had told all of them of their personal fates, be they triumphant or disastrous, but none of the events she had described were graven in stone. They were all a part of the future as Alyss saw it and understood it; in what she was saying to them so casually now she was acknowledging that her vision of the future events might well be wrong – that *nothing* foreseen about the future in this universe could ever be guaranteed to prove

131

correct. And hence the melting away of their memories of what the song had told them. Had they been able to remember it all, they might through their own conscious volition have been able to alter the events of their own futures; alternatively, perhaps worse, they might have found themselves caught up in a single future, trapped like a rabbit in its run, their options reduced to a pitiful few rather than the infinity to which they were entitled. He Who Leads might well have been able to remember her predictions, however, and so she had chosen to come among them at a time when only he wasn't awake to listen.

'You're a clever man,' said Alyss, turning in Marc's direction and smiling her approval at him. 'Over the next few waking-periods, perhaps you can explain all this to the rest of them.'

Marc smiled back, then realised with a sudden shock that none of the others had heard what she was saying: indeed, they seemed frozen where they were – Marja half to her feet, Redin with a bottle above his mouth, the flow of wine a motionless downward arc. Above Redin's head a bird was poised, a worm dangling in its beak.

He looked back at Alyss.

'And you, you're a clever young woman,' he said, returning the compliment.

'I'm not as young as you think I am,' she said. 'Hmmm.'

He could see there was something else she wanted to say but that she was debating within herself whether or not she ought to. Her rather thin lips were stretched across her small white teeth in a visible reflection of her indecision. Then, within a second or so, she snapped out of it. Evidently she'd determined to speak her mind.

'Marc,' she said, 'you have it in you to become the new forty-seventh singer. I could teach you, if you'd like. Actually, you'd be the forty-eighth; I only added the bit about poor old Ghyt having had his tongue cut out because I thought it added a certain amount of, um, dramatic effect – and anyway, he really *is* a lousy singer, and he once tried to pinch my bottom.'

She grinned suddenly.

'I broke his arm in three places. It was a long time before he could even lift his sousaphone, let alone play it – even as badly as he normally does.'

'That's not the only lie you told,' Marc reminded her.

'Yes.' She tried to look contrite, but giggled instead. 'I knew you'd notice that.'

'There aren't lots of you, are there, in all those millions of worlds?' he said.

'No.' Suddenly she was more sombre. 'There's only one. But I, you know, get around a bit. In some worlds I have one name, in others another – it all depends how the fancy takes me.'

'Are the other singers like you?'

'No. They're different from you,' she waved a hand to indicate his companions, 'but they're different from me as well. There's one whom you won't meet, Barra 'ap Rteniadoli Me'gli'minter Rehan, whose voice is so sweet that nightingales have been known to get really depressed on hearing it. Singers like him are a part of Albion, and always have been. I'm not. But you're dodging what I was trying to ask you, aren't you. Just a bit. Hmmm?'

Those acute eyes were on him. He felt as if he were being held up for close inspection. Whatever he said she would know what he really meant.

'Yes, you're right, I've been avoiding giving you an answer,' he said.

'Think of the advantages you would have if you were a singer, Marc,' she said earnestly. 'You'd be like He Who Leads, able to remember the past, able to name people and things, able to give all of this to the people around you through the songs you'd be singing. The *right* movements of your fingers across the strings and the learning of the songs so that they become almost like instincts to you – both of these would give you memories of everything that's gone before. Best of all, you'd have the delight of being in my company while you learnt the singer's arts. It'd be a big gift I'd be giving you, Marc, if you wanted to take it.'

'I don't,' he said simply, spreading his hands wide in his lap as if in apology.

'I thought that you wouldn't, but I had to give you the option,' Alyss said, a little frown of annoyance momentarily crossing her brow: *reject the offer of my company, huh?*

'I swore to follow He Who Leads and help him destroy the power of the Ellonia. What you're proposing is something more than I've ever dreamed of, but it's not enough.'

'More than I've ever dreamed of.' That's a bit more like it, thought Alyss.

'Aye,' she said, 'you're a good man.'

'I also know that I'll die quite soon because of the oath I swore.' He smiled ruefully, as if the prospect of imminent death was something far too trivial ever to have given anyone any cause for concern. 'I'm not a brave man – don't get me wrong about that – it's just that promises are things that can, or should, shape the future.'

'Oh, but *I* think you're a brave man.'

Her eyes were at the core of him. He had no secrets of past or future from her. He knew this, and accepted it easily.

'Will we see each other again before I die?'

'I . . . I don't know. I think that whatever it is that moulds the passing course of events hasn't decided yet.' Alyss looked almost embarrassed at her admission of ignorance.

'Well, if not, thank you.'

'And thank *you*.'

She winked at him once, and then all was bustle around them once again. Marja came to a fully upright position; the wine gurgled down Redin's throat; the bird flew away bearing the wriggling worm.

Alyss clapped her hands, quietly but with authority, so that everybody stilled.

'Thank you for realising how lucky you've been to have me among you,' she said. 'I'm glad you were able to appreciate my entertainment.'

She bowed.

'And now, I'm afraid, you must love me and let me leave you.'

She raised her thin arms above her head so that the

fingertips of her two hands were just touching, gave the little gathering one last smile, and vanished.

Marc waved to the empty air, bidding her farewell.

The others looked at him as if he must be insane.

Redin found that he couldn't sleep, despite the amount of wine that he'd drunk. Alyss's song had stimulated him, and he found his thoughts were weaving a never-ending tapestry of half-forgotten snatches of music and eerie little cadences matched to words that were infuriatingly just beyond his grasp.

He rolled over onto his other side, smelling the fruity scent of fallen leaves. He ran his fingers through his beard, grinning quietly to himself.

Besides, he thought, *I want to get laid*.

He analysed this emotion. Often he wanted sex purely for the physical sensations it gave him; sometimes he took it just because it was there. But it was different this time. He didn't want to become part of any relationship as intense as love or infatuation, but he did want to spend a part of this sleeping-period – what was left of it – having some loving form of sex with a woman. Someone with whom he could share caresses and smiles just for a short while, so that they could . . . love each other temporarily.

And that brought his thoughts around to Sinede. Joking or not – and he wasn't sure how much she had been – she'd been openly seductive towards him earlier. And he knew that he could share lovingness and reassurance with her: hadn't he done so several times before? Many of the villagers had mocked the girl because she constantly slept around but Redin didn't join them. If she had any fault it was that she was capable of loving so many men, rather than confining herself to just the one, and he respected her for it: if only more people would love widely rather than hate widely . . .

He sat up and climbed creakily to his feet. Next sleeping-time he must make the effort to construct a pallet from the heather before throwing himself to the ground.

He was fairly certain she'd wandered off to sleep somewhere to his right and so he went in that direction, doing his best not to make too much noise and wake the others. He almost stepped on Coll's sleeping form, but the neat little man didn't stir; Redin grinned as he discovered that even the fastidious Coll didn't escape the human frailty of snoring – although, to be sure, they were very polite and formal snores.

Finally he found Sinede. Through the maze of the tree-trunks he saw that he would have to do battle with wakefulness some other way.

Sinede was proving to Reen how spineless she could be.

Unexpected, thought Redin, *or maybe not so unexpected*. He paused for a moment, smiling at the two of them, his motives in no way voyeuristic, and then crept away.

This time he lay down in a site even more uncomfortable than his earlier one, but now sleep came to him easily. *What I really wanted to know*, he thought as drowsiness was overcoming him, *was that there was this sort of love between us all. I don't need to play any physical part in it myself: the very fact that it exists is enough.*

I love you all, he thought.

Chapter Six
Syor

The mob of soldiers standing around the courtyard and of aristocrats looking down from the surrounding windows was going wild. Men and women alike stamped their feet, shouted encouragement or derision, punched the air with their fists . . .

Garndon, the Army-Master, sat alongside the Despot on an only slightly less ostentatious throne and smiled benignly beneath his bushy eyebrows. His shoulders were stooped and his head now completely bald, but there was still a powerful gleam of vitality in his aged eyes.

Another roar from the watchers.

The Despot nudged him.

'That was a good one, eh, Garndon?'

'Indeed, sire.'

The two thrones were set above the platform used for executions, and Garndon wrinkled his nose against the stench of old blood. He and his ruler were, as tradition demanded, the judges of one of Giorran's regular spectacles: the fights held among army officers eager for promotion. A win or a loss in any of the bouts did not guarantee elevation of rank, but it could make its mark on a man's superior officers and affect their future decisions.

The two young men struggling in the courtyard were both strong and obviously fit. Their faces and bodies bore bruises gained during the day's earlier encounters. They fought naked, and there were no rules of combat: feet, hands, heads, knees and elbows could all be used, and frequently were. It was no coincidence that the most prominently bruised parts of both of their bodies were around the groin.

The young lieutenant with the fair hair swung round and now raked his toenails viciously across the genitals of his darker opponent, drawing blood. The other officer hardly flinched, instead reaching out with his hirsute arms, his hands grasping to attempt a stranglehold around the blond man's throat.

Both were off-balance, but the fair-haired man more precariously so. He fell backwards onto the white stone paving, clutching at the thumbs that pressed ruthlessly against his Adam's apple, trying to prise them away. His adversary fell on top of him, bringing a knee up to his crotch and bearing down yet harder on his throat.

The crowd yelled their enthusiasm. This looked to be the decisive strike. The blond officer's face was turning blue and his tongue was lolling uncontrollably from his mouth. But then he seemed to find a new source of strength from somewhere. He shifted his hands away from his throat and down over the buttocks of his opponent, then twisted both of their bodies so that they rolled over and he was now the one on top.

Almost as if they were lovers, thought the Army-Master, watching the scene with a benevolent gaze.

'That lad's got talent,' said the Despot. 'See that he's promoted, will you, Garndon?'

'Certainly, sire,' Garndon replied respectfully, thinking: *I'll see the bugger dead first. He's too dangerous. I've no desire to feel his dagger in my spine.*

The fair-haired man was now using his opponent's own stranglehold to beat the back of the man's skull against the stone. Both of the combatants were near to unconsciousness, but still forced themselves to continue the struggle.

There was another flurry of movement, too swift for the mob – or even the judges – to follow, and the blond officer was being thrown head-first against the front of the platform beneath them. Although Garndon knew it wasn't possible, it seemed as if the whole stone dais was jolted upwards.

Somehow the man survived the impact and staggered away, blood flowing from his forehead, his lips drawn back in a vicious snarl.

He's become a real killer now, thought Garndon. *He'll want my place before too long. If he does what I've asked of him, he'll be wanting it even more.*

A kick to the blood-covered groin and the swarthy man was gasping and crouching. Another kick, this time to the throat, and he was down. His opponent deliberately jumped in the air, landing with both feet on the man's head. Blood came spurting from his mouth. A series of ruthless kicks to the abdomen seemed to swell the flow of blood.

An ear-shattering boom came from the mob.

The Despot stood and held his hand, palm-outwards, to halt the contest. The loser was near-enough dead, and almost certainly would be within the next few minutes. The Despot did not regard himself as a sadist, and saw no reason to prolong the man's agony.

'The contest is over!' he shouted over the baying of the crowd. 'I declare the victor to be . . .'

He paused.

'Lieutenant Haka,' Garndon whispered.

'. . . Lieutenant Haka!'

There was widespread cheering. Surgeons rushed to the fallen man and, although they shook their heads at the futility of trying to save him, carried his choking body gently away from the arena. Some of the watching aristocrats spat on him from the safety of their apartments above.

Haka raised his arms to accept the accolades of his audience. Blood was pouring into his eyes from the wound on his forehead, but he soaked up the adulation of the crowd and felt no pain.

It was a long while before the applause died down. The Despot resumed his throne and gestured towards Garndon, motioning him towards the front of the podium. The Army-Master followed his ruler's silent instruction, and stood swaying above the blood-splattered combat area, right at the edge of the dais.

'Haka,' he shouted so that all could hear him, 'you now have the right of challenge!'

The young fair-haired lieutenant, a wet cloth stemming the flow of blood from his brow, looked up at Garndon with a bruised smile. He had obeyed the Army-Master's orders so far during the contest, and was confident that soon he would achieve high rank. He winked a puffed eye.

'I accept!' he shouted.

'Who do you challenge?' asked Garndon, almost meekly.

'I challenge Nadar!'

There was abrupt silence among the mob. To challenge the Deputy Army-Master – this was something unheard-of.

Garndon smiled yet again.

'Your challenge is valid,' he said.

That was the truth. It was the right of the winner of the competition to challenge any member of the army to a final bout. Garndon had promised Lieutenant Haka immediate, albeit modest, promotion, plus generous judgements in the earlier rounds, should he issue this particular challenge. Of course, the poor boy would be dead before the promotion could be effected. Garndon's lips pursed.

Nadar, who had been watching from a high window with a wife on each arm, looked down in consternation. He looked from one to the other of the women, as if by so doing he could somehow spare himself the ordeal to come; they both looked back at him, equally horrified. If Nadar died fighting Haka they would lose their status forever: in the House of Ellon, widows were held in low esteem when the men of high rank came to choosing their harems.

But there was no alternative; the challenge had been issued.

Nadar pushed the two women away and prepared for combat. In front of their critical eyes he stripped off his red and green uniform to reveal a body that was going to seed: the skin was ashy, almost deathlike, and the stomach protuberant. The hairs of his chest and groin were grey. Nadar was not an old man yet but he soon would be.

'You can refuse the challenge,' said one of the women.

She was extremely pretty and had been a wife of his for some time now but, blast it, he couldn't even recall her name: she was the one with the lips, that was all he could remember.

'Of course I can't,' he said, his voice harsh as he threw away the final garment. *A sock: of all the ignominious things to be wearing last before my death*, he thought wearily. *That cunning old bastard Garndon has set this up; I hope his soul burns very slowly in the eye of the Sun.*

Then he chuckled.

There might be a way of turning the tables.

All I have to do is kill this upstart lieutenant.

The thought speeded his steps down the spiral stone stairs, hot sunlight flushing his body each time he passed one of the slit windows. People moved aside to let him pass; a few of them – but only a few, he noted – applauded him as he went by. Some of the women and most of the men looked critically at the wrinkled knot of his genitals, shrivelled by the thought of the encounter to come.

The sunlight beat him as he emerged into the open. A path was cleared hastily to allow him to reach the combat area without having to push and shove his fellow-soldiers – he still regarded them as his fellows, even though now they were howling for his blood, aching to see their second highest officer toppled from his post.

He raised his arms in salute to the ranked masses as he entered the arena. The response from the mob was muted – especially, he realised sourly, from the window through which his two wives and himself had been watching the earlier fights. Should he succeed, there were going to be some early divorces. It was in his power to reduce them to harlotry among the common folk and, his smile tightening into an artificial grin as he faced the crowd, that was exactly what he proposed to do, whatever the result of this bout – even to the one with the lips.

'I accept the challenge!' he shouted defiantly up at Garndon.

'As you must,' said the old man.

Over to Nadar's right, Haka prowled restlessly, like an

141

untamed animal eager to escape from its pen.

I've experience on my side, thought Nadar. *Besides, the Wind once told me that my doom wouldn't come until I'd achieved what I thought was the pinnacle of my glory. Becoming Deputy Army-Master isn't enough for me – I'm reaching for higher peaks than that. Perhaps the attainment of the Despotism . . .*

Haka threw himself towards Nadar, his feet high in the air and his body almost horizontal. He seemed almost to be flying.

Nadar stood back smartly and watched the younger man crash painfully down onto the paving. Haka's body skidded across the stone, leaving red smears behind it.

'You could admit defeat now,' said Nadar softly enough so that the crowd couldn't hear his words. 'I wouldn't hold it against you.'

Haka tore himself to his feet, his face contorted with hatred.

'Watch the old man die!' he shouted to the crowd.

They yelled their enthusiasm.

To Nadar, quietly: 'You're going to die, very soon.'

'People have said that before.'

There was a smile on Nadar's lips.

It disappeared swiftly as Haka launched another assault.

This time Nadar saw a glitter of sharp steel between the young man's first and second fingers in both hands.

Fuck it! Garndon's cheating!

This time, as the young man ran furiously forward, Nadar seemed first to turn away, as if to cower from the attack, and then suddenly whipped around with his right leg to send the lieutenant sprawling across the paving for a second time.

So far Nadar had suffered not a single bruise. His opponent, by contrast, was bleeding copiously, both from the wounds he had received in earlier bouts and from his hands, where his own dishonest weapons had slashed him.

But Haka was far from done yet.

Grinning gleefully through his pain, he advanced on Nadar, letting the tips of the little hand-daggers he held show between his fingers to the older man. Suddenly he threw himself through the air, the points of the daggers aimed directly towards Nadar's throat.

It was easy enough to step away once more. Nadar smiled at the crowd, raising his arms, as if to say: *It's all so easy*.

The soldiers gave him their approval, resoundingly. The aristocrats were less enthusiastic: their women were critically comparing the body of the young man with that of the old.

A long time passed before Haka was able to pull himself to his feet; he staggered exhaustedly as he approached Nadar, the small blades now more obvious. Nadar had relaxed against the base of the dais, waiting for his adversary to recover. Earlier combatants would have moved in for the kill: Nadar chose simply to laugh at Haka.

As the young lieutenant stumbled uncertainly towards him, Nadar got to his feet and again hissed, 'You could give up now, you know, and that'd be an end of it – I wouldn't hold it against you.'

'You'll die,' Haka said, loudly enough for the two old men above the dais to hear him. He was having difficulty finding his feet. A sudden punch at Nadar's head missed by several centimetres, gouging a small groove from the stone and destroying the blade of one of the little daggers with which the lieutenant had been armed.

Nadar, stooping, took Haka's legs out from under him with a swift move of his right arm, so that Haka's face smashed yet again onto the stone. Pieces of teeth flew to either side and, more importantly, the younger man lost control of his remaining dagger.

The weapon flew away some metres from them, but Nadar was on it in an instant.

He held it high, then plunged it into Haka's back. The younger man gave a scream. Nada twisted the knife, crouched over Haka's buttocks, grinning.

His chest and loins covered in Haka's blood, Nadar slowly pulled away, drawing his knife from the still-warm flesh, wishing that the cheers of the crowd didn't sicken him so much. *I've killed a man I'd rather have had as a*

143

member of my troop, he thought. *That's not such a great achievement.*

Garndon, seated above, controlled his fury. He'd intended that Haka should slay Nadar in open combat, so that there could be no question of him, the Army-Master, having played any active part. Instead, the silly young shit had got himself killed – and without Nadar having done more than break into a slight sweat.

'Nadar's a bit of a one, isn't he?' said the Despot, nudging Garndon yet again. 'The boy had knives, but still your deputy killed him easily. A well chosen deputy, I say: this will not go unrecognised. Congratulations.'

The fat man waddled to the edge of the podium.

'The contest is over!' he shouted in the ritual words. 'I declare the victor to be my Deputy Army-Master, Nadar!'

'Nadar,' he said into the void of the crowd's silence, 'you now have the right of challenge!'

'With all humility,' said Nadar, bowing deeply as the surgeons lugged Haka's corpse away, 'I beg to challenge Garndon.'

Seven minutes after this Nadar was undisputed Army-Master.

'Lian!' shouted a voice behind him, and he pulled his horse Anan to one side.

Several hundred waking-periods and an untold number of villages had gone by – even Lian was beginning to lose count – and, by his dubious reckoning, it was time for them to start turning in a loop towards the east. He now rode at the head of an army that was almost two thousand strong, although many of the would-be warriors were unskilled and ill equipped. Encounters with platoons of Ellonian troops had frequently swelled their supplies of weapons, horses and red and green uniforms, the latter proving occasionally useful when luring the servants of the House of Ellon to their murder.

Lian was particularly pleased about two things. Firstly, it seemed that the larger his army grew the more volunteers there were emerging from each subsequent village. Secondly, they were leaving the gift of writing wherever they went. This had been given by Terman to Mina, and hence to the villagers of Lianhome; the art had spread among the members of the army, so that now each time they left a village Lian was able to order a couple of – usually gratifyingly reluctant – followers to teach the people, especially the children, that scratches on bark or on leaves made from pulverised wood could mean the same as the words they spoke.

'Writing,' Lian told all of them, 'is another way of remembering. When I leave here, your memories will start to fade again, but your writings will remain. Run your fingers and your eyes over them every waking-period, repeating the words to yourselves, and you'll be able to recall some of the things that have happened to you – and, once you have those in your mind, you might be able to fill in the rest.'

The peasants nodded, cheered, and did most of the other things he expected of them, and some of them even agreed to learn to write.

Wherever the army had been he'd generously given names – to people, to villages, to homes and even to trees and wildflowers.

He Who Leads looked up with a smile as Reen approached, slapping her small mare to greater speed. He had become very fond of her. His mind flew back to when he had, just for a moment, hoped to become her lover, and he was glad that she had rejected him all that time ago.

'You called me?' he said courteously.

'I haven't damn well got this damn pony to chase all this way after you just to say "hello",' she shouted over the thudding of their horses' hooves.

'Look up ahead!'

He obeyed her numbly. Ever since the death of his mother he'd found himself doing whatever Reen told him to.

Far away there was a cloud of dust rising lazily into the opalescent air.

An army of cavalry was coming towards them. Nothing

else could kick up a pillar of clouding earth like that.

'Hide!'

Lian's voice was cracking. There was nowhere to hide.

'Fight, you fool!' said Reen, riding by his side. 'It's the only thing we can do.'

He looked at her, then obeyed.

'We fight!' he shouted.

His army roared behind him.

'He Who Leads! He Who Leads!' the men and women yelled incessantly, as he sat there doubting his own ability to lead anything more than a flock of sheep to a new pasture, far less an unskilled rabble into battle.

Nevertheless Lian pulled his proud Ellonian sword from its sheath and waved it above his head. He patted Anan on the rump and the stallion sped along the track the army had been following.

'We fight!' he shouted again, slapping Anan so that he broke into a gallop. Those on horseback behind him followed suit and the foot-soldiers broke into an eager run, doing their best to keep up with the riders.

The two forces met at the crest of the hill.

It was clear that the Ellonia had been expecting this encounter – and equally clear that they'd underestimated the size of the army raised by He Who Leads. At best there were three hundred of the Ellonia, most on foot: despite their training they could not hope to match a collection of irregulars six or seven times that number.

Lian, with Anan rearing beneath him, flailed with his sword at the face of any Ellonian who came close to him; soon he found himself in an open space surrounded by bleeding bodies, the Ellonia preferring to attack the riders who came behind him. He looked around and saw Jonn toppled from his horse by a thrown dagger that caught him through both cheeks: as the tall man fell, his horse, terrified by the shouting and clash of arms, trampled his chest, shattering his ribs. Jonn gave a scream as he died, but the noise was lost in the greater sound of the battle. He Who Leads forced Anan through the crush and took great pleasure in lopping the head from the man who'd killed his comrade. As he moved away he saw Fil pierced through the stomach by a sword, looking down in astonishment at the hilt of the weapon and pulling it out of his body, watching his own blood follow. There was little point in trying to save him, so Lian charged directly at the circle of Ellonia, wielding his sword in one hand and his felling axe in the other, controlling Anan with his knees.

A blow from the hind-end of a pike caught him on the shoulder and, as he twisted to avoid it, he found himself tumbling down from Anan's back. He hit the ground hard.

That's it, he thought. *That's the end of it all.*

He waited for the killing blow. But it didn't come.

He looked up and saw that Lanyor, the least likely of all his original party, stood over him, her legs astride him, a stolen Ellonian sword almost invisible as it flashed from side to side, removing an eye here and a hand there, pressing back the Ellonian troops.

He Who Leads got to his feet groggily, hoping that a wild blow of Lanyor's stolen sword wouldn't accidentally cut him in half; the woman had seemed to be so easy and placid, but now she was as if possessed. Lanyor screamed in ecstasy each time she slaughtered one of the Ellonia; her sword was a liquid thing, not touching the air as it whipped through it.

An Ellonian officer was coming towards He Who Leads, his left leg a mess of blood; clearly he'd been dismounted by an upthrust stab to his calf. He limped as he advanced and Lian, feeling no mercy, sprang at him, cutting him fatally across the belly.

Lanyor parried a man's sword-blow and then, using one of the unorthodox repartees Lian had taught them, severed his hamstrings so that he fell screaming into the slimy mud. She put her foot on the soldier's chest and stabbed downwards, killing him.

Andia died when an axe removed most of the upper part of her face. Daif took an arrow in the breast, the sharp point penetrating easily through his leather armour. Coll lost his arm to a scything sweep of an Ellonian sword; he fell in agony to the ground, to be trampled by his comrades

147

as he died. Lian tried to reach the little man, to give him some comfort, but it was impossible to find a way through the solid wall of struggling bodies between them.

Lanyor had lost her sword and was looking around for it in bewilderment. Reen took the lives of two Ellonian soldiers with biting short stabs of her sword; from the second she grabbed, as he fell, his weapon. The big redheaded woman smiled faintly as she accepted it, then immediately skewered one of the Ellonia; with a deft twist of her wrist she pulled the blade away, leaving a gaping hole in the man's stomach.

He Who Leads was on his hands and knees again, this time deliberately so. He hacked out with his axe at any uniformed foot that came within reach, then finished the soldiers as they fell by stabbing them with his sword. He'd received a minor cut across the bridge of his nose – the wound produced a prodigious amount of blood which ran down over his lip to come saltily into his mouth, but he tasted nothing.

Marja was next to him now; he could hear her screams of triumph as she slaughtered Ellonian soldier after Ellonian soldier. She grabbed him by the hair and dragged him to his feet. 'He Who Leads,' she shouted above the din of battle, her breath punctuating the words, 'should be fucking standing, not on all fucking fours like a fucking animal!' Her axe darted into the eye of an attacking Ellonian so that he shrieked in pain and staggered away backwards, only to be hacked viciously down through the shoulder by a peasant sword and killed by a back-blow to the temple from someone else's axe.

After what seemed like hours, there was quiet . . .

The peasant army had been halved in number, but the few Ellonia left alive had fled. He Who Leads staunched the flow of blood from his nose using a scrap of cloth torn from the uniform of one of the fallen soldiers; the symbolism was deliberate. He looked around at the remnants of his army and at the corpses of those who'd fought on both sides, choking back his nausea. He leaned exhaustedly against Lanyor's shoulder, wondering if they wouldn't all be better off just returning to Lianhome and accepting the rule of the House of Ellon.

'We seem to have done rather well,' Lanyor said in her customarily languid voice. 'I'd say that at this rate we can take Ernestrad with ease.'

She wiped the blood from her sword on the grass, then returned the weapon to its scabbard.

'Hundreds have been killed here,' Lian said hoarsely.

'Yes. Good, isn't it?'

'I mean, hundreds of *us*.' The smell of the blood was making him feel even more sick.

'You didn't expect to win this war without spilling blood, did you?' Lanyor smiled at him and kissed his lips; he felt the softness of her breasts, through two layers of leather, pressing against his chest. *This is ridiculous*, he thought. *We've seen our companions die, yet I want to carry on kissing this woman until the end of eternity*.

They pulled apart, their eyes on each other.

The survivors of the battle were regrouping around Reen and Marja, who were holding an Ellonian standard upside down as a symbol of their victory. Many of the peasants bore wounds; surgeons were moving among them applying tourniquets and, on occasion, cauterising the more grievous injuries. He Who Leads heard the screams of those in pain as he and Lanyor moved to the centre of the group. Again he wondered if the entire exploit had been worth the suffering. He pressed the scrap of cloth to his nose, feeling like a fool in the eyes of his troops, his hair a mess of other people's blood.

Reen was shouting.

'Victory is ours!'

A wave of agreement.

'The Ellonia are dead!'

Another wave.

'And He Who Leads *leads* us!'

Stumbling and shambling, holding the cloth to the ignominious wound on his nose, He Who Leads found himself in the centre of the circle that Reen had created; Lanyor pushed him the last few metres, then retreated into

149

the mass of warriors so that she went unnoticed.

Lian made some kind of a victory speech. Afterwards he couldn't remember what he'd said, although he did recall the cheering of his warriors. And for the rest of his life he remembered making love with Lanyor that sleeping-period as the two of them laughed about their wounds. His own started to bleed again, but she kissed the seeping blood away. She told him that she wanted to bear his child, and he didn't believe her.

By this time they had moved a long way from the scene of the battle. The last thing they wanted to do was to arouse the wrath of the Ellonia against innocent nearby villages.

The treetops looked very pretty through Lanyor's fronds of red hair. He forgot all about the pain of his wounds.

Some waking-periods later they were camped beside one of the biggest villages they'd yet come across. The dampness in the air told them that the rain-time was soon to begin, so most people spent the while painstakingly erecting tents fabricated from rough branches and captured clothing. He Who Leads went on foot with Reen into the village, scrambling down the rough rocky slope.

At one point he took her slender hand, to help her leap over a stream, and found himself recalling the aromatic voluptuousness of Lanyor, who had looked at him the waking-period after their love-making as if he had been a stranger. For a while, taking Anan for his regular exercise, he had wondered if the whole thing had been a dream, even though he still could smell the closeness of her body on him. Now he began to wonder if it had been true, what she'd said, that she wanted to have his child. Perhaps that had been her only purpose, and all the rest a sham? The sunlight was too hot for his mind to concentrate on the thought for long, so instead he watched appreciatively as Reen's trailing foot kicked up diamond-like sparkling drops of water from the surface of the stream.

He bent low to the side to put his heavy arm around her shoulders.

She jabbed him in the ribs with a sharp elbow.

'Less of that, buster!'

He giggled.

Reen was Marja's and Marja was Reen's; that had been established a long time ago. Except on the rare occasions when either Reen or Marja decided that it'd be all right for one of them to be Sinede's.

They pushed on through a mass of gorse to reach the outskirts of the village, feeling the tough vegetation pulling at their clothes. The sharp smell of broken stalks surrounded them, making Reen sneeze. He looked sideways at her, watching her thin body convulse, her shoulders shaking. Her calves were covered in old and new scratches, long red lines that looked like some kind of primitive writing. Under her leather armour he could see the firmness of her body; her bare arms moved powerfully as she cleared the gorse-branches ahead of her.

Lucky Marja, he thought.

On the far side of the gorse a belt of rough grass formed a natural cordon that separated the village from the outside world.

Reen ran ahead of him, her arms outstretched, pretending to be a high-flying bird, whooping and jumping from hummock to hummock. Lian grinned as he followed her more slowly. *She can kill a man with her bare hands, if she wants to, and yet at the same time she's just a child. Come to think of it – so am I.* He imitated her, both of them laughing as they ran down the slope, their hair flicking at their eyes.

They sobered as they approached the outermost houses of the village, and walked hand in hand the last hundred metres or so, not looking at each other's faces.

Clearly the peasants had sensed the nearness of He Who Leads. The central pathway, under the strong white granary tower, was filled with men, women and children looking confused; it was a sight Reen and Lian had seen innumerable times before. Each time they came upon a fresh village there was this period of muddled awakening, as the inhabitants discovered that there was more to life than a succession of swiftly forgotten moments.

The peasants in some ways hardly noticed their arrival;

151

they talked eagerly – sometimes angrily – among themselves. A small black and white dog watched Reen and Lian approach; studiously it squatted back on its hindlegs and shat, still staring at them as if to defy criticism.

At last the human population began to realise that there were visitors among them. Tongues were stilled as faces turned to look at these bizarre outsiders: the man was tall and broad, his fair hair catching the sunlight so that it seemed as if his head were surrounded by a ring of fire; the woman was little more than half his size, but seemingly every bit as strong. Her face, embraced by her searingly black hair, was as thin and small as that of an undernourished child. They were holding hands, yet clearly they were not lovers.

The villagers had never seen outsiders before, other than the Ellonian requisitioning convoys, and so hardly knew what to do about these intruders. Kill them? Welcome them? Worship them?

Wearily, He Who Leads read all of this in their faces. *Just like all the others.*

As they'd done so many times before, he and Reen gestured that they wanted to keep on walking until they reached whichever part of the village served as its command centre. The peasants, as always, melted away on either side of them. A naked little girl, her long hair flowing behind her as if it were a part of the sea, ran ahead of them, leading the way.

Lian felt something strange – something indefinable – emanating from one of the nearby hovels. He glanced inquiringly at Reen to see if she'd noticed anything but it was clear that she hadn't; she was smiling comfortably at the jigging brown bottom of the child ahead of them.

He put his head to one side, uneasily aware of the soft footfalls of the peasants who were shyly following them. There had been a *touch* in his mind. It certainly hadn't been his imagination; the sensation was lingering. The others had described to him how, many scores of waking-periods ago, the singer called Alyss had come among them, and how she'd put out subtle feelers into their minds. *This must be the same sort of thing that they felt*, he thought.

The heart of the village was a hump of grassy earth, perhaps twenty metres across. Still concerned about that wisp of invasive thought, he meekly allowed Reen to lead him to the crest of the mound. The two of them waited there as the peasants gathered in sinister hush around them. He Who Leads looked out at a sea of brown-woollen-coated bodies and vacant tanned faces. *The business as usual . . .*

In the distance a blanket was pulled back from a doorway and a woman emerged. He felt the tug of her thoughts, and again he was disquieted. Motionless on the threshold, she was looking at him sombrely. He was more aware of her distant presence than even that of Reen standing beside him. In his eyes the muddy brown track between them seemed to provide her with an impossibly long skirt, tapering at last to her waist.

She began to walk towards the gathered crowd – towards *him*. The feeling that her mind was somehow inside his own grew stronger, as if she were speaking to him, coming ever closer. He knew that Reen was beginning the standard recruiting speech at his side, but he couldn't hear any of the words she was saying. His attention was totally concentrated on the approaching figure of this small woman.

It wasn't that she was particularly pretty – in fact, she was rather plain and mousy. Her figure was trim enough, but it lacked both the crispness of Reen's and the exuberance of Sinede's or Lanyor's. In the normal way of things he wouldn't have noticed her among the throng of villagers, but for some reason she seemed to be filling the whole of his vision. As she walked she appeared hardly to touch the ground; her progress towards him was entirely silent.

Stop it! he told himself, forcing his head to turn so that he was looking in a different direction. *Stop what?* It seemed to him as if there were another voice in his mind, as cool as chilled milk.

His eyes darted back to the woman.

Her face was bland and – yes, blast it – she really *was* as plain as he'd surmised from the distance. But her eyes were laughing at him.

Only a little bit plain, that other voice seemed to be saying. *You could turn that on its head and say I was quite a lot pretty, you know.*

Reen had stopped speechifying and was looking at him expectantly. He hadn't a clue what to say.

Humiliating moments passed.

Eventually he said, brokenly: 'I come to lead you.'

The peasants seemed unimpressed.

Then the woman at the back raised her voice.

'We will follow.'

The three words were enough to change the mood of the assembly entirely. Suddenly Lian and Reen were surrounded by eager volunteers, hands reaching to touch their leather armour, mouths tumbling out words in an incomprehensible roar.

Lian heard nothing of it. All he could see was the slender woman, standing there, distancing herself from everything; all he could hear was the sound, inside him, of her laughing at him.

Funny little soldier-boy, aren't you?

He found himself grinning for a moment. Then he set his face.

'I am He Who Leads!' he shouted at the skies, breaking himself free from her, punching his clenched fists upwards.

'He Who Leads!' echoed the peasants, their voices making ripples of sound.

Standing there with one foot crossed over the other, smiling at his face, radiating the cool essence of herself towards him, the woman seemed to be saying *All right, He Who Leads . . . for a while.*

The Despot was not so much in his bath as filling it to capacity. He had called his recently appointed Army-Master here for a meeting; Nadar hardly knew where to look. He'd never been overly concerned about nudity, but there was something actively repellent about the broad and clammy expanses of the Despot's naked flesh; if anything, the sight was made worse by the fact that a couple of nubile women, themselves scarcely covered, were washing the man. Nadar thanked the sun for the fact that the room was so filled with steam that his sight of all this was blurred and diluted. Even so, he found his gorge rising.

I mean, you have to work really hard at it to get that fat, dammit, his internal voice agreed. *He must have to use a mirror to check his prick's still there – hmmm, or maybe he uses one of those bloody women to check it out for him.*

'We sent a force into north-west Albion searching for the rebels,' the Despot was saying in his odd squealing voice. 'They haven't returned.'

'When were they due to return, sire?'

Nadar adopted a pose of determined respect.

'Nine waking-periods ago.'

'Perhaps they have found the rebels and slain them, and are now subduing pockets of unrest as they return to Giorran.'

Nadar was speaking the words just for the sake of it.

'I think not.'

The Despot eased his body higher out of the water as one of the women used a sponge to wash his hairy, dead-looking breasts.

'I think,' he continued, looking into her blue eyes but plainly still speaking to Nadar, 'that my forces met some kind of rabble of peasantry.'

'What makes you think that could even be possible, sire?'

'The mages tell me as much.'

Nadar snorted before he could stop himself.

'Laughter?' said the Despot with apparent interest. 'And from a Deputy Army-Master?'

'Army-Master,' Nadar corrected deferentially.

'No,' said the Despot. (And 'Yes, just exactly *there*,' to the woman scrubbing between his shoulder-blades.) 'I meant what I said, Nadar: *Deputy* Army-Master. Kloot will take your place, at least for the moment. He's a capable enough man, I think – don't you?'

'Of course, sire.'

'I could, of course, simply have you executed instead. Would you prefer that?'

Nadar shuffled his feet. It was such a bloody silly question, yet to fail to answer the Despot might bring his death.

'No, sire,' he said, hoping another snort of laughter wouldn't escape.

'Then listen to me. While Kloot's here, pretending as best he can to organise our troops, I want you, as his deputy, to take a hand-picked force – one thousand, two thousand, I don't care how many – out into Albion and find these renegades. You can have as much by way of provisions for the men as you want, but ensure you hand-pick them all. I want an end to this insurrection. Soon.'

Nadar was startled. It seemed that his demotion was a promotion. No Army-Master in history had ever been given as much of a free hand as this.

'Yes, sire,' he said gravely. 'I'm sorry, sire, that I failed to find the root of the insurrection long ago.'

Nadar was finding it hard to concentrate. The two women were washing the Despot's genitals, and a consequence was rising above the scummy surface of the water. The Despot seemed not to notice.

'I'll do your bidding at once, sire,' Nadar said, bowing deeply and backing away from the room.

'Good,' said the Despot's squeaking voice.

Chapter Seven
Spies

Lian tells me that our army is now as large as it can be. All of us have to keep close together – even during the sleeping-periods, which is sometimes embarrassing – because otherwise those warriors furthest from him begin to lose themselves. Some of them have wandered off, apparently, and haven't been seen again. I pity them. I couldn't bear to go back to Albion as it was before, where everything was constantly shifting around me and when all I could remember was how to work in the fields, or to piss or shit, or to be violated by one of those Ellonian swine.

Syor paused, trying to force some of the images out of her mind. She sucked one end of the twig she was using as a writing implement, then dipped the other end into a small pot of ink. Not long after she had joined Lian's forces they had captured an Ellonian patrol and found – among various other items whose purpose they could not fathom – a few score sheets of parchment and several pots of rather watery ink. She had been the one to realise what these things were for, and so, with the approval of He Who Leads, she had appropriated them for her own use. She had explained that it was vital that an account be kept of their campaign; should it fail, as Alyss the singer seemed to have predicted, the record might survive and assist those who rebelled in the times to come. It was all rather a long shot, she admitted, but it was worth doing nevertheless.

Lian had started teaching her to write only a few waking-periods after they had become lovers; he described his tutelage as his love-gift to her. In fact, he'd been astonished at the speed with which she had learnt the art he'd been taught by his mother. The vocabulary used in Terman's homeland had been designed for simplicity, and its breadth had been further curtailed in the version he'd brought to Albion – mercenaries and sailors were not literary folk – yet the ease with which Syor understood first the principle and then the practice of writing had been such as to make her mate look at her with renewed respect. Either she had a natural gift, or she was more intelligent than anyone else he had ever met – himself included, he rather ruefully thought. From that time onwards he consulted her about every major decision.

She looked out now across a broad plain of uncultivated grassland, dotted with small clusters of trees. In the distance was a line of hills, their slopes looking purple-violet through the heat-haze. She was sitting on the side of a small, amiable swell of ground, a hill in miniature, which separated her from the main body of the army. She could hear the men and women chattering and clattering as they prepared a meal or bedded down for the sleeping-period. When she'd finished writing of the events of this waking-period she would scramble back over the mound and see, at her feet, an expanse of handmade tents and smouldering fires.

It was good to know that her comrades were so close to her, and at the same time good to be separated from them. Especially during the sleeping-periods, she missed the solitude she had experienced so frequently in her home village. On the other hand, there was Lian, He Who Leads.

Or who had had to be led. He had seemed almost reluctant to become her lover, and she understood why. At Reen's urging, he had been sleeping with more and more of the women, hoping to create a whole new generation of offspring possessing his own abilities; with Syor's blessing, this practice continued. No pregnancies had resulted, and the fear of them all was that He Who Leads might be incapable of fathering children at all. He had confessed to her several times that one cause of the lack of pregnancies was his frequent impotence: the whole process of having sex with a stranger, purely with the aim of trying to fertilise her, was too impersonal, too clinical for him.

She smiled fondly; in her own arms, after a first chaotic sleeping-period during which they had both been nervous, he had always been the very opposite of impotent. They had laughed together, that sleeping-period, over their mutual inadequacies – for her own part, she'd been as dry as the parchment that she wrote on – and it was then that Syor had realised why Lian had been so loath to become her mate. They had both recognised, from the moment they'd first seen each other, that there was a sort of inevitability about it; yet he had felt that to bind himself solely to one woman would be, as it were, a dereliction of his duty. And he'd known that their becoming lovers would symbolise a more permanent union. For many waking-periods he had treated her in every other way as the person closest to him, yet resisted her physical approaches. Finally she had said outright to him that she wouldn't regard his 'duty' as any act of infidelity, and that it was stupid of him to carry on resisting what was so clearly destined to happen.

Again she smiled.

He was so foolish in so many ways. What went on between bodies wasn't in itself relevant; it was what went on between the minds of lovers that mattered. On one level there was simple sex between two people who found each other physically attractive; she found it profoundly unsatisfying in emotional terms *afterwards*, however much pleasure she might have experienced at the time. Then there was lovemaking between two friends, which was a physical way of expressing trust. She'd slept with several people among Lian's closest entourage, and had never felt that she was being in any way unfaithful to him. Although nowadays she took care not to risk becoming pregnant by them, for it was important that any child she bore should be Lian's. And, of course, there was Reen.

But making love with He Who Leads was something else entirely. In strictly technical terms, he wasn't the best of lovers. He was often maladroit and over-earnest until she started to smile at him, hoping he wouldn't notice, at which point he would start to smile himself, and hold her with the affection he wanted to express. Often – many times each waking-period – she conjured up in her mind the image of his face so close to her own. He was grinning in this inner picture of hers, and feeling a part of him becoming a part of her. He was her lover. She was his.

She loved him. He loved her.

She'd give up all physical contact for the rest of her life if it'd mean an extra minute talking with him.

The tip of her crude pen had soaked up enough ink for her to carry on writing.

Wherever we encounter the Ellonia, we destroy them. I loathe the destruction of my fellow human beings . . . but I suppose it has to be done. He Who Leads says that the only way Albion will be released from their grip is if they're destroyed entirely. Alas, I think he's right. It'd be good if we could establish some kind of understanding with them, but that seems to be impossible. The peasants have been subjected for far too long to listen to any cries of reason when we come across the Ellonian convoys; the soldiers are dead as soon as they're seen.

Why did it have to be like this?

Recruits from the House of Ellon would be useful to them. Aside from the ability of the Ellonia to spread their mental facilities among the army, as He Who Leads did, there was also the fact that they could teach the warriors some of the weaponry skills they'd learnt during their training.

Syor's eyes looked sorrowful as she dipped the twig once more into the ink. Her writing on the parchment was pitifully tiny, as if a minuscule insect had crawled across the sheet, leaving a trail of wispy lines behind it. The army of He Who Leads might never discover a new supply of parchment. She was doing her best to conserve what she had.

Lian tells me that we now have nearly three thousand warriors. He believes that this is more than enough to capture Giorran. I'm not so certain. From all I've heard, Giorran is well defended, and its soldiers, while they may lack compassion, certainly don't lack sense and weapons. I think it's likely that we'll be defeated in the long run, but of course I say nothing of this to He Who Leads. I believe I'd be happy if he and I died in each other's arms, holding each other by the hand until there's no such thing as reality for us any longer.

It wasn't a very cheerful thought, and again she sucked on the end of the twig, staring out over the swaying stalks of grass. If she went down there onto the plain she'd have to stand on tiptoe to see where she was going. Some time during the next few waking-periods the army would trample down that proud grass. She was certain that she would be creating a wide swathe through it, conquering its pride. She wished that somehow the troops of He Who Leads might leave it the way it was. It looked so tranquil to her, so much the way it was supposed to be.

We killed more people today. I believe in Lian's aim to conquer the Ellonia, but I find it hard to cling to that belief as I watch the men and women die. They feel pain, the same way that I do – or anyone does. Most of them look astounded when they find themselves surrounded by a horde of peasants with swords, as if somehow the whole thing was an offence against nature. I find myself wanting to reach out a hand and pull them away from it all, to tell them that it's all just a nightmare and that they'll wake up soon. But I can't do that. I know as well as anybody that they'll just pretend to listen to what I'm saying and then, as soon as they can, attempt to destroy all of us.

161

It perturbed her that she couldn't read Ellonian writing.

I want an end to the deaths. I want an end to the Ellonia – or at least to their omnipotence. I want to see an Albion where everybody can enjoy the kind of love that Lian and I share together.

We visited a new village today. Lian and Reen and I entered it, just the three of us, and explained that our army was already as large as it could be. There was an old shaman there, covered in the blood of animals and their ordure, and he cursed us loudly while the villagers looked on. Almost at once Lian realised that the shaman had the same sort of ability that he has himself, and tried to persuade him to create an army like Lian's own, or at least to join us. The fool just spat on the ground, muttering imprecations and, I think, garbled spells. I got the impression that he's content with having exerted his control over all the rest of the villagers around him, and doesn't want to find himself in the shadow of someone else. I may be doing him an injustice, but I don't think so. We came away with a young girl and a boy even younger. They seem friendly enough, but they're in no sense soldiers. I hope they don't die too painfully.

Syor gazed dreamily around, wondering if there was anything else of note concerning this waking-period that she should write down; she saw movement in the grass several hundred metres away. A large animal of some kind must be approaching; probably a cow that had strayed away from its herd. *In many ways*, she thought, *a lot of cows have more sense than their herders*. Even so, it might be some more dangerous animal. Deciding that she'd written enough, she set her sheet of parchment aside, blowing on it from time to time as she capped her valuable pot of ink. The twig she threw away; it tumbled down the slope and off into the base of the tough grass. Next waking-period she'd chew the tip of another twig.

162

Smoothing her woollen skirt over her thighs she got to her feet, holding the parchment in one hand and the ink in the other.

The movement in the grass was coming closer to her, but she didn't consciously notice it as she turned and, with a quiet song on her lips, began to walk easily up the side of the mound to rejoin the army and her lover.

Nadar had seen the smoke of peasant campfires several kilometres away, and he'd smiled, the pinkness of his lips splitting the freckled whiteness of his face.

We have them.

The trouble with peasants was that they were so bloody *stupid*. His own force could have quartered this region of north-west Albion forever and never found the rebels if the dimwits had only had the sense to abjure the use of fire, as the Ellonia under him did. Instead, they sent out a great signal to anyone wanting to see it, indicating exactly where they were.

A sudden moment of doubt: perhaps there were so many of the peasants that they didn't care if the Ellonia found them? He knew that there must be at least a thousand: the few Ellonia who'd escaped their massacres had spoken of vast legions of highly armed warriors, so Nadar had divided by a notional ten and concluded that this was something more than a band of marauders but nevertheless substantially less numerous than his own force.

'Garine!' he shouted. 'Come to me!' His most trusted commander was a slight man, seemingly ineffectual yet possessed of a wiry strength. He spurred his pink and grey horse to join Nadar.

'Sire?'

'See. Over there.'

Garine's eyes followed Nadar's pointing finger, then widened. Like his superior, he began to grin.

'We have them, sire,' he said.

'It seems that we do,' Nadar rubbed his chin, feeling the prickly ends of his stubbly half-beard.

163

'"Seems", sire?'

Nadar looked at the man and saw his yellowing teeth and the brightness of his eyes.

'Yes, "seems", my friend. There are too many fires for my liking. A few hundred peasants – or even a thousand – should put up little more resistance than a sparrow's fart, but I've still no inclination to throw away the lives of our men unnecessarily. There may be several thousands of them.'

Garine looked confused. The upper echelons of the Ellonian Army were not normally concerned about casualties. Perhaps this was because they so rarely suffered any, being able to exterminate with ease any small pockets of rebellion that might occur. He pulled his helmet more firmly down onto his oily black hair. Yet the army *had* suffered losses in recent times: far too many requisitioning patrols had failed to return from routine village visits.

'Another thing,' said Nadar, more to himself than to Garine, 'is that those might not be the fires of a camp.'

The commander looked at him blankly.

'They may be razing empty villages,' Nadar explained, 'destroying the crops and the hovels so that there's nothing there for us when the convoys arrive.'

Garine nodded as if in understanding.

'But we've not found any trace of that having happened anywhere else,' he said.

'True, true.'

Nadar, still rubbing his chin, was thoughtful. Garine knew better than to say anything more.

'We need to send out scouts,' Nadar said suddenly. 'I'm not going to attack until I know exactly what it is I *am* attacking. Choose two of your best men and send them ahead of us. Tell them to report back to you – no, better, directly to me. I want to know what's beyond that ridge. Post a few sentries in case the peasants start moving towards us, but tell the rest of the soldiers they can rest for a while. I want to relax, myself.'

Garine turned his horse away and started to bark orders. Nadar pulled off his helmet and threw it to the ground, then wearily climbed down from his horse, soothing the beast with a few affectionate words and a pat on the withers. A small thought came to him that the scouts might be caught, but he dismissed it impatiently: the peasants were surely too stupid to suspect that spies might be sent among them.

He was dog-tired – as tired as he'd ever known himself to be – and he wanted to get some sleep. It'd take the scouts a while – at least a waking-period – to cross the plain and see what they could see before coming back to report to Garine. There'd be time enough for Nadar to sleep and refresh himself for an assault at the start of the next waking-period.

If there *was* to be an assault, of course. When he'd talked to Garine about the possibility of the peasants burning villages he hadn't really been taking himself seriously, but the more he thought about the scenario the more plausible it seemed. He realised that he was even more exhausted than he'd thought, his mind neurotically swirling around to settle on the unlikely rather than the likely. He'd seen the distant smoke from the campfires of the Ellonia often enough before to know that this wasn't just a village ablaze. There was an army on the far side of that low ridge. Soon he would lead his soldiers to destroy it . . .

Soon he would . . .

Soon he would . . .

Yet the Wind had said . . . Maybe his moment of triumph could be delayed . . .

Soon . . . Eyes closing. No way to keep them open.

Falling softly into a bed of black warmth.

They move through the long grass on hands and knees, barely aware of each other except for the loud sounds of their breathing as they watch the soil under their hands and wonder if a sudden fall of arrows might descend upon their backs. Little love the two of them have for their leader, who seems too remote from them to exist as a genuine human being; a faraway figure giving orders they can't usually hear over the whine of the wind. A few metres further forward, trying to brush the tall stalks as little as possible. The raw earth that their fingertips pull from its hiding-place smells at least as fragrant as the grass; both of them experience its sweatiness and watch as the small animals living inside it scuttle or squirm away towards some hidden refuge. The sun beats down on them as they push the ears of grass aside, letting its heat hurt them. Surely they're safe from observation still – surely none of the peasants will be this far from the camp – but still, it's as well to take full precautions.

They watch the tan of the backs of their hands moving forwards. They slide from side to side, slithering through the stems of grass, hoping that they're invisible. On one occasion their little fingers accidentally overlap, so that they spring away from each other, terrified by the contact.

A young soldier who's never seen combat, an older man who has scars on his face because he's fought a few times in the contests for promotion that they hold at Giorran. Neither of them is keen to admit that they wish to avoid, at any cost, the coming battle; at the same time, neither of them wishes to be left, afterwards, unblooded.

The smell of the brown earth is strong in their nostrils.

Heads between their shoulders. They feel the touch of the soil as they move slowly forwards.

A fall of dried seeds on one of their heads. An annoyance, nothing more. Or so it seems. Perhaps one of the peasants has been looking out over this grassy plain and seen their movement? It's hard to tell, and the two of them simply giggle to each other, because there's nothing either of them could do about such an eventuality. They keep pushing themselves onwards, watching the bases of the reeds come closer to them and then pass them by. They see the clammily greenish-brown half-leaves of the reeds clinging to the shafts as they move past.

One of the men is Onir; he's very unpopular among the soldiers of his patrol because he prefers games to warfare of any kind. The other is Remen. They'd like nothing more than to find a way of escaping from the place where they now find themselves. In this they're no different from the majority of Nadar's troops – except that they're both Ellonia: common troops would lose their memories so far from the others. It's been a long time since they've been in any real danger.

But if they go back now they'll face death, so they keep on moving forward, smelling the soil and the grass as they go. They don't find it easy, and they hate the stink of the stuff, and they try very hard not to create too much turbulence in the long grass because otherwise they'll send a signal to the peasants, which is the last thing they want to do. But then there's a shuffling from Remen, and the stalks toss uneasily, unnaturally.

Onir and Remen fall to their faces. Against their cheeks they find warm earth. All they can hear is their own terrified breathing, the cry of a distant bird and the ears of grass rustling in the light breeze above their heads.

They hope against hope not to hear an outcry.

After many minutes they are both breathing more easily.

'Forward again,' hisses Onir. 'Only this time take a bit more bloody care, you halfwit. OK?'

He sees Remen nodding at him through the curtaining stalks.

'I'll lead,' says Onir.

He crawls forward cautiously, trying to pretend to himself that he isn't really here, hoping this will make him disturb the grasses even less.

It was only later, as Syor was fastidiously stowing away her writing materials in their woollen bag, that her mind began to register the curious motion she'd seen in the grass.

She bit her lower lip and tried to concentrate, stopping in a half-stooping position, one hand still absent-mindedly holding the bag open while she unconsciously pulled her hair back from her brow with the other. She was in the tent she shared with He Who Leads, but he wasn't around. *The wind can play funny tricks*, she thought. *That must have been all it was*. She tried to expel the memory from her mind, and continued putting away her parchment and ink.

But the memory refused to be expelled; the more she

tried to forget all about it, the larger it grew in her mind, until she could think of nothing else.

She tied the bag neatly and set off in search of Lian.

He was sitting near one of the fires, sucking grease from his fingers, when she found him. He looked up at her with a smile. *You look just like a little boy who's been caught raiding the pantry*, she thought fondly, watching his unshaven face crease within its frame of gold. He patted the ground beside him.

'Look,' said Syor, 'it's possible I'm just making a fuss over nothing, but . . .'

She explained about the grass and the way she'd hardly noticed it until afterwards, when the recollected image came into focus.

At once he was alert. As she'd said, it might just have been a prank of the wind. But there were other possibilities. Wild animals perhaps – although there were few dangerous species in Albion. The random workings of the land's inherent magic. Enemy vanguards of an Ellonian scouting party. All three eventualities had to be considered, because all three presented danger to the people under his command.

'You were right to tell me this,' he said after she'd finished her brief account of what she'd seen. 'Here!' he shouted to the other peasants eating around the fire. 'You, you, you, and yes, you! You've just volunteered to come with me.'

'Us,' muttered Syor crisply.

The peasants He Who Leads had designated gathered around them. The woman was wearing a captured Ellonian sword; the three men had felling axes and primitive daggers. All four were heavily muscled. Syor felt inadequate in their presence, despite her own Ellonian sword and the bow that she had learned to use so well.

He Who Leads told the others about what Syor had seen. In moments they were a committed band of six. A small time later, sentries had been posted at the outskirts of the camp to warn of any attack. The word spread like wildfire: they should prepare themselves for battle. Some panicked at the news, but most rather gloomily looped their swords into their belts and slung their bows onto their shoulders.

Lian whistled for his great white horse, Anan, and the beast soon came trotting into view. Other horses were ushered forward for the rest of the small band of scouts.

'If you hear us scream,' cried He Who Leads with a cosmetic laugh, 'join us!'

There was a shout of approval.

Perched nervously on a piebald mare which moved restlessly between her thighs, Syor looked around her. She found it hard to estimate the number of peasants thronging about them, waving clenched fists of defiance in the air. The people were preparing for battle, and her heart was sinking. Yes, of course, she and her kind had been subjected to humiliations since long before history had begun, but at the same time she had no desire to witness further bloodshed. She just wished that those of the House of Ellon could be persuaded to change their ways. She wanted . . . she wanted peace to come to her homeland, but it seemed that any peace would come about only through warfare.

He Who Leads was thinking rather less sophisticated thoughts. It was time for his army to kill large numbers of the foe, if only to boost morale. Ideally, he should slaughter several of the Ellonia himself. For too long the peasants had been satisfied with overwhelming small parties of requisitioners; now they should be blooded in a full-scale battle. He dreaded the possibility that what Syor had seen might prove, after all, to have been nothing more than an antic of the breeze.

He drew his sword, holding it high above his head.

Another cheer from those around them.

He tapped his feet gently backwards against Anan's rump, and the horse moved obediently forwards, the others following. They trotted sedately through the camp until they reached its boundary, where the newly posted sentries beckoned them through. Once away from the tents and the fires, they slipped their horses into a canter up the side of the ridge. He Who Leads smelled the sweat of Anan and the sweetness of the grass crushed under the horses' hoofs. He turned his head to look at Syor, riding abreast of him.

Her green eyes were shining as she turned to meet his gaze, saliva oozing from the corner of her mouth as she edged her piebald on to keep up with Anan as they ascended the slope.

'I love you,' he whispered.

She heard nothing, but she read the movements of his lips.

They burst over the shallow crest with a scream of vengeance. Thirty metres ahead of them, there was still movement amidst the grass.

He Who Leads waved his sword, gesturing for the rest of them to follow as Anan charged forward. The horse brushed through the long grass easily.

Please don't let there be any killing, thought Syor, urging her piebald into the channel cleared by Anan. *Please let it be just the way the wind has tickled the tops of the grass.*

Onir was the first to try to bolt for home.

He stood up, so that the top of his head was just visible, threw away his weapons and tried to spring off towards the place where Nadar's men were gathered. One peasant arrow caught him in the shoulder; a second killed him as it entered his skull just behind the ear. He fell into a mess of his own blood, one arm flailing uselessly for a second or two before it collapsed down onto the ground.

Remen stood up, holding his hands in the air, palms towards the oncoming peasants, showing them that he no longer bore any weapons. His face was sweating as they gathered around him; strands of hair were glued to his forehead. He felt that death was very near. He silently cursed the Sun for having betrayed them.

He Who Leads reined in Anan, gesturing to the others to stay clear.

'Who are you?' he snapped.

'A friend,' said Remen hesitantly. His voice was hoarse.

'I disbelieve you.'

He Who Leads sensed at once that this was another like himself who had been blessed with the ability to retain reality.

Remen looked up at Lian, towering on horseback above

him. This was no peasant – no minor irritation on the flanks of the rule of the House of Ellon. The man had the dignity of a leader.

The recognition of who and what they were affected both men.

Remen's heart seemed to stop for a moment.

'Give me my life and I'll prove that I'm a friend,' he said humbly, a tear forming in his right eye.

'Prove you're a friend and I'll give you your life.' He Who Leads waved his sword imperiously in the direction of the dead Onir, and added: 'Your comrade didn't seem to regard us as his friends.'

Syor found herself grinning. The man they'd captured was somehow pathetic. The death of the other one had sickened her, but she could tell from the timbre of Lian's voice that this trembling little fellow would be spared.

'He was . . . he was . . . oh, bugger it.' Remen paused a second or two for thought. 'Can we do a deal?' he asked, looking apprehensively at the faces of the band surrounding him.

'Depends on the deal,' said Syor before He Who Leads could speak.

'Let's discuss his fate back at the camp,' said Lian, his voice cutting across hers. He looked at Syor vexedly.

'Wherever you wish,' mumbled Remen, allowing his arms to slip lower.

'Bind him.' Lian's voice was ruthless.

One of the warriors leapt down from his horse and swiftly tied Remen's hands behind his back, then knotted the long end of the cord to his horse's stirrup. Remen watched them as the backs of his hands swelled up from the tightness of the binding. The pain was not intense, but felt to him as if it would last forever. He shut his eyes for a moment, begging the Sun to release him. But the Sun was deaf.

Remen felt himself being tugged mercilessly through the tall grass, its spiky ears slashing at his face. He kept his gaze firmly directed at the ground as he was drawn up and over the hillock.

Once he felt a horse close beside his ear and the touch

of a hand on his head. He looked up for a moment and saw the woman's eyes on him.

'Don't be so frightened,' she said, her voice barely audible over the harsh panting of the horse. 'You may've been told that we're just barbaric savages, but we're not. Really.'

Remen forced his face into a ghastly imitation of a smile, acknowledging the woman's kindness, then turned his head to look at the ground again. He was feeling physically sick.

Soon they were in the camp.

The horses took them to a space that had been kept clear in front of Lian's and Syor's tent, and several score of the peasant rabble gathered around, hooting and jeering at the dismal captive. Some of them gathered up scattered vegetables and spheres of horse excrement, preparing to bombard Remen, but He Who Leads stopped them with an angry word. All Remen himself could see was the blazing fire. He was convinced that the barbarians would cast him into it. Or maybe they'd heat their swords and brand him cruelly, keeping him alive for waking-period after waking-period, rejoicing in the sound of his screaming.

His bowels loosened and he felt warm clamminess slithering down both legs of his uniform breeches.

Tears sprang to his eyes. This was ignominy.

'Let him loose.' It was the woman's voice again. 'Cut his hands free.'

A man with a long black beard and a cynical smile appeared in Remen's vision. The man was dressed, like most of the others seemed to be, in a muddy-coloured woollen garment of indeterminate shape topped by a crudely stitched leather jerkin. Remen didn't like the look of that smile, and cringed away, but all the man did was sever the cord that had been holding his wrists together; then he retreated, throwing the cut ends casually into the fire.

The peasant muttered to the mob in an exaggerated *sotto voce*: 'Little arsehole's filled his nappies.'

There was loud laughter.

Looking up, Remen noticed that neither Lian nor Syor was joining in his humiliation. They were regarding him gravely. He persuaded himself that he could see sympathy in their faces.

'You told me you were our friend,' said He Who Leads, rather quietly, once the derisive hubbub had died down.

'Yes.'

'Then, for the while, we'll treat you as if that is what you are.'

The big blond man beckoned one of the peasants.

'Bring fresh clothing. And see if someone can spare a bucket. Our new-found friend will need to wash the stench from himself.'

Remen wished he could trust the peasant's words. Instead, his instant assumption was that this meant he was going to be boiled alive. He fell down on the churned mud and raised his hands in the direction of He Who Leads, pleading for mercy.

'Oh, don't be such a *clot*!' said Syor severely. 'If we'd wanted to kill you we'd have done so by now.'

Lian looked at her, riding proudly high on the piebald, and laughed openly. She reminded him in some ways of his mother: she had the same frankness, the same need to get straight to the hub of the matter rather than dress every issue up in unnecessary words. Syor, hearing his mirth, at first looked at him with disgust; then she began to smile with him.

She eased her piebald over so that it was close to Anan.

'You will spare him if you possibly can, won't you, Lian?' she said.

'I can't promise,' he said, his face clouding.

'He's such a little fool of a man. Killing him would be like killing a puppy.' She put her fingers in his hair, stroking the top of his ear.

'I'd like to be able to' – Lian moved his hands futilely to try to convey his feelings to her – 'but if he proves to be a devoted servant of the House of Ellon, I don't see what else we can do but kill him. We can't keep him with us.'

'Why not?'

'Syor, love of mine, it can't be long now before we're at

173

war with the Ellonia. This man's presence is the proof of
that. He's obviously a scout – an incompetent one, but
nevertheless a spy of sorts – and that means that there must
be an Ellonian force searching for us. Soon they'll find us.
Unless we're convinced that he really wants to come over
and help us, the man'll be nothing more than a burden to
us.'

Syor stroked the piebald's mane, then tickled it under
the chin.

'And what if I gave you my bond that he'd serve us –
or, at least, that he wouldn't betray us?' she asked, not
looking at him.

'That bond might not be enough, my love.' He cast his
eyes around the low hillsides.

'At least, if it comes to it, kill him cleanly, won't you?
Don't torture him.'

'No.'

'Please. I told him that we weren't savages. Don't betray
my word.'

'I told you, Syor. I'll try not to.'

He was clearly becoming impatient with her. If she tried
to defend the Ellonian spy any longer she'd likely do him
more harm than good. The smoke from the fire was puffing
up, making the piebald's sensitive nostrils dilate and her
own eyes water.

'I love you,' she said, 'but I won't see you put that man
to torture. We're not the Ellonia, dammit.'

'Syor . . .' he said.

But already she was moving away swiftly, the piebald
kicking its heels as she rode it off through the beaten paths
of the camp.

Lian sighed.

That's the trouble with lovers, he thought. *They twist you
around until you've discovered that you've half made promises
you're not certain you can keep*.

He watched her as she disappeared. Soon she was nothing
more than a distant silhouette.

Then he turned his face back to contemplate Remen.

'Prove you're our friend,' said He Who Leads harshly.

The man who had earlier cut free Remen's bonds was now heating an Ellonian sword on the fire. The steel was glowing redly.

The man winked conspiratorially at Remen.

'I am your friend,' said the spy desperately, his eyes searching the sky. *Why has the Sun forsaken me?*

'Well,' said He Who Leads in a matter-of-fact manner, 'we'll soon find out about that, won't we?'

Syor hated herself each time she dug her heels into her horse's ribs: it wasn't the animal's fault that she felt so angry with He Who Leads. She wanted to get as far away from her lover as possible, and as quickly as possible. Peasants scattered to either side as the piebald picked up speed, the white gunge from its nostrils forming a slimy trail up over its forehead and onto her hands. Lian had taken her word of honour and treated it as if it were little more than a joke. If he wanted to become a petty barbarian warlord who demanded the slaughter of everyone who stood in his way then there was nothing she could do to stop him. If he genuinely felt that the torture of a poor fool like this was a contribution to his cause then she no longer wanted to be his lover, or to fight alongside him. There was no point in defeating the House of Ellon if all that would result was its replacement by a tyranny that was every bit as bad.

She was outside the perimeter of the encampment now, perched high on a crag. She eased herself to the ground, reassuring the piebald with mumbled words of endearment and rather brusque caresses. Leaving the horse where it was, she walked over to look down at the sheer drop.

It wouldn't take too much persuasion to make her jump from here, she realised. She felt as if there was something drawing her to the rocky ground so far below. What was the point of carrying on living this repellent life that she'd been forced into? No one, it seemed to her, had ever asked her opinion: Lian had just been pretending all this time. She wondered if he regarded her as anything more than just a good screw . . .

There was a slope of scree about twenty metres beneath

her, and it stretched out a long way until it fringed a rim of bent trees. If she threw herself out from the edge to fly like a bird, her death – as she was buried in the loose rock – would be a painful one, but at least it would be quick.

Syor sat down and wriggled forwards on her buttocks until her lower legs were dangling out over the chasm. She discovered suddenly that, ridiculously, she was in high spirits: for the first time in all of her life she was totally in control of her own destiny. She could die or she could live; the choice was entirely up to her – and her alone. She had a freedom she'd never experienced before. If she died then she'd no longer have to concern herself with the misery that was Albion.

Although she was as much an atheist as all the other peasants, Syor had an image of herself somehow defying death, to live again on some different plane where the trivial squabbles of mortal human beings – peasants or Ellonia – would come to have a vanishingly small importance to her.

Yes, but that wasn't the whole of it.

The peasants whom the Ellonia killed and raped had no choice in the matter. They accepted their lot because they'd never known anything else; in truth, in a curious way many of them were happy with the way things were because the thought of change – of the unknown – terrified them. But surely they were still human beings. Weren't they?

Moving her legs from side to side agitatedly over the void she watched the distant fields of Albion, their boundaries constantly changing like the flow of water droplets down a window.

She kicked away her boots, watching them bounce over the scree until they disappeared beneath her. She liked the look of her feet. She waggled her toes, watching the haze beneath her through the gaps between them, feeling the upsurge of wind stroking the joints of those ridiculous little appendages.

Shall I die or live?

So easy to tip herself over the edge of the crag; so easy to keep herself poised where she was; so hard to make the choice.

She had no particular affection for the human race as a whole, no sense of obligation to serve it as fully as she could. She saved lives whenever she was able to, but purely because she felt it was her ethical duty to do so and because she disliked witnessing slaughter. In her heart she didn't care what happened to the slimy little Ellonian capture; but in her head she did.

Whatever . . . whatever . . . it was hard to remember the grudge.

Another reason for living was her mate – the man – his name escaped her for the moment. She recalled a cloud of fair hair, a readily mobile face, promises that were made too easily . . . but other aspects of him were beginning to become indistinct.

It was fascinating to watch the way the landscape in the distance altered its shape.

More than fascinating: it was spellbinding.

Her mouth dropped open.

Behind her, the piebald whinnied unhappily.

The sound drew some of her personality back into herself. Horrified, she pulled herself backwards from the brink. It seemed to her now as if Albion itself had attempted to lull her towards death. Stray memories came to her now. They weren't enough for her to be able to build up a complete picture of her past, but they told her as much as she needed for her to be able to find the motivation to drag herself towards the horse.

On the third attempt she reached the saddle. She clung there, gasping, groping through her mind to find the right words to say.

Lian – that was a familiar word for some reason, but she was sure that it wasn't the right one for the occasion. She rejected *Syor* for the same reason. Other words came and went, but all of them seemed wrong. Some of them she spoke out loud, but the piebald made no movement in response.

In the end she tried saying, 'Home.'

Luckily the piebald set off in the right direction, and as they came closer to the camp she found she was able to explore more and more of the areas of her mind that had been temporarily concealed from her.

Lian, she thought. *He Who Leads. I have no choice but to be led by him.*

She'd loved him for what seemed to her now to have been a very long time, and she still did love him. But mixed in with the earlier emotion there was something new.

I have no choice but to be led by him.

No choice.

So there was a trace of hatred in her mind as she guided the horse past the crookedly hand-stitched tents at the outskirts of the camp.

The sleeping-period had finally come.

Remen had been bruised a little by his captors, but had been spared the more gruesome tortures they'd threatened to apply: after a few punches in the face he'd eagerly told Lian and the others everything they'd wanted to know. Probably it was the sudden arrival on the scene of a vicious-looking black-haired woman, her cruel eyes alight with the prospect of inflicting torment, that had melted his spirit so readily. Or so he told himself now as he lay huddled on the earth, his hands and feet bound but not to each other; another rope attaching his hands to a firmly secured stake some feet away.

The pain of the bruises made it difficult for him to get to sleep. One of his teeth had been loosened, which meant it was even more difficult – however much he told it not to, his tongue kept probing at the wobbly tooth, so that he was brought back to wakefulness every time he seemed to be on the verge of sleep.

The peasant camp was quiet. Doubtless there were sentries posted, but he could see none of them through the puffy slits of his eyes. He searched his brain, trying to recall from the calendar in his mind whether or not rain might start to fall during this sleeping-period.

The rain might put out the last embers of the dying fire.

That gave him pause for thought.

He looked at the rope that attached him to the roughly

hewn stake and swore silently. Might the next waking-period's festivity for the peasants be watching him being burnt to death? Remen could think of nothing else for a short while – he even smelled his own flesh roasting – but then, after a prayer to the Sun, he found himself thinking of his situation more rationally. His tether was just long enough that he might be able to . . .

He slithered himself across the ground, snakelike, trying to make as little noise as possible. Turning himself over on his back and crooking his arms behind him as far as he dared, he found that he could just reach the heat of the fire with his feet.

He kicked a smouldering log clear, dragging it back towards him. Straining against his bonds, he was able to separate his ankles by a couple of centimetres. He brought his feet cautiously down on either side of the log, forcing himself to ignore the pain. His feet seemed to be cooking inside his leather boots. He was rewarded by the stink of burning rope.

It seemed to take an eternity before he felt a slight click as the first strand succumbed to the fire. He was able to stretch his feet just a little wider now, so that the pain on his ankles subsided slightly. With increased confidence he pushed the cord down onto the log, as strand after strand of it burnt away.

Once his feet were free he crawled back to his huddled position, pretending to sleep. From a distance, at least, it would look as though he were still immobilised. He just hoped that none of the prowling sentries – if there were any – would come here too soon, or that any of the other peasants would wake; although there was a slight breeze, the smell of smouldering rope was still strong enough that their suspicions would be immediately aroused.

No one approached him.

He thanked the Sun for its goodness. He deliberately kept out of his mind the thought that the Sun could have expressed its goodness a little while earlier – ideally, before he'd been selected by Garine.

Once the stink had abated a little, he crawled towards

the stake. It took him no more than a few moments to unpick the last few knots that had been keeping him checked.

Again he kept himself curled up on the ground for a short while, waiting for the alarm to be sounded.

Nothing.

The log he'd initially heeled back from the fire was still hot but it was no longer alight. Moving more confidently now, he rose to his feet and kicked away another. This was going to be more difficult, he knew; the last time his boots had protected his ankles from the worst of the heat, but now he was going to have to steel himself to accept it directly on his wrists.

Better than being burnt alive, he thought.

In fact, it proved to be not so bad as he'd expected. Within a very short time he was able to manipulate his hands out of the binding.

He was free, thank the Sun.

Yes, but free for what?

Neither Nadar nor Garine was a merciful man. They wouldn't look kindly on a spy who had lost his companion and who had been so easily captured by the enemy. He could try lying to them – 'Onir betrayed me to the peasants, and then they killed him; I escaped only because of my skill at weaponry.' But, if he was anything less than convincing, he would be put to serious torture, this time by the Ellonia – and they wouldn't be satisfied as easily as the peasants had been.

No, he must bring back a prize with him.

His cunning eyes scanned around him; everything he looked at seemed slightly reddened because of the beating he'd received.

Over there stood the tent of He Who Leads.

He Who Leads.

That was the name he'd heard the other peasants call the tall man.

A head would be a great trophy to take to Nadar. The Deputy Army-Master would regard his achievement as such a great triumph that he'd be safe.

But did he dare? He was weaponless, and far smaller than He Who Leads. Yet, if the man was sleeping and his weapons were in the tent with him . . .

There seemed to be nobody around. He would have to remember to report to Nadar that the peasants were lax on camp security during the sleeping-periods. The more useful information he could give to the Deputy Army-Master, the better his chances.

He crept forwards, crouching so that he was almost on his hands and knees, and within seconds was concealed beneath the tent's rudimentary flysheet. Still there was no cry to indicate that he'd been spotted. All he could hear was gentle snoring from inside.

There were cords tying up the cloth door. His hands fumbled with the knots even more than they had with the one binding him to the stake; he had to reach in through the gap between the flaps and work blind. The beating of his heart seemed to him loud enough to wake even the most drunken of sleeping sentries, but still there was no sign of the alert being sounded.

Luck? He could hardly describe it as good judgement on his part. Luck it must be.

One knot undone, the lowest of them. It was easier now that there was more space in which his hands could work. He cursed his fingers for the way they trembled. However much he tried to force them to work smoothly, they shook and shivered as if they had a life of their own.

The second knot came undone.

He felt more confident now. These weren't knots painstakingly designed to repel intruders; they were tied simply, mere devices to tell visitors that their presence was not desired.

That must mean that he's got a woman with him, thought Remen briefly, starting to work on the third knot. *Is it the black-haired one or the rather shy-looking one? Shit: fucking fingernail. Hope it's not the dark bitch; she looks as tough as a wrestler. Hope there's a sword or a dagger I can find. Hope the two peasant bastards aren't light sleepers. Hope this buggering knot will give way . . .*

Ah, at last.

Untying the three cords had been enough. Stooping down, he made his way as quickly and quietly as possible into the coolness of the tent.

Directly opposite him there was a grass pallet. On it, covered in a thin sheet, was only a single body.

The mousy woman! he thought angrily. *The bloody chieftain is somewhere bloody else. Thank the Sun it's the timid one he's left behind him.*

For a moment he was motionless, wondering what to do, listening to the softness of her snores. The sunlight coming in through the flaps painted a dark picture of the lower half of his body on one of the badly made rugs that floored the tent.

He looked around him and saw a scabbarded sword leaning against a stinking wooden commode. He moved silently across to draw the weapon from its sheath.

He could take the head of the woman – a mate of He Who Leads – back to Nadar as proof of his courage, but would that be sufficient? The Deputy Army-Master might laugh off his claims: the head could be that of any peasant woman. She was plain enough.

If He Who Leads was absent from the tent where his mate slept, he might return at any second. Perhaps he'd simply been out checking the sentries, or something like that. Remen couldn't stay here any longer.

He took a step forwards.

The woman woke.

Her green eyes opened slowly and hazily, then suddenly became alert as she saw him standing there, sword in hand.

Her mouth opened to scream.

'Say nothing!' he hissed, raising the sword. 'Say nothing, and you might live.'

A lie, he thought sadly. *Nadar will never let her survive. Assuming I get her to him.*

She shrank under the sheet, her eyes pleading with him. But at least he'd been able to stop her shouting for help.

He tried to look fierce.

Syor felt as if she were paralysed. This was the funny little man at whom she'd laughed at the start of the last waking-period, and now she was at his mercy; he could kill her with a single jab of the sword he held – her own sword. If he'd been a sturdy warrior she'd have been less terrified; but she remembered the peasants' emasculating mockery of him, and realised that he might take dreadful revenge from her. And yet he'd said she might live.

'What do you want?' she whispered.

'Get dressed.'

'I *am* dressed. More or less.'

Remen was a courteous man in many ways. As she climbed out from under the sheet he took a single glance to make sure that she wasn't armed; after that he turned his eyes away, using his peripheral vision only enough to check that she wasn't trying to deceive him by snatching up a concealed weapon. He saw the blur of her body moving smoothly and carefully as she put on the only garments she'd removed before tumbling into bed – her boots and a hooded halter. He could feel that she was trying to reassure him by her actions: there were no sudden jerks of motion; everything was done in a rhythmical fashion.

Does this mean that He Who Leads will be here soon? he thought.

'Get a move on.'

Fully clothed, she stood up, and Remen was nervously aware of the fact that she was several centimetres taller than he was. The feel of her heavy sword in his hand, however, seemed to give him the greater height.

'You'll come with me.'

'Yes, I'll come with you.'

She smiled at him, unexpectedly, and suddenly he realised both why she was a mate of He Who Leads and why he was beginning to loathe her.

I'm the person with the weapon. I'm the person who's in total control. And yet now she's confident enough to make me feel as if it's her who's taking me hostage. I may not shed too many tears, after all, when you die, peasant.

'Move round here, slowly now.'

He gestured with his free hand over his shoulder towards the tent door.

Holding her hands out to her sides, showing him that they were empty, she obeyed, treading slowly and silently in order not to antagonise him. The sharp tip of the sword followed her in a slightly trembling arc.

Remen moved up close behind her as she bent down at the low opening he'd made at the door. This was the moment when she might have been able to escape him for at least long enough to yell for help.

Ruthlessly he cut up through the cloth of the tent, creating a gap through which they could both walk upright.

'That could have been your spine,' he observed, very quietly.

'I'm all too well aware of that,' she muttered, but she didn't seem concerned.

Syor's calmness was beginning to infuriate Remen even more. The ways of the peasants seemed to be very different from those of the Ellonia, but surely even here the women should show due deference, due subservience. By now, one of the fledgling aristocrats of Giorran would have fainted or offered him the pleasures of her body – almost certainly the latter. He wasn't accustomed to this self-assurance in a woman. It was unnerving him.

She stepped out into the open air and politely held back one of the flaps for him.

Does she want *me to kill her?*

'You wish to take me to the leader of your army, little man. That's it, isn't it?' she said softly.

'Yes, bitch.'

'Address me more courteously and I'll take you there.'

He was astonished.

'What do you mean?' he said.

'Only a few people could take you safely out of our camp. I'm one, and obviously He Who Leads is another. Redin or Marc could do it too, but of course you haven't met either of them. Reen has the authority as well; He Who Leads told me that you seemed not to like her very much.'

The black-haired woman, thought Remen miserably,

remembering how the very appearance of her had demolished what little resistance he'd had. *Pray to the Sun we don't encounter her, that she's sleeping soundly.*

'Others of us wouldn't be able to help you like this,' Syor continued. 'Sinede or Bruiss, Marja or Lanyor – they'd probably have to discuss the matter with the sentries, and it might take them long enough that the alarm went up.'

She was walking away from him as easily as if the two of them were setting out for a leisurely stroll. He hurried to catch up with her.

A couple of skeletal dogs looked at them with interest for a moment, then turned back to nosing for scraps of food in the middenish mess of the camp.

'What do you mean?' he said, trying to keep his voice under control. 'Why are you doing this?'

'Because I want to get you out of here.'

'What do you mean?' he repeated.

'Little man, you have corruption in your thoughts – Ellonian corruption. I can sense it, and I'm certain that Lian – He Who Leads – can sense it as well. He might kill you for it – in fact, I think he came close to doing just that after they'd beaten you – but I'd rather you lived.'

She pushed away hair from her brow. For once she noticed the habit and was annoyed with herself for it.

'Besides, it's too late for you to harm us,' she carried on. 'It's nearly the new waking-period now. By then we'll have raised our army and be marching on your forces. You won't have enough time to reach your army and rouse it. If I were you I wouldn't even try: I'd run off and find somewhere to hide. If our warriors come upon you they're not going to allow you to live very long. So you see' – again that enraging smile – 'there's no reason why I shouldn't expend just a little bit of effort to save your rather revolting little life. On top of which, you've made me laugh; there's not enough laughter in this life, so it'd be stupid of me to allow one source of it to be cut off. No?'

She looked at him, her head at an angle, her eyes sneering at him.

'Bitch!'

'I've been called worse.' Calmly.

'Fucker of horses!'

'Now there's a thought. I must try it some time. Do you find it fun yourself?'

He cast his mind around for some other apposite insult to hurl at her.

'Slut!'

'You should be so lucky. Shall we end this particular aspect of the conversation here and concentrate on getting you out past the sentries?'

Her eyes were on him again, taunting him. He could see in them that she had no fear of death. Besides, he needed her alive if he was to survive himself. And it was all too obvious that she knew this. But, once he'd hauled her up before Nadar . . .

'Right,' he said at last. 'All right.'

She put her left forearm on his shoulder.

'Friend,' she said, 'well, friend for the moment. You're very lucky you shat your pants, you know. It'll be easy enough for me to persuade the guards that you're just another of us, now that you're rigged out in the same sort of clothes as we are. I'm surprised Lian didn't think to put you in one of the Ellonian uniforms we have; then even I would have found it a bit of a problem to get you away.'

Remen miserably watched the tip of his captured sword tracing a thin line through the mud. Maybe he should have run like Onir, after all. Death itself must be preferable to being patronised by the mate of the foe's leader.

Then he brightened slightly.

On second thoughts, living is better than dying. Probably. I've no wish to be gathered to the Sun before my appointed time. And she hasn't yet thought out the position she's in. She probably thinks I'll simply release her once my own safety's secure. Well, let her keep on thinking that until we're past the guards.

The tents were thinning out, and Syor was still walking confidently, about half a pace ahead of him.

'I'd put that sword away now, if I were you,' she said out of the corner of her mouth, and then sensed his sudden confusion.

'Just stick it through your belt, you bloody idiot!' she said, a little louder this time. 'A lot of us don't have scabbards, so the guards won't take too much notice.'

A couple of seconds later there were two sentries in front of them. Both towered over Syor and Remen; the spy was terrified. So much for his great plan. The woman could betray him with a single word. Why had he ever believed her deceiving tongue? Because he'd wanted to – that was it – and now he'd let her lead him straight into the simplest of traps. *May the Sun burn her to a crisp.*

She was saying something to one of the sentries; at first he couldn't hear what it was through the tumult of his own thoughts.

'I want to reconnoitre briefly beyond the camp's boundaries,' she said casually. 'I've brought a warrior with me in case I've got need of protection.'

The sentry looked dubious.

'Mightn't you be better with more than that callow little fellow? The two of us could come along.' He waved a hand at his companion.

'No, I should be all right. He mayn't look much, but he's as tough a fighter as they come.'

She kissed the sentry lightly and with genuine affection on his sweating cheek, even though she'd never noticed him before.

'But I haven't brought my sword,' she added. 'Perhaps if you could lend me your dagger . . . ?'

He passed the weapon to her, but a little reluctantly: he was still uncertain about the situation.

'I'll give it back to you when I return,' she said with a little laugh. 'I shouldn't be long.'

It's as if she were doing nothing more significant than going to the privy, thought Remen, *but instead she thinks she's altruistically saving my life.* He knew that he was being irrational – if she'd acted otherwise the sentries would have seized him – but the comparison raised him to a new height of rage. Dammit: he'd make her tell all that she knew and then he'd watch her face as the sharp blades descended . . .

And then the two of them were out of the camp, the

sentries looking inquisitively after them as they retreated. He turned to look back and was rewarded with a friendly wave. Syor was almost skipping across the turf up the shallow hillside, as if she hadn't a care in the world. He saw the easy movement of her hips ahead of him and felt a tiny surge of lust, which vanished almost immediately. Once they were beyond the crest he would have to take the dagger from her. True, he had much the better weapon in the form of the stolen Ellonian sword at his belt, but he couldn't afford to use it to kill her. The suggestion she'd made that he should hide from the ignorant rabble of peasants had been a reasonable one, but the Ellonia were far more ruthless; they'd raze the land from one horizon to the other once they'd won the battle.

Which they would.

Surely they would?

He was grateful for the fact that she seemed to prefer walking a little ahead of him.

Syor came to the crest of the ridge and stopped, waiting for him to catch up.

'Your people are over there, are they?' she said, smiling at him as if the question were nothing more than a commonplace. She pointed at the distant trees.

'Yes.' He was immediately furious with himself. Unwilling as he was to admit it, there was always the chance that she might escape. He should have lied to her, or at least kept his mouth shut.

'Then our armies will probably meet among the grasses. Be hidden well away by then, little man.'

Her booted foot kicked gently at a buttercup.

'I'm not hiding.'

His voice was weak.

'You're going to fight us? Yourself?'

He cursed those green eyes and the way they looked at his face.

'I may.'

'You can't reach your comrades before our army starts to pour over here.'

'I don't wish to. All I need to protect myself is – you.'

188

Before he could see what she was doing the dagger was in her right hand.

'But you won't have me, will you?'

She moved to her right. He could hardly believe her speed. She was half bent over, her right arm moving the small weapon easily from side to side, drawing his eyes towards it.

It seemed to take him forever to lug the unfamiliar sword away from his belt, as if the garment were trying to resist his efforts.

Suddenly the dagger was hurtling towards him, spinning through the air. He heard the whistle of its passage.

Instinct saved him. At the last moment he ducked his head away. Behind him there was a thud as the blade plunged into the ground.

Syor looked confused and bitter.

'All right, little man, you've won,' she said.

But then she laughed.

'You've lost, too.'

He pointed the sword at her.

'You're my prisoner,' he said, trying to keep any doubt out of his voice.

'Yes,' she said, sitting down, 'but I'm not a very useful prisoner, am I? He Who Leads already knows about your troops, doesn't he? By the time I'm as far away from him as your encampment I won't be able to remember anything that might help you. Oh, I'll be just a vegetable before you even start to hurt me.' She grinned at him, hoping he wouldn't spot the lie. 'And I won't really feel the pain, because I'll forget it as soon as it's over, moment after moment. Pain only hurts you when you can remember it long enough.'

'I need you.' The sword's tip now at her throat.

'That's what all the boys say. But it's a pretty bloody ineffectual line, isn't it? You'd be wisest to let me go.'

She picked a few stems of grass idly, threw them into the air, and watched them spiral dreamily away in the breeze. She seemed unconscious of the sharp blade so near to her face.

'No.'

He surprised himself with the firmness he'd managed to muster into the single syllable.

'Silly man.'

'Look at me.'

She turned her head obediently.

'I could kill you here and now,' he said, turning the hilt of the sword over and over in his hand.

'So you could,' she said, looking away again, 'but you're not going to, are you?' Far in the distance she could see a curlew making a black arrow in the air.

'I might.' Deliberately making his voice gruff.

'Oh,' she said impatiently, 'let's end this silly nonsense, shall we? Kill me now, let me go back, or make me walk through the grass until we reach your troops. To tell you the truth, I don't much mind what you decide. I just wish you'd decide *something*.'

'Stand.'

'All right.'

She seemed totally unconcerned. She got to her feet and turned her back on him. He saw the paleness of her flesh showing through the gaps in her knitted halter.

'Nadar will deal with you.'

'Nadar?'

'Our Deputy Army-Master. There's no one more cruel.'

'Oh yes there is.'

'Who?'

'Me, of course.'

The tip of his sword touched her shoulder, urging her down the slope towards the yellow-green grass.

He allowed himself to laugh as he followed her.

After a moment, she started to laugh as well.

It wasn't a sound he much liked.

Soon they were in among the tall stalks. She was walking cheerfully towards her doom, pushing the grass away from her. He did his best to keep the sword between her shoulder-blades, not hurting her in any way but nevertheless reminding her of its threat.

Then, clumsily, he tripped on a root, his legs still uncertain because of the tightness with which they'd been bound, and fell flat on his face, the sword slicing away from him.

Syor's foot stamped down on the back of his neck, killing him instantly. His death was almost silent; there was just a soft 'plunk' as his neck broke.

She groped about in the dimmed light among the long reeds, trying to find the sword. It must be nearby.

Over the ears of the grass she could see faces looking at her. The men were on horseback and she registered the green and red of their uniformed shoulders.

I wish you well, Lian, she thought. *I only wish I could be at your side when you ride into Ernestrad.*

'You killed the man.' The voice was ragged.

'I saw him die – that was all.'

'*We* saw him die. Who are you?'

'A woman. Trying to stop him from . . . from . . .'

The soldier's pointed shoe caught her in the throat.

Chapter Eight
Encounter

The two sentries were worried, although they didn't quite know why. They sat on the grass, companionably sipping from goblets of thin, astringent wine, expressing their concern over Syor's departure by the fact that, though they weren't talking about it, they weren't talking about anything else either. From time to time one of the other sentries sauntered along to join them from her station further around the perimeter of the camp, but she found herself frozen out by their non-conversation, and eventually desisted.

'I think I'll have a chat with He Who Leads,' said one of them at last. He remembered Syor's light kiss on his cheek. She wasn't in the habit of kissing people as casually as that. Was this what was making him so uncertain? Had she acted out of character in order to try to convey to him that there was something amiss? He hadn't liked the look of the little runt who'd been with her. The sentries' suspicions were inchoate, and perhaps that was what was disturbing them the most.

He put down his goblet and stood up.

The other sentry looked at him with a studiedly quizzical expression.

'A chat,' he said. 'What about?'

'You know bloody well what about.' Stretching his arms in the air sleepily, doing his very best to persuade himself that there was nothing to be concerned about, and failing.

'Yup.'

A short pause, and then the seated man added: 'I'll guard the post while you're gone.'

'Thanks.' Brusquely. His fellow had an irritating habit of stating the obvious. 'Do you know where He Who Leads is this sleeping-period?'

'I heard on the grapevine that he was with Reen and Marja, but I may be wrong.' He spat inaccurately at a money-spider that was laboriously crawling across the churned grass.

'Reen? Marja? I thought Reen and Marja were . . .' A twisting movement of the hand.

'I wouldn't know. But that's what I was told. Maybe they feel it's their duty: He Who Leads sorely needs an heir.'

This time his gob of spittle covered the little spider, which floundered for a moment and then expired, killed by the impact. He looked satisfied; his companion turned away without another word.

The tent that Marja and Reen normally shared was almost at the other side of the camp; near to it was the one in which Redin and Sinede dwelled together. It took the sentry a long time to pick his way among the sprawling tents and the smouldering fires, and almost as long to pluck up his courage to intrude; this was a sleeping-period, after all, when privacy should generally be respected. But by this time he had made himself very concerned about Syor's safety, and that had to be more important than social considerations.

'He Who Leads!' he shouted through the knitted walls of the tent.

'Go away.'

It was Marja's tight little voice.

'Syor. She might be in danger.'

There was consternation within.

A few moments later Lian emerged, still pulling his breeches on.

The sentry quickly explained what had happened. Within seconds He Who Leads was rousing Sinede and Redin, gesturing them angrily towards the sentry, who was baffled by the amount of attention he was receiving. He answered their questions as quickly and accurately as he could. He Who Leads was in the meantime yelling out for the other members of his original troop. Marc came stooping out of his eremitic tent, stumbling in his half-sleep. Reen and Marja looked resentful, but strapped on their swords nevertheless. Bruiss put on a good pretence of being wide awake. Of them all, Reen and Redin seemed to the sentry to be the most dangerous; Redin was shaking his long brown hair angrily while Reen's eyes were flashing in the way that had so terrified the spy.

'Taken hostage?' said He Who Leads tersely to the sentry.

'Possibly so. I don't want to be a scaremonger, but . . .'

'Assume she is. By the memory of my mother, but there may be blood spilt this sleeping-period.'

The tip of his sword whipped uncomfortably close to the sentry's belly.

'Where's Lanyor?' shouted He Who Leads.

'Sleeping,' said a muffled voice in the distance.

'Leave her where she is,' said Reen. 'She'd be of no use to us anyway.'

The dark eyes of the small woman were shiny with unspoken contempt.

'Eight of us,' said He Who Leads, his expansive wave embracing the sentry. 'Enough?'

'It depends,' Reen replied.

'On what?'

'On whether or not Syor's actually in any danger. On whether or not she's really been captured by the Ellonia. On whether or not – oh, on a hundred or more whethers or nots.'

She looked as if she wanted to hit him, and he retreated a couple of steps.

'What if there's an Ellonian force of hundreds – even thousands – out there?' he said limply.

'Then we come back, thicko.'

The sentry was amazed that anyone could have the temerity to speak to their leader like this.

Reen was building herself up into a high fury. She had never disputed Lian's right to be He Who Leads but, at the same time, she wished she'd been given his gift of retaining reality; she considered herself a much finer military leader than he could ever be, possessed as she was of considerably greater powers of strategic thinking and of a ruthlessness that Lian would never be able to emulate. Right now she wanted to feel her sword shearing through human flesh and bone.

He Who Leads was in imminent danger, and had the sense to realise it.

'Reen, Marja, Redin, Bruiss, Sinede – come with me,' he said peremptorily. 'The rest of you stay here. If things go wrong, Marc will be your leader: he has an element of my gift, and the singer may return to help him.'

'Stay here yourself,' said Marc, shocking himself by the force of his words. 'Lian, it's important for all of us – the whole of your army – that you stay alive. Otherwise everything'll be wasted.'

For a moment it was Marc's turn to be the leader among them, dominating Lian with his forcefulness, but then He Who Leads shook his cloud of hair decisively.

'No. No, Marc. I know what you're trying to say, but there's no use in it. I'd be nothing if I didn't try to help Syor myself – assuming she does need help.'

The sentry looked on, amazement becoming dismay. These were his heroes and they were bickering like children.

He Who Leads gave a curious whistle and Anan trotted into view. So, curiously enough, did the piebald that Syor had adopted as her own. Reen looked at the beast sceptically, then threw herself up onto it, happy to ride bareback. The horse tossed its head but accepted her presence. She scratched it behind one of its ears and it settled.

The others were soon mounted.

The sentry they passed as they left the camp was feeling very sick. The wine he'd been drinking was never particularly tender to the stomach, but the quantities he'd poured down his throat were such that his whole body seemed to be rebelling. He watched the five horses' tails flicking as they receded from him up the hillside and wondered how he'd ever been persuaded to allow his companion to set off in search of He Who Leads. Syor generally knew what she was doing. Now there was all this ridiculous alarm. She'd be back soon, and without the help of her pursuers.

Perhaps she'd kiss him on the cheek, like she had his friend.

It was a nice thought.

He took it with him into a nightmarish sleep where it seemed as if people were pressing inwards on his head from all sides, and that others were beating him with wooden staves. From time to time he whimpered as he watched the dream images dancing in front of him.

'You're not exactly a work of art yourself,' said Syor with a friendly smile.

Nadar had just remarked that she was singularly unappealing to the opposite sex, and she'd decided it was time to reply in kind. After all, blast it, she was going to die anyway; might as well upset this puffed-up squirt before she went. Getting him angry could well foul up his judgement and so help Lian. She looked at the man's reddish-grey hair and his feeble attempt at a beard, and she laughed.

It was one of the few things she had to laugh about. Her throat was a single agonised bruise; it felt as if her Adam's apple had been reduced to a pulp by the kick she'd received. Before she'd recovered her wits she'd been pegged out among the stalks of grass, her hands and feet bound tightly to small wooden stakes so that she was spreadeagled and helpless.

It had been by pure accident that Nadar had come here. He had woken refreshed to discover that the scouts he had sent forward had failed to return. Garine was more than usually obsequious as he told his commander the news, then suddenly remembered that he had important duties elsewhere. Nadar had thought of calling him back and ordering him to take charge of a rescue party, but had dismissed the idea almost as soon as it had occurred to him. He no longer trusted the twisted little man; that was the trouble. There'd have to be changes in the chain of command once this uprising had been quelled.

So Nadar had gone out to search for the scouts himself, leading a few volunteers.

Well, here was one dead spy, killed before their very eyes, killed by a stab of the woman's foot. She pretended to be a peasant, but that could hardly be true: no peasant would have had the quickness of mind to see the momentary weakness of the Ellonian and to react to it so effectively.

On the ground she looked much less threatening. Pegged out, she was not only helpless but also in a position where her helplessness could hardly fail to be the dominant factor in all of her thinking.

It could hardly fail, as Nadar had thought, but for some reason it was doing so.

The blasted bitch had the insolence to smile at him.

Again.

'Who are you?' he said angrily.

He and his men were now standing all around her. Their horses had wandered off but could be heard selecting the more succulent grasses.

'I think you're the one who ought to be answering that sort of question.' Syor was very serious. 'I've not got the slightest idea who you are, but you seem to think you're very important. If I met you somewhere in these grasslands and didn't much like the look of you, I don't think my first conversational gambit would be to have you kicked in the throat and then have you staked out like this.'

'Impertinent little slut, aren't you?'

He drew the forefinger of his right hand across his upper lip, just beneath his nose.

'If I'm impertinent, what're you?'

Nadar smiled cruelly.

'I'm the person you should be pleading with, that's who I am. Right now your life is worth less than that of a flea.' He snapped his fingers to emphasise his words. 'You're just a peasant girl, and not a very pretty one at that. You're not

198

in a very strong bargaining position.'

'Your spy – the little man you sent among us – was in a *very* strong bargaining position,' she said almost lazily, 'until he suddenly stopped being so. I'd remember that, if I were you.'

'Would you?'

He laughed sarcastically at her, and she shifted her gaze away from his face, nauseated by him. Far up above her, through the waving ears of grass, she could see clouds moving serenely across the azure sky. She wished she could somehow be away from here, flitting around and through those clouds. This petty little sadist seemed the type who would make her death a painful one, just for the fun of it. And she certainly would feel the pain . . .

Nadar couldn't believe the level of hatred he felt for her. It seemed to him to be an abuse of all natural laws that a peasant should show such defiance.

'We're going to kill you,' he said.

'I know that.'

'And before that . . .'

The threat was left unfinished.

'I don't care too much, shithead,' Syor said. 'Do whatever you want to – in the long run you'll still be the loser. And I'll be dead by then.' Relaxing back into the ground, feeling her shoulders and bottom creating comfortable hollows in the soil, she was trying to persuade herself almost to welcome the onset of the pain the red-headed man seemed prepared to administer.

'I could have you tortured indefinitely.'

She smiled.

'No. I'd laugh at your torturers. I've been at their mercy before, when some of your arsehole ilk came to our village and thought they were clever as they hurt us all.' She hoped he wouldn't think too hard about this. 'Do *you* think they were being so clever? In your heart of hearts, do you really believe it?'

He was furious to find that he couldn't find an answer to her question; his anger with himself eclipsed the surge of rage he'd felt when she'd insulted the Sun-blessed House of Ellon. 'Is that what you thought when they were hurting you?'

'Yes. That's exactly what I thought.' *Or hope I would have thought*, she added mentally. 'They believed that the power they had to cause me pain in some way meant that they were superior to me. But they weren't. It was the other way round, because if I'd had that power I'd never have used it. And you, with your stupid warnings, you're less than me, too. You're just a powerful *nothing*.'

Her green eyes were on his face.

She wasn't comely, but for some reason he wanted to take her – forcefully. Maybe it was the way that, even though she was helpless, she was presenting him with arguments he couldn't counter. He didn't know. Was it that he wanted to humiliate her violently before she died or was it that a certain spark in him was responding to the bravery of her defiance? She was totally at his mercy.

It had been a long time since he'd felt this *need* – especially for a peasant.

He wanted her.

No, he needed her. Needed her.

'Want' was the wrong word because he didn't actually want to do what he was going to. Despite his threats of torture, he'd hoped that she'd tell them what she knew so that he could have her killed quickly, because torturing rebellious peasants was scarcely worthwhile. He'd never considered himself to be at heart an especially cruel man – his cruelties he regarded as duties – and he believed that he found little pleasure in causing unnecessary suffering.

So why did he need so much to possess her dowdy little body?

Because she represented the opposite of everything he'd always believed was true. He looked around at the waving grasses and at his silent, expectant soldiers for a moment and had the honesty to admit this to himself. The admission didn't decrease his need in any way, but it gave him a sense of justification. Yes, it was *her* fault: she was provoking him intolerably, so that he hardly knew what he was doing. And any time he thought about it later he'd be able to tell himself this. That it had all been *her* fault.

He leaned forward and touched her on the ankle. She squirmed away, as if his fingers were wasp stings.

She stopped laughing. She threw her head to one side, her hair spilling out like a wave, and he found himself smiling again, now with anticipation.

She was at his mercy.

He needed her, and he was going to enjoy her.

It wasn't a matter of his having any choice in the matter. He hadn't asked for her to be here, it was her own fault, peasants who acted against the Ellonia should . . .

All of his justifications seemed to melt away.

I want to humiliate her because I can, he thought. *She's right, but I don't care.*

He was reaching for his belt when there was a cry of whooping triumph from a rider he never properly saw. The edge of a sword cut across his thigh, so that he spun away from Syor, clutching a hand down to stem the flow of blood. One of his soldiers fell sideways, gurgling his life gorily out into the grass.

Suddenly Nadar was on all fours, creeping backwards, feeling the resistance of the sturdy grass against his feet. He cursed himself for his stupidity: here he was crawling away from an ill-led rabble of peasants, and the only reason was that he'd underestimated them. He heard the *chock* as a peasant sword lashed into the neck of another of the Ellonia. *That should have been* my *neck*, he thought. *It was* my *fault that we were so stupid, not his; he gave away his life so that I could carry on making bloody silly mistakes.*

A horseman came cantering by and dropped a rock on the small of his back.

He shouted and rolled over.

A hoof landed just beside his ear, and he twisted away again.

The arrow missed him. It appeared suddenly directly in front of him, sticking up out of the ground like some strange plant.

He was up on his knees by now, slapping out on both sides at the grass, doing his best to hurt it.

The punch almost broke his jaw.

He rolled away, putting his hands up to his face.

'You'll never kill me,' said He Who Leads, stooping over Nadar's face. 'Once upon a time the Ellonia could have done it, but those times are too long ago.'

Nadar turned to the left and found himself looking directly into the eyes of a severed head. There was a salty taste in his mouth.

The peasants had released the green-eyed woman. She was smiling at him, yet again. It seemed as if she were sorry for him in his predicament, and that hurt him more than anything.

'Lian,' she said, 'don't be too harsh with him.' She hurt Nadar with her words.

He Who Leads beckoned her away. 'The Ellonia don't deserve to live,' he said softly to her. 'You wanted to spare that little runt, and look what happened.'

'Everyone deserves to live,' she said, suddenly angry. 'That's a right we all have.'

Lian left her standing there and kicked Nadar viciously, breaking several ribs.

'Stop.'

Syor grabbed He Who Leads by the shoulder, pulling him away.

'Why?'

'Let him go back.'

'Back where?'

'To his shoddy little army. He's not anyone to worry about – just a little jumped-up simpleton the Ellonia have sent to annoy us.'

Nadar would have been glad to have been killed. He was sprawling in the long grass and these peasants were talking about him as if he didn't exist. To make things worse, an ant walked up over the bridge of his nose and into his hair.

'Leave him.' Again it was the woman speaking.

'Kill him,' said one of their companions loudly and peremptorily. He was a big man and he held a blood-covered sword. He moved purposefully towards Nadar. 'I'll do it myself.'

'No,' said He Who Leads abruptly, reaching out an arm, palm upwards, to stop Bruiss in his tracks. 'We'll meet him in battle in the next waking-period, and then you can kill him.'

'Why not now?'

'Because Syor's right. The man's defenceless. Killing him now would be murder – we're peasants, not Ellonian scum. Send him back to his own people.'

Bruiss picked up Nadar and threw him over the back of his horse. The other peasants said nothing, turning away to mount their own horses; Syor climbed up in front of Lian, feeling his reassuring hands on her hips as she took the reins. She turned and kissed him on the lips.

Soon she and Lian were in their tent, Nadar was at the head of his army, and Bruiss was dead. His horse, too, had been casually slaughtered by the Ellonia.

It would soon be a new waking-period.

Behind Nadar there was a host of red and green banners that seemed to cover more of the land than his eyes could see. He fondled the ears of his horse briefly, hardly realising that he was doing so, then turned again to look at the army he'd brought here. Most soldiers lived their whole lives through and never saw the magnificence of a full-scale Ellonian army prepared for battle. He felt privileged. The air seemed sharp in his nostrils as he stroked his freckled forehead contentedly. He hardly noticed the throbbing of his bruises or the sharper pain of his ribs. Wherever he looked, sunlight glinted from naked blades. This wasn't going to be a war; it was nothing more than a clearing-up operation, putting a few peasants to death and then returning home to Giorran to report the success to the Despot. There would be great praise for him, he knew, and the likelihood that he'd be restored to his position as Army-Master.

One day he might become Despot himself.

This waking-period could decide it.

He'd never felt more *alive* than he did now. Nadar had few fears of the peasant army – if army it could be called.

Yes, his aching ribs testified that the peasants could be occasionally dangerous, but he was certain that his disciplined force could conquer them with ease. Oh, sure, there might be a few losses – that was the way in any military campaign – but by the next sleeping-period his men would be singing and drinking as they celebrated their simple victory.

I wouldn't like to be a peasant wench then.

The peasant wench . . .

That was the thing that was spoiling his belief in himself.

He'd needed her. He'd needed to humiliate her, but instead he'd been humiliated himself.

His smile faded.

His wives were drawn from the aristocracy of the Ellonia; only minor aristocracy, perhaps, but aristocracy nevertheless. They were women of great beauty and educated in all the social skills; their garments were of the softest silk. It had been many years since he'd had to make use of one of the peasant girls kept in Giorran for such purposes. Yet a little green-eyed runt in a coarse, badly knitted woollen skirt had turned him into someone he didn't recognise as himself.

Garine walked up and nudged Nadar's leg.

'Ready?'

'We're ready.'

Nadar adjusted his helmet.

Her eyes were green, and she laughed at me . . .

'I said "We're ready"!'

'Sir.' Garine saluted, then walked back to his own horse, looking back over his shoulder from time to time.

She was just a peasant – not worth any more thought . . .

He drew his sword and held it high above his head.

'To victory!' he shouted.

'Victory!' came the ragged chorus of the soldiers behind him.

She laughed at me . . .

'Forward!'

He dug his heels gently into his horse's flanks so that it began to move slowly forward, out of the trees. Soon the animal was moving more quickly, although he pulled it back from breaking into a canter. The sound of the army behind him was almost deafening – senseless shouting, clattering armour, frightened horses, bloodthirsty whoops and cries.

She laughed at me . . .

Something had gone from him. Only a little while ago he'd *known* that he was going to lead his army to an easy victory, but now he had to admit to himself that he was frightened. He remembered how the Wind had told him that he would be destroyed at the moment when he believed he'd achieved his greatest triumph. It was the laughter of the woman that had weakened him like this.

Her eyes were green. Her hair was brown as she lay among the long grasses, totally at my mercy. That's what was wrong, wasn't it? She shouldn't have been there. And I shouldn't have been there, either. She won.

Won.

He shook his head to get rid of the thoughts. His horse was trotting smoothly beneath him yet he felt insecure, as if the beast might change its mind at any moment and throw him.

He looked ahead of him at the ridge beyond which the peasants were encamped.

And then it was as if someone had spilt black liquid all across the horizon. The liquid began to flow rapidly and smoothly down the ridge towards him.

One in ten of the Ellonia died as a result of the first wave of peasant arrows. Twice that many were injured, falling screaming from their horses, desperately trying to remove the crude barbs from their bodies. Only the officers in their metal armour were relatively safe, though some of them died when arrows found chinks or pierced through visors. Garine was one; blood spouted from his helmet as he fell backwards, his hands half-raised towards his face.

He Who Leads had set out his troops in the earliest hour of the new waking-period. The peasants were no more than a poorly trained rabble and they were facing a well drilled army; it was therefore necessary to seize the initiative by assaulting Nadar's men before they were fully ready. Lian had put his archers in a great circle, several layers deep, around the plain, and had instructed them to wait until the Ellonian forces were nearing its centre. He'd walked among them all, quietly encouraging them.

Nadar, as soon as he'd realised the trap he'd led his army into, turned and shouted, 'Form!'

At once the shape of the phalanx behind him began to change. The men split up into seven groups, each with a single leader, and raised their leather shields so that the peasant arrows could no longer have any effect.

The second wave of arrows killed only four of the Ellonia.

Nadar was now the only soldier unprotected. Ahead of him the bulk of the peasant warriors were still coming on, shouting now, waving their weaponry. They seemed to be on foot, which puzzled him; he'd seen with his own eyes only hours ago that they possessed horses and ample riding skills.

He reined in his own horse and looked back nervously. There were too many dead and injured for his liking. The noise of his army was now compounded more of the screams and moans of the dying than of battle-cries. He started to wonder if he might have underestimated the leader of the rebels.

Nadar reluctantly turned his horse and spurred it into a gallop back to the protection of the shields. A few arrows chased him, but he was never in any real danger.

Under the barrier of shields, the familiar smell of leather and men's sweat was reassuring; this was the smell he had known since first he'd entered the army. He looked at the torn ground, at his sword and at the wild-eyed head of his horse, and he cursed himself for his own stupidity. Long ago Garndon had told him that any peasant uprising was likely to be led by an incursor from the outer world, and he'd paid too little attention. He'd perceived rebellions as potential but empty threats to the reign of the Ellonia; it had never occurred to him that he might have to face a leader with any genuine military skill.

Another cascade of arrows.

No fatalities this time. All the shafts fell uselessly into the grass or rattled on the leather shells the Ellonian troops had created for themselves.

The battle would soon become hand-to-hand.

Nadar pushed away the shields around him, cutting one of his own soldiers across the cheek as he sheathed his sword, hardly hearing the man's yelp of pain.

After his few minutes in the shade, the light out here on the plain was intolerably bright, seeming to stab at the backs of his eyes. Nevertheless he allowed his horse to trot easily forward, directly towards the advancing wave of peasants, watching the grass parting in front of him, shouting wordlessly in order to encourage the men behind him to follow.

To his relief they responded with military discipline, obediently beginning to move forwards purposefully, gathered back into a single phalanx, swords in their hands ready for the slaughter. Nadar waved his hand almost nonchalantly and within moments the mass of foot soldiers was surrounded by a protective ring of horsemen.

The body of men looked like a flexible green and red insect as it moved forward inexorably, the sounds of the wounded once again drowned by surging cheers, incoherent chanting and screamed threats, and the heavy, rhythmic pounding of men's feet as they trampled the long grasses flat. In places the insect had erect spines – the banners held proudly aloft by the younger soldiers – but most of its carapace was composed of sleekly polished leather interspersed with brightly gleaming metal.

Once again Nadar looked behind him.

Pride. I feel that emotion, and yet there's something wrong about it. The Wind – what the Wind said. No, that's not it. This will be a waking-period of bloodshed, but I'll feel no glory in it – just a sort of job-well-done sense, that'll be all.

But where are the peasant riders?

He waved his arms and within seconds a pair of his commanders were by his side, soothing their horses.

'They're all around us,' said the Deputy Army-Master.

One of the commanders, a man who looked as if he was even older than Nadar, chuckled unconcernedly; the other, a youth of high Ellonian rank who had been promoted with astonishing speed, looked terrified.

'Of course they've surrounded us,' said the older man. 'They'd be fools not to.'

He looked up at Nadar suddenly, 'Do you know how many of them there are?'

'No. More than I thought, maybe.'

'Too many?'

'I doubt it. They seem to have a leader – although I can't see him anywhere. But they still can't be much more than a disorganised mob.' Nadar gestured with a mailed hand.

'Depends on the size of the disorganised mob,' said the commander.

'Get them to spread out,' said Nadar impatiently to the younger man. 'So long as we all stick together we're vulnerable to these bloody arrows. Yes, we can fend them off, but merely fending off doesn't win battles. I want the whole of this plain covered by our soldiers.'

'Sire.'

'Just do it.'

The youth turned his horse away and began to bark orders.

'It's a pity about commanders like him,' commented the older man, quietly.

Nadar turned to him. 'I want you to do something as well. Split off a hundred of the infantry, under a good commander, and make them look as if they're fleeing. I want them to go right back the way they came. Tell them to shout any kind of insult about me they want to – the peasants should get the idea that they're mutineers who've lost all confidence in my leadership.'

'Really?'

The man looked at Nadar again. This time his eyes, through his visor, were clearly troubled.

'Really. Yes. That's what I want them to think.'

Her eyes were green, could see further than most people's eyes. It was unfair. That was what it was.

208

'And why?'

'Because I want you to circle round and attack those archers from behind. I want those bastards dead.'

The odd thing was that he didn't, particularly: he just wanted this conflict to be over. If the Sun would have listened to him he would have asked it to transport him instantly back to Giorran so that he could spend the rest of his life among his wives, never having to think about anything more weighty than where the next goblet of wine was going to come from. But the Sun, he knew, would ignore him.

'Do it.'

'Sire.'

'Go on, man! Get it done!'

'Sire.'

Nadar was alone again. The racket behind him – the shouts and the oaths – did nothing to make him feel that he was surrounded by friends. These men were just the tools he'd use to eradicate this menace to the House of Ellon: their allegiance to him was nothing more than a matter of their duty.

Tapping his horse on the shoulder so that it kept up its slow, high-stepping trot, he wondered about his foe. Somewhere out there, on one of the edges of this damnable bowl, was the big fair-haired man who commanded an army that obeyed because they *wished* to do so. Nadar resented it. The army he led obeyed his orders because it had been knocked into them that they should. The difference was hardly a subtle one: if one of his men ever had to choose between preserving Nadar's life and preserving his own, he'd probably opt to save his own; yet if one of the peasants had the same choice . . .

He wished he'd been someone else – preferably someone who'd never thought of entering the army or setting his sights on the throne of the Despot.

He wondered if any of his wives loved him . . . *She had green eyes, and I could have learnt to love her, but she saw me for the fool that I was – am – and she was right. I needed to have her beside me, telling jokes with me; but all I could*

209

think about was fucking her. This stupid little piece of baggage between my legs was telling me what to do.

Green eyes.

Yet another shower of arrows rained down on them, but the Ellonia coped with them easily.

The grey-haired officer was out of sight.

The Ellonia started to chant. The infantry, each in their separate units, were marching in perfect time. The men on horseback were leading those on foot out towards the rim of the plain, shouting exhortations. It was as if a stain was spreading across the bowl – a stain made up of a million busy mites, none of them paying any attention to each other but each acting in complete concord with all the rest.

Overhead, the Sun kept its silence. It had done so ever since Nadar, as a boy, had been taught to pray to it.

My soldiers think they're invincible, and I want them to keep thinking that. We'll conquer but . . .

Green eyes.

Lian's hordes suddenly appeared from all sides. They were poorly armed and most of them were in rags, but the sheer size of the mob made Nadar sick to his stomach. *My men are going to be butchered, overwhelmed by sheer numbers.* Even from here he could see that many of the peasant army were women; the sight disgusted him.

The man with the great cloud of gold hair – the man who'd beaten him so savagely and humiliatingly last waking-period – was at the head of a wedge of cavalry that plunged with horrifying speed into one flank of the expanding ring of Ellonians; he was wielding an axe around his head with brutal consequences.

Those of the Ellonia who weren't screaming were still trying to keep up their chant, but there was now a dismal, imposed tone to it.

The peasants were, by contrast, very quiet.

Nadar felt panic beginning to dominate his senses.

He'd been trained to lead men to battle, but he'd never before been *in* a large-scale battle. What was his role?

For the moment, to kill peasants . . . to lead by example. Raising his sword, he charged his horse towards where

210

he could see the blond man's reddened axe-blade hacking through Ellonian flesh.

Far away, in the northernmost corner of Albion, a dreamer was sleeping.

Most often, dreamers were not allowed to sleep, but this one had slipped away from the little peasant village where he'd spent the last few sleeping-periods on the pretext that his digestive tract was in disarray and that he'd like a little privacy, please. In part this was true; the greasy food served up as the peasants' standard fare was twisting his intestines into knots, and he'd spent an embarrassingly noisy hour or so squatting in a patch of bracken, revolting himself by this fresh evidence of his humanity. His main aim, however, had been to be allowed to *sleep*; it had been so long since last he'd given in to the temptation – or been permitted to – and his body had been heavy and aching with fatigue, his eyes itching foci of pain. He hoped he'd come far enough from the village. He knew he could walk no further.

He'd stumbled down from the bracken to fall face-first onto sweet-smelling grass; almost before he'd landed his eyes had been closed, and the first snore came seconds later.

Everyone knew that dreamers were dangerous. The only reason that they weren't shunned from all other society was that they could also, in the short term, be useful.

He was dressed in the obligatory garb of a dreamer – a grey and purple robe with a translucent green metallic star pinning the cloth at the shoulder. He was unarmed, of course. He was only a small man, and although he seemed never to age he always looked older than any human being had any right to be. His name was Joli.

That he had a name at all marked him out from the peasants – and herein lay his usefulness to them. He journeyed from village to village, being welcomed by the inhabitants – fed, sheltered, honoured – but never for more than a few waking-periods. After that, he would pick up his meagre belongings, throw his satchel over his shoulders, and set out again across country or along one of the Ellonian

211

dirt-tracks, plodding through the heat towards the next village on his ceaseless itinerary.

He could name people and things. He could tell the peasants what had happened in their region of Albion. He could make them feel, at least for a short while, the delirious ecstasies and agonies of existence as a complete human being rather than as a barely sentient creature who just happened to take human form, doomed to the endless drudgery of a domestic animal.

Of course, soon after his departure, the peasants would have forgotten all this – all except the vague recollection that they had had an experience so brightly shining, so intense, that it surpassed everything else in their normal existences.

The trouble was that he was dangerous to them, too, as if his presence were some kind of a narcotic drug that brought a few hours of rapture but then an endless and chaotic nightmare of misery.

He rolled over, snuggling down into the grass.

The crucial word was 'nightmare'.

As dreamers slept, their dreams came to predominate over the fluctuating reality of Albion, stamping themselves so firmly onto the fabric of spacetime that they transcended the normal flow of events. The effect was localised around them – a few kilometres away all would continue as normal – but it could be intense.

He shifted restlessly in his sleep again, his thumb moving childlike towards his wizened mouth.

Most of the dreams were benign. But the others, the nightmares . . .

All the vile abominations of the dreamer's subconscious could crawl forth from their earthly lairs, the skies could crack open to hurl fire down on those below, the ground could open up to swallow men, women and children into a freezing-cold limbo of neverness from which there was no escape through all of eternity, babes in the womb could turn into sharp-fanged creatures that ate their way up voraciously through their mothers' bodies to spit themselves eagerly out into the sunlight, relentless and invulnerable pursuers could follow a person with a silent, invisible malevolence . . . The worst of it all was that the dreamers *knew* what was going on and what they were visiting on the innocent, but were powerless to stop it by forcing themselves into wakefulness.

Dreamers were never permitted to sleep when they were near human beings – either peasants or Ellonia.

His ancient-seeming forehead was even more deeply furrowed than usual as he tossed and turned, occasionally making little uneasy whimpering noises and once or twice screaming out loud.

This was not an ordinary nightmare – he could sense that. The lurid images passing across the screen in front of his eyes were quite different from those he had experienced in the past. They were neither more nor less hideously real to him, but they had a different *kind* of realism; they were less immediate, less all-consuming, and yet they possessed a sort of cold precision and sharp delineation which made him feel as if somehow, for once, the nightmare was coming not from inside him but being sent into him from somewhere else – somewhere many kilometres distant.

It seemed he was being both drawn to that place and sent images from it. The picture of a small thinnish face with close-cropped reddish hair darted across his inner vision – too swiftly, maddeningly, for his mind to record what it looked like.

A singer, some part of him thought. The singers, he'd been told, were nobody's enemies, but neither were they anybody's friends – they were outside all such considerations. He had heard of them and of what they could do; he'd hoped never to encounter one of them. *Yet, is this what singers are really like?* that same part of him asked.

His nightmare was of a battle. Although he could see the carnage and bear the sounds, he was sensually divorced from it, as if he were looking at it through some mental sheet of glass. The rapid succession of different scenes was being guided by someone, something . . . and at once he knew why. Through all his life he had remembered everything that had happened to him or that he'd been told; it was impossible for him to forget. And this was true also of his dreams.

The singer – she? he? – was using his mind as a logbook. The purpose was unclear.

A severed arm catapulted straight towards his face, and he tried to raise his arms to fend the object away from him; but he had no arms to raise, and suddenly he was somewhere else on the battlefield, watching another agony and feeling another brutality.

Here's a dream:

Reen and Marja are heading a small column of what they rather grandiloquently call cavalry up to the rear of the Ellonian army, the riders quietly picking their way through the debris left by last night's camp. Once among the trees they are completely hidden.

Nevertheless, they see a few score Ellonians riding towards them. They must have been observed.

But no. That doesn't seem to have been the case. The Ellonians look terrified and are shouting obscenities about some officer of theirs, but from the expressions on their faces Reen and Marja can tell that all of this is a pretence, a ploy, a pretty military tactic. The soldiers' gestures are too enthusiastic, too self-satisfied to be genuine.

Marja looks at Reen and Reen looks at Marja. They grin at each other.

'They don't even realise we're here,' says Marja, fondling the shoulder of her horse. The animal seems completely unconcerned by all that is happening on the plain ahead of it; it takes the opportunity of this hiatus to chomp at some tender shoots of a nearby bush.

'Soon will,' says Reen. She giggles briefly, just a single short burst of quiet sound, almost instantly cut off.

'What d'you think they're trying to do?' It is Sinede who has come almost silently up behind them. Her breathy voice is barely audible.

'At a guess, they're using a rather rudimentary trick,' says Marja. 'The bastards are taking a lot of casualties out there, so they've sent back a bunch of cavalry to try to pretend that some of the Ellonians have had enough – you know, sort of leaving their army without the formality of a resignation letter.'

'Letter?' says Sinede.

'Ask Syor, later,' says Reen impatiently.

'*Later?*' '*Letter?*' *Why the two pronunciations?* thinks Sinede. She shakes her curly hair confusedly.

'But of course what they're really going to do,' Marja continues, 'is come around behind us, so that we're caught between the two forces.'

'Well, they're not *really* going to do that,' says Reen, her white teeth showing in determined anticipation. There's a tone of comradely mockery in her voice as she glances across at Sinede. 'What's *really* going to happen is that they'll all be dead before that happens.'

'But there are only about twenty of us,' says Sinede. For the first time since the battle started, she's looking worried. She's never been very good at thinking about the future, but now suddenly she can't help doing so. As far as she's concerned death is a great mystery that can remain permanently unsolved.

'True,' says Reen, rubbing her chin. Above her mouth there's the faintest trace of a moustache; it accentuates the loveliness of her face. 'But we have the minor advantage that they don't know for certain that we're here. Sinede, lead away all the horses, as well as ten of our warriors. I want them all well back from here, in case something goes wrong.'

She slips easily to the ground and Marja follows suit, understanding Reen's thoughts immediately. Sinede copies them rather more slowly.

'Why?' says Sinede.

'Tell you later,' Marja snaps impatiently. 'Get a move on. We haven't much time.'

'We'll need Redin here,' says Reen. 'Ask him to pick out some more to stay here with us. They must have bows.'

Sinede looks worried, but leads their three horses back towards the others. Moments later, a score more warriors, including Redin and Sinede, pad up to the two women who

215

look so startlingly similar, their feet making little noise on the browning detritus of the ground beneath the trees.

Reen says nothing, just taps her bow and gestures upwards with her thumb. The peasant warriors take her point immediately. Each begins to clamber up a tree, trying to keep its trunk between themselves and the rapidly approaching band of 'deserters'.

The grey-haired officer is first to reach the copse. The ruse seems to be working: none of the peasant rabble have broken away from the main combat to follow them. He's halfway through the clump of woodland, still grinning confidently, when an arrow strikes directly down through his skull until its tip pierces the top of his spinal cord. He slumps forwards onto the neck of his horse, which trots on, avoiding any hidden obstacles that might trip it, seemingly oblivious to the fact that its master is dead.

After that, things happen too quickly for the dreamer to know exactly what's going on. He sees a kaleidoscope of different images: dying horses, their hooves thrashing at the shrubbery; men lying in the undergrowth with blood and vomit pouring from their mouths; a peasant dropping with an exultant scream to land on an Ellonian, snapping the man's neck.

Only four of the soldiers are able to escape from the copse. Three die instantly, transfixed by arrows. The fourth, sharper-witted than the others, turns his horse sharply to gallop off to one side, his sword whipping evilly through the air to either side of him.

His blade takes Sinede, moving far too slowly out of his way, just above her nose, and she collapses backwards to lie motionless.

Marja's arrow skewers the Ellonian as he tries to escape.

The peasants regroup, all of them panting not so much from their exertions as from the shock of realising what they've just done.

'We must wait here a little while longer,' Reen says at length, not looking at Marja.

'I agree,' says Marja, and there's a steely bitterness in her voice. 'We wait here. It's a pity the shit died so quickly.

216

But there'll be others who won't.'

Now Reen turns towards her.

The look in Marja's eyes terrifies even Reen.

The dreamer wanted to wake himself, but he couldn't. He'd been a fool to leave the village and allow himself to be taken over in this way. He should have stayed among the peasants, allowing them to goad him constantly away from sleep. He was hoping that he wouldn't see what the black-haired woman called Marja would do to some poor feckless soldier who fell into her merciless hands – and he had the inescapable forboding that one of them would.

But the sequence of dream visions had taken him away to somewhere else, some new vantage point.

If he'd been awake he would have been able to close his eyes, curl up into a little ball, hope all of these images would simply shimmer away into nothingness . . .

Here's a second dream:

Nadar's sword chops down into a peasant's neck and the woman stands there for a moment, not realising yet that she's dead. He puts his booted foot in her chest and pushes her away, so that she topples into a heap, freeing his sword. His horse skitters, unable to understand its master's intentions. He shouts furiously at it, digging his spurs cruelly into its sides so that blood immediately begins to bubble down its flanks.

The noise is deafening, here in the thick of the conflict. Few of the peasants are prepared to attack him, so he must go after them. His sword is so covered in blood that he tries not to look at it. He's slowly working his way closer to the place where the golden man is slaughtering the pride of the Ellonia. That's all he knows, except for the fact that there's a barrier of human flesh between himself and the renegade peasant leader. He tries to pretend, as another body falls, that this means nothing more than hacking his way through a forest.

But the subhumans scream so much, he thinks, and then, irrelevantly: *And she had green eyes.*

The peasant archers have recovered their poise, and once again their deadly rain descends among the Ellonia, killing three of the soldiers for every ragamuffin warrior who dies at the soldiers' hands. Nadar knocks away a shaft with his shield, almost instinctively; his right arm cuts his sword into the belly of a warrior.

There are so many milling people about him now that it's hard for him to force the horse forwards through the crush; the beast itself is terrified by the noise and the crowding.

Nadar severs someone's arm. The man looked almost friendly before trying to slash at Nadar's stirrups with his crudely forged iron sword.

Ploughshares into swords, thinks Nadar. *Seems like the other way round would be a better idea then all this. Maybe if we . . . no, they'd slaughter us all.* He deflects an axe with ease, so that the weapon goes tumbling away into the midst of the fighting people, perhaps killing one of them: who knows? His own attacker is trampled in the kidneys by the rear hooves of Nadar's horse.

These are people, in the Sun's name, Nadar thinks as he kills another person. The ground beneath his horse's hooves is a horrible reddish-brown now; the flax green of the grasses that once grew in this plain has almost completely disappeared; the mixture he sees beneath him is one of mud and blood.

His horse inadvertently stamps on a corpse and Nadar looks to the sky, wishing he could get away from the place he's found himself in.

An arrow strikes his horse in the rump. The injury isn't serious, but it reminds Nadar that there's no longer any way out: he must gain victory or he must die; there's no other alternative.

Behind his visor he's almost weeping. He can hardly see the people he's killing with his sword, which now seems not so much a weapon as an independent being, controlling the movements of his arm so that it can inflict most damage upon the barrier of flesh.

218

His right arm hurts. The sword's heavy and it's been used too often.

Another peasant woman dies, screaming.

Another part of the barrier.

Someone sneaks up and cuts the throat of Nadar's horse, so that the animal moves on only a few more paces, spraying blood over its attackers before collapsing forwards.

Nadar's on his feet, his eyes alight, his sword moving faster than the speed of sight as he attacks the peasants. One moment he's stabbing backwards to remove the groin of an ill-clothed elderly man; the next he's chopping successfully at the ankle tendons of a red-headed woman whom he'd have welcomed as one of his wives.

She falls away from me, yelling the fact that she's dying, and all I can do is keep pushing on towards the man with the fair hair. And the House of Ellon is supposed to be civilisation. Yes, but it has been blessed by the sun. These are animals, remember, nothing more, that we're culling. Yet maybe the Sun is wrong; that's a woman who's bleeding to death, not a slaughtered animal . . .

Lanyor dies as an Ellonian boot, unmindful, treads on her face.

Another shower of arrows. More screams.

Is there no way out of here?

Killing the leader is a minor matter: it can be done any time. Killing the rebellion is something else.

The battle has to be won.

Nadar backs away and looks around to see which of his officers have survived, all the time reflexively cutting at the peasants.

Garndon would never have approved, but there is just a chance that . . .

The dreams are becoming nightmares . . .

Through Lian's eyes Joli sees nothing but a mist of pain.

Not the pain of those dying as the axe-blade hurtles from one side to the other, puncturing veins and arteries so that Anan's white chest is now coloured in a browning red, but

219

the pain of Lian himself. The son of Terman wanted to dethrone the House of Ellon and end their tyranny over the peasant. Now, brought face-to-face with the slaughter of ordinary foot-soldiers, he considers the human cost. Before it seemed to him a fairly simple matter: once the Ellonia were gone, the peasants would be able to control their own futures – ruled, if they needed any rule at all, by someone strong; perhaps, but not necessarily, Lian himself. Such grandiose dreams are a long way away from the dirty business of thrusting the point of an axe into the throat of some poor fool who thought that joining the army was a quick way of getting laid a lot.

The poor fool dies.

Too many poor fools have died.

On both sides.

The dreamer began to scream a thin whining scream as he slept, saliva dribbling from his lips as he rolled on the grass. Within his dream he wished that he could reject these nightmares but knew that that was impossible . . .

Anan has taken a cut on his fetlock, and that enrages Lian more than anything that has gone before, shocking him out of his introspection.

The Ellonian whose sword hurt the animal looks with astonishment at the place where his sword-hand used to be. He Who Leads hardly notices as he turns, his axe still moving in the same deadly swing to chop clean through the leather armour that should have protected the chest of an Ellonian lieutenant.

And the Sun gazes down benignly.

Lian rips away the axe and swings it around, not really looking at where the blade's going. A head spins away and he feels sick.

Yes, Lian thinks, *I'm called 'He Who Leads', but this isn't what I'd wanted to lead my people to.*

Another victim. And another.

Back in the village . . .

The arrow that, from nowhere, strikes him in the buttocks is nothing more than a minor irritation. He snaps it off just above the flesh, hardly noticing the pain as he pushes the point of his axe firmly in through the visor of an Ellonian horseman, so that the man yells his agony before he falls to the ground; Lian has to jerk twice at the haft of his axe before he's free to raise it again.

The dreamer hated what he was seeing.

He knew that the whole thing was a dream and at the same time that it was a reality.

He Who Leads has no idea where Syor might have got to. She's no great fighter, so by now she might be dead, cut apart by an Ellonian sword, her corpse bruised into unrecognisability under the feet and the hooves of the two armies, her face pressed into . . .

No. He doesn't want to think about it.

His cloak is covered with slimy stuff, most of it red. This offends him even more than the necessity of killing, as a flick of his axe chips through to a man's skull and he swerves his body out of the way of a whistling Ellonian sword and hopes that Reen and the others are being successful in their attack from the rear.

A man in a helmet is fighting his way on foot towards He Who Leads with an obvious determination.

The man who was hurt so badly the previous sleeping-period?

Lian's mind wanders for a fraction of a moment, and he almost loses his life as an Ellonian horseman leaps screaming from the saddle, trying to grapple his throat. Then the two of them are on the ground, kicking and punching until He Who Leads knees the man firmly in the balls and one of the peasants leans down obligingly to press, almost gently, a dagger into the soldier's temple.

He Who Leads is on Anan's back again. He's not quite certain how he got there. He has a stinging cut on his left cheek, but he doesn't have time to worry about it.

A sweep of the axe.

Someone's arm.

Rolling away towards the dreamer, although Lian doesn't know this.

The dreamer awoke, screaming into the unsympathetic skies. The blueness seemed to swallow his cry, sucking it away until there was nothing left of it.

But he was too tired, too tired . . .

A final dream:

Marc looks down on the battlefield, his thin face looking worried. He hears the sounds of war and they turn his stomach. His horse moves beneath him. It looks as if the peasants are winning, from here, but he knows in his heart of hearts that, by the end of this waking-period, the war will be lost.

Alyss the singer said almost as much.

Smiling sadly, he pulls a dagger from its sheath at his belt and draws the sharp blade across his throat.

No more dreams.

Nadar was at last free of the throng.

'House of Ellon!' he screamed at the top of his voice. 'House of Ellon – push the peasants back from the golden-haired man!'

A few Ellonian soldiers turned to look at him just long enough to die.

'Scatter them!' Nadar yelled. 'Don't bother killing them – just get them away from their leader!'

It was hard to make his voice heard above the noise of the battle. He looked around him and saw a bugle on the blood-covered grass.

It took him only a few moments to reach the place where the bugler lay dead, his eyes wide open, showing only the whites.

Nadar leaned down, reaching with his left arm for the instrument, and fell heavily.

He told his shoulder firmly that the pain would soon go away, grabbed the bugle from the dead man's hand, and with some effort scrambled back upright.

His vision was swimming, but he put the mouthpiece to his lips and produced a strangled noise.

There was a sudden cessation of movement as peasants and Ellonia alike wondered what was going on.

'Scatter the peasants!' Nadar shouted again. 'Drive them away from each other!'

More than half of the Ellonia died, but the battle was theirs by the end of the waking-period. The further across the open countryside from He Who Leads the fleeing peasants were forced, the less they remembered about why they'd come to this place originally. Nadar watched the whole process with something approaching pity; during the battle he'd learnt that even peasants could display valour and something else, the something his own troops could never achieve: the belief in a cause.

As I expected it'd be, it was just a mopping-up operation, he thought sadly as he saw peasants wandering away bemusedly, not knowing why the soldiers were continuing to chase them, slaying far too many of them with their harsh swords. There were a few groups, near to He Who Leads, who resisted until the bitter end; they died bloodily.

Nadar surveyed a plain filled with corpses, and smiled the cruel smile his troops expected from him.

Green eyes.

The smile hardly wavered.

Lian was hauled in front of him and Nadar gestured that he should be tied up, hand and foot, and taken back with the army to Giorran.

Nadar called to his side a junior officer and detailed him to command a working-party to finish off those soldiers – Ellonians or peasants – who were anyway dying. The officer saluted, rounded up a few suitably callous men, and set about the gory task.

Green eyes . . .

The Ellonia failed to find the woman with the green eyes. She'd buried her head under a corpse, and they assumed that she was dead as well.

A long while later, as they left the plain, none of them

noticed her moving to follow them – to follow the golden-haired man strapped over a horse, his back bleeding from the beating they'd given him.

The wind blew across the plain . . .

The Wind blew across the plain.

The Wind blew across the plain and some of the dead peasants found movement returning to their minds and their limbs. Syor found herself the leader of a small and silent band stalking the Ellonia. The others were warriors, she knew, although she could see them only out of the corners of her eyes – when she tried to look at them directly all she could see were wispy columns of climbing smoke.

Memories were her warriors.

Not enough of an army to save He Who Leads.

No, not enough.

All the same, Syor followed the Ellonia.

PART TWO
She Who Leads

Chapter One
Writings

Now it is a time of nothingness for Syor. All around her the scenery is constantly changing, and therefore constantly the same. She is dimly aware that somewhere, locked away in a dusty attic in her mind, she has memories of these past tumultuous times; but it is an attic to which there are no stairs, so it seems that those memories will remain forever out of her reach. They're like an itch that she can vaguely feel but about whose location on her body she's uncertain.

Sun: the glaring sun. It's watching her as she walks, alone, along the edges of shifting fields or along paths that seem to writhe like serpents ahead of her. The brightness of the light is like a physical force pushing against her, as if she were trying to run through deep water. She's walking very slowly. Syor knows that for some reason she's deeply unhappy; the reasons for her misery are locked away with her memories in the attic. The hot air is trying to crush her, press her to death; perhaps it is her resentment towards it for this gratuitous cruelty that keeps her legs ticking on and on – tap, tap, tap on the hard paths whenever she follows them – so that she can allow her instincts to guide her.

They took a long time to reach Ernestrad, but she has no clear recollection of this now. Nor can she remember what happened there.

Something flits across her vision. It's the image of a fierce dog impaled by a sword. The picture is meaningless to her, and she giggles mindlessly at its absurdity. Two waking-periods later she sees, for an instant, a man's body with blood streaming from it, and she retches into a ditch without knowing why: she has little memory of people with bodies that are unlike her own, and assumes that the blood at his groin indicates that he's menstruating, because that is something she herself has done so often that the knowledge has become a part of her.

There are times of waking and there are times of sleeping. She has no compunction, during her times of waking, about stealing vegetables from the fields through which she rather uncertainly walks. Often the vegetables – mainly cabbages and turnips – taste tart to her, and she frequently suffers agonies of indigestion, so that sometimes she sprawls, squirming, clutching her belly, fouling herself. She walks around each of the sparse villages, avoiding them and their inhabitants without really knowing why she does this.

Moments.

Here's a moment when cattle are watching her dourly. Here's another when sheep run from her footfalls. She can smell her own smell, but doesn't know where it comes from and is hardly concerned. She's more worried by the insects that circle her and sometimes bite or sting her, but the pain lasts for only an instant, after which it is forgotten; she looks at the scabs on her arms and legs and wonders where they've come from.

In another moment Alyss visits her and smiles at her and talks with her, telling Syor that soon, with the foetus growing steadily inside her, things will change for her – although Syor cannot understand the word 'soon' when she hears it and her encounter with the small woman will be immediately forgotten . . . except for one thing. Alyss reports to her that she has transported the writings Syor so painstakingly created to Lianhome, where they are safely waiting. The memory of this remains within Syor only as a dim, deep knowledge that she must try to go to Lianhome and recover the writings: why this should be important, she doesn't know.

Syor kneels beside a stream, reeds moved by a slight wind

tickling the backs of her legs and the soles of her feet. She ignores the sensations and cups her hands to raise some of the lukewarm, crystal-clear water to her lips. Somewhere, in another lifetime perhaps, she swam with someone in a stream like this, but she can recall nothing of it except the feel of the water caressing her naked body as she moved like a seal, flipping herself upwards and downwards through the ripples, touching the soft pebbles with her feet.

She drinks more of the water from her hands and tries to force her mind to concentrate on this memory. The hot sun up above her does its best to pull her away from the picture she had of something that happened in her own past (the sudden concept of 'past' shocks her). She slips off her dress and lowers herself cautiously down into the cold water, her toes recoiling from the soft mud that squelches up between them. The stream is not very deep – certainly too shallow for her to swim in – yet she's able to lie back, supporting herself on her elbows, and feel the water washing over her body. The water invades her, and yet she doesn't resent the intrusion. It fondles her like a lover, without malice, so that she can trustingly lean her head backwards and let her dark hair be spread out by the current. Momentarily losing her balance, she pushes her fingers through her hair, painfully untangling the knots; her face goes under the water at the very moment that she sighs with relief, and she laughs at herself as she splutteringly gets her head up above the surface.

She kneels up in the stream, facing towards the current, and uses her fingers to wash her crotch. She takes a long time over this, loving the experience of the chilly water making her feel clean. Her bottom is a mess, and she knows it, but she can't think of any way of cleaning it that wouldn't repel her. After a while, though, she grabs a handful of reeds from the bank and does the best that she can. The broken stalks of the reeds swirl away down the stream.

Still naked, she drags her besmirched clothing to her and kneads it under the water, half-weeping as she does so. Puffs of greenish-brown swirl up into the water, like clouds of midges. At one and the same time she's revolted by what she's allowed to happen to herself and relieved by the fact that at last she's cleaning herself from the mire of however long it might have been. With great satisfaction, she urinates copiously into the stream, feeling as if poison were being drained from her.

She flounders clumsily towards the bank, dragging her heavy clothes behind her. She suddenly remembers that she has a name and that that name is 'Syor'. The whole concept is mystifying to her as she feels the soapy touch of the mud on her feet and then the harshness against her breasts of the coarse grass.

Throwing her clothes away from her, she relaxes on her back, spreading out her limbs so that the hotness of the sun can dry her.

Yes, she is Syor.

There once was a man called Lian.

He's dead now, killed by the Ellonia.

Nadar.

Nadar tried to rape her, and would have succeeded had it not been for Lian. Isn't it stupid that the attempt to invade her body against her will should now seem so much more important than anything else that happened?

Lian was often so gentle and sometimes, when she wanted him to be, so strong.

Another image in her mind. This time it's a blue-eyed face with a smile crossing it; at first what she sees surrounding it is a halo, but then she realises that it is a tangle of golden hair. Then it's as if she's been thrown backwards, head over heels, so that she can see this man mounted on a huge white horse. *Anan*, she thinks. *Yes, that was the name of the horse: Anan*. Once the stallion had tried to kick her, and Lian had crossed its milky flank furiously with his whip, almost drawing blood.

She is becoming quite frightened. There seems to her to be something *wrong* about these visions that her mind is calling up, as if she were somehow blaspheming. She tries to banish them, but they insist on thrusting their way into her mind. Her eyes closed against the light, she lets a hand wander down over her belly towards the tangle of her pubic hair.

Lian is with her and he never left her and he never will.

Heat brushes her skin and she turns over onto her stomach, hating the sandy feeling of the coarse grass and the scratching of the reeds. A moment later she turns so that once more she's on her back. The cloudless sky is an endless expanse of blue light and looking at it makes her eyes feel as if needles were being gently probed into them.

Syor knows that Lian is still with her, and that she is now possessing him.

For the next few waking-periods Syor had the uncomfortable sensation that someone had painted all of the colours of Albion in far more brilliant hues than any she'd been accustomed to. The cold air she was breathing seemed as refreshing as water. Now she was walking with confidence, rather than following the whims of her feet. She felt as if there was a voice in Lianhome that was calling her towards it, and she paused only to eat or to sleep. Wherever she walked, the land stilled itself, so that no longer was she constantly distracted by seeing, out of the corners of her eyes, the melting horizon and the shimmering fields. She was able to remember in all its miserable clarity the war that Lian's sorry peasant rabble had attempted to wage against the House of Ellon, and the hideous execution that he'd suffered. The memories should have saddened her, but instead they raised her spirits, making her somehow feel more alive. There was a certain spring to her step now as she moved ever more rapidly in a direction that she *chose*. That Lian and so many of her comrades had died was a minor source of sorrow, but no more than that; its pinpricks were as nothing to her overwhelming sensation of exhilaration that she could remember their futile heroism and that she could rejoice in the way they had all been so very much alive for those few years, rather than simply enduring the mistiness of the semi-life to which the peasants had been condemned since the beginning of eternity.

231

As she walked the fields and the lanes and the mountain passes she often found herself singing.

She also discovered that the wild animals had begun to trust her. One waking-period she whistled cheerfully at a hare which had been watching her from the crest of a ridge, its ears bold darts pointing towards the vivid sky. To her astonishment it raced towards her, its body moving fitfully as it came swiftly through the mossy grass. For some time it followed behind her, letting her move a short distance ahead and then pursuing her as fast as it could to be beside her. On one or two occasions she paused when it overtook her and reached down to stroke her fingernails through the fur between its ears and down the bony line of its spine; then it would lean back, showing its yellowing teeth as if it were smiling at the touch of her hand. The hare stayed with her in its stopping-and-starting way for most of a waking-period; then she was joined by a kestrel, which fluttered down rapidly to settle itself on her shoulder, its claws digging into her with comforting pain. The hare slunk away. She looked behind her and saw it staring at her as if she'd betrayed its love.

For a short while the presence of the kestrel's sharp beak so close to her eyes made her feel uneasy, but then she became accustomed to it. She talked to the bird from time to time as if it were a blind companion who needed to have the landscape described; sometimes she explained that she was going to Lianhome in the hope that somehow she could discover her writings there. It was a wan hope, she knew; but it was the only hope she could sustain. As the kestrel moved its head twitchingly from side to side, its flicking orange-specked eyes seemed to be telling her that it understood what she was saying. She grinned at her own foolishness, but carried on talking nevertheless.

'Have you a name, my friend?' she said, stepping carefully around the crumbling edge of a huge pot-hole that stretched almost the full width of the road. The bird made a small hissing sound, startling her so that she almost lost her balance.

Once she'd left the pot-hole behind and her heart was

232

beating more easily, she resumed the one-sided conversation.

'Everyone should have a name,' she said, beginning to giggle at her overreaction to the bird's whiffling noise, 'and I don't see why animals should be any different. Do you?'

This time, to her relief, there was no response.

'Lian, and his father before him, said that names were the greatest gift he could give us – greater even than release from those shits of the House of Ellon. Would you like me to give you a name?'

The kestrel looked bored.

'I've got a name. Lian gave it to me.'

They were passing under a tree whose leaves and smaller twigs were dancing to soft, tuneless music. She paused for a moment and watched the shadows moving across the packed earth in front of her, creating patterns that never stayed the same for longer than the time it took to glance at them.

'Yes' – walking on again, her brief fascination with the shadows having evaporated – 'he gave me his love and more than that, but the best thing of all the things he gave me was my name. Let me introduce myself. I'm called Syor.'

Again the bird didn't react. She looked sideways and was fascinated by its cold, unemotional eyes and by the brown and grey tapestry of its feathers.

'No,' she said. 'It's more than that, you see. It's not just that I'm *called* Syor – it's that I *am* Syor. Before Lian gave me my name I wasn't anything at all . . . just another woman from my village, which was just like all the other villages until Lian named it, too.'

She stopped suddenly. To her right was a vast field of rape-seed, its colour such a vast expanse of brilliant yellow-green that it seemed impossible that such a thing could exist in nature. From the base of the primitive wall that separated her from the field came the distinctive tang of wild garlic. She breathed deeply.

'I suppose I could have been happy, like that,' she said, her eyes feeling salty, 'and I suppose most of the other women were. Living out their lives, I mean. No, "living"

233

is the wrong word. Just existing. Tending the fields until their backs broke, and then working on a little longer – not really feeling the pain of what they were doing, because pain only hurts you if you can remember what it was like in the past and know that it's going to last into the future. If you pecked at me now, my friend – and I do ask you not to – I'd feel all the pain of the wound you'd given me. I'd probably also wring your neck, because I'd be angry with you: I'd know you'd committed me to some days of pain. If I'd stayed in my village with the others – women *and* men – I'd never have felt either the pain or the anger.

'Without pain, you see,' Syor continued, exasperated with herself because Lian would inevitably have explained it all so much better, 'you can never feel the opposite of pain. Right now I enjoy the fact that you're with me – gripping my shoulder a little too tightly, if you don't mind me saying so. Lian gave me joy as well, and the joy was that he took away the endless greyness of the existence that was all that I had had before.'

Now the kestrel looked at her, and she persuaded herself that it was asking her to keep on talking. She half-tripped on a stone that protruded from the road's surface, and the bird flapped its wings nervously.

'So Lian gave me happiness. Sadness too, of course. And the way he did it was to tell me that I had a name, and that it was my own. It was the first thing that had ever belonged to me.'

Syor looked left and right, her eyes moving swiftly. The call of Lianhome was coming from *over there*. Without having to make any conscious decision about the direction in which she was going, she waded through a shallow but swift-moving stream; she felt the coldness of the water rushing against her shins, but it seemed to be a long way away. Moments later, as she walked across a field of grass that had been chewed almost down to the soil by hungry cattle, the droplets of moisture had vanished from her legs and from the hem of her skirt.

'So, would you like a name? At a guess you would.'

It was good to have someone to talk to.

The kestrel leaned sideways and plucked a hair from her head. The momentary pain was a pleasure.

'Well, whether or not you want one, here it is. From here on, my friend, you'll be known as . . .'

Her self-confidence fled.

For the first and last time she thought she heard the kestrel speak.

'I don't want a name,' it said in a rather hoarse voice.

Then it flew away from her shoulder, fleeing across the bright blueness of the sky that hovered above the flat landscape of Albion.

Once upon a time, as Syor would later recall it, *there was a woman who stood at the top of a ridge, smoothing back her hair from her forehead, annoyed with herself because she felt she should be more beautiful. Spread out before her was the village she would come to know as Lianhome; even from here she could see a few of the people moving about their business listlessly. One or two of them were obviously confused, although none of them looked up towards the place where the woman was standing.*

'Yes, Mummy,' said the little girl to whom Syor was telling the story, 'but who was the woman?'

'It was me.'

'Why?'

'Because . . . look, blast it, because it couldn't have been anybody else. If it hadn't been for you I'd never have reached here. I didn't really know why at the time, but I do know now. You were a part of me, Anya, but also a part of Lian, and Lian passed on to you something his father had given to him.'

Anya was very proud of the fact that she was now old enough to walk properly, the same way that grown-ups did. She demonstrated this by hopping off her mother's lap and teetering around in an uncertain circle. On her return she threw herself down on Syor's thighs, breathing heavily as if exhausted from the heat, even though she was wearing nothing more than a light woollen dress. Syor felt the tight little tummy of her daughter against her flesh and ran a teasing finger down the ridge of her nose. Syor loved the way the laughing child wriggled like a fish at her touch.

'You were there when my father died?'

Half of the words were serious, half of them spoken in laughter.

The smile left Syor's face.

'Yes, I was there when he died.'

'Why is it that you knew how to come here?' said Anya, still laughing, ignorant of the new stiffness of her mother's body.

'Because I learnt to remember things,' Syor said after a while. She was sitting on a poorly made bench just outside the door of a house that had once been occupied by a pair of people called Lantz and Gred. Someone called Terman, of whom Syor knew only what Lian had told her, had given them those names. For all she knew, he'd also created the bench, in which case she directed her petty hatred towards him; it was extremely uncomfortable.

'I could remember things because you were growing inside me, and that meant I could find my way back to Lianhome.'

Syor ruffled her hand through her daughter's hair, feeling its smooth silkiness.

With the memories had also come, not glimpses of the future, but a recognition of what the future must hold. In her mind's eye she had seen the columns of smoke, riders dressed in red and green, and the flash of reflected sunlight from sharp blades, reddened and rusted by blood. But she kept her dark premonitions from Anya, wondering at the same time if she were doing the right thing. After all, the child would learn, one day. *And let that day be a long way from us*, she breathed, *a long time after I'm dead and forgotten*.

When she'd first come to Lianhome the people had forgotten Terman and Lian altogether; they had some vague recollection that once, a long time ago, people had been among them who had made things different; who had allowed them to know that what happened in the next waking-period might not be the same as what had happened in this one. That was all. By then she'd known that she was carrying Lian's child. She didn't know whether or not she ought to be proud; for all she knew or cared, there might be a thousand women in Albion who could make the same claim.

But Alyss had said she'd brought the writings here.

And she seemed to have brought Reen, too.

At first Syor didn't know how Reen had made her way to Lianhome, let alone how she had discovered the house where Lian had been born to Mina. The dark-eyed woman had simply appeared on the doorstep as Syor arrived and had embraced her as if the two of them were sisters – which, Syor thought, in a way they were. So many of their comrades had died; of Lian's initial band of inexperienced volunteers, it seemed likely that only she and Reen had survived.

'Careful,' Syor had said, pulling away after a while. She had touched her belly, which was just beginning to show a new roundness. 'Is it the same with you?'

She bore no rancour. It had been Lian's duty to try to father children, and she knew that he and Reen had occasionally been lovers. Still, she felt a tiny pinprick of grief, just for a moment.

'No,' said Reen. 'I'm not pregnant.'

She led Syor through to the kitchen, which was a mess.

'Housekeeping's never been one of my fortes,' she said, for once seeming a little nervous, perhaps even guilty. She swept some litter off a wooden chair and sat Syor down, then brought her a cupful of warm water.

'Lian and I . . . well, it just didn't work.'

She pointed at her groin, her hand drooping flaccidly, and shrugged.

'With Marja it was different, but Marja's dead now.'

'I'm sorry,' said Syor. 'So many of us died.'

She drank the water in a single draught and put the empty cup down on the cluttered table. There was a long silence between them, both of them thinking about Marja. She'd always been in the shadow of Reen, somehow – as if she'd spent much of her energy trying to be *like* her lover.

'I'm not,' said Reen a while later.

'Not sorry that Marja's dead?' said Syor, incredulously. She crossed her legs and leaned forward, balancing both elbows on her knee.

'No. Of course I'm sorry about that.'

Reen waved her hand angrily at a wasp. It seemed to be buzzing in terror as it fled out through the window. Her eyes were glittering as she looked almost sternly at Syor.

'Never say that again,' Reen's voice was cold. 'Marja was my lover, and while we were together I thought that no one would ever replace her. But she's dead now, and there's no way of changing that. For a while I thought I should just do my best to forget her, but then I thought no, that's wrong: why should I try to forget her? Instead, wasn't it better to remember her? In a while I'll probably have another lover, and give that person all the love I have; but giving love *now* doesn't depend on the forgetting of the love I felt *then*.'

She shifted awkwardly.

'In fact, it's the very opposite.'

'I know,' said Syor, her voice very quiet. 'Lian was my life, but when he died I felt nothing. No, "nothing" is the wrong word. I felt a lot, but most of it was selfishness: I wanted him to continue to live because I wanted him to be beside me whenever I felt lonely. The touch of his hand in mine – that kind of thing. Sometimes I think I was never really in love with him at all, just told myself that I was because for a time he was like a light that shone over everything I saw.'

She stared at the dirty straw on the floor.

'You felt nothing for him?' Reen took more water from a pail in the corner, refilling Syor's cup and this time taking one for herself.

'For a while I felt his pain as if it were my own. Later, things changed. When he died all I could think of was that he was dead and that I'd been deprived of him. As I told you, it was selfishness. I'm sorry that he couldn't make love with you.'

Reen interrupted.

'He loved you.'

Syor smiled and was annoyed that the smile was a sad one.

'He loved you,' Reen continued, 'but he loved the rest of us as well. You're deceiving yourself if you think anything else. You were the cornerstone of his life, and if you'd ever insisted that you be his only lover he'd have accepted that. But he had too much love in him to confine it to just the one person. When I was in bed with him and Marja I could *feel* his love for her. He wanted to give, not to take. One time when he wanted to express his love to me and – to be blunt, couldn't get it up – he was nearly weeping. He felt as if somehow he was insulting me by not wanting my body. I stroked him all over his back until he fell to sleep; then I fell asleep with my arms around him and Marja's arms around mine. That was love. That was the love he wanted to give to everybody. Just the closeness. Don't pretend to yourself that he was using his women as breeding stock.'

'You're frank,' said Syor, wishing that she could take some of the harshness out of the words.

'True. Would you rather I lied to you?'

For a few moments Syor held her breath.

'No,' she said, half-reluctantly.

'Good. Can we be friends?'

Syor giggled, suddenly feeling as if she were walking among the clouds.

'Of course. What else could we be?'

They walked around the house, exploring its clumsily built wooden staircases and rooms. A half-feral cat that had adopted Reen, its fur coloured in a curious mixture of grey and pink, scampered around their ankles, so that they had to move cautiously. The tension that had been between them had now evaporated, and they were laughing as they swore at the cat.

'Where did you get it?' asked Syor.

'It got me.'

The house was a small one, as Lian had told her. What

he hadn't told her about – *couldn't* have told her about – was the thick layer of greasy dust that covered everything. Reen had made an attempt at cleaning out one of the bedrooms, so that the white-painted walls were now streaked with dark stains where she'd tried to wash away the filth. At least the sparse bedding didn't stink of ancient dampness, as it did in the other room.

'I think I'll wash this,' said Syor glumly.

'No,' said Reen. 'Let me do it.'

'No,' said Syor firmly. '*I'll* do it.'

She picked up the crudely woven blankets and smiled a little wistfully at the patches which someone – Mina, she guessed – had worked into them. The patches were what affected her. They had been clumsily done, but Syor felt as if they represented a strand of life that ran down from Mina through Lian to the child she herself was carrying. They represented a bond between the next generation after hers and the one before hers.

There was more than sentimentality to this feeling of hers, as she recognised. Had it been Mina's grandmother who'd repaired the bedding, Mina or her parents might never have realised who had been responsible. To Syor, by contrast, the repairs were messages handed down to her through time. And they also told her that Lian and the army that he'd led had succeeded in taking something from the House of Ellon: a gift – time itself – that the tyrants had hoarded for their own exclusive use.

For a while it had been a gift that she'd lost, but it had now been returned to her by the foetus growing inside her.

Lian's child.

Perhaps, only one of many of his children.

But *his* child, nevertheless. And, more importantly, *hers*.

She bundled the blankets against her chest and laughed at the expression on Reen's face. 'Yes, they stink. It showed, didn't it?'

'Too bloody right it did. Let me help you.'

'No. They're mine, now.'

They descended the rickety stairs, where darkness seemed to be trying to spread. Reen went first, her feet rattling down the steps two at a time. Syor followed more cautiously, her mass of bedding clutched in front of her, looking over it circumspectly at each new tread in case she lost her footing.

It was good to be back in the brightness at the bottom of the stairs.

'There's a stream or a river where I can wash these?'

'Yes. Let me help you.'

'No. I told you: they're mine. But come with me. I'd be glad if you came along with me.'

Syor had sudden visions of Lian with his hair an incandescent torch against the ever-bright sky. Her eyes glistened, but she refused to allow herself tears.

Reen's black hair had grown since Syor had last seen her, and now she tossed it impatiently away from her forehead. She looked angry.

'I'll show you the way.' The words were spoken dully.

'Thank you.'

Syor wondered what she'd said to offend the smaller woman. The two of them would be lost – both to the world and to each other – unless they learned how to read each other's emotions better.

'Come on,' said Reen. 'If we go now they'll be dry by the end of the waking-period.' She gestured at the blankets in Syor's arms. 'Let me carry some of them.'

'If you're sure . . . ?'

'Yes.'

So soon, thought Syor, *and already we've developed a strange parody of formality between us. We might be mistresses at Ernestrad, locked in a duel over some puffed-up minor scion of the House of Ellon, yet constricted by the formalities from going with tooth and nail for each other's eyes. All this over washing soiled blankets.*

Syor dropped the mass of bedding onto the floor and immediately wished that she hadn't. The untreated planks were filthy, covered with smudges of earth where Reen had blithely walked to and from the door, insouciantly ignoring any marks that she made.

'Thanks,' said Syor, pretending.

Between the two of them they divided up the patched blankets. Each of them now had two. It seemed to Syor that the division of labour was ridiculous – all four blankets together weighed little enough – and then she recognised that what Reen was searching for was a symbol. They were sharing something. It didn't matter how trivial it was: all that was important was the sharing.

'Thanks,' she repeated as Reen stood up, and this time she put more warmth into her voice.

'Thanks for saying "thanks".' Reen's voice was brusque and patronising.

Syor stopped where she was and stamped her foot. In the enclosed space the impact on the planks was almost deafening, and both of them flinched away from it.

'Fuck it, Reen! We have to help each other, don't we? Stop taking up these positions that I can't understand.'

Reen looked at her with a gaze that was a mixture of arch knowingness and fright. She remembered Syor as a very gentle person – ruthless in the field of combat, sometimes, but outside it quiet and often withdrawn. There was something new about Syor, and Reen both liked it and disliked it. Lian's mate seemed to have discovered a strength that Reen had never seen in her before.

'We're friends,' she said curtly.

'Yes. Friends. We need to be. If not, we're nothing.' Syor looked down at the blankets she was holding. 'If we're not friends we might as well . . . oh, I don't know, just go and drown ourselves in the river and leave these bloody blankets on the bank for someone else to use. At the moment it's as if we were competing for the ghost of Lian, or as if we were trying to score points over each other in order to establish a pecking order. A pecking order of *two* is a bit on the ridiculous side, isn't it?'

Reen patted her on the shoulder, and there was affection in the gentle touch.

'I told you, we're friends.'

'Let's not fight against each other,' said Syor, 'and especially let's not fight against each other over Lian. We loved him in our different ways: let's respect the difference and leave the rest of it alone.'

The stream, when they reached it, was moving reluctantly between banks of great rocks that had been smoothed over the ages until they were like grey-green mother-of-pearl. Syor guessed that sometimes the waters must move into spate, washing over the banks to harry the soil and the stones. A small group of children watched the two women with open mouths, and Syor grinned to herself. *If I've brought nothing else back to the people of Lianhome*, she thought, *at least I've instilled in the children some sense of inquisitiveness.*

Then her lips thinned.

Well, for a little while, she thought.

The mate of Lian, who had once seemed to have Albion at his feet, and the great rebel's most trusted lieutenant soaked the blankets in the moving lukewarm water and beat them against the slithery rocks, time and time again. The children continued to watch, although a few of them became bored and peeled off from the others to find new games to play. Every now and then either Syor or Reen would stop to ease the aching muscles in their backs, putting their hands just above their hips and stretching backwards until it seemed that their spines might crack; then, after a few moments, they returned to their task.

Until at last the chore was done. The brown bloodstains and the grey, spotty incursions of mould had finally disappeared.

Reen held one of the blankets to her face, water running down over her tunic, and laughed.

'Smells all right to me,' she said, pulling the cloth away from her mouth.

'You can't tell when it's still wet,' muttered Syor with difficulty, grunting as she industriously hammered a blanket down onto the marbled stone surface.

'We've done enough,' said Reen. 'This is as good as we're going to get them.'

Syor privately agreed, but to prove some obscure point she continued to beat the blanket for a short time longer. Then, her whole body aching with fatigue, she stopped.

'Perhaps you're right.'

They spread the blankets out over the yellowed grass some distance back from the stream, flattening the long stems, and glared so ferociously at the few remaining children that they fled in terror. At least the blankets wouldn't suffer their inquiring, but none too clean, fingers . . . The sun beat down everywhere, and steam rose in wisps and trails from the wet cloth.

Syor and Reen lay down on their backs on either side of the expanse of damp cloth, as if it represented some tacit boundary between them. Both stared at the cloudless blue of the sky, their hands behind their necks. A dandelion tickled Syor's nose irritatingly and she moved to pluck it away; then she stayed her hand and instead moved her head. The dandelion was a part of the Albion in which Lian had taught her to believe. Let the dandelion live.

'You're carrying Lian's child,' said Reen at last, stretching in the heat of the sun.

Syor smiled. Reen was saying something they both already knew. It wasn't like Reen to utter truisms, so clearly the intense young woman was using the statement as a way of introducing some topic about which she was nervous.

'Yes,' she agreed, addressing her words to the sky.

'That,' said Reen, 'is why you can remember things. That's why we're here speaking to each other right now.'

'I think that's true. Yes.'

'No, it's not quite true,' Reen brushed away an inquisitive fly from her face. 'It's why you can speak to me. It doesn't explain why I was able to find my way here.'

'I know. That's why I thought you might have been bearing Lian's child, too.'

For a short while there was little noise around them except the whirring of small insects and the soft stroking of a breeze through the grass. Syor felt as though she were looking upwards through a long chimney of browning stalks, seeing the waving, spiny heads at the top of the chimney and, beyond them, a roughly defined circle of blue. To her surprise, a feathery edge of thin cloud was intruding into the circle.

'I'm not,' said Reen at last, her voice seeming to Syor to be coming out of that halo of sky. 'I told you that. No, something else brought me here. Something in the house.'

Syor sighed.

'What was it?' she said.

'That's the worst of it: I don't know. Truthfully, I just don't know. After Lian died I wandered: I can vaguely remember drifting wherever the wind took me, sleeping in fields or in crofters' cottages and being given food by the people I met. For a time, my memories tell me, I trailed along as a camp-follower of a band of the Ellonia – I think I could probably remember more about that, but I try not to. Anyway, it wasn't *me* that was the Ellonians' whore, if I was: it was only the "me" that existed between the times that Lian was among us and this time now.'

Syor was astonished to hear the emotion in Reen's voice. She herself had grown so familiar with her memories of her occasional whoredom, born of necessity, that they no longer troubled her; it was like trying to recall, a long while later, a meal of boiled grain or stewed pulses. She had eaten because she'd needed to be fed, and she'd given her body from time to time for exactly the same reason: if the only way to be fed had been to sell her body then she had accepted the situation, finding the act as boring as the eating of her reward. To Reen it had clearly all meant a lot more.

'I'm sorry,' she said.

Another pause. The cloud, a tiny patch of striated milk, swam across the frame of blue that Syor could see and vanished as slowly as it had arrived.

Reen cleared her throat.

'I've no idea how long that lasted,' she said. It sounded to Syor as if she were speaking more to the sky or the grass than to anyone else. 'Then there was a waking-period when everything seemed to alter. It might have been easier if it hadn't – easier for me, I mean. I can remember exactly the moment when things changed. I was sitting at a badly made wooden table which rocked abruptly whenever you put your elbow on it. Of course, I was a guest in this hovel, and I kept forgetting, so the broth the family who were looking after me had served up was slopping around in the bowls. They laughed at me every time it happened, and I laughed with them because the crass humour of what I'd done seemed to fill all of Albion for that moment. I guess you know that feeling.'

'Yes,' said Syor, picking a stalk of grass and playing with its soft end against her upper lip. *When Lian died it was like that, only the sensation was the antithesis of sensation: I was staring into a vacuum that was all creation and all eternity.*

'And then something tugged at me.' Reen breathed so deeply that Syor could hear her. The warrior, more at home with stabbing blades, was searching for words. 'It was as if,' she said eventually, 'I was a fish in the river, swimming lazily along and not noticing the water going by me, and then a hook had snagged me by the gill. The fisherman was asleep, so he didn't immediately start drawing in the line. The hook had nocked close enough to the edge of the gill that it wouldn't have caused me too much pain to pull away, leaving a scrap of my flesh behind, but I chose not to. I just hung there in the water, moving my tail easily from side to side, holding my stillness against the push of the current, and felt the sting of the wound, rolling over and over in my mind what this new sensation could mean. Sorry, I'm not explaining this very well.'

'You're doing all right,' said Syor, imagining Reen's dark, concentrated eyes screwing up against the light as she tried to express something that couldn't be described in terms of death or glory.

'Hmmm,' said Reen noncommittally. Nevertheless, she continued.

'Any wise fish'd have pulled away then: the wound would've been forgotten almost before it had been felt. But I wasn't a wise fish. That tug at me had stirred up something in my mind that I'd forgotten was there, during the time that I was drifting. I was *curious* to know what it was that was tugging at me.'

She laughed briefly, as if angry with herself.

'I can't imagine a fish turning its head around to have a closer look at the hook,' she said, 'but that's what I did. I looked at the hook and, although I didn't at first recognise it for what it was – it had come here from another world entirely, a world I'd never known, the world above that mirror-like surface above my head – I knew in a misty sort of way that there was some purpose for it being there. So for a while I kept hanging there in the water, not so much thinking as letting the presence of the hook create thoughts inside me. This was a messenger from somewhere I could never go to . . . and yet there began to grow inside me a sort of half-conviction that I'd *been there*.'

Syor took the stalk of grass, its tip now chewed until all the sweetness had gone, and held it delicately between her thumb and first finger. Smiling to herself, she threw it like a spear.

'So you turned,' she said. 'You turned and you swam in the direction of the line, just to see what was at the other end.'

'That's right,' Reen agreed eagerly. 'I pushed away my broth, stood up, said farewell to the farmer and his family, and left. Was that what happened to you?'

'Not exactly, no. But the same sort of thing. And what did you find when you pulled yourself up through the surface of the water?'

'I found I was near this place – near Lianhome. I was in a glen somewhere back in the hills, so I couldn't see the place – and, even if I'd been able to, I wouldn't have had a clue as to where it was. I'd no idea where I'd come to or why I'd done so. I was just there – that was all. But the fisherman had me now: there was no way that I could escape. I went tripping and scrambling through the heather and gorse as if I were being physically dragged here. When I arrived I wasn't so much a human being as a butchered animal that could still walk. The children screamed and ran away.' Reen chuckled. 'So did the adults.'

Syor pictured the scene: the half-flayed woman staggering along the dusty road through the centre of Lianhome, the blood bright against her torn muscles.

Syor didn't echo Reen's chuckle. Instead she said: 'But you're cured, now.'

'Yes. There are no such things as miracles, of course, but I was lucky enough to find one.'

Syor sat up abruptly. 'What do you mean?' she hissed.

Reen raised a hand above the level of the grass and waved it with teasing delicacy.

'All in good time,' she said. 'There I was, more dead than alive and mainly wishing that I was the former. The place seemed to be occupied just by ghosts, although I knew that there were people watching me from every dark corner. And I also sensed that the fisherman's creel was not so very far away. I turned, thinking of running – oh, how I wished I could run away from here – but there was no escape. It wasn't me but the fisherman that drew me through the dust and the packed earth until I came to a dingy little house, half-way up a side street that curled a little way towards the hills. I was crawling by now: all I could see were the soil and pebbles of the roadway and the slashed flesh of my splayed hands as they moved, one behind the other, over and over again. Then something told me to look up, and I did.

'There, barely an arm's length ahead of me, was a grey wall of badly joined wooden boards. I forced myself back onto my haunches and made my eyes focus properly on it. I could see it was a rickety old door, sagging on its hinges. For a moment or two it seemed to me as if there was a "taboo" symbol burnt into the wood, but as I watched it faded. I crawled a little further forwards and pushed at the door and it opened wide to let me in. There's a sort of blank after that; then I was sitting in one of those uncomfortable chairs Lian's grandfather must have made, looking around me at the room.'

Syor relaxed back into the grass. If the warrior didn't want to be hurried, she wouldn't be. There was no point in pressing her. Letting her eyes glaze over, Syor listened to Reen's descriptions of the filth, of the shafts of sunlight glowing softly in the floating motes of dust, of the way that the pain seemed to ebb from her while she sat there. The few cotton furnishings there had been in the cottage had long since rotted away, leaving curious corded patterns across the bleakness of the grey floor. A misshapen mirror hanging on one wall was distinguishable only as a blacker mark against its background.

And then suddenly Syor was awake again.

'I was by the side of the fisherman's creel,' Reen was saying, 'but I wasn't yet actually in it. I could feel his hands around my belly now as he picked me up; the grip wasn't unkind, but it was firm – I knew throughout me that I would be unable to break it, no matter how hard I might try to struggle, so I simply acquiesced.

'I pulled myself up off the chair and shuffled towards the foot of the staircase – barely more than a ladder – that led to the upper storey of the house. The rungs looked dangerously weak and rotted, but I was hardly giving a thought to my own safety by now: as far as I was concerned, although I'd been brought back to life, I'd already died once; even if I died a second time, I'd still been given that gift of a little extra life.

'I needn't have worried. The old wooden cross-bars protested in a crotchety sort of way, but despite their grumbles they bore my weight. I suppose I'd expected to see something dramatically new, but all there was was another stretch of dusty floor. There was a wall just to my right, with a door in it. To my left was a desert of dust which was interrupted only by the legs of a couple of beds and the bottoms of the two uprights of a second ladder. If the one I'd just climbed had looked dangerous, this one looked positively suicidal.'

Reen giggled again. Syor smiled. She liked the sound. Reen was exorcising old memories that had clearly haunted her for far too long.

'Well?' she said.

'Well,' said Reen, 'I forced myself across that fucking floor – I still haven't got rid of all of the splinters – until I got to the bottom of the ladder, and then I pushed myself up against it until I was standing erect.'

The timbre of Reen's voice changed.

'That was very painful – more painful than anything I could remember. I felt as if I were leaving my guts behind me on the floor, and I would have looked down to check that I wasn't except I knew that looking down was the last thing I should do. The fisherman still had a grip of me, you see; he was still dragging me towards the inside of the creel.

'So I made myself start climbing. Again. There were only three rungs this time, so it didn't seem to be so bad – or, at least, the pain didn't. Pain *hurts*, but it's something you can force yourself to conquer, to cope with. No, what was worse was this terrible feeling of *fear* that started to seep through me. At first I didn't even notice it was there, but then it became so great that I almost turned back. Maybe fish feel like that, right towards the end. "Fear" – perhaps that's the wrong word. Perhaps "dread" would be better.

'Whatever the word you want me to use, I could feel as if pushing on towards the little attic was something that I *had* to do, not just for myself but for the whole of Albion; and at the same time I knew – as clearly as I know I'm lying here in the grass – that by going into that attic I was going to start things all over again. I was going to be responsible – me, no one else – for people dying in starvation or under the sword or stabbed by the sharp daggers of the flames. It was going to be worse this time around, worse than it had been when Lian led us.'

Syor punctured the moment by laughing out loud, pressing the flats of her hands against the ground and swivelling her heels into the friable soil between the grasses.

'Reen,' she said after she'd calmed a little, 'you're supposed to be the warrior of the two of us. You're supposed to *like* the idea of blood. Don't you know that, ever since I realised I was bearing Lian's child, it was obvious to me that the times of destruction would be upon us once again? I've learned to live with it, Reen!'

'Don't,' said Reen grimly. 'Don't ever learn to live with death. Once you start doing that, you're a part of death yourself.' Then she paused for a short time.

'There was a small skylight in the attic,' she continued at last, 'and it let in a surprising amount of the sunshine. It had also let in a surprising amount of rain since anyone

250

had last been here. I was astonished that the ceiling beneath me hadn't collapsed. There didn't seem to be much up there but dribs and drabs of assorted junk heaped up around the walls, against the slopes of the roof. Except for one thing: right in the middle of the floor, as if someone had cleared a space for it, there was a small, untidy pile of curling bits of bark. The fisherman. I knew it was the fisherman as soon as I saw it.

'It took me half a lifetime before I was touching one of the bits of bark with the tip of a finger, and then I just lay there, waiting for death to take me.

'And I lay there, and lay there.

'For the smallest moment the worst agony I've ever known made me scream out loud. Everything disappeared except the pain.

'When I could see again, I was crouched up against the barks, holding them as if they were my child, being infinitely gentle with them for fear of reducing them to tinders. And I felt my body becoming whole again. As I watched, the ribbons of flesh along the backs of my forearms knotted themselves together into broader strands and then smoothed down, coalescing to form strong skin beneath which I could see the curve of my muscles. My shoulders, which had been aching for as long as I could remember, tingled so strongly that I almost started laughing – it was just as if someone were tickling me – and then I could feel the pain melt away to be replaced by a strength even greater than they'd had before. It was the same all over.

'The fisherman. This pile of dried-out bits of wood. I couldn't understand it. Yet the funny thing was that in a sort of a way I *could*: it was as if the whole thing was somehow quite natural, just that it wasn't the sort of "naturalness" we're used to. It's hard to explain.'

Syor shivered. Sometimes she, too, had felt that, beyond the curtains that marked the edge of the world, there might be a different sort of 'natural'. Every now and again she'd feel as if the skin between herself and it were wearing thin, and she'd move mentally away as quickly as she could, chilled by the closeness of the almost-contact.

251

'They were just barks, you say?'

'No,' said Reen, 'not *just* barks. There were magical carvings on them. I tried to look at them more closely, but every time I did so they sort of curled up and wriggled away until they were just outside the scope of my vision. That's not what really happened, of course – just what it felt like. It was as if my eyes could see them, and they could tell my brain what they were seeing, but that my brain didn't want to *know* what they were seeing. I've thought it all over several times since, and that's the nearest I can get to describing the sensation to myself. I doubt if I can . . .'

'My writings!' yelled Syor. 'They've come here!'

She leapt to her feet, her matted hair slapping her cheeks and the nape of her neck. Without looking behind her, she bolted towards the outskirts of Lianhome.

'My writings!' she shouted yet again.

'The blankets are dry now,' muttered Reen, gathering them together.

Crouching in the attic, the tops of their heads just touching above the pile of fragile wood and parchment. Syor's breath coming in swift, shallow pants; Reen breathing more slowly, but nevertheless infected by her comrade's elation. *Syor*, thought Reen, *is like a seducer who, after many years of courtship, is finally and almost reverentially peeling away the garments of the only woman she has ever loved, and the only woman who has never before freely given up her body in response to the blandishments*. Reen wondered where the thought had come from and then, looking inside herself, she knew the answer. *To think I'd never realised that before*, she thought, her eyes flicking towards Syor's brown knees. The insight seemed to have come to her from the old barks that Syor called her 'writings'.

'Writings.' It was a word that Reen knew she had encountered before, and yet maddeningly it refused to come into focus in her mind. Words always had meanings, Lian had taught them. In the same way that names reified people and objects, so words captured ideas – and sometimes made

252

them bigger than they'd been before. Once upon a time in the long ago, when Lian had been among them, Syor and Lian had often talked about Syor's 'writings', but Reen had paid very little attention; at the time it had been her duty to help win a war, not toy intellectually with the new words and concepts that Lian created every waking-period. She had learnt the words if they had any applicability to their military position; the concepts she'd almost always dismissed as irrelevant to her activities.

Then she realised that the sounds Syor was making were more than just little gasps. There was an undertone of something else mixed in with the green-eyed woman's urgent breathing. As Syor moved from one piece of bark to the next, sometimes holding a parchment open, handling each of them with a delicacy Reen had never known her to possess, there was a steady flow of words. The words weren't spoken: they were simply formed instinctively by Syor's lips, tongue and vocal cords, so that as she breathed out they could be faintly heard.

Too faintly, like a conversation held just tantalisingly too far away.

All Reen could do was to let the warm glow of the words touch her skin and seep through into her. Just the knowledge that those bizarre and still somewhat frightening scratches on the bark could *mean* something filled her with a new confidence. Who had made the scratches was something she still didn't fully comprehend; why that person had made them was even further beyond her understanding. Through the misty barricade of the time when she had been mindless – the no-time between the death of Lian and the call she had received to come here – she captured blurred images of Syor, her back against a tree or a bank, her face twisted into a parody of itself as she concentrated on the bit of wood in front of her and the sharpened twig in her hand.

Could the pieces of bark be speaking to Syor? Was that what Reen was hearing? Maybe it was just an illusion that the susurration was coming from Syor's mouth – maybe the bits of wood were themselves infested with such magic that they could speak, and Syor was drawing the words *in* through her lips, rather than breathing them out?

'Reen,' said Syor at last, squatting back so that her buttocks rested comfortably between her heels and looking intently into Reen's dark eyes. 'Reen, there's something wrong here.'

'Wrong? How?'

'You know what these are.' A casual gesture towards the carefully arranged litter of barks. Of course Reen knew what they were.

'No,' she said.

'My writings.' Syor looked impatient.

'I don't know anything about writings except that they cure people. Well, they cured me.'

'I *made* these writings.'

'Then you're a great physician.' Reen kept the sarcasm out of her voice. Some of the peasants could help superficial injuries heal more quickly by applying carefully chosen and usually noxious selections of herbs, but only the House of Ellon could call upon those mystics who had mastered the magical arts to the extent that they could restore people's health. Reen's attitude, when wounded, was simply to wait until the sore scabbed over and healed itself.

But you'd have died if you hadn't been drawn here to the writings, said a voice inside her. *The sores would never have scabbed over, and they'd never have healed themselves.*

'*Are* you a great physician?' asked Reen after a little while, this time with less authoritativeness.

'No,' replied Syor. Lifting her gaze to study Reen's face, she grinned again.

'I'm just another peasant girl like yourself, Reen,' she said. 'I've got no more idea than you have why just touching these bits of bark cured you.' She slowly waved her hand, palm-downwards, several times above the heap of parchment and thin-shaved wood. 'If I had, I'd probably conquer all Albion just like that' – a rather poorly timed snap of the fingers, so that the sound was a muffled fumbling noise rather than a crisp click – 'and then, heh heh, woman, you and all your kind would be mine to do as I wished with.'

Syor produced a melodramatic cackle and clawed her hands.

'Don't joke with me,' said Reen.

'"Don't joke at my expense," you mean.' said Syor, abruptly serious again. 'I'm sorry – I didn't intend that.

'This is more serious than curing people. Yes, yes, I know what you're just about to say – please don't say it.' She waved her hand as if to ward off Reen's unspoken words. 'If I could be a physician, I would be. If my writings can be used to heal people, then of course I'll use them for that. But that'll be only something *else* that they can do: it won't be their main purpose.'

'I don't know what you mean.'

'But you can learn.'

Syor grabbed Reen's right hand. The soldier's first reaction was to pull it away, but Syor clung tightly and in the end Reen gave in to her will.

'When I ask you again,' whispered Syor, 'give me your hand willingly.'

'I will.' There was sweat breaking out on Reen's brow and she dragged the sleeve of her arm across her forehead, hoping that Syor wouldn't notice. The brown-haired woman was seeing nothing, however, except the shards of bark and scraps of paper that she was carefully replacing, right-side-up, as they had been on the original pile that Reen had discovered in the attic. All that Reen could see was the cleft that ran down the centre of Syor's hair, where once it had been lovingly combed to either side.

'Give me your hand.'

Reen, who had firmly instructed herself to feel no fear when fighting against the armoured soldiers of the House of Ellon, found herself having to force her arm out towards Syor against the cries of every instinct in her body.

'Now,' said Syor, 'touch the markings I made so long ago, and let your body *feel* what they have to say to you.'

And all at once Reen *did* feel – as her rough fingernail was pressed into the grooves and then run along them, guided by Syor's cool but unremitting hand – what the markings had been trying to tell her. Her memories of the time when she had served alongside Lian had been fragmentary – some of them good, some of them bad, but few of them knitting together to form a coherent whole. Now she saw, with a clarity that was almost too bright for her to tolerate, the way it had really been – the petty squabbles all mixed up with the incredible deeds of self-sacrifice, the way that a loosely knit collection of inarticulate peasants had come together under the leadership of the man who had seemed to have spun gold into his hair, so that its bright light shone across all the land of Albion.

Syor was speaking.

'I wrote these things down – all of them. The pictures you're seeing in your mind aren't pictures I created. I found from Lian a way of making the words we speak into marks that could be carved into bark, or written with ink on parchment, and when I saw something I made a few markings to remind me of what I'd seen. You're making the pictures yourself. All my words are doing is reminding you of what you saw yourself.'

Reen pulled her hand away, at last.

'You're in league with the Ellonia,' she said, shifting backwards awkwardly across the attic floor.

'No,' said Syor absent-mindedly, instantly forgetting Reen's presence and looking in perplexity at the little mound of writings in front of her, 'I'm not that. Perhaps there's magic in my writings – that must be what it is. Must be.'

'What do you mean?' said Reen, shuffling forwards again, despite the fact that she had become frightened of Syor – or, rather, of the power that Syor seemed to wield.

Syor tilted back onto her haunches once again and glared at Reen's face.

'You think it's magic that my writings can recall the past for you. That's not magic to me. While we were marching under Lian I wanted a way of setting things down so that people after us could learn of our attempt to overthrow the House of Ellon. I never thought we could succeed, although of course I never said anything like that to Lian. I just wanted us to leave something more permanent than fickle memories behind us, so that there'd come a time when peasants like ourselves would be able to pick through my writings and eventually discover that there was a way of banishing the Ellonia from the shores of Albion. That was *all* I wanted.'

'The pictures I saw?' said Reen, calmer now, resting her sharp chin in one hand as she squatted in the filth.

'It was *you* that created the pictures for yourself. I told you.'

Slowly Reen began to understand. When people had told her stories, she'd done more than just hear the words: she'd seen all the colours and heard all the sounds of what they'd been describing. Syor had found a way of doing this by using mean little scratchmarks. Somehow she'd managed to encapsulate happenings and people and places and names and things in such a way that all you had to do was touch the scrapings and the pictures were released into your mind. Syor was content to call these her 'writings', but this was something far greater than the indecipherable scrawls that the Ellonia frequently daubed on rocks and on the walls of their stockades and palaces.

There was a magic in Syor's writings, yet Syor was rejecting it. It all depended, thought Reen, on what you regarded as magic. To Syor the writings were simply recordings of past events, yet to Reen they were magical cryptograms whose power, once unlocked, unleashed forces that no mortal could control. The same could be said of spoken words: a single word could be just a description to one person, and yet evoke a million images in somebody else's mind. This was what these markings were about: they were trying – or, at least, Syor had been trying – to pull together the whole of existence so that the people and events of the past had some permanence. Lian's mate had been attempting nothing more than that during the campaign against the House of Ellon, and yet she'd succeeded in doing something else altogether.

Pictures. Pictures in the mind. Syor's writings could create those.

But they could also cure the worst of wounds, as Reen knew from her own experience when first she'd arrived in Lianhome.

'Why do they cure?' she said.

'Because . . . because they do.'

'Why're you looking so worried?' Reen leaned forwards. Now that she'd been able to understand the effect that the touch of Syor's writings against her fingertips had had upon her she was no longer scared of their magic. Instead, she wanted to help her friend, if any help were needed.

'Let's go downstairs,' said Syor, turning her face away. Her voice was strangely muffled, as if she were speaking through tears that daren't show themselves in her eyes.

'We'll go down there,' said Reen soothingly.

Carefully avoiding the pile of bark leaves and curling parchment sheets, they took each other by the shoulder and scrambled towards the opening that led to the damp-smelling bedrooms.

'Wait here,' said Reen, leaving Syor sitting on one of the beds, and feeling it creak dangerously beneath the suddenly small-seeming woman's weight, 'while I go and get those blankets. A shame to waste all that effort we put in down by the river.'

She disappeared, and Syor could hear her knocking around below.

'Food?' shouted Reen.

'Perhaps in the next waking-time,' replied Syor, just loud enough for Reen to hear. 'You go ahead and eat.'

'You still haven't told me,' Reen shouted, 'why you were so terrified by your writings.'

It was a statement of fact, but Syor recognised that it was really a question.

'Because,' she mumbled to herself, 'some of the later ones weren't mine – they'd been added by somebody else. They paint pictures of the daughter I will one day bear to Lian. She'll be called Anya, and she'll have his golden hair and my green eyes. But before that she'll be a child playing in the mud or crapping thoughtfully on my knee, the way that children do.'

258

She stood up, turned over the mattress of the bed on which she'd been sitting on the basis that the underside couldn't possibly be worse, and then hastily turned it back again.

Syor held up her right hand towards the window, through which the light was a searing gold. As she spread out her fingers, it seemed as if there were molten-copper threads joining each fingertip to the next. The writings had painted for her the picture of a child, but instead she saw a slight figure, a mocking grin on her face, clinging to the neck of a great grey horse and armoured from head to foot; the young woman was holding an axe.

'Welcome, Mother,' said the rider. 'I've been waiting for you.'

'Spare them,' said Syor beneath her breath, hardly knowing that her lips were moving.

'Spare who?'

'Everyone you *can* spare.'

The horsewoman disappeared from the nexus of light created by Syor's hand, and instead Syor saw the great surface of Albion slowly lurching up into the heavens until it was upside-down above her, threatening to crash down on her. She shrank away for an instant and then steeled her body. If this was the way that she must die, then she would offer her defiance.

But the image of Albion began to recede, rapidly and ever more rapidly, until it was nothing more than a bright point in a purple-black sky. Syor was floating in nothingness – the same nothingness she had known before she'd come here to Lianhome.

Here.

To Lianhome.

There was no sense in the words, now. Wherever she looked, all she could see in the velvet darkness was the pricked point which represented Albion.

'Mother, you're frightened. Don't be frightened.'

Syor screamed.

There were no echoes.

The voice all around her.

'Mother,' it repeated, 'you're frightened. Don't be frightened.'

Anya.

Anya here with her. The daughter she and the dead Lian had created. So much greater than Lian would ever have been. Lian. Lover. But almost like a son.

Tumbling over and over, but always Syor's eyes were fixed on that point of incandescent brightness, so intolerably harsh that it pierced into the eyes and sparked off radiating chords of exquisite pain.

'Mother . . .'

This time the soft voice was only an echo.

'Anya!' shrieked Syor. The force of the scream seemed to be trying to haul her vocal cords from her throat.

'Mother . . .'

The distant light winked out.

The soothing voice had gone.

Syor, knowing that she was falling head-over-heels but not knowing how she knew, was confronted by a loneliness she'd never met before.

She was nothing – less than that, if such a thing were possible. And at the same time she was something much greater than all of Albion itself. As she twisted and turned through the emptiness that surrounded her, she found herself realising that she'd become some kind of a deity. A deity for good or a deity for evil? She'd seen the smile on the face of Anya, the woman who would grow from the child born of her womb, and she'd seen evil in that smile. Yet that could have been an illusion. How many people had she encountered who'd had friendly smiles and who'd nevertheless tried to rape or even kill her? And how often had she dismissed a person because of their overt disingenuity, only to discover that they were almost obsessively faithful to whatever they perceived as the truth?

Was it fair for Syor to judge her unborn child on the strength of a vision of a smile?

Chapter Two
Soldiers

Anya, running through the dust of the street, knowing that somewhere far behind her (a couple of hundred metres is far to a child) someone is laughing. Her hair is gold, an inheritance from her father; her skin's sheen is a rather darker gold. Her nose is a little snub button, begging to be pressed firmly-but-not-too-hard by some grown-up's thumb. Her mouth is a little too broad to accord with the Ellonia's accepted standards of beauty, but we're a long way from Ernestrad.

The child will be thrashed when her mother finally catches her, as catch her she inevitably will, but Anya doesn't care very much. Thrashings are part of the daily round, like meals; also like meals, sometimes they're not very pleasant, but they have to be endured. The joy is to prolong as far as she can the time before her mother's strong arms surround her, pulling her to those great breasts of hers and scolding her in that thin, taut little voice Syor has developed, then dragging her back, with Anya caterwauling piteously in a vain attempt to alter the stone faces of the tall people who watch unmoved as she's taken home again.

It's a game, this running away.

Ah, when you're Anya's age, it's the grandest game of all.

She's passing a little store where the food the Ellonia allow the villagers to keep for themselves is handed out, and the storekeeper waves at her. He's a big fat man, far fatter than he ought to be. The rumour is that some of the

261

food that he's in charge of goes 'missing' in mysterious ways, ways that would have been inconceivable in the greyness of the past, before Syor returned to Lianhome. He gives her a grin. They're fellow-criminals, fellow-conspirators. She waves back at him, but keeps running.

Anya can almost smell the open countryside from here. Lianhome is not a large settlement, but crossing it from one side to the other is a long way for short legs to travel: she's never before managed to get even as far as this. The breath is painful in her chest, and it sounds in her head like a stream in spate, but she ignores it.

'Stop her!'

Syor is slow-moving these days: Anya wouldn't be able to outrun her in a straightforward race, but in these circumstances she has a chance. She hopes that was Syor yelling because Reen is something different. There may be streaks of grey in the hair that was once jet-black, but Reen's figure is still compact and firm. Anya waited until Reen was sleeping before she made this latest dash for freedom. She grins at the thought of her own cunning and foresight.

Thumpety thumpety thump go her woollen-shod feet on the packed earth of the road. Now she's near the edge of the village, fully seven hundred metres from home. The feeling of freedom threatens to burst her heart.

But her lungs are threatening to burst, too, and she's aware that she's running more slowly now. She can see the open country ahead of her, and she crams all the energy she has into her legs, *willing* them to move more quickly. Out there in the great openness she'll make her own home, camping in caves or in the lee of bushes, catching wild animals for food and drinking the sweet waters of tiny streams. She'll become a wild woman, and people will scare each other and their children by talking about her in hushed tones: *Go to sleep, my lovely, or that Anya will come to get you*. She'll be the younger sister of the sky, and the friend of the ospreys.

All that separates her now from her dream is a narrow ditch, a black line crossing her view. Even though her legs are near to collapse, she'll have no trouble jumping the small distance across it to freedom.

One last great effort and . . .

Reen threw the squirming child over her shoulder and trudged resignedly back through the village, ignoring the catcalls of some of the urchins (and some of their elders) who'd been watching the whole drama as if it had been a regular sporting event – which, in a way, it was.

Reen was annoyed with the child. Not for running away: she was pleased that Anya was, even at this age, displaying what Reen regarded as the right temperament. No, her concern was that the child had chosen her moment so badly – on two counts. First, she'd tried to make her escape during a waking-period – right at the beginning of one, to be fair, when many people, including Reen herself, hadn't yet woken, but nevertheless at a time when there were too many people around. Anya should have learnt by now that, if one wanted to do things by stealth, it was much better to do them during a sleeping-period, when anyone who was still awake was probably out working in the fields, so that one's chances of detection were minimal. It wasn't easy for a child to stay awake during a sleeping-period, but it could be done – and Reen had spent some time trying to show Anya *how* it could be done. She didn't want the child to escape from the village, of course, but she was furious with Anya for not at least making better attempts at it.

The second reason for Reen's anger over the child's choice of timing was that it was widely suspected in Lian-home that a convoy of the Ellonia was near. Should the soldiers ever be given grounds to suspect that . . . Reen shuddered at the thought of the carnage. They'd destroy the village and every living creature in it, raze the houses to the ground and leave nothing but drifting smoke and the stench of scorched flesh. Anya had been aware – or should have been aware – of the doom she might be bringing down not just on her own head but on those of her friends. The child had either shut off her mind to the risk, callously ignored it, or been too stupid to recognise how very real it was.

Stupidity, as Reen recalled only too well, was the way to lose wars. Anya could not allow herself the self-indulgence of stupidity.

Reen sighed, and reflexively slapped the girl's bottom yet again.

'Shut up!' she snapped over her shoulder as Anya renewed her wailing.

One of the children laughed. Reen gave him a glance. The child's face changed as he noticed something monumentally interesting on the ground somewhere near his foot.

Anya was pummelling with her sharp little fists against the base of Reen's spine, knowing precisely where to strike in order to cause the most pain. Reen ignored it.

Syor had returned to the cottage, and was sitting with her elbows on the downstairs table when they arrived, her forehead in her hands so that Reen couldn't see her face. It was obvious that she'd been weeping and was trying to conceal the fact.

'What,' she said in a thick voice, 'have we done wrong?'

'Nothing,' said Reen bluntly, plonking Anya unceremoniously down on the floor.

'The child's evil!' said Syor, spreading out her arms and lowering her head so that her face rested on the backs of her prone hands. 'How many times has she done this? Twenty? Thirty? More?'

'Counting's a trap, if you let it be,' said Reen, looking so sternly at Anya that the child was too terrified to make the slightest noise, instead glancing nervously backwards and forwards between the two adults who had reared her.

Anya loved them both, in their different ways: Syor all soft and motherly smelling; Reen equally soft once you discovered it, but outwardly as hard as metal. Anya would listen with her mouth open to Syor's dreamy fables of times long gone and times that could have been, then go out with Reen to kick a ball around and get dirty.

'Why does she want to leave us?'

'Because she's an intelligent child,' said Reen vexedly. 'No' – as Syor let out a small sob – 'don't take that wrongly.

264

Of *course* she's got to show us that she's a person, not just a doll, and the only way she can do that right now is to defy us by running away. When she's a bit older she'll learn that there are other ways of running away from home; that's when we'll start to be her friends rather than her parents.'

Anya looked confused. She thought she'd discovered all the ways of running away from home there were. Was it possible that Reen knew of some quite different escape route, and wasn't telling?

Reen promptly switched her attention away from the child. She drew up a stool to the table, swept aside some poorly crafted earthenware pottery, and put her face close to Syor's. All she could see was a mass of brown hair streaked with silver, but she could envisage the red lines and the dampness of the cheeks behind it. Syor had changed since Anya had been born, Reen mused, worrying for her friend as she had countless times before.

Reen had long recognised Syor's instability: the way that her smiles could mask either insecurity or sometimes, by contrast, steel, but motherhood seemed to have drained those smiles away and the shafts of steel were becoming increasingly rare. Reen sighed. It was a cliché that women inevitably drew strength from motherhood; it was a convenience to forget that so many were weakened by it.

Reen realised too that for some time now Syor had been becoming increasingly morbid in her memories of Lian, filling her mind with miserable and futile questionings – endless what-ifs that decayed inside her and spread their poison throughout every aspect of her life. Syor herself knew, deep down, that it was this self-administered poison that was responsible for her unhappiness, of course, but her mind, loth to admit its own failings, automatically sought out something or someone *external* to be the culprit – and had chosen to blame Anya.

Now Reen sensed that Syor's eyes, hidden by hands and hair, were open, staring furtively at her.

'Syor,' she said, 'Lian is only dead so long as you keep killing him every day. I think he's alive. Not alive in the sense that he's walking around and talking to all of us, but alive in your daughter. If Anya stopped running away – stopped doing all the other things she shouldn't, some of which I haven't told you about – then Lian really *would* be dead. You'd have been his executioner.'

Anya, seeing both her parents engrossed, relaxed: it looked as if the anticipated beating had been crossed off the agenda; even if it was administered later, it would be a half-hearted affair, performed more as an observance of the proprieties than as a genuine physical punishment. She felt hungry, and looked around to see if perhaps some bread had been left lying out.

'She'll lead us,' Reen was saying. 'Or, if not us, then others like us. But only if you allow her to be herself now.'

'It's so fucking difficult!' said Syor into her fingers.

'Yes,' murmured Reen soothingly. Then her voice stiffened. 'Yes, of course it's bloody well difficult. Getting along with Lian was bloody difficult a lot of the time. It *had* to be. If he'd been everybody's friend as a boy – if he'd never done anything "naughty" – he'd have lived out his life in this village as a curio. And a short life it'd have been, because the Ellonia don't like curios: they distrust them.'

'I suckled that child!'

'Do you love her?'

The starkness of the question clearly shocked Syor. It was a few moments before she replied. Anya watched, entranced by the dramatic spectacle which, she assumed, the two adults were putting on for her entertainment.

'Yes,' said Syor in a whisper. 'Yes, despite it all, of course I love her. Deeply. I love her more than I love you.'

'Then let her be a rebel, dammit,' said Reen intensely, leaning forward until her nose was almost touching Syor's hair. 'Sure, we can beat her every time she does something like run away, but we mustn't beat the spirit out of her.'

Syor raised her head and looked at Reen through watering eyes.

'But it's so *difficult!*' she said again.

'Capturing Ernestrad is going to be difficult,' said Reen quietly.

Anya's hand, hovering over a crust, froze.

'D'you think she'll . . . ?'

'Yes,' said Reen. 'I think there's a chance. But not if she becomes a good little girl, every mother's dream, one who does what she's told and can always be relied upon to help about the house.'

She glanced briefly in Anya's direction. The hand was swiftly withdrawn. Anya looked at it innocently, as if wondering how it had come to be where it had been.

There was the blast of a trumpet outside the house.

'I'll speak to you later,' Reen hissed to Anya. 'Grab that bit of bread and get up to the attic at once. As soon as I've got your mother into some sort of shape I'll come and board you in. Don't forget to take some water . . . and *don't* make a noise once you're in there.'

At once the child's face became an adult one. Moving with swift efficiency, she gathered together food, water and a shabby woollen doll and scampered up the stairs.

In the attic, trying not to fidget while listening to Reen disguising the hatch, she thought over all the things she'd heard her parents say. It seemed that they expected her to lead somebody – but who? Countless times she'd tried leading the thin cat that had adopted their home as its own, but it had refused to follow, preferring either to sneak off into its own hiding-places or just to sit in the sunlight, smugly licking the pink soles of its paws, ignoring her completely. She'd tried leading some of the village children, but they'd just laughed at her as she'd strutted around; she still had the bruise where a clod of earth had hit her on the elbow a few waking-periods ago. She knew that she was able to lead her mother, any time she wanted, but that didn't really count.

So she was to be a leader. Reen had said so, over and over again, when she'd thought Anya was out of earshot or safely asleep. A leader of people, Anya surmised, but where were the people? The solid, stuffy people of the village she discounted at once: they were grown-ups, and lived in a different world, a world filled with the preoccupations of bringing in the crops, tending the animals and generally being boring. She'd noticed from the attic window that the villagers became even more boring when the Ellonian patrols arrived, as if they'd lost all their powers of speech and thought. Leading them would be like a shepherd's job – perhaps that was what Reen intended.

But Anya suspected from what she'd heard that Reen had something quite different in mind.

Anya was to be a leader. She was to be kept in secrecy until she was big like most of the other villagers were, and then she was to lead some of the big people so that they could hurt other big people.

She had cramp in her left leg. She moved as quietly as she could, stretching it out and extending the foot, making no noise as the momentary pain faded. She grabbed the hunk of bread and took a mouthful, her sharp white teeth seizing at the coarse crust. The grain was gritty, and she was tempted to spit it out, but she forced herself to chew it until it was a pulpy mass that she could swallow.

A spider ran across the floor. It paused in the middle, and Anya concentrated her mind on it, trying to persuade it to obey her will. It stopped for a little while longer, its threadlike forelegs making patterns in the air, then scuttled away to its new hiding place.

Her first mouthful of bread had tasted miserable, as it always did. She'd tried to explain to Syor and then, more optimistically, to Reen, that the corn could be better ground if the stones were smoother, but neither of them had seemed to hear her; it was as if they wanted things to stay the way they'd always been. Anya took another bite, chewed, then doused the unpleasant taste with a gulp of water. At least the water was fresh.

Then the screams had started.

Anya rather enjoyed the sound of screaming. Her mother screamed quite often, almost always because she'd discovered something *interesting* that Anya had done – like create a new and mystical artefact using common household objects – but aside from that it was a rare noise in Lianhome. Anya found the musical cadences of screaming quite fascinating. She wished that the Ellonia would come to Lianhome more often. She understood that the screams usually meant that someone was experiencing pain, but as long as the somebody wasn't her she didn't mind too much.

She was about to get to her feet, confident that she'd grown enough just to be able see out of the skylight, when she realised there was someone else in the attic.

Anya peered around. There was no corner that she couldn't see into.

No. Her senses had misled her. There was no one else there. She turned back towards the skylight.

There *was* somebody watching her.

Again she darted her head around. Still nothing.

Nothing except for the fact that the blue-grey shadows in one corner of the attic were just a little more extensive and a little deeper in colour than all the others.

Anya stared at them. The light was bright enough, even in the corners, for her to be able to see everything that was there, and yet she had the uncanny sensation that there was something extra in that one – something present in reality but nevertheless invisible to her.

Without being aware of it, she took another bite of the rough bread. Her eyes were fixed intently on the suspect shadows as her jaws chewed automatically.

More screams from outside. Anya hoped, with a side-corridor of her mind, that the Ellonia weren't raping her mother. Syor was weepy quite a lot of the time, but never more so than after she'd been raped. Anya made a mental resolution to find out, once she was old enough, what it was like to be raped. Reen had told her that it was most unpleasant, but then Anya wondered if Reen was speaking from direct experience: Reen was strong enough to lift things that two men couldn't lift, so no one – even, Anya assumed, the Ellonia – ever tried to do anything to Reen that Reen didn't want them to do.

The shadows were still there. Anya had the uncomfortable feeling that, just as she was watching them, they were watching her.

She was surprised that she didn't feel frightened. She was wary, yes; but not frightened.

'Well,' said the shadows a little huffily, 'we might as well be friendly with each other.'

'Sh!' said Anya instantly, her alerting finger flying to her lips. She carried on in a whisper: 'We've got to stay absolutely silent up here, or the Ellonia will find us. That's what Mummy says, and . . . and Reen says it as well.'

'Don't worry.'

The voice was louder now, and there was a ripple of laughter sheltering behind it.

'Sh!' said Anya again. She hauled herself up to peer out of the skylight, but as far as she could tell the Ellonia hadn't heard them.

When she looked back she saw that there was a young woman patrolling the attic, peeking inquisitively into this corner and that. The woman had closely cropped red hair and was dressed entirely in green: green jerkin, green breeches, green shoes and a green tunic. She glanced at Anya for a second and the child saw, set in the woman's narrow face, a pair of eyes even greener than her mother's.

'We don't have to worry about noise,' said the stranger. 'We could set up a dance band in here and the Ellonia still wouldn't hear a thing. I've a way of making sure that no one notices me unless I want them to. Did you realise that you've got some really quite interesting junk up here? If I'm not mistaken, that's a seal of the Despot over there under the dust – yes, it is.'

The dust cleared away from where she was pointing her bony little finger, and Anya could see a small disc of a dark red waxy-looking material.

'Now,' said the stranger, 'I suppose you're wondering who I am?'

Anya nodded, speechless, then took another precautionary glance out through the skylight before turning to examine the woman more closely.

'Well, Anya, you shouldn't really need to be told, but if you're very good I'll tell you. I don't mean good at being good: I mean good at being bad. Because you're going to have to be very bad during your life. You're going to have to be so bad that you'll just grin whenever you hear the word "naughty".'

The woman was now sitting in the middle of the floor, her legs crossed, turning her head so that the sunlight from the window would catch her face to its best advantage. Her hands, whenever they weren't moving to emphasise her words, were resting on her pointed knees.

'Don't speak so loudly!' said Anya, loudly.

'I told you not to worry,' said the woman with a smile. Her teeth were disconcertingly white and even. Anya was accustomed to grown-ups having broken, discoloured teeth. 'Nothing the two of us say to each other can be heard outside this attic. I've . . . I've arranged it that way. I told you.' A shrug of the shoulders dismissed the matter as being of little importance. 'Shall I sing you a song?' she asked eagerly.

'Who are you?' Anya asked, at last finding her voice.

'Alyss, of course. Hadn't you begun to guess? I arrange it so that most people know who I am even before they've met me: it saves so much time over formal introductions.'

Anya couldn't remember having heard the name before, and yet she was aware that it wasn't totally unfamiliar to her. She seemed to hear it spoken in her mother's soft voice, at the end of a waking-time as Syor was telling her a story about Lian and the others while she shoved herself down under the tattered blankets that Grandma Mina had left here for them. Then she remembered – there'd been an encampment, and . . .

'You're a singer,' said the child.

Anya settled herself down into a squat, mirroring Alyss's position.

'A singer, yes – from time to time. Probably the best there is, when I want to be. Oh' – with an impatient snap of her fingers – 'let's forget all this "probably" nonsense. Of course I'm the best. If you're extremely lucky I'll sing you a song. In fact, I'm going to sing you one anyway.'

Alyss reached into one of the small pockets of her jerkin and pulled out of it a clarsach, the strings of which she immediately began to tune using a key which had suddenly

271

appeared in her other hand. The clarsach was almost as large as Alyss herself, but it wouldn't be until many waking-periods later that Anya would begin to think about the strangeness of this.

'The Ellonia . . .' the child began.

'I told you not to worry about them. Oh, well, children will be children. Here, if it reassures you.'

Alyss uncoiled her body and stood with her head just out of the skylight. She pulled Anya up beside her. The flag of the Ellonia fluttered in the wind, the dog seeming to be struggling to escape from its impalement. A line of rather somnolent-looking soldiers was passing baskets of grain from the storage tower back to the cart, then handing the empty baskets along the row again to be refilled. One of the horses was urinating copiously onto the road; Anya was interested to see that the village woman who was currently on her back seemed more concerned by the horse and its steaming urine than by the soldier on top of her.

Alyss moved her fingers and the entire tableau froze.

'There,' she said, 'now we can talk, just you and I.'

'What do you want to talk about?' asked Anya. She didn't like to admit it, but she'd been impressed by what Alyss had done. Her mother would never have been able to manage it, and even Reen would probably have had difficulty.

'About your future, of course,' said Alyss. Her face twit-ched; she was obviously thinking. 'Hmmm,' she said after a little while, 'on second thoughts, we can leave the song for another day. Songs are like wines: the longer you leave them the better they get.'

Anya had never heard the word 'wine' before, but she accepted the statement. She watched as Alyss moved her hands deftly so that the clarsach folded itself away until it was no larger than a purse, which Alyss daintily slipped back into her pocket.

'There aren't very many people called "Anya" in Albion, you know,' Alyss said abruptly. 'Do you know what the name means?'

'No. Yes. It means me.'

Another bite at the bread.

Alyss looked on approvingly.

'It means a little more than that,' she said, once she'd judged that Anya could hear her voice over the noise of her jaws. 'It means that you're She Who Leads.'

'Mummy and Reen talk about me leading,' said Anya, her mouth still half-full, 'but I think they're being silly.'

'Have they told you about your father?'

'About Lian? Yes. Lots about him. He was He Who Leads. They've told me that he was a great hero, but that I mustn't ever mention his name.'

Anya's thumb was now in her mouth; she had to remove it whenever she wanted to speak. She was entranced by her new friend, who seemed to know what she was thinking even before she'd thought it herself.

'Who're the people who've told you that?'

'Why, Mummy and Reen, of course.'

Alyss drummed her fingers on the wooden floorboard in front of her. Anya noticed that the nails needed cutting, but that they were clean.

'I want you to start mentioning Lian's name.'

'I can't. I've been told not to.'

'I don't mean you should shout it from the rooftops – that'd be a sure way of killing yourself. No, what I'm trying to say is that you should accept the fact that Lian was your father. Don't let Syor and Reen forget it.'

Alyss put a hand to her temple, and then seemed a little surprised to discover it there.

'Reen wouldn't,' said Anya firmly. 'Mummy . . . I think that sometimes Mummy tries to forget it. She wants to worship his memory, and at the same time she wants to forget all about him.'

Alyss bent forward and patted Anya on the thigh.

'Talk about Lian with Reen,' she said. 'Ask Reen to take you up into the hills, so that you're far away from other people's ears, and ask her to tell you everything she knows about Lian. Then this nonsense' – she gestured in the general direction of the village's main thoroughfare – 'this nonsense can be put to an end forever.'

'Who shall I lead?'

'For the next few hundred waking-periods? Wooden ducks on wheels, if you're lucky. After that? Well, it's up to you. Reen'll tell you the things you should do. I can't. All I can do is point you in a direction and hope that you go that way; if you choose not to, I'm powerless.'

Alyss was gathering herself into herself, so that she seemed to be becoming smaller and smaller.

'I'll be with you when you lead, Anya,' said a soft sigh of a voice, which the child hardly recognised as Alyss's.

In one corner of the attic the soft shadows were darkening as the figure of the singer slowly ebbed away. Now Anya could quite clearly see the joins of timbers behind where Alyss had been sitting.

'Come back!' the child shouted.

'Hush,' said a whisper of dust. 'The Ellonia might hear you.'

It wasn't, the Despot kept telling himself, that he *liked* having people put to death as such; it was just that he enjoyed watching them die, especially several at a time. He suspected that the tribunals set up by the House of Ellon were deeply corrupt, and that many of the people who were condemned were in fact innocent, but this only enhanced his pleasure as he sat high above the execution platform and watched human bodies being tormented to the point where death seemed to be a wide-open gate, beckoning them to a paradisiac garden beyond. The Despot was proud of himself in this respect: had it not been for him the poor peasants would have lived out their futile existences in a long eternity of grey sameness, whereas he was giving them, through his courts and through the due processes of law, a way of remembering, if not the dull courses of their drab lives, at least the spectacular manner of their exits.

The Despot's courtiers described him as 'slight' or even, depending on the extent to which they felt it necessary to toady to him, 'diminutive'. In fact, as they constantly failed to notice, he was so fat that his deputy throne, upon which he was now sitting, strained to take the weight. This paradox was, the Despot reflected, as it should be: respect should transcend the piffling details of reality. When not listening with a wry smile to their compliments, he gloried in his grossness. It proclaimed to all the land that he was a man of immense wealth, who could afford to gorge himself on the richest of foods. More, even, than the richness of the cloth of which his garments were cut, the rolls of fat on his neck, chest, stomach and legs conveyed to the few commoners he allowed to see him that the House of Ellon reigned supreme over all of Albion.

His obesity kept the peasants in their subservient place, he ruminated as he stretched out a hefty arm to take another piece of sugarloaf. He was doing a good job.

The torturers were being rather unimaginative today, he decided, and he made a mental note to order their executions on the morrow as punishment for boring him. Watching torturers facing their own deaths was always especially interesting to the Despot: the torturers knew precisely the effects that their red-hot irons and their sharp knives had on human flesh, and it was fun for him to watch their faces as they recognised the full enormity of what was about to happen to them.

A frown crossed the breadth of his face, taking several seconds to do so.

He could still remember the time when he'd been sitting up here, the father of his people, watching benignly as some upstart peasant had slowly met his end. A fool of an Army-Master called Nadar had determined to make some kind of a spectacle out of the whole affair, and had been slaughtered by the mob for his asininity. Infuriatingly, by the time the hubbub had died down, the peasant had been dead, so that the Despot had missed all the best bits. It had been a poor consolation to see nothing more than his Army-Master being pulled to pieces.

The Despot shifted in his throne, irritated by the memory, and it creaked its wooden protest.

He leaned forwards, elbows on the window-ledge. After a little while he removed one arm and used it to beckon for his favourite concubine. Mid-beckon, he remembered that, blast it, he'd had her executed a few waking-periods ago. He altered the subtle phraseology of his beckon, so that he was now gesturing that his second-favourite concubine should approach him. Except, of course, that presumably she'd become his first-favourite concubine, now.

It was very confusing, being the Despot. And it was all the fault of the concubines.

He felt the softness of a silk-clad body by his ear, and relaxed. With studied gentleness he raised one of the woman's large breasts, because it was obscuring his sight of the ongoing torture.

Despite the apparently carefree leer on his face – placed there for the benefit of the adoring if seemingly sullen members of the peasant classes who thronged the courtyard beneath him – the Despot was worried. The long-ago death of Nadar had disconcerted him, not because of the loss of the man – the Despot had long had suspicions that Nadar's ambitions centred on the throne – but because it was a blatant demonstration of how vulnerable the Despot's own position was. If the peasants could realistically threaten to topple the House of Ellon, and if then they could come within a hair's breadth of rescuing their barbaric leader from the execution which he had so justly earned . . . Why! Nothing seemed to be sacred any more. For a time the Despot had put all such considerations away from him, preferring to ignore the fact that there might be factions among the peasants – and even among the army – who might like to see him deposed, but recently rumours had reached him from several of his most trusted spies that the peasants were in turmoil once again, that they were expecting the coming of a new leader.

Hah! Peasants in turmoil, thought the Despot contemptuously. *Might as well talk about* cabbages *in turmoil!*

He wondered if it might be sensible to put a few of the nearby villages to the sword, just to make it plain to any would-be rebels that all thoughts of revolt were doomed from the very start, then decided that it was hardly worth the effort. The rebellion led by the fair-haired peasant whose name the Despot could no longer remember had come to nothing, and there was little reason to believe that a revival of ferment among the peasants would fare any better. His spies had been unable to identify any potential leader of the mobs, although, just to be on the safe side, they'd killed several hundred peasants whose brains had seemed to them to be composed of anything more imaginative than the usual silage.

The Despot watched the torture with renewed attentiveness and idly wondered what the plural of 'scrotum' was.

He looked at the crowd.

Of course, his subjects loved him: everybody knew that. Still, sometimes he wondered why the people were so recalcitrant about showing their adoration. Perhaps they didn't want to embarrass him by being over-effusive. Yes, that was almost certainly the reason.

Another satisfied smile meandered oleaginously across the breadth of the Despot's face.

Far above – unseen by the Despot, his courtiers, the gathered peasants, the executioners, and those who were suffering the last agonies of their lives – a curlew circled easily, banking its wings against the updraughts of air.

A little later, it turned and flew away from Ernestrad until, even if anyone had been looking at it, it would have been invisible against the backcloth of the searingly bright sky.

It had been decreed by the mages that this waking-period should be a time of rain, although they had neglected to announce this fact beforehand to the Despot's court at Ernestrad, or to transmit the information to the leaders of the army. As on all such occasions, they explained disarmingly that they preferred to preserve their mysteries – indeed, that their incantations would be ineffectual should their secrets ever be betrayed to the uninitiated. The Despot believed them implicitly, and therefore so did everyone else.

Here in a ravine in northern Albion the normally dry earth was being churned by a flash torrent of floodwater that rushed and thundered down the narrow channel, tumbling stones, uprooted shrubs and the branches of fallen trees along with its powerful current. Overhead, the sky was purple and tormented, heavy-looking clouds hurtling at seemingly improbable speeds from one horizon to the other. Colossal thunderclaps appeared to be doing their best to split the sky wide open and allow the immensity of the unknown beyond to come gushing into Albion, drowning it in a sea of chilly emptiness. Sheets of lightning judderingly lit up the land, showing the silhouettes of tormented trees quailing impotently against the fierce attack of the gale.

At least the wind isn't too bad down here, thought Barra 'ap Rteniadoli Me'gli'minter Rehan gloomily. *But that's about the only good thing you could say about this place.*

He'd been walking easily down the dry channel, playing his flute and listening to the interesting echoes from the ravine walls, when, without any warning, the storm had struck. At first he had paid it little attention, except to play sound games, trying to blend the notes of his cane flute, the echoes and the unpredictable crashes of the thunder – the combination was giving him ideas for a new composition, and he was engrossed in it – when he realised that there was a new component to the cacophony: an angry, growling noise from behind him.

That was when he'd turned around and seen the advancing wall of grey-brown water.

So here he was, perched halfway up the side of the ravine on a narrow, muddy ledge, his knees pulled up to his chest and one arm wrapped around an etiolated bush, the other hand clutching his precious flute and bodhran under his cape for protection from the elements. His normally soft, long, wavy red hair was plastered flat against his head – the feathered hat he usually wore had long since been lost. He was cold, wet, miserable and frightened. If the rain kept up for too long his roost was going to become intolerably slippery and he would inevitably slither into the madness beneath him. His other concern was that he might accidentally fall asleep. Much of the time he spent singing songs he didn't like – songs by singers other than himself – so that the irritation of what he regarded as their clumsiness and flawed progressions would keep him awake. He was thankful that no one could hear him.

He had been given his name, Barra 'ap Rteniadoli Me'gli-'minter Rehan, as a boy by a peripatetic singer who had come strolling through the village where he had spent all his life up until then. He had been amazed by the arrival of the old woman, because it had never really occurred to him before that, apart from the brutal Ellonia (who, he'd assumed, came from somewhere outside reality), there were any human beings at all aside from the few hundred inhabitants of his village. Eyes wide with amazement, he'd watched her sitting cross-legged in the dust, her twig-like fingers manipulating the double-ended stick of her bodhran so swiftly that it was as if she were holding a handful of mist. She'd smiled at him, her face a spider's web and her eyes like little points of light, as she'd sung ballads of strange places that were far, far away from his little village. At first he'd thought that her songs were like the stories he was sometimes told by his parents or his elder siblings when he had difficulty getting off to sleep, but it had slowly dawned on him that the tales her songs told were about real people and about things that had really happened.

Gates opened for him. Albion was far more than the area contained within the confines of his village. It was a vast world populated by untold thousands of people who dwelt in countless villages just like his own. The world was ruled by the invincible House of Ellon from their huge village of Ernestrad, surmounted by a vast house called Giorran. The leader of the Ellonia was a person called the Despot, whose capricious cruelty knew no bounds. This was the way it always had been; although still only a child, he had been alone among her audience in noticing that none of her songs stated unambiguously that this was the way it would always have to be.

The old woman had observed this in his face, and nodded approvingly.

Through this gate his mind had gone, finding itself at ease in the outside world. The first things his mind had seen were other gates which the old singer's ballads had pushed tantalisingly open for him. Tentatively he stepped through one of them, and discovered that people and places could be given names. In her songs, heroes and heroines were not just described as 'the one with the broad shoulders and hips who has long fair hair and generous breasts, who has given four children to the man who has black hair and a club foot': they were named, and therefore they became people. Some of the names had meanings; others were just ways of distinguishing one person from another, a concept that hitherto had been totally unknown to him. Immediately he had started ascribing names to the people around him, and discovered that he could conjure up pictures of them in his mind even when they weren't present. Of course, he'd kept the names he'd created to himself, as secrets, because he was sure with the confidence of childhood that he was committing some great sin, and that he'd be punished if ever the grown-ups found out.

The other gate had revealed a more dramatic vista. Some of the people about whom the old woman sang were dead.

Death had been another totally new idea to him. Life lasted for eternity, surely? People changed as life progressed: the singer herself was showing in her body and her face that she had been living since a time before he himself had been born – he had seen few people whose bodies had progressed to this particular stage of life, and he'd wondered what the next step of the process made people look like. But he couldn't recall anyone in his village having taken that step. A question had appeared in his mind as it gazed through this gate. *Children are born into this village, yet there never seem to be more of us than there were before. Does this mean that other people disappear to make room?* This had been immediately followed by another question. *I'm the child of my parents, but surely they, too, must have had parents? What's happened to those parents of theirs? Where are they?*

Afterwards he'd asked a number of the grown-ups, including his own parents, but all of them had just looked at him blankly: it had been obvious to him that they regarded his question as utterly meaningless, like 'Why is an apple?' or 'Where is nowhere?'. And so in the end he'd sought out the old woman to ask her, and had discovered that she'd been expecting him. Her fingers had played lightly and absent-mindedly on her bodhran as she listened to him, and her taut reptilian lips had twisted into a smile.

'You're a singer,' she'd said at last. 'Born to be a singer.'

That was when she'd given him the name of Barra 'ap Rteniadoli Me'gli'minter Rehan, which she'd explained to him meant 'the little boy who wonders long enough to step through the gates which other people open for him'; but she'd also told him that, if he wanted to peep through more gates, he should discipline himself to use his full name only for formal purposes, and not to think of himself by it, but instead to select a single element of it. At random he'd selected Rehan, and she'd smiled again.

'Yes,' she'd said, 'a true singer. You've called yourself "the gates which other people open". In your life you'll open gates yourself, but those'll be gates for the singers who follow you to go through.'

A few waking-periods later she'd left the village, and Rehan had gone with her as her apprentice. She'd never told him her name, and he'd never asked her for it: he'd guessed that, just as he was allowed to think of himself by only part of his name, the greatest of all the singers, having learnt how to take names to themselves, then learnt the even more difficult skill of abjuring those names altogether. And he'd found that he never needed a name for her: she'd always known when he was addressing her, or calling for her help.

She'd shown him how to make his first flute, but she'd refused to show him how to play it: that, she said, was something he would have to learn for himself – which, after much difficulty, he'd done. She'd also helped him learn to play the bodhran, and had taught him how to play her own; which, she'd told him, would be his on her death, to do with as he chose. The two of them had wandered from village to village, playing and singing together to vacant-faced villagers who found in them a temporary focus of reality in the midst of their indeterminate lives of never-ending changelessness. Like the old woman, Rehan had learnt to look out for those sparks which she had recognised in him, and from time to time they'd felt a surge of enthusiasm which was inevitably followed by the anticlimax of disillusion.

And then one waking-period, when he'd been a youth on the verge of adulthood, she'd died. It had all been quite peaceful, and she'd resigned herself some hours beforehand to the fact that her existence on Albion was ending. She'd laid down beneath a tree and told him to leave her there among the grass and the daisies, then closed her eyes. He'd watched the life drain from her parchment face.

Feeling reverence but no grief, he left her body there as she'd requested but buried her bodhran reverentially in the chalky soil. He'd felt that he was preserving her spirit – partly in the buried drum and partly in his own living body. Since then, wherever he'd journeyed, he'd experienced her by his side, encouraging him; sometimes, when he played his flute or sang soft old words which he himself could barely understand, he could hear, distantly but quite distinctly, the sound of her bodhran – so much mellower in sound than the one he'd since made for himself – keeping perfect time with the bubbling glissades of his flute.

She'd been the first to call him a 'true singer'; there'd been others who'd said the same since. Some were fellow-singers whom he occasionally encountered on his travels; a few were village wenches whose sophisticated musical perception he had fostered at whatever personal cost in terms of physical exertion.

A true singer, Rehan thought now, *but, if I'm not very careful, a dead singer as well.*

If anything the water level beneath him seemed to have crept rather higher up the walls of the ravine. He looked upwards for the thousandth time, and for the thousandth time realised that the muddy, almost vertical wall was unclimbable: if the waters swept him away from his perch he'd have to trust his luck to the whims of the current.

The current, he thought glumly, looking downwards once

more, *doesn't look over-imbued with, um, the spirit of humanitarianism.*

Rehan wished that the rain would stop. The prospect of death – even death by drowning – wouldn't be nearly so unbearable if he weren't sitting here being drenched from head to foot by the deluge from the skies. Besides, the impact of the rain was hurting his back, his shoulders and the top of his head, despite the layers of cloth and hair that were supposed to shield those parts of him. He grinned at himself as he recognised the paradox of his thinking: he didn't mind drowning as long as he was able to stay dry.

'Barra 'ap Rteniadoli Me'gli'minter Rehan!' shouted a sharp-edged voice from above him.

For a moment he assumed it was an aural hallucination, just a trick of the way that the downpour was creating a solid wall of sound all around him.

The voice came again.

'Barra 'ap Rteniadoli Me'gli'minter Rehan!'

This time he paid it a little more attention. Making extra sure of his grip on the bush to which he'd anchored himself, he swivelled his head and shoulders around in order to look upwards, narrowing his eyes against the driving rain. He could dimly see against the darkness of the sky what seemed to be a person's head looking down at him over the lip of the ravine.

'Barra 'ap Rteniadoli Me'gli'minter Rehan!' said the voice yet again, and this time he began to wonder if perhaps some form of rescue was at hand. Maybe not. Although he'd never met any, he'd been told that some of Albion's wildernesses were the haunts of spirits who delighted in watching travellers lose their lives to the elements.

'I don't usually answer to that name!' he shouted, knowing that his words were being stolen from his lips by the gale. He shut his eyes, feeling the lukewarm water pouring down over his exposed face and into the neck of his cape.

'Wait there, Barra 'ap Rteniadoli Me'gli'minter Rehan,' said the person about him. 'I'll come down to join you.'

'Don't be a fool!' he yelled. 'The cliff's a slick of mud! There's not room here on the shelf for both of us!'

'Thank you for your courtesy, young man,' said a crisp voice beside him, 'but I assure you I'm a better judge of slipperiness than you'll ever be.'

The noises of the rain and of the turbulent waters had waned until they were no more than an aggrieved murmuring, as if they were very far away. For the first time in ages Rehan began to feel warm; he felt his cape and found that the cloth was dry.

The woman who was sitting beside him was disconcerting, with her high cheeks, her bright yellow-green eyes and her short russet hair. She looked at him with smart friendliness, and he found himself smiling back at her. It was then that he noticed that she wasn't sitting beside him on the ledge but was instead hovering, cross-legged, in mid-air at the same level as his perch.

'You're a mirage,' he muttered resentfully. 'I've spent all of my life hoping to see a mirage so that I could tell other people they really exist, and now that I finally see one it happens when I'm about to die. Thanks a bundle, mirage.'

The mirage laughed.

'Don't worry, Barra 'ap Rteniadoli Me'gli'minter Rehan,' she said, throwing her head back so that he could watch the muscles move along her throat, 'I'm no mirage. I'm really here. Later, if you like, I'll show you a mirage, and then you'll be able to write a song about it.'

She must have come here through the worst of the storm and yet she was totally dry; her boots showed no trace of splattered mud and her hair showed not a strand out of position; on her shoulder she carried a clarsach whose wooden soundbox gleamed from polishing. Rehan sensed that there was a little frame of light surrounding the two of them, so that the rain couldn't penetrate. No, he realised as he looked around them: it was more as if the falling rain, instants before reaching them, suddenly discovered that it had always intended falling in a completely different direction; it swerved aside and followed a new course.

'My full name is Barra 'ap Rteniadoli Me'gli'minter Rehan,' he said tightly, 'but I hardly ever use it. It's personal to me. Those who know me well call me Rehan; to others I have no name at all.'

'Make room on that shelf,' said the woman impatiently, patently ignoring what he was saying. 'I'd like to sit beside you.'

'There's not enough room,' said Rehan, making a token display of shifting to his left while still maintaining his hold on the bush.

'Of course there is,' said the woman peevishly. 'See?'

She was sitting alongside him on the ledge and there was plenty of space for both of them. Her clarsach balanced easily on the muddy shelf beside her.

'Now, Barra 'ap Rteniadoli Me'gli'minter Rehan . . .' she began.

'I've told you,' he interrupted annoyedly, 'I don't use my full name except on formal occasions.'

'I'm sorry,' she said, turning to face him, her eyes large and her face drawn into a caricature of apology. 'You're Rehan, of course. I tend to forget these things, Barra 'ap Rteniadoli Me'gli'minter – '

'Rehan!'

'Rehan. Yes, of course. But why does it matter so much to you?'

Nobody had ever asked him the question before, and he was furious to find that it embarrassed him. *Because the use of my full name makes me feel as if you're stripping me naked, intruding into my privacy*, he wanted to say, but he realised from the mockery in this woman's eyes that she would tease him by deliberately misinterpreting his explanation.

All he said was, 'It does.'

She looked away to one side, towards the thin sheen of water pouring down the opposite wall of the ravine, and nodded her head very slightly.

Then she turned back to him, her lips taunting him once more.

'Well,' she said, 'each to their own. Myself, I always use my full name.'

'Which is what? You still haven't told me.'

'Alyss, of course.'

She looked at him crossly.

'You've obviously heard of me,' she said with acid force.

'Well, not in so many words,' Rehan muttered. He knew that he was in the presence of a singer whose powers were very much greater than his, who could topple him off the ledge into the roiling waters with just a flick of her fingers, and he was wondering how to be suitably servile to her while at the same time not offending her: the two aims were incompatible.

'Never mind.' She was smiling. Her moods seemed to be mercurial. She plucked a twig from the bush Rehan had been clinging to and threw it out above the water, watching it spin in the air as it fell to its doom.

'Tell me,' he said. 'Tell me why you're here.'

'Because we need to protect Anya, of course.'

'Anya. Who's Anya?'

'The woman who'll change Albion. The child of Lian – do you remember him?'

'No.'

Alyss sighed.

'If things had been only a little different, Lian would have taken away the throne of Albion from the Ellonia. But he was too stupid to call upon the allies he could have called upon, and so he failed.'

She threw another twig into the maelstrom, and watched with interest as it was tumbled and twisted away downstream. Still there was an unnatural peace surrounding them. Rehan felt the urge to push out with his fist, to press against the silvery bubble that seemed to be protecting them – not because he wanted to burst it: all he wished to do was feel its surface against his knuckles.

'You're *sure* you don't remember Lian?'

'No,' said Rehan. 'I haven't heard the name before. I'm sorry.'

'Forget it, then.'

Alyss looked at him as if he were something undesirable she'd discovered on the road.

'You're a singer?' she said, a little while later.

'Yes,' he agreed. 'I am.'

'Then let me teach you a song.'

He laughed.

The ledge tilted alarmingly, and he stopped laughing.

'That was deliberate,' he snarled.

'Perhaps,' said Alyss vaguely, her head bowed over the keys of her clarsach. She was using a wooden key to adjust the tuning of the countless strings. The long nail of the little finger of her left hand was touching the strings gently, so that she could hear their soft noise through the wooden soundbox. Against his will he blew a note so that she could tune her instrument to his flute.

The rumbling of the waters was a long way in the distance. For the moment the two of them were in a place where there were just themselves, their instruments, and the voices they might use.

'I want you to do something for me,' she said, listening critically as she flexed a string and the note rose and fell.

He ran his fingers up and down the holes of his flute, hearing in his mind the notes that he might have been playing.

'I might,' he said grudgingly.

'I want you to join the daughter of Lian, and help her.'

'The daughter of someone I've never heard of?'

'That's right.'

A flattish note suddenly became perfect as she twisted the key. To Rehan it was as if Alyss had plucked unexpected light from the sky.

'Who is this person?'

'At the moment,' said Alyss, 'nobody much. She's a pleasant enough child, but there are plenty of intelligent children in Albion. She'll tell you all about Lian, if you ask her to; and you can find out more from a parent of hers called Reen. Anya's mother . . . well, Anya's mother has served her purpose. That's a harsh thing to say – this string is likely to break soon – but unfortunately it's true.'

'This Anya's the daughter of the Lian you've mentioned?'

'Oh, yes.' Alyss looked at him with wide eyes before turning back to her tuning. 'Yes,' and now her voice was more muffled as she pressed her face again to the soundbox, 'you won't understand Anya unless you realise that she's

Lian's daughter. Lian led. Had I been the leader in his place I'd have done a whole lot better, but of course I wasn't asked – we singers never are. Still, he made a good fist of it, all things considered. Anya is likely to do much better than her father did, but only if she has help.'

'And you want me to help her.' Rehan said the words flatly.

'I do declare,' said Alyss with a deliberate burst of thespian over-emphasis, 'but we have an intelligent man among us.'

Rehan flushed.

'Why?' he said. The cork inner lining between the two tubes of his flute had dried out a little too much – strange, since only a little while before it had seemed to be becoming too wet – and he rubbed his fingertips over the surface of the mud before applying a little of the moisture. Of course, this meant that he'd now put himself out of tune with Alyss's clarsach.

'Lian,' said Alyss, 'made a great mistake. All of the people whom he gathered around him were warriors. He built himself up an army of soldiers, and he led it against the soldiers of the House of Ellon. He knew he was trying to conquer well armed professional soldiers using amateurs with home-made bows and arrows, but he still believed he could succeed unaided. Anya will have, I hope, more sense than that. There, I'm in tune. How about you?'

Rehan asked her to sound a note and he readjusted the tubes of his wooden flute until he could match it exactly. Letting go of the bush, he played a little riffling scale, feeling his fingers create the notes.

'Who is this Anya?' he repeated. 'You've told me that she's the daughter of a failed rebel. That's hardly a recommendation.'

'She's She Who Leads. But the army she'll lead won't be anything like the one her father did. I'll be in it. So will you – don't pretend that you won't. There may be other singers apart from ourselves. And there'll be a dreamer as well.'

'Yes,' said Rehan, feeling his flute become a part of him

yet again as the notes that it created reached up into the sky, where the clouds heard them. 'You still haven't really answered my question. Who's Anya?'

'A child, right now,' said Alyss. 'Her breasts are budding and she's started to menstruate, but it'll be a while before she becomes an adult. If you'll let me come into your mind I'll show you where she is, so that after the storm is over you can make your way there and offer her all the help of your music. I can't promise to be with you then, but I'll follow as soon as I can.'

Rehan blew up a whirlpool of liquid notes on his flute, and Alyss matched them with hastily plucked notes on the clarsach, her fingers seizing the strings as if they were her enemies. The bubble of calmness that had been surrounding them swelled outwards, until it crossed the entire ravine. The music stopped the flood of the water, and then made it retreat back up the ravine until there was nothing left but the sounds the singers made and the echoes that returned to them from the walls of the ravine. Alyss and Rehan, swaying towards and away from each other, wove tapestries of music; they smiled at each other every time they discovered a new blending of serendipitous notes.

The wrath of the spate beneath them slowly abated until it was nothing but a mumbling.

Rehan held his flute out in front of him and looked at its long shaft. He twirled it through his fingers, remembering the old woman who'd been so kind to him.

'I'm not going to die,' he said to Alyss.

'Not yet,' she said.

'I'll climb the cliff.'

'Climbing's a mug's game. I'll take you up there.'

He found himself clutching her left ankle as she scrambled up a ladder of air by the side of the ravine until the two of them were lying on the coarse grass at the head of the cliff. He felt the sharpness of the blades scratching against his cheeks.

Both of them turned around and looked down into the ravine, where the surge of the water was now growing greater than ever.

'That's a pretty chord,' said Alyss, producing one.

Rehan looked at her with undisguised dislike: she was much too sure of herself.

'Listen to it again,' she said, pretending not to notice his stare, 'and remember it. Every time you try to find the child, imagine you're hearing this chord. It'll guide you to her.'

Rehan was alone on the clifftop, the rain once again beating him about the head and shoulders. He looked around him, but Alyss was nowhere to be seen. There was nothing but the flattened, wet, sad-looking grass.

He brought Alyss's chord into his mind and immediately knew the direction he had to follow.

Later, once the rain had stopped, he composed a new tune on his flute – a merry jig that bore nothing at all in common with his turbulent state of mind.

It was difficult for the mages to find a place for the singers, like Alyss and Barra 'ap Rteniadoli Me'gli'minter Rehan and the dreamers in their heliocentric cosmology, and so, wisely, they didn't attempt it – besides, singers and dreamers almost always gave the Ellonia a wide berth, not wishing the slivers of magic they possessed to be enslaved and ruthlessly exploited by the tyrants. The Despots had always regarded tales of such folk as mere legends, and the mages encouraged such a belief. Let the Despots continue to think that the only people empowered with magic were the mages themselves – that way lay security. The truth was rather different.

No one knew how long ago it had been that the shores of Albion had been open to traders from the World; with no measure of the passing of any span of time longer than that of a human life, even the Ellonia couldn't be more specific than to say that the guardian shroud of mist had encircled the land for all of eternity. Yet the Ellonia's own legends told them of how it had not always been like this, of how in a primitive time crude ships manned by the peoples of the World had sometimes found harbour on Albion's coast. One of these, the *Ellon*, had brought a cargo of pioneers from a place called the Nameless City; the duty of these people had been to explore the little known land and then, if they found it hospitable, to return to their home and bring a fleet of other ships bulging with further colonists. Instead they had found an island realm ripe for conquest and had stayed, abandoning their compatriots to whatever fate might befall them.

For in those times Albion had been unlike the World. The society indigenous to the country had been dispersed and agrarian, pacific and heedlessly anarchic – although it had been no paradise, for hunger and disease hadn't spared the natives. More to the point, however, as far as the intruders had been concerned, magic had seemed to be almost totally absent from its people. The healers who were to be found in every village effected their cures through the use of concoctions of herbs and minerals, rather than by calling upon more arcane powers. Deeds were performed as a result of human endeavour rather than through the recitation of recondite incantations. The stars were lights in the night-time sky, not pathways to power. The colonists were too restricted in their minds to see that each and every native of Albion was joined with the land by a magic which, although passive, was none the less powerful for that.

The people aboard the *Ellon* included sorcerers. Their ship was laden with weapons. The peasants of Albion had never formed a large-scale, coherent society. The conquest was easy.

The last and greatest spell of the sorcerers required them to call upon all the World's resources of magic. They created the barrier that surrounded Albion, dislocating the island in time so that, while the years succeeded each other in all the other nations of the globe, in Albion the sun remained perpetually overhead, never straying far from the zenith – the moons and stars were never seen. Almost always the passage of time in Albion was separated by several seconds from that in the World – a few short seconds that represented an unbreachable wall. But the spell was imperfect, and so this differential varied continuously, in the same way that the sun's position diverged from the zenith. And sometimes – rarely – time within Albion coincided with that of the World for a short while, creating rents in the seething mist of sheared air molecules that marked the barrier. A mathematician of the World might have been able to predict these moments, given specific knowledge of the details of the spell that the sorcerers had employed; the practising magicians among the original Ellonia knew those details, of course, but lacked the scientific expertise of the World to go alongside their knowledge . . . And, as they soon discovered, magic was a creature that they could not tame. The parts of it that they had been vain enough to assume they possessed left them, rendering them impotent, magicians without magic. These shards joined with the wild inherent magic of the land itself to form an abstraction of both that had little regard for the doings of mortals: the Ellonia's temporal rule became a mere charade, for the sole ruler of Albion was magic itself.

And magic is capricious, it has a childish love of play – and a childish proclivity for breaking its toys.

The ancient bonds between the natives and the land were, with a few exceptions, sundered – *had to be* sundered, for in the playful hands of magic the land itself was no longer a stable entity, but was instead in a never-ending state of flux. Its constant geomorphological ebbings and flowings were a reflection of the uncertain nature of reality that came about in Albion. The natives both suffered the worst and gained the best from this, for, since much of the past was no longer immutable, they could have no knowledge of it . . . and yet, under the tyranny of the Ellonia, such ignorance was a blessing. The future? If there were a multitude of choices as to the truth of the past, then for the future that number became infinite.

And as for the Ellonia themselves? Magic chose to reject them entirely, choosing to withdraw its beneficence from them (a situation which the mages in due course chose to describe to each other as a rejection by the Ellonia of the entreating whore that was magic). To the remainder of the Ellonia, those not privy to the mages' secrets, it seemed as if their dynasty was possessed of, rather than rejected by, magic, for was it not the case that wherever they went the ferment of the land ceased and reality became fixed?

This magical abstraction was not internally consistent: its whole had been made up from many parts. Like any conscious diverse entity, parts of it dissented from the others, and a few of these rebels bestowed themselves in small measure upon mortals. There were singers among the natives of Albion, men and women who had no real knowledge of the power that inhabited them yet found that they could draw words and music from the empty air and use them to express the concepts of the magic within them. They, too, as concentrations of single-minded magic, were foci for consistent realities. As were the few dreamers, whose minds possessed the often unsought ability to invade the territory of magic and bring back elements of it as hostages.

The abstraction as a whole did not trouble itself with such trifling aberrations. Instead it laughed and cavorted as it played with the realities and with its mortal toys. Only sometimes did it choose, for purposes that were not human and are hence incomprehensible to humans, to make its presence more directly known to those of its playthings whom it normally shunned. Knowing that the nakedness of its abstraction would make communication impossible, for the benefit of the stupid, unimaginative mortals with whom it conversed it took on a physical guise, as one of the natural elements. It could have chosen fire, water or the ground, but in fact it selected the air.

Sometimes the wind became the Wind.

The Ellonia believed that they understood the motives of the Wind, that its purposes could somehow be comprehended in human terms. They believed that the Wind was their ally – a fickle ally, but an ally nevertheless. It was impossible for them to recognise that the Wind was no one's ally. Stuck in the mire of their own pragmatism, they could not conceive of – let alone aesthetically appreciate – the fundamental indefinability of the magical abstraction. Had they realised the depths of their misunderstanding they would, due to their lack of imagination, have been irritated with the inexplicability of it rather than enraptured by its beauty or transported by the possibilities that its limitlessness would have opened up to their minds.

The dreamers and the singers could and did explore some of those possibilities; even a few of the natives did, although they could not realise that they were doing so. But magic had slammed its doors in the faces of the Ellonia, and the Ellonia themselves had turned the keys.

On those infrequent occasions when the time barrier between Albion and the rest of the World was penetrable, it was possible for traces of the World's greater magic to come into the land. Most often these traces were directly absorbed into the abstraction but sometimes, when they were absorbed by mortals, they retained their independence. Those mortals became singers who had no need for song, dreamers who had no need to dream. They brought with them knowledge from the World which, in conjunction with their own unconscious magic, had the power to effect change. To say that Albion's magic feared or respected their influence would be to ascribe human motives to it – to make the same blind error that the Ellonia did. Instead, all we can say is that it recognised the existence of these entities and responded to them.

Somewhere, deep in the heart of Barra 'ap Rteniadoli Me'gli'minter Rehan – and of every other singer of Albion – there was an indigenous shard of magic that knew and comprehended all this. Rehan himself didn't, of course. Even though he'd had his first meeting with Alyss – who, like the magical abstraction, regarded Albion as her playground – he would know nothing of such matters for some long while.

If ever.

Even for Alyss, the future didn't exist yet.

Most of the villagers had decided they didn't like Anya. They'd been prepared to accept her unfeminine roughness for quite a long time, but then she'd made a point of beating the shit out of Bartqa, the village bully, to the extent that Bartqa had had to wear a sling for a score or more of waking-periods. Nobody liked Bartqa very much, either, but it was considered unseemly for a small girl, barely entering puberty, to have caused him such considerable damage. Bartqa's family would have exacted vengeance had it not been for the fact that the vigilante force they'd sent out had just happened to encounter Reen who, by the purest of chances, had been out for a stroll at the time. Reen, too, had abruptly become unpopular, even though she'd immediately set about preparing splints and bandages.

Syor had reluctantly thrashed Anya for fighting. Reen had later, creeping secretively up the stairs, brought her a couple of cakes, a couple of kisses, and whispered advice on how better to use her right uppercut. Bartqa had stopped being a bully – any time he tried to intimidate a smaller kid he'd see Anya's wrath-filled face and suddenly think of something else he ought to be doing – and so Anya began slowly to regain popularity among the children, even though their parents continued to regard her with deepest distrust. She was, after all, a child who had come among them from nowhere. They had only the word of Syor and Reen that she was Lian's daughter.

Anya spent much of that sleeping-period sobbing loudly, long after the pain had gone, doing her best to make her mother feel guilty. Eventually Reen clambered once again up the ladder to the attic where Anya was supposed to be sleeping and told her to shut up. She muttered the words with such intensity that Anya, terrified, turned over, stuck her thumb in her mouth – even though she was far too old for this – and fell immediately to sleep.

At the start of the next waking-period there was a newcomer in Lianhome. He was thin enough to show that very few people had loved him sufficiently to feed him, and his clothes were a collection of tatters: torn breeches, a stained tunic, a cape that he'd probably discovered by the side of the road. Yet he capered and danced happily, playing tunes on his flute or beating out rhythms on his bodhran, so that Anya felt her body begin to move in response to them. He was still able to play on the instruments while performing cartwheels down the village's main street, the dirtiness of his cape periodically hiding his face from the villagers. Anya found that her fingers were moving in sympathy with the singer's, almost as if she were playing the flute alongside him.

He stopped tumbling for a few moments and put aside the flute, beginning almost immediately to beat on the bodhran. He opened his mouth again and sang a song that he'd composed just a short time ago.

Seven women rode down through the town of Starveling that night,

he sang,

Horses' hooves spitting galaxies in the pale moons' empty light,
And their eyes sought out the corners where the shadows grew
As deep and as dark as wine.

To Anya the words and the music were nectar; she held them close to herself. Syor and Reen had told her about the magic that music could create, but neither of them had ever been able to do more than fumble clumsily with a tambour. This person – Rehan – could pull musical instruments from his various unpleasant-smelling garments and bring from them the sounds of the sky.

He stopped playing and singing, a boyish grin on his face. Anya was beside him, aware of the fact that her eyes were at the level of his shoulder. He glanced at her briefly, recognising her as the girl whom Alyss had described, then turned away to acknowledge the plaudits of the villagers. They were cheering and shouting in a way which normally he'd have relished. He raised his arms to them, his flute in one hand, and bowed deeply. At the moment all he wanted to do was to speak with this little fair-haired girl. Alyss had told him that, if he followed the chord across Albion for long enough, he'd find the child. Now he'd done so he was filled with impatience: according to what Alyss had said, he was standing next to She Who Leads, the girl who would become the woman who'd build an army that would defeat the House of Ellon . . .

'Not an army,' said Anya.

'Um,' said Rehan, startled.

'There'll be only a few of us. At most a few thousands, but more likely a few hundreds. Forget your dreams of columns of infantry. That's not the way to conquer Albion. Honest.'

'That's what you say now,' said Rehan, making sure that there was no one else within earshot. 'But you're only a child.'

'Speak with Reen. She was at Lian's side as he led a great army against the House of Ellon. He lost. She tells me that we have to use different ways if we're going to defeat the Ellonia.'

The child was squatting, finding fascinating stones in the road. Rehan knelt down beside her and ran his fingers through the soil, feeling its grittiness against his fingernails.

Anya pointed her finger towards the sky.

I've lost the love of my daughter . . .

Below Syor, down to the left, was the village of Lianhome, its few pathways seeming to melt and flow in the heat-haze. She held her face in her hands, struggling to keep her fingers out of her eyes. Beneath her there was a long drop, at the bottom of which she could see harsh rocks.

I've lost my love for my daughter . . .

It hadn't been a sudden thing, this feeling, just a slowly growing sensation that Anya was not really of her flesh. More and more, Syor had found herself acting out the role of motherhood rather than being a mother. This child whom she'd watched grow from babyhood had become almost a stranger – almost a *foe* – to her. Too many small things – Anya so mercilessly beating a bully, Syor thrashing Anya and feeling hatred as she did so – had amassed together, had conspired to torment her. She should have been able to tell Anya of her pain, but one doesn't tell one's innermost secrets to strangers. She might have confided in Reen, but she wanted to merit Reen's respect, not beg her pity.

I'm alone. I've always been alone. When Lian was with me I thought I wasn't . . .

Imprisoned in a room with many doors, all locked except one, Syor leaned forwards and felt herself falling downwards through the air.

She spread her arms and her legs, so that she was flying free.

Chapter Three
Newcomers

At first the bowstring had cut into her fingertips but now, after long practice, the skin was callused and hard so that she no longer felt any pain. Anya squinted along the length of the arrow, feeling that it was an extension of her body. She focused her eyes alternately on the arrow's tip and, in the distance, the stylised deer that Reen had painted in white on a tree-trunk. All around the throat of the image were the marks where Anya's arrows had struck.

She loosed the string and saw her arrow fly, as quick as light, to stand proudly between the deer's eyes. Almost immediately she had a fresh arrow nocked in the string and was ready to fire again. She was annoyed with herself: the exertion was making her breathe heavily, and Reen had told her that the main skill of archery was to perform every action as efficiently as possible, so that she could spend a whole waking-period shooting arrows and still feel relaxed at its end.

The second arrow almost split the first. The third thudded into the wood between the first two. Had the deer been a real one, rather than just a painting, it would have been dead three times over.

'Enough,' said Reen peremptorily. Her hair had become grey but she was still as trim as ever. 'Now we must practise with the sword.'

Almost before Anya was ready, Reen's wooden blade was whipping the air above her head. Anya dropped to her knees, throwing the bow from her, and drew her own wooden practice sword from its sheath, striking out at the same time with her left hand towards Reen's ankles. The warrior dodged adroitly but lost her balance; she was staggering uncontrollably backwards when she found the sharp tip of Anya's sword uncomfortably close to her throat.

'Surrender.'

'I surrender,' Reen said.

The two of them sat down on the cushioned turf and grinned at each other. Reen had brought some bread and meat, and for a while they concentrated on eating. Anya was conscious of the flow of oil down the right-hand side of her chin; she wiped the mess away with her sleeve and saw the slick sheen of the fat on the woven cloth.

'You'll do,' said Reen. 'You're not half the soldier that your father was but, still, you'll do.'

'Was Syor a great fighter?'

'No. She'd courage, all right, when she was driven to it; but she lacked the skill.'

'Why do you want *me* to have it?'

'Because you're going to have to lead us.'

Anya threw her sword into the air, watching it spin end-over-end, and caught it by the hilt. 'I don't want to lead,' she said, throwing the weapon like a spear so that it plunged into the ground.

'You have no choice.'

'Why not?'

'The people of this village – they're why you have no choice. Now that you're here, some of them remember Lian and the way he led the peasants against the House of Ellon. You're expected to do the same, whether you like it or not.'

Reen picked a daisy from the grass and held it to her nose, appreciating the flower's humble scent.

The two women exchanged food.

'I don't want to kill people,' said Anya after a while.

'You'll have little choice.'

'Why?'

'Because of the way the Ellonia *are*. They've kept us down too long.'

300

Anya studied the grass in front of her.

'Do you think you're my mother?' she asked shyly.

'In a way.'

'What do you mean by that?'

'Your mother's dead. You know that. I'm your "other mother". I do my best.'

'In which case, I'm your "other daughter".'

A pause. 'True. You could say that.'

Reen picked up a sharp-edged stone and threw it at the painted deer. The stone was perfectly aimed and shattered the cluster of Anya's arrows. Splinters of wood flew to the ground, littering the forest floor.

Reen pulled herself up to her feet and flexed her shoulders; then, conscious of the way her muscles were creaking, she touched her toes once, twice and a third time. Anya laughed at her.

'Back home,' said Reen. 'It's time we went back home.'

The two women gathered their weapons and stowed them away in their haversacks; the wooden swords were returned to their sheaths.

'Next time the Ellonia come here to Lianhome,' said Anya, 'we'll slay them.'

'Yes. Next time. But haven't there been rather a lot of "next times"?'

They were trudging through the woods, pine needles squashily soft beneath their feet.

'I don't *care*,' said Anya forcefully. 'You keep telling me I'm supposed to be a leader, a killer, but every time I get ready to do something about it you stop me. You tell me I've got to take precautions, or to be careful.'

'Yes.'

'Why?'

Reen looked around her at the blueness of the sky and the greenness of the deciduous trees. Raising the child, after Syor's death, had not been cosy. Adolescence is a miserable time for all concerned, but in Anya's case – Syor having been so brutally taken from her – it had been doubly bad. Reen had tried to be both mother and father to Anya, and was convinced that she'd succeeded in neither role.

'"Why?" That's the impossible question. It seems pretty obvious to me that, if you're to lead us, you need to stay alive.' She skirted a cowpat, feeling angry. 'Until you're ready to battle the Ellonia it'd be madness to reveal your existence. But I think you're ready now. It won't be long until they're among us again.'

Anya said nothing for a while. She'd been there when the villagers had discovered her mother's battered body at the foot of the cliff, and had watched as the bruised meat was interred under an anonymous clump of grass. Reen had explained to her that, had Anya not been there and had Anya not been Lian's daughter, the villagers would have forgotten Syor at the moment she died. Instead they'd accorded her the honour that they might have given to a monarch. Anya, as a child, had watched the ceremony with tears in her eyes but with very little passion: Syor had always seemed far more distant than Reen had. Syor had seemed in some obscure way to dislike her, even as she held her on her lap, whereas Reen had played games of ball with her, or taught her the skills of arm-wrestling.

'Then we strike?' Anya said.

'Yes. We must strike them soon.'

They were entering the village, feeling the hardness of the earthen road under their feet.

'Must we kill them?'

'I don't see what else we can do. The alternative is that they'll massacre everyone in Lianhome. They wouldn't think twice about it – they've been trained not to.'

Anya saw a mushroom in the grass ahead of her. She stooped to pluck it and stowed it away in her shoulder-bag. Reen hardly broke stride as she watched Anya half-run to catch up with her.

'I don't like killing,' said Reen, 'any more than you do. But the Ellonian soldiers would kill us without any compunction: as far as they're concerned, we're just animals ripe for slaughter. They don't think of us as if we were human beings like themselves.'

She tossed her head so that her grey hair made a curve in the air.

'Do *you* think of us as human beings?'

Reen stopped in her tracks and looked at Anya furiously. 'Of course I do,' she said. 'Why do you ask that?'

'Because sometimes you can seem so cold.'

A few moments passed before Reen started walking again.

'I loved your mother, you know,' she said. 'When she died I had to readjust all the thoughts I'd had before. I wanted her to be alive, but of course that wasn't possible, so I had to go for the next best thing, which was making sure her death hadn't been for nothing.'

'What's that got to do with slaughtering the Ellonia?'

'A lot, child. A lot. Your mother saw what the Ellonia did to your father, and she would never have been able to forgive them. If she'd had the courage she'd have stayed alive in order to kill them herself. She wasn't the most forgiving of people, your mother: that was probably why she killed herself.'

Now they were in the centre of Lianhome. They turned left to climb the hill towards the house they shared. Anya tossed the mushroom from hand to hand, enjoying the feel of its soft clammy dampness against her palms.

'She never forgave me for becoming her lover,' said Reen, kicking at a stone, 'even though it was something she wanted more than I did.'

'But you've never tried to become *my* lover,' said Anya.

'I don't fancy you,' Reen replied, not looking at the girl.

'Thanks.'

'I love you, but that's something different. I think Syor would love you the same way that I do, if she were still alive. As far as I'm concerned, you're my daughter, and that's an end of it.'

Anya pushed open the badly hinged door of the house they shared, filled the kettle with water from the pump, and lit a flame beneath it. Reen sat down on the settle and pulled off her boots appreciatively, murmuring to herself as she smelt the warm perspiration of her feet. She stretched out her legs, feeling the coarse matting beneath her heels.

There was someone else in the cottage.

They both became aware of this at the same moment.

Reen's dagger was in her hand. Anya took a little while longer because she had to remove the kettle from the heat.

'Hello there,' said a voice from one of the upstairs bedrooms.

'Sounds friendly,' said Reen, although she failed to sheathe her dagger.

'It's me,' said the voice.

Anya's face was white. Since childhood she'd expected that Ellonian soldiers would invade the house purely because she was Lian's daughter. Now her worst dreams seemed to be coming true.

'Forget it,' said Reen. 'That's no one from the House of Ellon. The accent's all wrong.'

'Then who is it?'

'That bloody singer, at a guess. The one who was here when your mother died.'

Reen raised her voice.

'Where are you?'

Her dagger was still in her hand.

There was a clattering of footsteps down the wooden stairs and the tall man appeared. In his left hand he held his cane flute, which he obviously regarded as more important than his own life: the instrument was nestled to his side and held well clear of the steps. On his right arm he bore his bodhran. He looked at the flute and the bodhran and then smiled at Reen.

'You're Anya,' he said, over-courteously.

'Try again.'

Reen looked to her right.

'Ah, so *you're* Anya.'

'Yes.'

She couldn't remember having brought the bow to her shoulder, but it was there. Anya was seeing the centre of the man's forehead down the length of her arrow, just as she'd seen the deer's throat.

'Put the bow away, Anya,' said Reen quietly.

Anya obeyed.

'Who are *you*?' she said.

'Barra 'ap Rteniadoli Me'gli'minter Rehan,' said the man, 'but generally I prefer to be called "Rehan". You don't remember, but I was here before. I was told to come to your assistance, but I was too early, the first time. Well . . . now I'm back.' He smiled brightly.

'Who told you?'

Reen was still tense.

'A singer, like myself. She told me her name was Alyss, but I don't know if I can believe her.'

'I know about Alyss,' said Anya. The kettle, now back over the flame, was beginning to boil. 'She met some friends of my father's once. And she came here to see me, too.'

Reen pulled out a chair from the table and gestured Rehan towards it.

'Why are you here?'

'As I said, because Alyss told me that I should be,' he said.

'Will you take tea?'

'Of course.'

He settled down in the hard chair, resting his elbows comfortably on the table. He smiled at the two women, one after the other. Through the window sunlight poured, painting the floor yellow. Barra 'ap Rteniadoli Me'gli'minter Rehan watched the movement of the light for a few moments, then looked away.

'My friends call me "Rehan",' he repeated.

'No wonder,' said Anya.

The tea was tart and Rehan didn't like it very much, but he drank it anyway, hoping that somehow it'd start to taste nicer. He was disappointed: the last gulp tasted just as bad as the first.

Anya smiled at the man.

'You've been introduced to Reen?' she said.

'Not as of this moment, no,' Rehan replied.

'You've met Anya before?' said Reen sarcastically.

'. . . No.'

Anya giggled.

When she woke at the start of the waking-period Anya

felt sore between the legs. Beside her Rehan was snoring soundly, and she snuggled her body around his, feeling the warmth of his back against her stomach and breasts. She ran her fingers up and down through the short hair at the top of his neck, watching his vulnerability as he slept. She cupped her hand around his loins, caressing his balls, until she managed to generate a sleepy reactive twitch.

Rehan did his best to simulate sleep but without success.

Later, leaving Anya snoring on her back, he crawled out of the bed and put on a gown. He peed briefly, then found himself some food: a few raw mushrooms followed by some fistfuls of bread. A couple of raw eggs finished his meal; then he drank a litre of cold tea.

Reen was already there.

'Alyss told you,' she said.

'Alyss told me what?'

'To become a part of us.'

'Yes. She said that I should do that.'

He watched her as she prepared mushrooms for herself. He was embarrassed by the fact that she was so much more efficient than he had been.

'You made love with Anya?' Her half-question was nervous.

'Yes.' His answer was equally so.

'You're a lucky man. She must like you very much indeed.' Chop, chop, chop went her swift-moving fingers. 'She's never slept with a man before.'

'I could tell.' Rehan wished the conversation were over – or, better still, that it had never started.

'I'll miss her,' said Reen with slightly forced matter-of-factness.

'She's not planning to leave here, is she?' Then Rehan realised that this was not what Reen had been meaning. 'Oh,' he said, flummoxed for words.

'I knew the time would come,' said Reen, chewing a mushroom fastidiously. He'd never seen anyone able to speak gracefully with their mouth full before.

'You were her lover?'

'Not in any physical sense, no. It'd have seemed all rather incestuous, somehow, seeing as I was her mother's lover and Anya has always regarded me as a parent.' Reen was no longer showing any of the hesitancy or embarrassment she'd displayed a moment before; Rehan wished that he could have said the same for himself. 'But we've been closer than many a pair of physical lovers. If it hadn't been for circumstances . . .'

Barra 'ap Rteniadoli Me'gli'minter Rehan could think of no response. He sat at the table, his chin in his hands, looking at the older woman compassionately. His own love life had been less extensive than he could have wished, but he could remember only too well that feeling of utter desolation when it becomes clear that the object of your love will be forever denied to you. He reached out one hand and very gently brushed the backs of Reen's fingers with his own.

'I'm sorry,' he said inadequately.

'Don't be. Part of me wants to sing and dance for her sake. I will tell you one thing, though. She's a very precious person, our Anya. I don't mean just in the sense that she's She Who Leads; I mean for *herself*. I don't expect you necessarily to commit the rest of your life to her, but if you're ever cruel to her . . . well, I have little doubt that I'm abler with the sword than you are.'

Rehan could think of nothing he wanted to do less right now than harm the smallest hair on Anya's body. Reen saw this in his face and nodded slowly in satisfaction.

A few waking-periods later there was another newcomer to Lianhome, also sent here by Alyss. Strangers were rare enough that Reen could tell from the shouts of excitement outside that she should put on her sword-belt – its scabbard this time containing her iron, rather than her wooden, sword – and go to investigate. She felt weary as she felt the pommel to make sure that the weapon was exactly where she wanted it. *In some other world*, she thought, *perhaps things are different and you don't always have to assume a*

*visitor's an enemy until you're able to prove otherwise. I'd like
to be able to just relax and welcome strangers to our house with
a goblet of cider or tea.*

She shrugged. A vain hope.

She squinted her eyes against the brightness of the sunlight as she came out into the open. At first she couldn't
work out what all the commotion was about, but then she
saw a bedraggled, haggard old man lurching wearily
towards her, ignoring the chorus of high-pitched questions
from the gaggle of children surrounding him. He looked
up and saw her standing, legs apart and hands on hips, ten
or fifteen metres in front of him, and a great tide of relief
crossed his face.

He gestured futilely at his unwanted entourage, and Reen
took the hint.

'Get away with you!' she shouted at the children, waving
her hands in sweeping movements. 'Can't you see this trav-
eller is weary from his journeying?'

Cowed, the children crept away to find shadows from
where they could watch what happened at a distance.

'Is this Lianhome?' gasped the old man. He had long,
greasy grey hair that clung stickily to his shoulders; an
equally long and filthy grey beard tangled itself among the
coarse blood-coloured wool of his cloak.

Reen nodded.

'Praise be to all that's good in this world – although
there's precious little of it,' he said. 'Right now I'd even
offer a minor paean to the Despot himself to be sure that
I'd finally reached here.'

He paused for a moment.

'I really have, I suppose?' he said just as Reen was about
to speak. 'I mean, you're not pretending or anything, are
you? You're not secretly a mirage, or something like that,
tormenting a poor old man's aching bones by imitating a
village?'

Reen laughed and assured him that she really was
a woman and that this really was the village of
Lianhome.

He looked at her with suspicious red eyes.

'Well, you *would* say that, wouldn't you?'

Reen smiled again and walked forward slowly, anxious not to frighten him by any too sudden movement, holding out her bronzed arm.

'Pinch me,' she said. 'Then you'll find out I'm real.'

He obeyed, with surprising strength, and she took a rapid step backwards, rubbing her flesh.

'Hmmm,' he muttered, scratching himself behind one ear contemplatively. 'I suppose you probably *are* really there, but it's hard to be certain. They're clever buggers, these mirages, and delight in deceiving people using all sorts of tricks – or so I've heard tell, never having met one in person, as it were, myself. Still, no one's ever said anything about a *solid* mirage before, so for the moment I'll take you on trust, young woman. But remember, you're still on probation. If you start dissolving into a cloud of mist, old Joli will notice and be onto you like a hawk on a fieldmouse.'

Reen began to laugh again at the prospect of this dotard threatening her, but then something in his eyes caused her laughter to trail away before it had properly begun. He wasn't as frail or as stupid as he seemed, this man. She would do well not to underestimate him.

He saw her eyebrows rising and smiled.

'I wish you no harm, wench,' he said.

'It's many years since I've been a wench,' she corrected, although nodding her thanks in acknowledgement of the compliment. 'Who are you?'

'Joli – as I said. I have many skills, but perhaps the greatest is that I'm a dreamer.'

He bowed with mock courtesy.

Reen drew in her breath. The last person they wanted among them was a dreamer. No wonder the old man looked so exhausted: it must have been many waking-periods since last he'd permitted himself to sleep.

Dreamers paid a terrible price for their gift.

'You will not sleep in this village,' she said sternly.

'Fear not,' he said, dismissing her words with a backwards wave of his hand. 'I'm not so much of an inconsiderate fool as I might look, you know. I've been sent to help you, not to put your scrubby little lives in danger. If I find I need to sleep I'll trek out into the hills and find somewhere lonely.'

Reen guessed that Joli had been sent by Alyss, but she couldn't imagine the underpinning of the woman's reasoning. It was a fairly safe rule to give as wide a berth as possible to dreamers, because they were dangerous. During the few sleeping-periods when they laid themselves to rest, their minds created bizarre images which obeyed no logical pattern. In their immediate area, these became manifest realities, affecting the people and places around them. Often this was harmless enough – their sexual dreams, in particular, created an innocent ecstasy that was far more intense than anything one could experience through the normal act.

But sometimes dreamers had nightmares. Then the story was very different.

Reen had never experienced a dreamer's nightmare, but she had heard enough stories about them. Boiling rocks plummeting from the sky represent the stuff of nightmare; implacably cruel generals, long-clawed monsters creeping unwelcomed from the fringes of the unconscious, gaping chasms suddenly appearing in the ground in front of you . . .

She shivered.

'You'll sleep a *long* way from Lianhome,' she said firmly.

'I told you: I will. It's a promise.'

He made a funny little shrugging motion, turning his hands outwards as if to show that they were empty of weapons.

Reen nodded doubtfully.

'I believe you,' she said.

'By the massed total of Ellonian genitalia, I sincerely trust that you do,' said Joli, suddenly angry. 'I'm a man of my word, and I expect you to remember that!'

A few of the braver children were creeping back towards them, some of them holding hands so that they could approach in mutually reassuring pairs.

'If indeed it was Alyss who sent you, then you have my trust.'

'Of course it was that blasted bitch who instructed me to come to this dump of a village! Do you think I'd have come for any other reason? She told me that I either had to cooperate with her or she'd transform me into one of the more unusual varieties of pond-slugs. She can be a very persuasive woman when she wants to be, you know that, Alyss.'

Reen was smiling again.

'You've friends to meet, Joli,' she said. 'Anya and Rehan. Come along with me and see if they're out of bed yet.'

He moved abruptly from aggression to companionability, and took her arm as if they'd known each other for most of their lives.

'Alyss told me about the girl-warrior called Anya,' he said, 'and instructed me that I must serve with her. If you're not a mirage after all, you must be Reen. Alyss mentioned another woman, Syor.'

'Syor's dead,' said Reen softly.

'Ah. Alyss chose not to mention that, the trollop.'

They walked back towards the cottage where once Mina and Terman had lived together as they brought up Lian.

'Her death caused you pain.'

It wasn't a question.

'Yes,' she said. 'It did.'

He didn't dwell on the matter.

'And you love her daughter as if she were your own.'

'Yes.'

'Who's this Rehan, then?'

'To give him his full name, he's Barra 'ap Rteniadoli Me'gli'minter Rehan; he's a singer, and prefers us to call him just "Rehan".'

She pushed open the cottage door and ushered the old man in ahead of her.

'A singer, eh? I've never met a singer I could trust.'

'I doubt if he's ever met a dreamer he could trust.'

Joli looked annoyed for a moment; then his face eased.

'Whoever taught you, woman,' he said, 'gave you a sharp tongue.'

'Have you eaten this waking-period?'

'I stole a turnip some while ago from an Ellonian stock-pile and ate it raw. I'd strongly recommend that you don't try the experience yourself: I lost more of that turnip than I can ever have ingested, and I'm still feeling the weakness of it. The world dropped out of my bottom.'

'You stole from the Ellonia?'

'Why! Of course! Who else could a man of honour steal from?'

'You're definitely a friend,' said Reen. 'Pull yourself up a stool. I'll call the others.'

A while later the four of them – Anya, Rehan, Joli and Reen – were drinking a thick vegetable soup and eating their hard-grained bread. Reen saw with some annoyance that Anya seemed instantly infatuated with the old man, and shot sympathetic glances towards Rehan, who ignored them. Joli, for his part, reacted coltishly to Anya's attentions until Reen kicked him firmly on the shin.

'Why did Alyss ask you to come here?' said Reen, ending a pause that had been interrupted only by the sounds of the four of them lapping their soup from their spoons.

'She didn't *ask* me,' said Joli, 'she *told* me. I had very little choice in the matter.'

'I remember the experience well,' murmured Rehan.

He briefly touched Anya's hand.

'She wants me to lead,' said Anya, putting her spoon to one side.

'All of us want you to lead,' remarked Reen, looking around the table at the others. Both of them smiled at her reassuringly. 'There's no one else who can apart from you, not in the same way that Lian did. Alyss places her trust in your leading us as well – otherwise she'd never have sent these friends of hers to help you.'

'Yes, but will I die the way that Lian died?' Anya looked into the meniscus of her soup as if she were looking for the answer there.

'No,' said Rehan.

'How can you be so certain?'

'Because Alyss is certain. If she thought there was any doubt she'd spare you.'

Joli lifted his bowl to his mouth and drank off the remainder of his soup noisily, then ate the last of his bread.

'Alyss has as much human compassion as an adder with toothache,' he muttered.

Reen agreed, but said nothing.

'She doesn't care if the four of us live or die,' Joli continued, 'so long as we help her destroy the Ellonia. That's the game she's playing at the moment. She doesn't have morals or ethics the same way that we have. Don't get me wrong. If she can help us she will. But it doesn't matter to her all that much, so if she decides that it serves her best if all of us should die she'll quite happily allow that to happen.'

'You're a gloomy person, Joli,' said Rehan.

'And you're wrong,' added Anya.

'How d'you mean?'

'Wrong,' she said. 'I can't say it any more plainly than that.'

She took a dark purple plum from the fruit bowl that Reen had placed in the centre of the table. The flesh of the fruit was a little hard but the flavour was sweet. Anya sucked at it, feeling the acerbic juice tumbling around the backs of her teeth and making her gums tingle.

'Alyss wouldn't send people here without reason,' said Anya, 'so she must have had a purpose for finding you two, wherever you were. She must have reckoned that you would contribute something important to the army that I must soon lead against Giorran and Ernestrad.'

'You stretch my credulity, maid,' said Joli, helping himself to a little more soup.

'I'm not a maid, and it is courteous to request permission before appropriating additional food.'

Joli looked at her balefully.

'Indeed?' he said.

'Indeed.'

'You're hardly hospitable.'

'Shut up,' said Rehan, surprising himself.

Joli's face turned nearly blue with fury.

'I mean it,' Rehan said. 'The people here are welcoming us among them, even though they have few resources of food or anything else. If it weren't for Reen or Anya you'd have been kicked out – and I wonder if that still wouldn't be the wisest thing for them to do to you. So show a few manners, my friend, when you're accepting their generosity.'

'I forgive you,' said Joli in a low and menacing voice, 'because I accept that you're young. When you're a little older, perhaps we'll see who's the stronger of the two of us.'

'Go,' said Anya to Joli. 'Whatever Alyss said, we don't want you here.'

Her face was dark.

'What do you mean?' the old man said.

'You're a pain in the bum, that's what I mean,' said Anya loudly. Rehan looked at her with admiration. 'Either you can start making friends with these friends of mine or you can leave us. Frankly, I don't care right now which of the options you choose: you're behaving like a malicious old bastard, and we can do without you. Go away and join the Ellonia: you'll find them a lot more to your taste. They're just as mean-minded and stupid as you are.'

Reen glanced at Anya. Her look was half reproach and half scepticism.

Joli seemed nonplussed.

'I'm a friend and ally of yours,' he said. 'Alyss told me to be.'

'Then start acting like one!'

Rehan suddenly began to respect the old man. Most people would have reacted in fury to Anya's outburst and stormed away from the village, but Joli instead considered what had been said to him, nodded, and apologised to the other people seated around the table. He gravely shook hands with Reen and Rehan and then, with a moue of apology, kissed the back of Anya's hand.

'Forgive me,' he said. The words were muted, so that

the others could barely hear them.

'Well,' he said after a little while, 'so much for all these bloody arguments, eh? May I have some more soup, ma'am, please?'

'Of course you may.'

'Good. I'm as hungry as a coastal shark in heat.'

He helped himself copiously, smiling at each of them in turn. When he'd finally finished eating he hauled himself to his feet and bowed towards them one by one.

'I must sleep now,' he said sadly. 'I advise none of you to follow me, because I can't predict what'll happen around me once I'm sleeping. I'll come back here as soon as I can – perhaps it'll be another couple of waking-periods, or perhaps it'll be even longer. I don't know.'

Rehan was washing dishes and goblets in the corner in the urn that Reen kept full of water for the purpose.

'We want to be your friends,' Anya explained apologetically, 'but you make it very difficult for us.'

'I said I was sorry, blast your tits,' said Joli. 'Let me go now. I must.'

He left them.

It didn't take long to clean the plates.

There was a new Army-Master, and the Despot wasn't sure he approved. In fact, the Despot was thinking of having the man executed on some trumped-up charge, so that someone a little more cooperative might be appointed in his place. This Ngur had, like his predecessor but one, an unpleasant habit of pointing out that it was a matter of record that some of the peasants had managed to form armies that had tested the Ellonia severely; moreover, he occasionally mentioned that the peasants had some slight grounds for their grievance, and that perhaps the Despot might rule a happier Albion if he accepted this and started to conduct negotiations.

The Despot looked upon these radical new ideas with as much favour as if they'd been a bucket of sick.

It wasn't that he wasn't progressive, he told himself, because of course he was: it was simply that he didn't want to find himself progressing too fast. As far as he was concerned, the people in his thrall could find long-term freedom only through short-term slavery: much as such a prospect revolted him – he was, after all, a libertarian – he saw little option to his planned course until some radical change occurred; for example, until after his own death.

He was happy for the new Army-Master, Ngur, to institute radical changes at that stage, but not a moment before.

He looked at the man with loathing. The soldier had instituted some insane new ideas. The worse of all of them had been the reduction in the torture of the peasants: was it not perfectly plain that the peasants went willingly to their ends no matter how unpleasant? Ngur had rejected all the Despot's received wisdom, and was actually displaying mercy to the animals. The Despot had had, several times during the past few waking-periods, to watch the dismal display of peasants being perfunctorily beheaded without even the most basic of preliminary disembowelments. The Despot recognised that this method of execution might just possibly be more palatable to the peasants, although, knowing the peasant mind, he doubted it; but it was the duty of the Army-Master to serve the Despot, not the peasants, and the Despot was becoming increasingly dissatisfied.

He drummed his pudgy fingers on the artificial gilt painted on the arms of his throne and stared at the man.

Ngur bowed. 'Your army has served you well, sire,' he said loudly. The courtiers gathered in the throne room moved appreciatively from side to side, nodding their heads.

The Despot realised that this was not the right moment to castigate his Army-Master.

'I hear you well,' he said.

'There are rumours abroad . . .'

The Despot sighed in his thunderously belching way. There were always rumours abroad, and most of them were nothing more than a farrago. The only time during his lifetime that the rumours had come to anything had been when that idiot whose name he now forgot had led an amateurish army against Ernestrad and been rewarded for his efforts by a lingering death. The Despot was generous enough to recall that the peasant had created panic among the Ellonia and that, even as he had died, his riders had mounted a desperate last-ditch struggle; but the fact was that the peasant had been comprehensively humiliated.

Any new peasant uprising would undoubtedly meet the same end, whoever led it. The problem with the peasants was that they had no brains, and so inevitably they lost out in any encounter with the Ellonia.

'We shall enter into consultations,' said the Despot to his Army-Master, thereby effectively making him seem small. 'We'll have to plan our tactics for the future.'

Ngur again bowed sceptically in his direction, and the Despot noted the impertinence. His courtiers did as well; they hummed loudly their disapproval of the soldier's behaviour.

With difficulty the Despot hauled himself down from his temporary throne, feeling his paunch rolling as he caught his balance, and gestured the Army-Master towards the official throne-room. He let a smile paint his face, and was gratified to see that the Army-Master accepted it as genuine. With his other hand the Despot beckoned one of his swordsmen to follow both of them.

The throne-room, as it was tactfully called among the Ellonian courtiers, was cool. Cloth hangings had been erected in pale greens and the windows were narrow, so that the light was rather like that in an underwater pool. The Despot made straight towards his throne of alabaster, pointing with his fingers that Army-Master Ngur should recline on one of the upholstered settles that nestled against the walls. The two of them made themselves comfortable while slaves served them with jellied sweetmeats and then retired, walking studiously backwards.

'We're too kind to the peasants,' said the Despot, spitting away the stone of a peach so that it flicked across the marble floor.

'I disagree. It may not be very long before the peasants rise up against us, and then all of us will be dead.'

'They tried before,' said the Despot.

'And they'll try again. This time they might succeed. Our spies tell us that they've got a new leader who's even more powerful than the old. Remember what h∍ nearly did to you: if he hadn't been unlucky he'd have ousted you from your throne. You'll be lucky if you esc∍pe so easily this time.'

'This is treason.'

Even so, the Despot hesitated from calling his guards to kill the Army-Master.

'No,' said Ngur, 'it's the exact opposite: it's loyalty. If you don't believe what I'm saying and you don't believe what I'm trying to tell you, then you'll find yourself in the tombs, watching the slaves tear you apart limb from limb. Is that what you really want? Despots have fallen before – not that, of course, I would wish in any way to contribute to your downfall.'

The Despot looked at him keenly.

It'd be nothing for him to have this man killed. On the other hand, Ngur had the loyalty of the Ellonian soldiery. The Despot forced his fury to the back of his mind and resolved to wait for his revenge until the time was right.

To make amends he called a slave to him and had the boy beheaded by the attendant swordsman, so that blood gushed out over a valuable carpet.

'You expect that the peasant army will threaten us?' said the Despot, feeling marginally more amiable.

'I think they might.'

'Why do you think this?'

'Because of the warriors they have. Some of them – I don't yet know how many – fought against us last time around.'

The Despot pulled a sticky truffle from the dish in front of him and popped it into his maw. He sucked on its sweetness until it melted in his mouth.

'They were rebels,' he said.

'You misjudge them, my lord,' said the Army-Master. 'They might have been your dedicated followers if only you'd given them some of your support.'

318

'I've heard that before.'

The Army-Master bowed again but this time there was an even greater note of sarcasm in the way he moved. He combed the dusty flooring with his hand, so that it looked as if he were laughing at the Despot. He stood up straight, smiling confidently. The Despot realised how impotent he was to retaliate.

A dreamer, at least one singer and two warriors had gathered an army about them, according to the reports of Ngur's spies.

The Despot knew very little of this. His ignorance held him in a limbo, so that he could only guess about the way they were rallying.

The dreamer rode a horse – unless he didn't.

The singer either rode a horse or ran until she was able to sling herself up onto a horse; if there were more than one singer – reports on this conflicted – they found themselves on horseback, one way or another. The warriors were natural horsemen, as one would expect; the word was that at least one of them had served under the brat Lian, but the Despot was sceptical about such tales and found all of this intelligence extremely confusing.

He wasn't frightened of the small force – in fact, he felt that he could put it to his own devious uses. The House of Ellon had, after all, put down a far larger uprising with ease, and was no longer concerned with rebellions. A few soldiers – and more particularly their officers – might die, but that'd be a small price to pay for the number of peasants who'd meet their ends. Dreamers and singers were difficult foes, he knew, but there were so few of them that he was barely worried: the men of his army, he was certain, would display their usual efficiency and destroy the enemy. Ngur had told him several times that, however fine the Ellonian Army looked on parade, its efficiency – through lack of practice – was largely confined to polishing buckles, but the Despot chose to ignore such objections.

Ngur would almost certainly lose his life, stabbed in the back by one of the peasants, as it would be reported throughout Ernestrad. That would please the Despot, since simultaneously he'd be rid of a reluctant commander and find a cause – treachery – against which he could expect his aristocrats to rally. Ngur must have entertained thoughts by now of usurping the throne of the Despot – it would be unnatural for a man elevated to the post of Army-Master not to start speculating in this direction. It was good for the continuance of the House of Ellon for there to be a fairly rapid turnover of Army-Masters; dismissal was customarily terminal, one way or another, although the protocol had to be preserved so that it wasn't too blatantly obvious to the aristocracy just who had directed the fatal blow.

It seemed to the Despot, as the sweat rolled down the rounded folds of his face, as if all the roads to the future were good ones. The periodic subjugations of the peasants were remembered by the singers and the dreamers, and through them the lesson was passed on to the mobs: rebels die painfully, so subservience to the will of the House of Ellon represents the best possible world for you. It didn't represent the best of *all* possible worlds, of course, but down through the centuries since the beginning of time generations of the House of Ellon had never troubled to pretend that – and, even if they had, the peasants wouldn't have remembered the pledge.

Yet Ngur was still smiling with unsatisfactory confidence, as if he were retaining some further knowledge to himself.

'We've heard about one of the singers before,' he said with a smirk.

'He's entertained us, has he?' said the Despot.

'It's a she, not a he; and no, she hasn't been here to Ernestrad.'

'What's her name?'

'We don't know yet. I'll let you know as soon as I find out, sire.' There was unpleasant sarcasm in the Army-Master's voice, but it was sufficiently well disguised that the Despot was forced, as usual, to ignore it. 'My scouts, however, have told me something about her.'

'Explain.'

'She's said to have come from another world – a world beyond Albion.'

'Gibberish! Balderdash! The fool Lian claimed that of his father, but it was all just a madman's fantasy.'

Ngur nodded with a sham of respect.

'It was convenient,' he said, 'for the House of Ellon to portray it among themselves as a fantasy, but the soldiers at your service were persuaded that it was true. They believe that there is another world beyond the curtain of the clouds, and that Lian's father came from there. I agree with them, sire: I can think of no other explanation for the turbulence that the man caused. He was neither peasant nor Ellonian; nor was he a dreamer or a singer. It's hard to think of any explanation for his existence apart from the one my soldiers give.'

'You test my patience with this nonsense.'

'I wish to serve you to the best of my ability, sire. To do so I must on occasion say things to you that you do not wish to hear.'

The Despot quelled his fury. The Army-Master was right, of course, but that didn't make accepting his statements any more palatable. His sausage-like fingers screwed on the sides of his throne as if trying to powder the alabaster.

'But Lian's dead. I saw him die myself. We have no need to fear other-worlders any longer.'

'I, too, saw Lian die, and I remember it well, even though I was barely more than a boy at the time. But Lian was a man, just like any other, and it must be assumed that he took lovers to himself. Is it not possible that one or more of those lovers bore him a child? And might it not be that that child has inherited some of his father's characteristics?'

'Rubbish!' snapped the Despot, out of reflex, while thinking, *That, alas, is all too possible. It may be that it will take a little more effort to put down this nascent rebellion than I'd anticipated. Ngur may have to live longer than I'd hoped, if only because he's easily the most competent among my army command.*

'I accept your judgement, sire,' said Ngur.

'It *is* rubbish, as I've ordained,' said the Despot, 'but

nevertheless I command you, just in the event that there might be some truth in these mindless rumours, to despatch a modest force – perhaps five hundred men – to scotch this rebellion before it can gather any impetus.'

Ngur bowed yet again.

'I respect your wisdom,' he said.

'You may leave me,' said the Despot.

He watched as his Army-Master backed away until he reached the ponderous marble door.

The man would be killed. Impertinence was not to be tolerated.

But he wouldn't be killed for a little while yet. Not so long as he was still useful.

The soldiers of the Ellonian convoy died messily. The first wave of arrows was met by astonishment, the second by a wall of shields. Most of the young men had never faced attack before, and so were incapable of effectively countering it. Just as they were beginning to think that the assault had all been nothing more than a nightmare, Reen led a gang of peasants from behind them to cut them to pieces using axes and swords.

When the last of the Ellonia was dead the peasants immediately started stripping away the uniforms and, under the directions of Barra 'ap Rteniadoli Me'gli'minter Rehan, washing them free of blood in a great wooden cauldron. Other villagers hauled the bodies to a mass grave that had been dug in preparation and then filled in the earth. The captured horses were tethered and the grain the convoy had been carrying was distributed to hiding places in various of the village's homes.

The whole operation had been carried out with ruthless efficiency, and Reen and Anya were proud of it. None of the Ellonia had escaped, so with luck it would be many waking-periods before the news of the massacre made its way to Ernestrad. On the other hand, news might travel rapidly . . .

As the sleeping-period neared, the four of them – Anya, Reen, Rehan and Joli – gathered together in the house they

322

were sharing. They had a small barrel of harsh red wine sitting on the table between them, and from time to time they topped up their goblets and drank, their eyes swimming with a mixture of triumph, sorrow and drunkenness.

'We must move from here,' said Reen, watching the room spin. The door opposite her seemed to be flapping backwards and forwards. 'As soon as the Ellonia discover where their soldiers have died they'll descend on Lianhome and kill everything living – woman, man or beast.'

She was depressed by the slaughter she'd just taken a part in helping: she'd seen too much killing, no matter how necessary, during her lifetime to find any satisfaction from seeing more of it. Anya, by contrast and despite her earlier reluctance, was visibly elated now that she had tasted blood for the first time.

'We'll need provisions,' she said.

'We've got plenty of food and wine,' said Reen, 'now.' She let the last word hang heavily, hoping that there would be some response from Anya, but the young woman just smiled as if she'd done something childishly clever. 'People died so that we could have the food,' Reen added.

'Yes,' said Anya, 'but only four of ours. Who cares about Ellonian soldiers? It's better for all of us if they're dead.'

Reen nodded sadly.

Anya was right – and that was the problem. Being right didn't make it any easier to watch young faces twist up in terror and pain as human beings became meat. Reen hated the House of Ellon and all of its willing servants, but she would have preferred, in an ideal world, to change them rather than simply to slay them.

Anya might, perhaps, learn in due course to understand her point of view.

Reen forced her mind away from the topic.

'Water'll still be a problem,' she said. 'We can't drink nothing but wine.'

'We have plenty of water,' said Anya airily, pointing through the wall in the direction of the village's well. 'Why should that be a problem?'

'Transporting it,' said Rehan, looking at her fondly.

Although it was obvious from Anya's every movement that she was a leader and utterly ruthless in that leadership, it was also plain that she was even more impractical than he was himself. As far as Anya was concerned, the things she wanted to happen happened because she wanted them to: it was up to the rest of them to work out the ways and means.

'We have vessels,' she said. 'Waterproof sacks and all the cauldrons.'

'Water's heavy,' said Rehan, stating the obvious. 'How're we going to carry it?'

'Best not to have to,' said Joli before Anya could reply.

'What do you mean?' asked Rehan.

'Wheels, that's what we can use. People can walk, so there's no need for them to ride on horses or be carried in carts, watching their bellies grow larger from their indolence. Thanks to the generosity of our friends the Ellonia, we now have six carts.'

'Seven,' Reen corrected, 'but otherwise you're right.'

She took another gulp of wine and pointed at Rehan.

'As soon as the last of the corpses has been buried,' she said, 'get a team of people to start raising water from the well, and another to gather any container they can find. Ideally we should all be away from the village before the start of the sleeping-period, so tell them to get their fingers out, huh? Anyone not involved in making sure we've enough water should be collecting up all our blankets. Don't bother with pillows – if someone's so pernickety that they need a pillow in order to sleep at night we'd be better off without them. Any space not taken up on the carts by water and bedding, fill with food – but don't bother too much: we can always take food as we travel. Leave the meat animals behind; they're too slow-moving. No, on second thoughts, kill a couple of the cattle – no more. If we have a feast tonight it'll help firm the resolve of some of the fainter-hearted among us.'

Barra 'ap Rteniadoli Me'gli'minter Rehan tried to remember all of the rapidly barked orders. He looked at Anya for confirmation of what Reen had said; Anya blinked her eyes at him to tell him that she concurred.

He left the house crossing his fingers: it was by no means certain that the villagers would obey his commands, even if he backed them up with Reen's and Anya's authority. He hoped he wouldn't have to come back to the cottage, tail ignominiously between his legs, to ask one of the two so very different women to take over from him.

He needn't have worried. As if they'd heard Reen's commands the peasants were already loading the wagons. To the front of each wagon they'd harnessed a pair of the Ellonian horses; some of the beasts were accustomed to such work but a couple, the horses on which the officers had ridden, were stabbing their forehooves into the ground and breathing loudly. Rehan wondered if it had been wise to hitch both of them to the same cart, but decided that it was better not to change things now.

He smiled amiably at the sweating villagers as they heaved casks of water and crates of food, and they smiled back equally amiably. *I'm glad to have been of help*, he thought ironically as he turned back towards the cottage.

'How many weapons do we have?' Reen was asking as he came back in through the door.

'We have nearly one hundred swords,' Joli was replying, 'but of those only seventeen are Ellonian ones – the rest are peasant-made and therefore less well balanced. Seven axes, including your own. Everyone has a bow and arrows, even the children; the bows vary from excellent to medium to bloody awful, depending on who made them.'

'Slings?' said Anya.

'A few. I didn't bother counting them.'

'We can make more slings,' said Anya abruptly. 'It won't take us long to cut up a few pieces of fabric. Besides, slings have the advantage that we can pick up our ammunition from the roadside as we go along rather than having to take it with us.'

'Yes,' Rehan interrupted, again noticing how impractical his lover could be, 'but how many of us know how to wield a sling? It's a difficult business; it takes a lot of practice before you learn how to hit a target.'

'We're going a long way,' she said coldly, turning towards him. 'We'll have plenty of time for practice.'

He shrugged, feeling flattened. She turned back to the other two, ignoring him.

'Anything else?' she said.

'Cloth,' said Joli reluctantly.

'What for?'

'You . . . um . . . well, it'd be a good idea to have some cloth with us. Also we may need bandages for any wounded we suffer.'

'I plan that no one will be injured except the Ellonia,' said Anya, leaning forward and pointing with a finger at Joli's nose.

'He's right,' said Reen, pushing Anya's hand away from Joli's face. 'He's thinking about the things that could happen, and you aren't. When it comes to the survival of all of us we need things like sanitary towels and bandages.'

Anya glowered, her eyes alight and her teeth showing.

Reen gave her a shrivelling glance.

'Yes, Joli,' she said. 'Get some of the children to gather as much cloth as we have. Tell them to keep it separate from the bedding, at least for the moment.'

'Will they obey me?' said the dreamer, bowing his head towards her.

'Yes. Of course they will. Just tell them that you're passing my orders on to them.'

'And mine,' added Anya, trying to seize back the initiative.

Joli looked at both of them in turn, then left.

'From time to time I tried to tell your father where he was going wrong,' said Reen absently, tracing a circle of spilled wine on the table's surface, 'but he'd never listen to me. Besides, I was only young then; I didn't have the confidence I should have had, and anyway I wanted so much to believe everything would be all right. Things'd have been a lot different if I'd been more forceful with him. I don't plan to make the same mistake again.'

'I am She Who Leads,' said Anya in a furious hiss.

'You may lead, if you want to,' said Reen mildly, 'but I

will tell you *how* to lead and what you must do.'

Rehan, standing near the door, felt as if he'd been forgotten. He cleared his throat in order to attract attention to himself, but neither of the women turned.

'You were part of the army that lost the war,' said Anya hotly. 'What do you think gives you the right to pretend that your strategies would be any more effective now?'

'I learnt,' said Reen. 'I saw the errors your father made and yet I fought alongside him, willing to risk my life to save his. In the time since then I've realised how foolish I was to have behaved like that: I should have had the guts to advise him, no matter how much he'd have shouted his wrath at me before accepting my advice. I let our people die because I didn't have the courage to speak up when I knew Lian was getting things wrong. One time there were nineteen people killed on a single hillside because I didn't tell Lian to lead us well clear of it.

'Those aren't very pretty memories for a person to have,' Reen continued, 'and there's no way I can "unremember" them. But what I'm not going to allow to happen is for you to make the same mistakes as your father all over again, so that I'm left with a new load of memories that are just as bad as the old ones. If you're not happy with that, I'll say goodbye to you right now. Lead your little army any way that you want to: I'll find somewhere in this benighted world where I can settle down and live the rest of my life out in peace. Maybe I'll farm potatoes, or be a shepherd, or . . . It doesn't matter what I do, does it, so long as I can be so far from the fighting that it doesn't affect me.'

Reen didn't look Anya in the eye, but continued to make patterns on the table with the spillage of wine.

'Yet I am still She Who Leads,' said Anya.

Now Reen did look up.

'Leaders don't need to lead from the front,' she said. 'What they need to do is to husband their forces to the best possible effect, and often that means allowing other people to make their decisions for them. You're green in battle, child, and I'm not. Your job as She Who Leads is to support every command that I give until such time as you've gained enough wisdom and experience to offer me a decent argument.'

Barra 'ap Rteniadoli Me'gli'minter Rehan watched, horrified.

'If you were anyone else,' said Anya quietly, 'you'd be dead by now for what you've said.'

'Two mistakes,' said Reen, lifting her goblet to her lips casually and draining the dregs. 'One of fact and the other of policy. First of all, if you tried to kill me you'd be dead before you even started to move. In almost all our pretend fights, I've been the one who's been doing the pretending. As I said, I've fought in battles and you haven't, so you'd never stand a chance if I really tried. Second, despite being almost certainly your best warrior, without a doubt I'm your most experienced tactician, so killing me, while it might give you a temporary feeling of omnipotence, would achieve nothing except helping the House of Ellon destroy all of you. If that's what you want . . .'

'No!' shouted Barra 'ap Rteniadoli Me'gli'minter Rehan. 'That's not what we want! Listen to her, Anya. Listen to what she's saying, not just your own anger!'

'I heard her,' said Anya. 'She's right. At least, she's right for now. Later . . . well, we'll see, won't we?'

She smiled sweetly at both of them and left the cottage to direct operations in person.

'I didn't like that smile,' said Rehan, reaching for the wine.

'Neither did I,' admitted Reen, 'but she's still got a lot of growing up to do.'

'I'll try to help her, in any way I can.'

'Do that.'

Chapter Four
Convoy

So relations between Anya and Reen began poorly; they got progressively worse. Relations between Anya and Barra 'ap Rteniadoli Me'gli'minter Rehan started off good but got progressively poorer, until the two of them could hardly bear to share the same tent together during the sleeping-periods. Rehan wasn't quite certain why this had come to be the case, because he'd done everything in his power to humour her. More and more often he found himself going to Reen to discuss his difficulty with the older woman. She listened to what he had to say, but contributed very few comments of her own. It seemed to him that he was falling out of love with Anya and that she was growing to despise him, but he couldn't understand why. It was as if she were just deliberately trying to spite him, to hurt him, for reasons that she had no wish to describe to him. And, for his own part, although he found her body and her lovemaking as enticing and exciting as ever, they no longer shared time staring at the sky, talking nonsense to each other as they slowly drifted off to sleep.

The sex he could do without, just, but that shared intimacy of conversation he missed desperately. In Reen he found someone to whom he could speak without any barriers, just as he'd used to be able to do with Anya. It felt strange to him, being one woman's physical lover and relying on another woman to be the lover of his thoughts. The first time he tried to unite the two by making a pass at Reen his heart wasn't in it, and anyway she just giggled at him and held his hand, as a mother might hold the hand of a precocious child, until he started giggling along with her and then began to cry. She held his forehead against her shoulder as he wept and told him to come back to speak to her as often as he wished, but it was obvious to him that she still loved Anya despite all the quarrels, and perhaps even envied him his place in her bed.

The army was now several hundred strong, thanks to Anya and the way she had of talking to the peasants in the various villages they came across. They had more food, water and wine than they knew how to consume but, as Anya had pointed out forcefully, they had no way of knowing what privations might lie ahead. Two further convoys of Ellonian soldiers had been put to the sword; now most of the army was clad in Ellonian uniform, while the rest acted out the role of peasants being taken back to Ernestrad for slavery.

The combination had proved to be effective. The last Ellonian convoy had come willingly to meet them; the soldiers had been astonished to find themselves being cut down. Reen was convinced, or so she'd said, that the House of Ellon's headquarters at Giorran had yet even to hear of their existence.

Barra 'ap Rteniadoli Me'gli'minter Rehan was less sure. During the time that he'd spent wandering the provinces of Albion, playing his bodhran and singing the songs he'd composed, he'd built up a healthy respect for the House of Ellon and its ways of obtaining knowledge about what was happening in Albion. Some of the singers, he knew, supplemented their income by acting as spies for the Ellonia, and there were a few Ellonia living in the villages as if they were peasants. Rehan was certain that by now the Despot and his Army-Master must know that another rebel army had been raised – and, for that matter, must have knowledge of roughly where it was.

Had it not been for Reen and Anya, Rehan would have left the army long ago and found himself a safe hiding-place somewhere in the hills. The fact that Reen had made the same non-decision didn't help. The two of them were following a leader because of what she represented, rather than because of what she was. To Rehan, Anya was a person whom he adored but at the same time despised; to Reen, although she loved Anya more intensely than perhaps Rehan ever could, she was the lesser daughter of her father. Lian had had many faults, but he had never borne malice towards any of those who had fought alongside him. Anya was failing to live up to those standards, and this fact threatened to bring tears to Reen's eyes every time she thought about it.

They were walking the horses and wagons carefully along a road that threaded cautiously among foothills when the attack came.

A horde of arrows stamped into the ground around them, so that most of the horses reared in panic.

One of the peasants lost her life, her blood spouting out onto her stolen Ellonian uniform. She screamed as she fell backwards, clutching at the arrow's shaft in the moments before she died.

Within seconds the peasants were sheltering behind their wagons, looking up nervously towards the hillsides. The attack had certainly come from there, but they could see nothing of the attackers.

Reen motioned with her head, trying to catch Anya's attention, but Anya was looking in the other direction.

Reen shrugged and slid away, grabbing at Rehan's cloak so that he followed her. Both of them drew their swords as they crept through the thin scrub that skirted the base of the hill. Arrows hummed overhead, the ones fired by the peasants often falling short; one of them missed Rehan's shoulder by no more than a few centimetres.

Soon they were in dense bracken, and therefore better concealed as they worked their way slowly uphill. The strong smell of the plant's broken stalks made Rehan's nostrils flinch as he encountered it, but he forced himself to carry on. Ahead of him, Reen was crawling eagerly, switching from side to side in order to disturb the heads of the bracken plants as little as possible. He did his best to follow her example.

A wasp flew at his forehead and stung him; he bit his lip and squashed the insect with a swift slap. Reen looked back at him critically, but smiled sympathetically when she saw the mess of green, yellow and blue-black on his face. He scraped away the sludge and followed her, trying to crawl as quickly as she was doing.

He had a sword; he also had a stone loaded into an old sock, so that he could use it to shatter someone's skull. He felt as if he had far too few weapons. Reen, up ahead, was carrying a bow across her back, a sword at her waist and a hooked axe in her left hand.

Rehan wished that he were a real soldier rather than just a hanger-on. Although he had no desire to kill people, a primitive part of him felt a shamed admiration for those who, like Reen, were good at the job. He resented that feeling: through his music he was able to create joy and passion, to preserve the past so that the present might be a better time in which to live, yet still there was that little voice inside him telling him that he was somehow inadequate because he lacked the skills to make the present a *worse* time in which to live. Was killing such a fine art? He was glad he was who and what he was, and yet at the same time he wanted to be somebody different – somebody he wouldn't much like if ever he met him . . . Yet he liked Reen.

'Come on!' she whispered.

Dust from some yellow plants made him sneeze, and he had to stop for a few moments. She turned around again and glared at him angrily until he stopped.

'I couldn't help it,' he whispered.

She said nothing to him. Instead she began to crawl at even greater speed up the hillside, so that he found it more difficult than ever to keep up with her.

The rabbit-trap caught her by the wrist, and blood began to ooze from her skin. Rehan was beside her in moments, muttering words that didn't mean very much but served to soothe her while he tugged the sharp wire down over her hand until she was free of it. The cut around her wrist would need to be bandaged later, he decided, but for the moment it could safely be ignored.

Now he took the lead up the hillside, Reen following him warily.

When they came out of the bracken they were still about thirty metres short of the summit. They sprinted over springy grass and heather until they found themselves hiding behind a roughly constructed granite cairn.

'Thanks for all your help, buster,' he said bitterly, peering down the hillside in an attempt to see the attackers.

All he could see was a sea of bracken.

'We'll have to follow them down,' Reen said. It irritated him that she still hadn't thanked him for saving her from the snare, yet he followed her as she slithered downhill away from him.

Her first arrow took an Ellonian in the nape of the neck so cleanly that none of the others noticed. Rehan wished that he could emulate her, but decided that, if he tried to, all he'd achieve would be to alert the Ellonian patrol to their presence. He watched as Reen killed another member of the convoy, again unnoticed, and this time crept forward himself to slit a soldier's throat. He sent a silly smile and an exaggerated goggle of the eyes over his shoulder at Reen, and was maddened when all she did was shrug uselessly.

Within a few moments the remainder of the convoy were dead, most of them at Reen's hands. Whooping as if they'd only just been born, Reen and Rehan stumbled down the hillside, waving their arms at Anya's army and shouting about their triumph.

They were received dourly. The majority of the peasants were clearly unimpressed. The two of them felt almost shy as they rejoined the column and carried on the march as if nothing at all had happened.

Reen took Rehan's hand as they walked alongside.

'Love,' she said.

'You don't mean that.'

'Yes, I do.'

That sleeping-period he went to bed with Anya and wished he were sleeping with Reen. Reen, for her part, was in bed with herself – generally her favourite person to sleep with. All she could imagine of Rehan was that he might be a nice boy to sleep with once, or even perhaps twice. She hoped he wouldn't intrude into her life any more than he already had. She hardly noticed when another body slid in beside her own.

She hoped that Joli was likewise sleeping, but far away, and that his dreams were less vivid than her own. She saw a flight of Ellonians soaring over their small army, loosing arrows downwards so that the peasants, including herself, fell dying into the soil. The Ellonians were riding astride great birds that were black like crows but a hundred times the size, their wings flapping slowly and lazily as they moved across the sky. The arrows fell in towards Reen's skull and split it into a hundred pieces. She fell from her horse, tortured by the slashes of the arrowheads, then felt the heavy creature trampling over her, destroying her stomach and her kidneys.

Joli was indeed dreaming far away from the rest of the camp. He was curled up in a bundle of blankets, enjoying their warmth as he lay with his body on the clammy ground and his head on a small mountain of grass.

It was Rehan who had come to be with Reen that sleeping-period. The two of them didn't have sex when she half-woke; instead they just smiled at each other, acknowledged each other's nakedness, and fell back to sleep again in each other's arms. He felt her twitching from side to side as the nightmares tormented her. As he teetered towards his own sleep he admitted his guilt and turned over so that his naked back was towards her. He felt her curl around him as she slept, one of her hands tugging gently at the hair of his chest.

There were worse times, some of them very much worse.

Reen saw far too many of them.

She saw the way that the Ellonia fired their shots at the little army of peasants that She Who Leads had raised. Then there was the time that Anya's people had gratuitously killed a hundred or more green young soldiers from the House of Ellon without any mercy whatsoever, showing no

334

remorse. To Reen, there could be nothing more saddening.

During sleeping-periods she curled herself against Barra 'ap Rteniadoli Me'gli'minter Rehan's tall body, felt his hardness against her, and often admitted him into herself.

She loved him for the pleasure he gave to her, even though his body itself was vaguely repellent to her. She loved him also for the jokes he made and the funny stories he told in between their bouts of lovemaking. She hadn't willingly been to bed with a man since her youth, when a field-worker had not so much made love with her as fucked her for the price of a meal in his house during the time she'd been picking her way to Lianhome; it was a delight to find that there was a man sensitive enough to arouse her, to consider her needs before his own. It made it easier for her to give him pleasure, however much her body was yearning for a different one.

Anya, by contrast, just rode him, her body a horse upon his. She took pleasure from him selfishly, giving nothing away, and yet he found it impossible to resist her demands. Reen was the more skilful lover, yet Anya was the more lovely. For a time he tried to deceive Anya about his relationship with Reen; when he eventually confessed he was astonished that Anya, normally so possessive, simply nodded and said that she'd known about it all along, because Reen had told her.

More Ellonia died.

In every second waking-period Reen conducted weapons-training with the peasant recruits. To her surprise, and to his own, Rehan proved to be an adept with the sword, often striking her own wooden practice sword with sufficient skill and force to send it tumbling away across the heath. She hoped that this wasn't just because he could read her reactions in her face – that he'd be able to face Ellonian soldiers with similar agility.

She was reassured when he killed five mounted soldiers with five blows. He crouched low as they charged on their horses, swords or morningstars held high, and then punched upwards to pluck away their intestines.

After battle, once the bodies had been buried, Rehan

would play his bodhran and sing his songs to those of the army who gathered around him. Always there was that one which had come to him from nowhere:

Seven women rode down through the town of Starveling that night,
Horses' hooves spitting galaxies in the pale moons' empty light.
And their eyes sought out the corners where the shadows grew
As deep and as dark as wine.

Each time as he finished pulsing the beat on his bodhran he'd look up and see both Anya and Reen watching him with their different variations of love. Each time he'd silently curse himself for having become involved with either of them, but then, later, he'd find himself drawn to one of their beds, feeling the need to be caressed by their hands.

Once he told Reen as they lay sweatily together, his penis becoming limp inside her, that he could no longer stand the stress of loving both of them during the sleeping-periods, then going out to wage war during the waking-periods. She moved lazily against him, rolling him over onto his back, then fell asleep. It took him a long time to realise that she'd given him no answer.

He was growing tired of killing.

When Alyss had told him to join She Who Leads he had for no good reason assumed that his part in the campaign would somehow be bloodless.

The opposite was true.

He'd lost count of how many Ellonian troopers had been cut down by his blade. Often they were little more than children, fighting in the army because that was what had been expected of them since their birth. Rehan wished that he could have spared them, but to do so would have been to give away his own life, something which he was frank enough to admit he regarded as more precious than anything – *anything* – else.

Joli showed no such compunction. Despite having been ordered to wash regularly, and despite the fact that he'd done so, he still seemed as filthy as ever. When the peasants

336

attacked the Ellonia he was always at the forefront, his sword high above his head before it swept down to draw blood, his face twisted into a smile of unabashed pleasure as he watched the weapon take its toll of human lives.

Blood.

There was too much of it for Rehan's taste.

He wondered if any form of justice was worthwhile if it involved so much loss of life to establish it.

He wondered, too, how he could watch Anya glorying in the slaughter and then, just a short while later, share her bed. Sometimes he felt as if they were making love on a mattress of corpses, whose blind eyes were staring up at their twisting bodies.

Reen saw the sea-change in him, and said nothing about it. Instead she took his hand when he needed his hand to be taken, or made soft love with him, murmuring tender endearments when he came to his unshared climax.

There were the four of them at the crest of the long escarpment, their horses restless. Behind them was a long shallow slope, at the base of which grouped the few hundred warriors of the army they had gathered during their slow promenade through Albion. Ahead of them was the first serious force they had had to face: nearly a thousand Ellonian troops, clad in red and green, well armed and restless for battle. Standards were held high, showing the insignia of the impaled hound. Even from here the four could hear the soldiers chanting their mindless cries of slaughter.

'They can't know how many of us there are,' said Barra 'ap Rteniadoli Me'gli'minter Rehan, patting the head of his stallion with a reassurance he hardly felt himself.

'No,' said Anya. 'They must think we're just a little convoy of upstarts who can be slaughtered to warn others of the folly of rebellion. The longer we keep them thinking that, the better off we'll be.'

'I feel sleepy,' said Joli, turning to stare at her. 'I wish to dream.'

Anya waved at him dismissively.

337

'Dream, then . . . if you're sure you can control your dream.'

'I am . . . this time.'

He spurred his horse away from the other three, down the steep slope towards the massed Ellonia, then threw himself off it so that the beast cantered on riderless. The soldiers laughed loudly, assuming that he'd been thrown. Joli rolled over and over until his head was resting on a soft clump of heather.

Anya turned her horse and beckoned to her followers that they should climb the hill. She mirrored their grins with one of her own, and watched them as they scrambled slowly and quietly up the slope, their weapons at the ready.

'Have no mercy,' Reen muttered to Rehan. 'The Ellonia would offer no mercy to us.'

Reen pulled her sword from its sheath and whipped it in the air; in her other hand she clutched the shaft of her axe. She twisted her head so that her grey hair went behind her ears, leaving her vision free.

It was clear that the Ellonia were expecting a simple massacre of the minuscule force that faced them: four armed soldiers, one of whom had already fallen off his horse. Their shouts became louder as they moved towards the base of the hill.

Joli fell asleep.

Almost immediately he began to dream.

He dreamt of fire falling from the skies, and of the ground opening up to swallow men-at-arms. He dreamt that the whole of Albion was shaking from side to side, and that lightning was hurtling its bolts at all those who carried the standard of the spitted dog. He dreamt that hearts were exploding from men's chests, and that heads were being twisted away by unseen forces to fly through the air and fall sightlessly among the heather. He dreamt of horses losing their footing and staggering downwards, throwing their riders and then trampling upon them. He dreamt of a wash of water springing up from the hill's crest and flooding down over the Ellonia, swamping their progress and drowning more than half of them. He dreamt of venom-

338

ous snakes that struck up from the newly created marsh to stab their poisonous fangs into the soldiers' legs or the horses' bellies.

He dreamt of death in many guises.

Anya, her mouth open, watched in amazement. Now she waved to her followers to keep well back.

Only a few moments before, the Ellonian army facing them had been a well disciplined force. Now it was a shambles. Most of the men were dead, and those who still survived were screaming and trying to escape from the carnage around them.

Anya smiled her ruthless small smile.

Alyss had been right.

The dreamer, however little she liked him as a person, was a potent weapon of war.

Ellonian skulls were beginning to explode, for no reason other than that such a thing could be imagined in dreams.

Again she gestured her troops to keep back. Although Joli had claimed that he could keep his dreams under control, she didn't yet trust him completely: she had no desire to see her own forces die in the way that the Ellonia were dying.

There was another great gush of water, turning the plain beneath them into a wash of mud and quicksand which swallowed up many more of the Ellonian horses and their riders.

Anya chuckled thinly.

She looked from one side to the other at Reen and Rehan and slapped herself on the thigh.

They looked back at her impassively. There was something wrong with all this, something that Anya couldn't understand. Reen remembered, long ago, how Syor had told her of her vision of Anya's savage smile, and of how it had frightened her; now she was reminded of Syor's description all over again. War, yes, that was something that Reen could accept, however much she disliked seeing people losing their lives. But this was something different: it was the use of occult powers to slay people who had no means of replying in kind.

Rehan's reaction was simpler. He just felt sick. As a singer his sole desire had been to spread pleasure among the people of Albion; the spreading of death, by contrast, was quite alien to him. Yet he'd sung to the peasants about past massacres as if they'd been perpetrated by people of glory and valour.

As the last of the Ellonians died below them, Anya started a cheer and gestured her army to join her on the hill's crest. They were soon beside her, as was Joli, looking fresher and cleaner than he had since before he'd arrived at Lianhome. Reen and Rehan looked at each other again and shrugged: what had happened to the Ellonia had been an act of inhuman cruelty, but there had been nothing they could have done to stop it.

'Next we take Ernestrad!' Anya shouted, holding her sword above her head.

'Next Ernestrad takes us,' murmured Rehan.

Reen heard him. She nodded.

The news of the massacre reached the Despot rather earlier than he would have liked.

He was addressing a gathering of his most senior aristocrats and other courtiers, people whose stated function it was to act as a check on the Despot's power, although it was rare that they tried to do so, bearing in mind what happened whenever they did. A small man with a fresh bruise on his cheek scuttled up to the Despot and handed him a sheet of paper, then fled from the hall. Light spun in through the stained-glass windows, painting the aristocrats' faces in curious colours as they watched the Despot reading the message. After a few moments he tore the paper into shreds, throwing them away from him so that they scattered across the marbled floor like lazy snowflakes.

'We're at war,' he said. 'At war with the peasants.'

His Army-Master, Ngur, rose to his feet.

'Sire, you'll recall that I warned of this.'

'I have no wish to be given untimely reminders,' said the Despot coldly, pulling his sleeve across his brow.

Ngur sat down again.

'We have few alternatives,' said the Despot. 'The rebels must be put to death, immediately, every last one of them.'

Ngur looked for a second as if he were about to speak, then decided that it was better to keep his silence.

'I call upon our Army-Master,' said the Despot, 'to tell us how this heinous uprising will be put down.'

There was a muttering among the courtiers, some of them agreeing as a matter of course with the Despot, but others of them sympathising with Ngur.

Ngur rose to his feet once more and this time stared his ruler full in the face.

'Killing the peasants won't solve anything,' he said.

Behind him most of the aristocrats shouted their protest, so that the noise built up until it was a thunder.

Ngur persevered.

'We may not be able to kill them all. Even if we could, all that'd happen is that a new army of peasants would arise to fight us – again and again and again. Is that the sort of future we really want?'

'Do we want the peasants to rule *us*?' said the Despot icily. 'Is *that* the sort of future we really want?'

Ngur smiled in an imitation of confidence.

'If too many of the peasants die, the fields will have to be tended by members of the House of Ellon. There aren't enough of us to do that, and fewer still who'd wish to; you'd have a revolt on your hands, my lord.'

Again there was shouting, but this time, miserably, the Despot recognised that much of it was antagonistic to himself. His aristocrats wanted to keep the peasants in their place, killing as many of them as was necessary to quell any uprising, but had no desire to find themselves forced to take to the fields. The culling of the rebels would have to be kept within strict bounds.

'You make your point, Ngur,' the Despot said reluctantly. 'What is your plan?'

'Our spies, as you know, have told us that there are at least four leaders among the peasant army: a singer, a dreamer and two warriors, the younger of whom is

341

descended from the man called Lian who presumed to make war on you many years ago.'

The Despot moved his hand dismally. It seemed so recently that he'd told Ngur not to mention Lian or any of his possible progeny; now it was too late for such proscriptions.

'Maybe,' added Ngur, 'there's another singer involved – we can't be sure. A woman – barely more than a girl. Some of our people say that there is and others that there isn't.'

'Why should we be frightened of these less-than-humans?' said the Despot, looking briefly at his Army-Master and then, more significantly and at greater length, at the courtiers swarming around him.

'The dreamer alone has killed at least a thousand of our soldiers,' mumbled Ngur.

'They were fools!' said the Despot.

'No,' the Army-Master said quietly, 'they weren't. They were destroyed by a force they couldn't find a way to counter. Your soldiers'll be in the same difficulty any time they try to combat a dreamer again.'

'You're trying to tell me that the forces of the House of Ellon are vulnerable to this bunch of peasant layabouts the four have raised?'

'That's exactly what I'm trying to tell you, sire. It's a pity that you do not always choose to listen to me.'

The Army-Master spoke in studiedly respectful tones, and yet the Despot felt that the argument was running away from him.

'We will destroy them,' he shouted.

'If that is your wish, sire,' said the Army-Master, 'then that is what we shall try to do.'

Chapter Five
Wanting

High above their heads fluttered the banner of the House of Ellon, its symbol of the spitted hound stark against the bright cerulean of the sky. Ngur looked at it with a certain half-resentful pride, then turned to regard the men under his command. Eight groups of five hundred stood in orderly fashion on the plain in front of him; at the head of each group was a commander on horseback with, alongside him, a trumpeter. It was an impressive host, the largest that the Army-Master himself had ever seen. The Despot could not complain of any lack of will to conquer the peasant rabble, but still Ngur felt uneasy in a way he couldn't properly describe, even to himself. There was a great gulf between gathering the means to conquer and effecting the conquest.

It was approaching the sleeping-period and the men hadn't yet eaten. Ngur signalled to his own trumpeter to sound the command for the army to break ranks, and watched with approval as they moved efficiently, some taking up posts as sentries, some lighting fires for cooking, some digging latrines, and some erecting the simple standard-issue tents. Within a short time the plain came to look more like a cloth village.

Ngur slowly rode around its perimeter, exchanging the occasional word with the sentries. He kept a smile of casual confidence firmly on his face; it wouldn't do to let the men have even the slightest inkling of his qualms. To his relief the soldiers unanimously displayed the same look of confidence. Perhaps he was worrying about nothing. What band of peasants, however well led or organised, could hope to prevail against a mighty war machine like the one at his command?

Over to his left there was a commotion. He spurred his horse in that direction.

Four of the soldiers were holding a red-eyed old man who was struggling with them while giving voice to a stream of obscene invective. Ngur raised his eyebrows: he was startled by the man's imaginativeness.

'Silence!' the Army-Master shouted, slapping his thigh for emphasis.

The diatribe stopped abruptly. A couple of the soldiers looked, if anything, rather disappointed: the man had just been getting to the end of describing their mothers' unusual activities with goats. Who would have thought that the sweet old dears could ever have . . . ?

'Who are you?' said Ngur to the old man coldly.

'An honest man who travels the land plying his wares to the best of his ability.'

Ngur looked at him with suspicion. It was his experience that people who described themselves as honest men were generally the most deviously criminal of all.

'And what are these wares? Pots and pans, or fruit and vegetables? Where are they? I can't see any cart sagging under the weight of the goods you say you sell.'

The red eyes looked at him with hostility. The old man really was a filthy fellow, Ngur reflected with distaste; if there weren't fleas in that grey straggle of a beard, then it must be because even they couldn't stand the environment.

'I have no need of a wagon for my wares, you privy-peeker, and I don't even sell them. I carry them here.'

Pulling loose his right arm, the man pointed at his head.

'I give them away in return for a drink or a meal or a bed for the sleeping-period. Preferably a shared bed.'

Ngur began to laugh, and the soldiers dutifully joined in.

The man spat on the ground between them.

'I'm more of a man than you are, I'll warrant. I can . . .'

The Army-Master let him ramble on for a while, ponder-

344

ing on the fact that, if what the dotard was telling them was true, it was strange that any other man in all of Albion had ever had to undergo the chore of deflowering a virgin. He raised a hand to stop the recitation when the subject turned to domesticated animals.

'For the sake of it,' he said, 'I'll believe you, just for now. But what are these goods that you have to offer?'

'Visions.'

'Visions?'

'Yes, but very special visions. I give people glimpses of their own futures.'

The soldiers instinctively took a couple of paces back.

'You're a necromancer?' said the Army-Master.

'No!' The word was said very firmly. 'What I do has nothing to do with magic – black, white or any other colour. I'm gifted to know not just the past but the future. Few enough of the people of this world are able to have knowledge even of the past; in all my time travelling, I have yet to meet another person who has the talent of seeing what the future holds. Yes, muttonchops, there are charlatans who pretend that they can do so – turn over any stone and you'll find a bundle of them – but they're just cheating bumswipes.'

'And you're not, I suppose?'

Ngur smiled.

'I told you. I'm an honest man. Perhaps the Wind was my father.'

'But how can you be honest? The future hasn't happened yet, so how can you describe it to people?'

The old man cackled and looked at the four soldiers, who were still keeping their distance and watching him apprehensively.

'That's why people are so glad to avail themselves of my wares. You're right: the future hasn't happened yet, so the events in it aren't inscribed in stone. If you know what the future potentially holds, prickwit, you know how you can change it. Imagine that I told you that, some time during the next few waking-periods, a traitor among your own troops would kill you by firing a crossbow bolt into your back, between your shoulders, shattering the upper part of your spine. You could make sure that the event never came to pass simply by keeping the traitor in chains and making sure that he wasn't allowed to get his hands on a crossbow. Couldn't you?'

The old man glared at Ngur and then, in turn, at the four soldiers.

Ngur considered. He decided he rather . . . enjoyed the old man, for all his insolence.

'So,' he said, 'you wander all over Albion making predictions of woe that, just because you make them, don't in fact come true?'

'What would be the point of making them if the events I describe couldn't be averted? Besides, numbskull, I don't predict only the griefs of people's lives. Sometimes I tell them of the joys and successes, and what they must do to achieve those joys and successes. You, for example, hope to defeat an army of peasants led by a rather attractive young woman. If you carry on your campaign in the way that you're planning, it's doomed, and so are you.'

The Army-Master was shocked. It was supposed to be unknown outside the House of Ellon that the army was massing to defeat the peasants. Did everyone in Albion know the truth? Had spies been at work? Or was the old man as honest as he claimed to be, and could he really see what the future held?

'You interest me,' said Ngur, reluctantly.

'But you can defeat her,' said the man, 'and without bloodshed. More importantly, perhaps, at the same time you can defeat the machinations of the Despot, who would dearly love to see you dead. If you change the passage of future events in the ways that I describe to you, it might be that you will gather the throne for yourself.'

'You're either the greatest fool I've ever met or the greatest liar.'

'Well,' said the old man, kneeling in mockery, 'it's good to know that I'm the greatest at something other than . . .'

Ngur laughed aloud.

'You're the greatest at audacity, if nothing else,' the

Army-Master said eventually. 'Don't you realise that it would take just a flick of my finger to have my men to execute you for your impertinence?'

'But of course,' said the man, regaining his feet and looking very serious, 'except for the fact that my knowledge of the future tells me that you're not going to give any such order. You're intelligent enough, just, to realise that if you had me killed you'd only bring about your own defeat. Or, to put it another way, killing me won't help you to victory, whereas listening to me might.'

'I see. And what's your advice?'

'Seduction.'

Ngur could hardly believe his ears.

'"Seduction"?' he repeated incredulously.

'Yes. The peasant girl, Anya, is not without her attractions – in fact, she's got quite a few of them – so seducing her should be a pleasure rather than a duty. Once you've done that, your army will be united with hers. There won't be a force in all Albion that will be able to counter it.'

The smell of cooked food was becoming compelling.

'Let's eat and talk about this further,' said the Army-Master. He wasn't very good at seducing women – or, at least, he'd been dramatically unsuccessful at times in the past – but . . .

'I can read the future in your eyes,' said the man happily. 'All I ask of you is a meal and a sleeping-period under cover.'

'That you shall have. But beware: plan no treachery. I'll have guards watching over you as I sleep.'

'What harm could an old man be?'

Joli did enjoy lying. He also liked eating free meals, and watching people making fools of themselves.

The pullets' eggs were acceptable, although perhaps he could have done with less of the butter sauce. The conversation over the meal was abysmal, but conversations with the military generally were: soldiers seemed to have little regard for the subjects that appealed to Joli. Every time he tried to introduce the topic of music, for example, he found himself being forced to discuss the highest note that trumpeters could reach, a matter that interested him not at all.

Joli's descriptions of Anya's beauty would have embarrassed her; his outline of her sexual proclivities would have astonished her. He had tremendous fun making it all up as he went along. Even Ngur began to have doubts: surely it was impossible for any woman to raise a man to such a height of ecstasy using only her earlobes?

Hmmm. Nevertheless . . .

Ngur slept on his camp-bed, thinking of the old man's accounts of Anya's beauty.

Joli lay, annoyedly alone, in the far corner of a subaltern's tent, thinking to himself: *They've let me get away with it twice, the imbeciles!*

And then he fell asleep and had a nightmare.

He liked lying and deception, but he liked a thoroughgoing nightmare in a good cause even better.

The sky became a mask of hatred, pouring down its venom onto the land. It had turned into blackness; the sun had been hidden away behind an unseen hand, and rocks fell to destroy the tents of the Ellonian Army, ripping through the canvas and pulverising the bodies of the sleeping soldiers. Then the ground welled up as a liquid mass, swallowing more bodies as they writhed and tried to escape; it fell upon them like a predatory animal, devouring them where they lay. There were also great beasts from whose fangs dripped bright red blood: they ate any meat they came across, whether it was animal or human. With their huge claws they picked up soldiers and threw them backwards and forwards, watching them twisting through the air as their limbs were torn from their bodies by eager teeth.

It was a top-hole nightmare. Joli was very proud of it, even as he slept.

He was less certain about setting the sky on fire, but eventually decided to go through with it. The red and yellow and blue light cast curious patterns of colour across the plain. Some of the flames spat down towards the ground, incinerating the Ellonians.

A little later there was nothing much left but Joli himself

and the pungent smell of burning. He slept right through until the next waking-period, a smile on his face as he snored, then got to his feet, peed blearily on the scorched ground, and left.

A few of the Ellonian troops were still alive to watch him go. One of them was Ngur.

'So the bastards used a dreamer against us *again*!' shouted the Despot, punching one of the whitewashed inner walls of Giorran.

'I don't blame them,' said Ngur mildly. 'In their position I'd probably have done the same myself. What angers me is not their perfidy but my own stupidity in not spotting at the outset what the old codger was. His eyes should have told me.'

'Then you should die,' said the Despot.

'In due course I suppose I shall,' remarked Ngur, 'for my folly in allowing so many of my troops to perish. However, I think it sensible to delay my entirely justified suicide until after I have seen the death of this barbarian minx and her treacherous horde.'

Ngur looked at the Despot with a feeling of profound insecurity. He had no intention of committing suicide: he had convinced himself that it had been no fault of his that he'd been deceived by the seedy old man. Yet the Despot wouldn't trust him unless convinced that he was planning to take his own life at the end of the campaign.

'Bastards!' yelled the Despot. 'Shits and bastards, one and all!'

'I wouldn't be surprised,' said Ngur, 'if most of them were bastards, these things being rather difficult to keep track of throughout most of our world; but I repeat, sire, that it is wrong to blame them for using any weapon at their disposal in order to act against us.'

'So you side with them?'

The Despot's words were spat viciously at the empty air.

'No,' said Ngur quietly, 'but I can understand their motivations. That's something very different, and also something much more valuable. The more I know about

what drives them, the better I'll be able to counter them –
the more likely, sire, that I'll be able to defeat their rebellion
against your magnanimous rule.'

The Despot looked as mollified as he ever did.

'I hate the thought of so many of my subjects dying,' he
whimpered unexpectedly.

'But you're responsible for the deaths of so many yourself,' said Ngur after a few moments. He detested hypocrisy
and self-deception.

'That's something different. That's a matter of individual
traitors being executed because of their treason. This rabble
is made up of peasants who're being fed delusions of martial
glory – peasants like the dreamer who killed those thousands of our royal army. They bear no ill will towards me
personally: all they want to do is rally around a charismatic
leader.'

'I think,' said Ngur softly, 'that in fact they bear you
and the House of Ellon considerable ill will. I'd go further
than that, if I might, sire. These people are no plaster
effigies of virtue, nor are they the dupes of a demagogue;
if you start to think of them that way you're as good as
dead. The woman, Anya, is cleverer than you give her
credit for – cleverer, in fact, than *I* gave her credit for.
She's mustered about her some skilled commanders and
allies – not just the dreamer but others as well.'

The Despot looked at him, enraged.

'Can you think of any reason why I shouldn't order your
instant death?'

Wearily, Ngur iterated: 'The delay of your own, sire. I
believe we can defeat these rebels, but it is something that
can't be carried out by any fool whom you choose to appoint
in my place.'

Had there been guards there at the time, Ngur would
indeed have died. The Despot's piggy eyes flashed with red
fury and his fingers flexed as if they'd like to rip the Army-
Master's throat from his neck. Instead he grabbed a pear
from a bowl on the window-ledge and bit into it with as
much force as he could.

'I do not appoint fools,' he said, spraying juice and fragments of peel on the rug.

'Precisely. That is exactly why you've got to listen to the things I'm telling you, however unpalatable you may find them. We can win this war, if you want us to, but *only* if you want us to.'

'What do you suggest?'

'There's no sense in our just amassing an even bigger army to counter theirs. That's exactly what they must expect us to do, and they'll be prepared to create exactly the same sort of mayhem as before. No, we must think in other ways.'

'Magic?' said the Despot. 'My mages can . . .'

'Sire,' said the Army-Master, bowing from the waist, 'with all due respect to your opinions, I place little confidence in the abilities of your mages. I suggest that instead we use a force that's much more fundamental to human nature than magic: corruption.'

'Explain.'

'The peasants in Anya's army have nothing of their own but their greed. If we offer them possessions, some of them may be persuaded to betray her to us. Perhaps to assassinate her, but even better to kidnap her and bring her here to Ernestrad so that she can see the wealth and power your concubines enjoy. She is very lovely, sire.'

The Despot looked at Ngur critically.

'I should take this whore to my bed?'

'There are worse fates,' said the Army-Master softly. 'Think of it, if she's seen as having allied herself to you purely through her own cupidity, all support for her among the peasants will evaporate. In particular, she'll lose the allegiance of her senior officers; those we can kill at our ease once the woman Anya has been discredited.'

'And her? Should she be allowed to live?' The Despot threw the core of his pear angrily towards a corner of the room.

'That would be for you to decide, sire. It might be better, though, for her to live – as a symbol of your might. Besides, as I've said, she's very lovely; you may wish her to live for that reason alone.'

'I have enough lovely women; in fact, sometimes I wonder if I have too many of them. Besides, she could betray me by pretending to accept the advantages of power and then stabbing me to death as I slept.'

The Despot considered another pear, then decided against it.

'Have you,' said the Army-Master, 'so little faith in your abilities as a lover?'

The Despot didn't reply; instead he decided to eat another pear after all. Chewing on the flesh of the fruit he nodded to his Army-Master peremptorily.

'I agree with you. Subtlety must be our approach, in this as in all other matters. Act as you believe best – but act swiftly, man. The longer this rising of the rabble continues the greater the support the woman will gain.'

The Army-Master bowed again.

'It will be a pleasure, sire.'

He backed towards the door, displaying with his hands his reverence for his ruler. Once outside he stood fully erect and grinned to himself gleefully, ignoring a sentry who glanced at him in surprise.

Ngur enjoyed corruption almost as much as he loved conspiracy. If things went the way he wished, the rebellion would be at an end . . . and so would the life of the Despot. The stakes were large, but the same was true of the likely gains. He envisaged himself in the role of Despot, and found the picture very pleasing.

'Here are precious stones enough for you to buy a palace and live the rest of your life in ease.'

A peasant bows his insignificant head and accepts the proffered leather sack of trinkets.

'With these coins you could have all that you've ever dreamed of – a mansion in Ernestrad, food ever of the finest quality, a large retinue of concubines . . .'

A humble shepherd, drawn away from the hillsides only by the prospect of a gleaming future, takes the money with a smile from the dapper young man he's never noticed before. With wealth such as this he can expect to become an honorary member of the House of Ellon. He has little thought of what the future might hold once She Who Leads is dead: all that he can encompass in his mind is the prospect of being a rich and influential person. If the Despot is willing to give him wealth such as this, then perhaps She Who Leads was wrong, after all, in insisting that the Despot was such a cruel and merciless tyrant.

The infiltrator who attempted to bribe Barra 'ap Rteniadoli Me'gli'minter Rehan met a sudden and rather brutal death. Minutes later Anya had been informed about what was going on. She'd been drinking rather a lot of cider and at first found it hard to comprehend what she was being told, but a little while later she was somewhat shakily on the move. By the end of the sleeping-period seven people were swinging from rapidly erected gallows: four were peasants who'd been tempted by the bribes of the Ellonia and three were the slick youngsters who'd been sent to corrupt her army.

It didn't stop there – in fact, it couldn't. Anya had no way of knowing if this was the end of the attempt to subvert her troops.

They were encamped in a pool of land amid a circle of mountains; there were several score tents, while a few hundred warriors slept in the open air. Anya had little idea of how many of them had been bribed – or, more important, of how many of them had accepted the bribes in the expectancy of being able to sell her army to the House of Ellon.

Hangings carried on throughout the waking-period.

Barra 'ap Rteniadoli Me'gli'minter Rehan was revolted by the executions.

Once upon a time he'd found Anya an affectionate lover driven by her thirst for justice. Now it seemed that she'd changed: it was a matter of little import for her to demand the killing of someone purely on suspicion. This was a woman far different from the woman he'd once known.

He said as much to Reen.

'I loved Anya once, too,' Reen responded. More than that she wouldn't say.

Everywhere he wandered around the encampment he saw gallows, and his stomach protested at the sight of the carnage. In the end he returned to his own tent and thrummed on his bodhran until the images of death disappeared from his mind.

Then, for a long time, he stared at his hands, wondering exactly why he was here.

He still wanted Anya, in a way. He couldn't escape the fact. He wanted to be in bed with her, curling himself around her body, feeling her small hard buttocks against his groin as they both drifted off to sleep. He wanted to kiss her on the nose as they woke up together, seeing her eyes open and then her lips curl into a smile. But the trouble was that he was no longer sure that he loved her – in fact, he suspected exactly the opposite; that in reality he hated her, but just enjoyed sex with her.

With Reen it was all so different, Reen *gave*. To be sure, she took as well, but only at the times when it was right to take. It seemed that they made love *with* each other; Rehan and Anya made love *to* each other, which was completely different.

But Anya's body inflamed him.

Reen's body was a friend. A friend not just to Rehan but to herself, in the same way that his body had become a friend of hers.

Anya had the harshness to have people executed even if it wasn't certain that they were guilty of betrayal. Reen could on occasion be as ruthless, but she'd never knowingly risk having an innocent person killed.

He put the tips of the fingers of both hands together and looked at the pattern they made.

Was he to be governed by lust or by love?

It was a difficult question for him to answer.

He heard, from outside, another strangled scream as a peasant died.

Barra 'ap Rteniadoli Me'gli'minter Rehan answered the question, and wished that he'd done so before.

He and Reen made love very tenderly several times during that sleeping-period. In between she told him, in carefully measured episodes, one of the most scatological jokes he'd ever heard.

Joli had tried to find his way as quickly as possible back to the place where he'd left Anya's army, but when he'd arrived there, after more waking-periods than he would have thought possible, he'd discovered that the troops had decamped. The ground had been cut up by their departure, and he was able to follow the track for many kilometres, running and walking alternately, hoping to catch them before too long. He swore while running and merely uttered imprecations while walking. It interested him that he should make such a distinction.

After a while he lost the trail. There was a broad tract of land made up of an unbroken sweep of flinty grey pebbles and it was impossible for him to work out which way the army had gone. He looked at the uninformative plain of stones and cursed imaginatively, then decided to cross it in the same direction he'd been following for the past few waking-periods: it seemed unlikely to him that the army would have changed course much. From time to time he paused to pick up a stone and throw it away from him, watching with pleasure the puff of dust as it landed. Here and there were the tall structures created by termites, and every time he passed one he dipped a hand into it to extract some of the wriggling insects for food; he also raided the nests for the succulent moisture of the aphids that the ants harvested.

The fare could have been more appetising, but aside from that he was perfectly happy as he trekked across the arid plain. He had long been accustomed to sleeping as infrequently as possible, so he was able to make rapid progress. There was never anyone else around; even so, he felt slightly guilty peeing or shitting in full view of anyone there *might* have been. He realised that he was beginning to smell quite strongly of sweat and shit, and wished that he could find a pond somewhere so that he could wash himself; it was the first time he could remember having had much concern about his personal hygiene.

There weren't any ponds. He stank.

And, after a while, there weren't any termite-mounds.

This was more of a problem. He could tolerate his own filthiness stoically, but hunger and thirst were less easy to endure.

The sunlight beat down on him remorselessly as he looked all around him, hoping to see another anthill.

There were none.

It seemed his only option was to turn back.

The difficulty was that it was impossible for him to tell, in this featureless desert, which direction was 'back'. For all he knew, he could have been wandering around in circles for the past few waking-periods.

Better to keep going on in the direction in which he'd been travelling. But which direction was that?

He looked around again, but there was no sign of his footsteps among the pebbles. The sky was cloudless and the sun directly overhead. Whatever way he looked there was just an endless waste that extended as far as the horizon.

He'd heard once that you could delude your body into thinking that it was taking in water by sucking a smooth pebble, so that your mouth salivated. Several kilometres later he spat the pebble out, with difficulty. There seemed to be nothing in this wasteland that could be used to replace the liquid that he was losing in the omnipresent heat.

Change things . . .

If Alyss had been there she could have changed things, perhaps creating an oasis.

But Alyss wasn't there.

Joli tried to lie down on the parched stones and dream of rain, but for once sleep refused to come. After a while he pulled himself back up onto his feet and staggered in the direction that seemed best to him.

Some hours later all he could think about was his own thirst. Everything else had disappeared from his mind. His dry eyes searched around the desert, desperately hoping for any source of liquid – a stream, preferably, although a plant or one of the anthills would have been almost as acceptable. Nothing.

The first time he stumbled on the stones he thought it was just a foolish act of clumsiness. He rubbed his knees, stood up, and walked on.

The second time he stumbled seemed more important. As he fell, he cut his flesh open in several places and lay on his face for some minutes squealing like a wild animal caught in a trap. Although the light around him was changeless, it seemed to be circling him, swooping in to attack him and then drifting away aimlessly.

It was far more difficult, this time, to pull himself upright. It was as if some intangible force were trying to push him back down against the ground.

Then he fell for the third time.

He managed to survive for most of the rest of the waking-period, lying there. His mind seemed to wander into different regions: sometimes he was transported by bliss into an aerial world where his face was washed by cool air, and sometimes he found himself in a hot netherland whose rulers were sadistic demons that delighted in tormenting him. As the waking-period wore on, he spent more and more of the intervals being tormented.

It was therefore with little reluctance that he allowed his essence to slip easily away from his desiccated body.

He felt himself being tossed high towards the sky. Joli was filled with an intense loneliness as this happened, but then he found that there was a warmth surrounding him, as if he were its unborn child. A million colours swam together across his memories of vision.

Who are you? the relics of his individuality thought to the entity that had taken him into itself.

The Wind, it replied, its voice like a tsunami that filled all of his thinking with its rushing water. *Welcome.*

Chapter Six
Nerve

The Wind swept itself to the high places above Giorran, and there it summoned the Despot to attend it. His immediate response was to rebuke it for its presumption; he was not accustomed to being told by anybody or anything what he should do. However, after a few of the grander houses of Ernestrad had been reduced to heaps of rubble, he reconsidered.

He was a ruler of human beings. The Wind, on the other hand, was a ruler of the elements which governed all of Albion and could scatter human beings before them. Although it was hard, the Despot forced himself to accept that there was a power greater than his own.

He was in a spacious room with one of his favourite concubines when the summons came. The floor was made of squares of different-coloured stones whose dull light created a reflected pattern on the ceiling, thanks to the brilliance of the sunlight that poured in through the room's unglazed windows. She was a woman of average height, just a little shorter than himself, and had been taken away from her aristocratic family, with their permission, in order to serve him while at the same time advancing their interests. It was the wish of her parents to create trade throughout Albion, so that other merchants would be compelled to purchase from them. It was the wish of the Despot to have as many beautiful lovers as possible. Naturally her parents had been executed as soon as the contract had been confirmed. The Despot had no complaints about the system

– indeed, it seemed perfectly equitable to him.

She was just discovering that his nipples were the part of his body that she most loathed, narrowly ahead of his armpits, when the Wind entered the room, throwing paintings from the walls and tearing up tiles from the floor.

The Despot pulled himself out of her.

'Away! Away with you!' he shouted. 'I'll attend you, as I agreed, but not quite yet!'

Under her legs, bottom and shoulders she felt the smoothness of the stone floor. Oddly, it seemed more loving than the despairingly passionate embraces the Despot had been pressing upon her until just a second or two before.

The fat man was now being thrown from one side of the room to the other by the Wind, so that bruises were beginning to form on his torso. She giggled as she watched what the gale was doing to him, especially at the wilting of the erection of which he'd been so proud. Now he was nothing more than any other man: rulers and peasants knew no distinctions when they were in terror. One of his ears was shattered against a stone wall, so that blood began to pour from it.

Lying there on the floor, she was spared from the worst of the Wind's wrath.

The Despot had told her that the Wind had tried to speak with him during the previous waking-period, but that he'd indignantly refused it . . . before confessing that, instead, he'd conceded to the requests the Wind had made. Now it would seem that the Wind had decided to make a display of its powers. The Despot was still being battered this way and that across the room, and one of his arms was droopily broken. She tried her best not to laugh again – then tried her best not to castigate herself for her failure. If the Despot survived this encounter she might find herself in deep trouble for her lapse.

After a long time the Wind carried the Despot spinning away out of one of the windows, holding his screaming body aloft as it fluttered him through the air until he found himself dropped unceremoniously on the plateau where Nadar had long ago spoken to the Wind.

The concubine, delighted to find herself alone, laughed to herself cheerfully again and pulled on her clothing, hoping beyond all hope that the Wind would destroy the Despot, so that she would no longer have to tolerate his clammy invasions of her body.

The Wind, capriciously, came back into the room just as she was leaving it and threw her down the stairs, so that her neck was broken in several places.

'Anya!' said a voice.

'Yes.'

She was hardly awake.

'Anya!'

The voice was more insistent.

'I'm here,' she mumbled.

She turned over, feeling the pillows soft against her ears.

'It's Barra 'ap Rteniadoli Me'gli'minter Rehan. Remember me?' He was shaking her shoulder, trying as hard as he could to waken her.

She kicked out at him and missed.

'Anya!'

Through the off-white canvas of the tent came sunlight that wandered into her eyes so that she could no longer convince herself that she was asleep but had to listen to what he was saying.

'Um,' she said.

He sat down beside her on the bed; she felt the heaviness of his body against her stomach.

'Do you still plan to be the leader of an army?' he said earnestly.

''Course I do. Am, dammit.'

'Not for much longer.'

Now she sat upright, fully awake.

'What do you mean?'

Her eyes were sharp little points as she looked at him. He hoped she wouldn't apply the principle of killing the messenger. The bedding dropped away from her breasts, which looked strangely youthful and innocent beneath the stern mask of her face.

'The executions. Your people are saying that no one's safe from you any longer, that you're just as bad as the House of Ellon. During the last sleeping-period several dozen deserted – just left – to try to find their way back to their homes. That's not so bad – we can do without a few faint-hearts. What's worse is that some of the others are plotting against you. They believe that you should die and that a different leader should be appointed in your place.'

'But that's bullshit! There's no one alive but me who could keep this army together! If I died it'd just dwindle away until it was nothing.'

She got out of bed, unconcerned about her nakedness, and started to throw on some clothes.

'That's not quite true,' said Rehan, gazing out through the open doorway of her tent. Some children were playing with a ball. One of them had just fallen flat on her face and was rolling over, laughing at her own clumsiness.

'How do you mean?' said Anya loudly.

'There's Reen, for one,' he replied, not looking at her. 'And for that matter there's me. Both of us can remember the past . . . and the dead.'

'Yes,' she hissed, 'but you can't do what I can do – give the abilities to those around you.'

'You're sure about that, are you?'

Barra 'ap Rteniadoli Me'gli'minter Rehan sensed that he was only a hair's-breadth away from death, but still he preferred to keep his back to her.

'Explain, you little shit!'

Now Rehan did turn to look at her.

'We have a new ally. It, too, can remember all of the past – in fact, it can remember everything back to the time when Albion first rose from the waves.'

He sat down on the bed again and watched her as she finished dressing. *Why*, he wondered, *do I feel so repelled right now by the body that, once upon a time, I was pulled towards just by imagining the touch of it? Why has Anya become an alien creature to me?*

'I don't believe you.' She clipped the words.

'But it's true.'

'Who is this fictitious ally, then?'

'The Wind.'

She stared at him disbelievingly.

'You've got to be joking. The Wind doesn't befriend humans – ever!'

'The Wind has told us that it wants to see the destruction of the House of Ellon, and that it'll act alongside Reen and myself – and maybe Alyss, too – in order to make this come about. Reen and I said that we'd consider the matter, but that first we'd have to consult with you. Unfortunately, the Wind told others of your soldiers what was going on, and they decided that the army would be better without you as its leader. Reen and I have tried during the last sleeping-period to talk them out of it, but it's been difficult, and there are still quite a number who want to see you assassinated and replaced.' He was enjoying lying to her. 'As I said, the executions are to blame: you should never have killed so many of our people.'

'But you and Reen would never betray me . . . Would you?'

He coughed, then wiped his sticky palm against his knee.

'Reen and I share a principle with the Wind: we would like to see the end of the House of Ellon's tyranny,' he said, pronouncing the words carefully. 'However, we have no wish to see one tyranny replaced by another that is just as bad. If the only way we can achieve our end is through your death, then that strikes us as a small price to pay.'

'Traitors!' she bawled.

'No, not traitors at all. That's the sort of accusation the Despot shouts at his minions. Our loyalty is firstly to our people and only secondly to you. But things could change, I guess.'

'How?'

He considered his words for a moment or two.

'If *you* changed,' he said eventually.

Anya emitted a stubborn and furious silence.

'If,' he said hesitantly, 'you could only return to the way you were before. People saw you as harsh and tough, but never as unjust: they loved you and some of them even worshipped you. Think of Joli, for example.'

'Joli's dead. I felt him die. Besides, he was a dishonourable old reprobate who stank of decaying fish.'

'He was also your friend. He died through trying to help you.'

Again Rehan's voice was very quiet. He was staring straight ahead of him, remembering how Joli would swear and spit at all of them at the same time as sparing a moment to tell a child a joke that was just too deliciously naughty to be passed on to its parents.

'Don't,' said Rehan, 'judge your friends by their personal appearances. And, for that matter' – his voice rising – 'don't judge them when they have to tell you things you don't much want to hear! Reen and I could have simply watched you being killed and then taken over command of the army, but we decided between us not to do that. We *want* you to be our leader, we believe in you – all of us do – but at the moment you're making it impossibly fucking difficult!'

Anya rubbed her hair back from her brow.

'What would you like me to do?'

'Remember that you're not some kind of goddess.'

'I've never claimed to be one.'

'But you've been acting like one – and a cruel one.'

'On occasion I've had to take Draconian action . . .'

'No. You've been needlessly cruel. Haven't you *noticed*?'

There was a very long silence, during which Anya walked to watch the kids playing outside her tent. She clapped her hands when a little boy managed to kick the ball up in the air and then head it off towards the feet of one of his friends. As she turned back towards Rehan she was smiling, and for the first time for ages he was able to accept her smile as genuine.

'You're right,' she said.

He took her hand in his, and clutched her fingers.

'Mercy,' said Anya. 'If I don't show mercy then there's no point in my existing at all.'

He pulled her down beside him and kissed her very chastely on the point of her chin. He'd doubted that she'd have the strength of soul to accept the criticism; Reen had been the one who'd had more faith in Anya.

'Let's go and say hello to the Wind,' he said.

What had happened on the plateau above Giorran had been humiliating for the Despot. The Wind had whipped the sky up into a frenzy, drawing together clouds of white moisture and forming them into the shapes of giant eyes that seemed to be staring at the Despot as he stood, trembling with cold and terror, feeling all the strength of Albion's elements raging against him. Despite the clouds, the sun shone mercilessly down at him, its heat touching his naked skin with the harshness of a knife. Viciously the Wind picked up loose seeds from the grasses around him and lashed them against his ankles severely, so that he hopped about uncontrollably in pain.

'I demand an end to this torment,' he shouted at the anger of the sky, shaking his fist at it.

You have no power to demand anything of me, said the Wind to him, the sound of its thought so strong in his mind that he stumbled to one side, clamping his hands over his ears as if trying to keep out a physical sound.

He staggered into the cairn, cutting one of his fleshy hips on its sharp rocks. He fell, pulling himself round at the last moment so that he landed on his bottom, sitting with his back against the pile of stones.

'I have,' he yelled, his eyes closed, 'a *right* to demand an end to this torment!'

And from where do you derive the right to make this demand? The nuance of the thought was cruelly teasing, as a child might be to an insect.

'I am the Despot of all Albion!'

Now he opened his eyes and glared around him.

'I rule all, and rule all with the consent of all.'

You lie.

'Ask my people.'

You lie. You may rule the people of Albion, but you do not rule Albion itself, and you cannot say that you rule the people of Albion with their consent.

The Wind blew sleet into his face and chest, and he

heard what he guessed to be its laughter.

You rule because people are either too terrified of you or too stupid to be terrified of you. Your empire is nothing but a field of death – a mountain of crap, with you sitting at the very top, proud of yourself because you can crap more than anyone else. Don't you understand the basic pettiness of tyranny? Only the pettiest, most trivial of people would derive any pleasure from holding power of life and death over even a single fellow human being; pettier still to rejoice in having that power over the entire world.

'I'm the head of the House of Ellon,' he said, trying to muster some dignity. 'We've ruled Albion for millennia in the best and kindest interests of all.'

The peasants?

'The cattle? The rats and weasels? The fishes in the streams or the sheep in the fields? Would you want the House of Ellon to be universally kind to *all* of them? If not, why are you complaining that sometimes the peasants are treated harshly? They're nothing more than animals, are they? Human-shaped animals, but animals all the same? They're not even very clever animals. A dog is more easily house-trained and can do more entertaining tricks.'

The Wind flipped a stone from the top of the cairn so that it fell on the Despot's shoulder. He flinched in pain but continued to stare his defiance at the sky.

They hurt just the same way as you do, said the Wind, *and they have the same knowledge of their pain as you do. When they're hungry their stomachs snarl at them the same way yours would if ever you allowed yourself to eat less than five times as much as your body can reasonably use. Yet you rejoice in the benevolence you show to these 'animals'? Would you starve a pet dog or work it until it was nothing more than a snivelling, cringing object with never a thought but keeping clear of the point of your boot?*

The Despot pushed himself to his feet, ignoring the pain as his back scraped against the rocks of the cairn. It was becoming difficult for him to see now against the blasts of cold air in his eyes. He felt as if blood were running from them down over his cheeks.

'I rule this world for the benefit of all,' he said.

The whole sky seemed to laugh at him.

You rule Albion for the benefit of you, said the Wind a little while later. *Besides, as I said, you don't even rule the whole of Albion. To take a single example, it's very obvious that you don't rule me, and nor do you rule any of the other elements.*

The cloud-eyes looked at him balefully.

And you don't rule the woman called Anya or the people of hers you choose to think of as 'animals', do you? All you rule are a few hundred members of the House of Ellon and a few thousand other people who find that life is safer and more comfortable in Ernestrad than in any other part of your realm.

'They love me,' he said. 'They tell me that they love me.'

Of course *they do, because what alternative do they have? A disembowelling, or just a quick hanging? Even the women you take to your bed both are revolted by you and laugh covertly at you, yet if ever you guess at their feelings you forget the blandishments you've lavished on them and instead have them slaughtered.*

'Should a man tolerate a false lover?'

You've had no lovers – just women who've been forced to share your bed.

The Despot shook his head.

'I've . . . I've . . . I've . . .' And the words just trickled away until he found that he wasn't saying anything any longer.

Can't you understand how insignificant you are, how paltry? To be ruler of the world is nothing: it's something anybody could do.

'I'm Despot by right. By right of my inheritance of the leadership of the House of Ellon, who have ruled this world forever.'

The Wind caught up his words and momentarily painted them in vast crimson letters across the sky. Then it wiped them away, so that they fell as rain.

Do I have to spell it out to you? You do not rule me. *To me you're just a rather pathetic little naked fat man, cowering on*

367

a hilltop because he's been told that the world as he knows it is drawing to an end. The woman called Anya is coming closer and closer to Ernestrad, and she will destroy you and all of the House of Ellon. You don't rule the rain, you don't rule the clouds, you don't rule the sky, you don't rule the Sun . . .

'Why did you bring me here?' He was too tired, now, for defiance.

To give you a chance. The future hasn't been written down yet – not that you could have read it even if it had been. For far too long I've watched the House of Ellon turn Albion into a slaughterground. Even so, if you wanted you could change things and then I'd fight with you against Anya and support the future promises of the House of Ellon. But you don't seem to want me to do that.

'Take your threats and . . .'

The Despot, his face bright red, couldn't find the words because, after all, the Wind didn't have any appropriate apertures.

The Wind picked him up and hurled him through the air for a sickeningly long time, his arms and legs churning against the air, until he fell with a crash onto the bed in one of his preferred bedchambers. He landed on his broken arm and screamed from the agony, nursing it with his good hand; then he turned over, instinctively pulling himself under the bedding, hoping like a child that sleep would bring him some measure of comfort from the pain and the freezing cold he had experienced.

He heard the door open behind him and turned back again: perhaps one of the slaves had heard his scream, and would fetch a physician to tend to his arm.

The person who entered was neither a slave nor even a fortuitously passing physician. Until recently she'd been one of his concubines; in fact, now he thought about it, he remembered that he'd been screwing her when the Wind had snatched him away.

Her head lolled uncontrolledly as she walked towards him. Her eyes were vacant. She climbed into the bed beside him and nestled her cold body against him.

As the Despot tried to struggle away from her, she tightened her arms about his chest, so that he was unable to move.

You see, said the voice of the Wind in his mind, *you do not rule over the dead, either.*

Reen stood beside Barra 'ap Rteniadoli Me'gli'minter Rehan as they watched a chunk of fresh venison scorching on the fire. It was late, and most of the soldiers had already eaten and gone to bed, but the two of them had got into the habit of sitting up later than the others and chatting about the events of the day. Although both were now reconciled in their different ways to Anya, they seemed to find more enjoyment in each other's company than they did with her. Often they talked long into the sleeping-period, then stumbled off to share a bed together. Occasionally, but not very often, they made love; usually they just fell asleep holding hands and telling silly stories.

The venison was beginning to burn, and Rehan dragged it out using a forked stick and a large cabbage-leaf.

'Can I cook tomorrow?' said Reen, looking at the venison steak. 'Perhaps, um, something accompanied by a selection of fresh vegetables, all served in an interestingly concocted sauce comprising various spices as well as, maybe, sour cream to add body?'

'Yes,' said Rehan, 'please. In the mean time, er, this is getting cold.'

They ate the meat, which was as tough as it had looked.

'Anya's changed,' said Reen between mouthfuls. 'Thank all the powers of goodness that she had the guts to be able to do that.'

'She's a better person than she seems. I remember, long ago, you telling me that you thought she was someone very special. At the time I believed she was just a person who was good with weapons and a brilliant bang – which she is, by the way.'

'You've mentioned as much before. Too many times.'

Fat from the venison running down his chin, Rehan grinned at her.

'Yes, but you're *different*. And I've mentioned that a

million times before, too. Does it matter all that much?'

'Some time soon, Barra 'ap Rteniadoli Me'gli'minter Rehan, you're going to find yourself killed. Nastily.'

'This bit of meat . . .' he said, struggling with a string of it.

'Prat.' Reen laughed at him.

'That's the difference,' he said.

He got the string free and was just about to throw it away before, on second thoughts, he ate it.

'What do you mean?'

'You call me a prat and it's just something for us to laugh about. That's a completely different sort of relationship from the one I used to have with Anya. The reason you and I usually sleep together hasn't got a lot to do with our bodies, has it?'

'True.'

'Now, if you said that to a lot of people they'd be profoundly offended – even more profoundly offended than if you said that this venison is bloody awful.'

'This venison is bloody awful.'

He reached out and touched her on the nose.

'Honest woman.'

'Honest man,' she said, rather more seriously.

Feeling guilty – because the soldiers were supposed not to waste food under any circumstances – they threw the remains of the venison onto the fire. It flared up briefly, then began slowly to turn into charcoal.

'You're . . . all right, you know,' she said as they walked through the silence towards her tent. Her fingers were interlaced with his. 'I've made love with a lot of women who were a lot less caring than you.'

He didn't say anything for a few moments.

'That's a very considerable compliment.'

She dragged him into her tent with a shout of laughter. They were neither man nor woman: just lovers.

Anya sat sleepily on the edge of her bed and looked at her fingernails, which seemed to her to be too pale. She spread her fingertips apart, as if somehow this would help, but it didn't seem to. They were still the same shells they'd always been – nothing more than things to be used for picking her nose, untying knots and other odd jobs.

The Wind.

The Wind had apparently said it would become a part of them, that it would help them bring the House of Ellon low. The three of them – Anya, Reen and Rehan – had gone to meet it in a copse not far from the camp, and at first she'd been absolutely petrified by the sheer power of the element's mind – and also by its patent potential for ruthlessness. Reen and Rehan, by contrast, had greeted it almost as if it were an old aquaintance: they'd casually sat themselves down on the grass and exchanged inconsequentialities with the Wind before discussing further plans.

And slowly Anya had begun to understand why they were able to do this.

They were not frightened of the Wind's power, because they knew that the Wind would not use it to harm them. The Wind might be ruthless and it certainly wasn't a friend – but it wasn't an enemy either. It explained that it would cooperate with them in their endeavour because it no longer believed that the House of Ellon was fit to rule Albion. That was all. It wished to help them because there seemed to be no other way of replacing the governance of the House of Ellon except by confusion and anarchy. It had very little interest in human beings as such, but it was trivially influenced by human grief. Being largely a creature of mind, it felt the grief as if it were a slightly aching tooth or a minor bruise. Now, after all the millennia since the House of Ellon had come into existence, the minor throb of pain nagged at the Wind until it had come to seem like a major torment.

The Wind was frank. Its motives were utterly selfish, it explained for Anya's benefit. It wanted the itch it felt to end and didn't care how that was brought about. If it had been within the Wind's power simply to exterminate all human life from Albion, it would have done that without the slightest compunction – in fact, it would have preferred to have been able to. But that option wasn't open to it:

without them its magic would be purposeless and hence shrivel and die. It didn't expect that eliminating the House of Ellon would remove the ache altogether, but at least it would make it so minimal that it could be ignored . . . at least for a few more billennia.

Which, Anya realised, was why Reen and Rehan weren't frightened of the Wind. It had no wish to harm them, any more than either of them would wish to harm a fly that had found its way into their tent: all they would have wanted to do was to get the fly out again, killing it only if necessary – and if they could catch it. Similarly, the Wind didn't care too much about what happened to humanity, but saw no particular reason to destroy human beings.

Except that it would help them destroy *some* human beings in order to remove that tiny ache.

Anya had never, except for a time she preferred not to remember, really wanted to kill people either, but then there had seemed to be nothing else that could be done if human grief, in the long term, were to be reduced. Unfortunately, Anya had confused cruelty with surgery.

It seemed that she had a lot in common with the Wind, and she began to smile. She had felt a flick of its thought in her mind – the brush of a horse's tail against her skin – and recognised that the Wind, reciprocally, was welcoming her.

And yet now, as she looked at her fingernails, they still seemed too pale. It worried her that somehow this figured in her mind as a more important matter than the fact that, earlier during this waking-period, she'd spoken on equal terms with the Wind.

Surely that was something she should remember as long as her life should last, while the colour of her fingernails was something that she would forget about before the end of the next waking-period?

The Wind had told them something else, and she was still finding it difficult for her mind to cope with it. Maybe Rehan and Reen were finding it easier – although she doubted it: they were probably just doing their best to forget it.

Before her grandfather came to Albion, the peasants had

had no memory, especially no memory of the dead. They could perform rote activities like tilling the fields, but they did so only as domesticated animals would have done. Yet – in the presence of someone like Anya, or like Barra 'ap Rteniadoli Me'gli'minter Rehan, or like the Wind, or like Lian, or like Joli – they became quite different: they turned from trained animals into human beings . . . human beings with as much awareness as those who could trace their ancestry down through many generations of the House of Ellon.

The Wind had watched all this.

It knew why.

It had told the three of them, there in that copse where the leaves had rustled so industriously.

At last a slave had heard the screams of the Despot. Nervously she opened the door of the bedchamber. As always, she was amazed by the splendour of the hangings and the furniture, and spent a few seconds looking around at them. It was only then that she recalled what had brought her here in the first place, and looked around for the source of the noise.

The tapestried bedclothes were threshing, and her first assumption was that the Despot was treating one of his concubines cruelly, and that it was the concubine that was screaming. She was just about to retreat backwards through the doorway, hoping that she wouldn't be punished for her intrusion, when she realised her misapprehension.

She smiled and closed the door behind her.

Next waking-period there was a new Despot.

Ngur.

Then the killings began in earnest.

Too many of the House of Ellon believed that the throne should have gone to a more direct descendant of the previous Despot, and there were plenty of claims by his concubines on behalf of their children; for obvious reasons, most of these claims were met with a hollow laugh. Why, some of the lesser scions of the House of Ellon could remember how they themselves had . . .

The children of the concubines died first; that sorted out the first argument about the succession. Then, just to be on the safe side, it was the turn of the concubines themselves. By now the critical voices were fairly muted, but even so Ngur felt threatened by the fact that anyone at all should resent his rule, and so those who made the slightest critical comment were executed with a degree of mercy appropriate to their rank.

The slave who had left the previous Despot to his fate was promoted to become a kitchen scullion, there by now being a shortage of scullions.

Within a few waking-periods the population of Ernestrad had been decreased by about one-tenth, but Ngur felt secure in his new position.

Before his elevation he had thought that, some time soon, the oppression of the peasants of Albion could be ameliorated. Now that he'd achieved the ultimate power, it was difficult for him to rush too hastily into making such changes. After all, although there was still the troublesome matter of the peasant army which was, according to all reports, once more growing in size, he knew ways by which it could be conquered and was only too ready to put them into practice – now that he was no longer shackled by his predecessor's unpredictability. The rebellion would be a minor matter now that he was in control: it was something that the Ellonia would natter about over the table of a banquet here and there for a long time to come, but it wasn't anything more than that.

He decided to call the Wind to his assistance.

That was when he first began to worry.

The Wind failed to respond to his summons. He had climbed to the plateau above Giorran and called the Wind to him, but nothing had happened.

He re-armed his soldiers, equipping them with crossbows and small, evilly sharp daggers, and giving them fresh young horses and new leather armour decorated in the Ellonian red and green. Once upon a time he'd believed that subtlety could be used to conquer the rebels but, now that he himself was on the throne of ultimate power, his instinct was to extirpate them with all the vicious heavy-handedness at his command. Their bodies would be scattered all over Albion; their disjointed limbs would be strung up high on every gibbet so that even the peasants from the fields would be able to remember that never again should they revolt against the might of the House of Ellon.

And then one waking-period he found himself on horseback outside the main gate of Giorran. The army arrayed before him was even more vast than the one that he had raised before – the one that had been massacred in such miserable circumstances by the dreamer. Everywhere he looked there was movement, as if all the surrounding hills were covered in busy insects. He wished for a moment that he had a paintbrush with him: he knew that with a few brief movements of the brush he could have caught the sensation of that mass of colour so that it would be preserved on paper forever as a testimony to his own might.

He was both Despot and Army-Master. He ruled every last hectare of Albion.

He felt as if he could reach a hand above his head and hold the sky, telling it that even it should bow in the face of his infinite power.

Instead, he told one of his commanders to give the order for the army to turn away from Ernestrad. He rode among the columns of men, listening to their enthusiastic cheers, until he was at their head. He touched his horse on its shoulder so that it pulled around. Again there was that sea of well disciplined humanity spread out in front of him. Some of the people near to him he recognised as of the pure stock of the House of Ellon; others wore the stolid expressions of slaves; yet others were merchants or shop-keepers or . . .

He turned his horse away again.

'Advance!' he shouted.

There was a cheer that didn't last quite long enough, but he heard them as they followed him.

Dutifully.

Chapter Seven
Warfare

The echoes of the flute die away, and Rehan resumes singing.

Here are a few facts that it's very improbable you'll like very much.

You're a peasant, you see.

There's a new waking-period and you fall out of bed and find yourself something to eat – usually a not very nice something, but at least it'll keep you going until the middle of the waking-period. You and your mate, your minds on your stomachs, leave your cottage or shack and those of your children who're too young to work, and you go to the fields. There, under the bright blue of the sky, you pick fruit or gather grain until it seems that your back wants to split into tiny splinters; after you've worked a little longer, you slowly head for home.

All you can think about as you climb into bed with your mate is your weariness. You can't recall why you're tired: indeed, you don't properly realise *why* you're tired, because that's the way you always are. Instead you think for a short time until the thinking stops and you're asleep.

It's different when the Ellonia come.

Those are waking-periods which you're likely to remember at least until it's the time for you to sleep, and perhaps even beyond that. They take things away from you and they invade your bodies. You think of the way that you've watched their invasion of your friends, and for a while the memory is fire in your mind, but then it seems to fade away until it's something you can no longer grasp.

Then there's a different waking-period.

Someone has come among you who has the power to give you back your memories and your feelings. The sudden exposure to your emotions is a bit of a shock, and is normally quite painful, but it's as if you'd been surrounded by a suffocating mist all of your life and abruptly it has retreated. Now all the colours of the world are different, almost like someone had taken the time to wash them so that they looked cleaner. The brightness you've never seen before sometimes hurts your eyes, but you find yourself glorying in it.

Your village is host to three peasants who have the power to open up your memories.

The three strangers have names. They have a request they'd like to make of you.

All of a sudden, you find that you're a warrior. You dig out the toughest clothing you've ever owned, and you're given a sword or a bow; in the unlikely event that your village has a competent smith, she or he will craft some sharp-ended implement for you. The luckiest of people – who are inevitably not you – will be supplied with horses.

Off you go from the village where you've lived for all of your life. The chances are you'll be dead soon, but that isn't something that worries you just at the moment.

All that's important, right now, is the fact that you're suddenly – bewilderingly – *alive* . . .

They were moving more swiftly now, even though the task of recruiting new warriors seemed to be taking up an inordinate amount of their time. There was also a strong feeling of fellowship among the members of their scruffy army, almost as if they were all out to enjoy a party together rather than to fight a war.

In some ways this worried Anya.

She knew that the forces of the House of Ellon would be tightly disciplined and would show little compassion in battle. Might it not be that her own army, singing lightheartedly as they marched, would be mown down with ease?

She asked Reen.

The older woman had been through all this before.

'Frankly,' Reen said, 'I'm glad I'm not up against this bunch of ours we have here: at a guess they're going to make pet food of the Ellonia, even though in general their weapons are bloody awful and their military skills are, to put it politely, somewhere so far beneath elementary that no one has yet invented an adequate word to describe them.'

'Um,' said Anya, trying to think of a polite way of pointing out the internal contradictions in what Reen had just said.

'The Wind,' muttered Barra 'ap Rteniadoli Me'gli'minter Rehan. 'Alyss. Me.'

'Great. Thanks. Especially for the last,' said Anya. 'The Wind says it'll fight on our side, but then we see nothing of it. Alyss wanders in and out of our lives ordering them as if she owns them, but all she's done so far is send us a dreamer who's now dead and a singer who might well be good at singing but who's not exactly a dab hand with any weapon more lethal than a double-ended drumstick.'

'And, as it happens, now with a sword,' muttered Rehan, 'but that's one of the things you wouldn't notice.'

'There's also the fact that our soldiers will willingly die fighting the Ellonia,' said Reen. 'Ever fought against someone who'll die rather than be defeated? Believe me, it's not a pleasant experience. They've got a distinct advantage, even if you're armed with an axe and all they've got is a wooden spoon.'

They were slowly picking their way through a belt of forest, working uphill. The horses were clearly unhappy, and Anya wished that she'd decided to lead the army in a different direction. Yet she was conscious of the fact that the Ellonia couldn't be far away, and she wanted to keep her people out of sight as much as possible: spread out in the open they were constantly vulnerable to an assault by the House of Ellon's archers.

The horses they were riding made their way daintily

among the trees, moving at no greater pace than a walk. Anya smelled the scent of leaves that had been recently rained on, and from time to time reached out to touch the smooth wetness of one of them.

'I'm more than you think,' said Rehan a while later, when their two horses again approached each other.

'I apologise,' said Anya. 'I was being deliberately rude. And, come to think of it, generally shitty.'

'No: don't apologise. I mean that.' He pushed his hand back up over his forehead, wishing he could think of some clearer way of explaining himself. 'I can create music.'

'True,' Anya said. 'I apologise again.'

There was a touch of sarcasm in her voice.

'You know something?' said Rehan. 'You're unusually repellent, even for you, when you apologise. It'd be really nice if you stopped doing it.'

'Sorry.'

A few moments later he added: 'There are things music can do that a sword can't.' He ducked to avoid a low branch.

'Make you do a sword-dance?'

He plucked a chestnut and threw it at her. He missed.

'Music,' he said, when she'd stopped laughing at him – and he at himself – 'music has powers of its own. It shares something with the Wind. I don't mean that,' he said, gesturing towards his flute, 'as some kind of stupid pun. What I'm trying to say is that music can take the air and transform it so that it becomes a weapon. Think about it. Why do the Ellonia sound trumpets when they come to the villages? It's not for aesthetic reasons, is it? What they understand – or used to understand – is the effect the notes of the trumpets have on the peasants. Music can be used to convey messages or even commands, whether or not the person who hears the music wants to hear it.'

'It's been a while since you've fascinated me, Rehan,' said Anya, her eyes mocking him and her mouth respecting him.

'Listen,' he said.

He played a gay little rhythm on his bodhran, gripping

the firm flanks of his horse with his knees, and she felt her toes moving in response in her leather shoes.

'That was nothing at all,' Rehan said, putting his stick automatically back into the pocket of his jerkin, 'except for the fact that, for a few seconds, I deliberately controlled you.'

'Nonsense,' Anya laughed. 'I was just tapping along with you!'

'Could you have stopped yourself from doing that?'

'If I'd wanted to, yes.'

'That's part of the point: you didn't *want* to. All you thought of doing was something I'd decided that *I* wanted you to do. I wanted to make you move your feet, and they moved just the way I expected. You didn't even think about the fact that your feet were moving at my command.'

'I think I begin to see what you're trying to say.' The gleam had gone from her eyes.

'But I could give you another command that you wouldn't notice, a quite different one.' Again he held on to the horse's sides with his legs, hoping that he wouldn't fall off and end the conversation ignominiously. 'I won't do this for too long, because it would frighten the horses.'

For a few seconds he made the drum produce regular and mournful notes. Anya found that she was having to pull in the reins of her own horse, and she heard nervous whinnies from around them in the woods. She herself felt scared by the sound that Rehan had produced: it had depicted, in some way, her own death.

'Don't do that again,' she snapped at him.

'But I must. That's what music has in common with the Wind. Both of us can talk directly into people's minds, and alter them so that they make the people do things they'd never otherwise have done. You've spoken with the Wind, so you know what *it*'s like; now you've listened to the bodhran, and so now you know what *it*'s like when it speaks to you in the same way. The sound is just a sound, and its measure is nothing more than a measure. But your mind responds to both of them, and it obeys whatever commands they give you.'

He clipped his bodhran back against his saddle, pocketed the stick, and pulled his flute from behind him.

'Proof,' he said, raising his flute to his lips.

His fingers ran along the keys, fondling them almost as a lover would. Then he pursed his mouth and blew a little dance tune that he'd once heard in the north of Albion.

Anya felt herself smile. It seemed as if her whole body was imbued with happiness, as if her heart wanted to beat twice as fast, as if the sun was shining its heat down onto her at just the right temperature so that her skin was being caressed into a tingling of appreciative pleasure.

Then Rehan stopped playing.

She looked at him furiously.

'Carry on,' she said.

'No.'

'Why not?'

They didn't speak for a few moments as they guided their horses with difficulty down a steep, slimy slope, at the bottom of which was a narrow stream. Once they'd climbed clumsily up the other side, Anya repeated her question.

'Why not?'

'Because I respect you.'

She snorted.

'That's no answer,' she said.

'Yes it is,' said Rehan, 'and, moreover, it's a true one.'

She thought for a little while.

'Yes,' she said eventually, 'I see what you mean. It'd be like when you're making love and want it to go on forever, so that you're really annoyed when your man comes and it's got to be all over for a while. Except then it could start again. But when you stopped playing the music it would never start again.'

Rehan looked at his flute with a sudden doubt, then stowed it away behind him.

He coughed.

'I'd never thought of that before,' he muttered. 'But,' a little more loudly, 'I trust you see what I mean about the way music can govern people – people and their emotions.

As I said, that's what I have in common with the Wind: I can speak directly to people's minds. I can speak directly to *Ellonian* minds.'

They were out of the trees and were nearing the top of the hill. Anya glanced behind her and saw an amorphous mass of coloured clothing and panting horses.

'So, you could be a weapon in yourself?' she muttered, looking towards Rehan.

'Yes.'

'Then soon I must *use* you as a weapon.'

He smiled at her.

'I know. We're coming near to Ernestrad. It can't be very long now.'

'You may die. Maybe within the next waking-period.'

'I'm not frightened of that.'

'Then you're a fool.'

'No. I'm a singer. Songs never die, and I'm no different from a song.'

Ngur moved restlessly up and down the hall in Giorran he'd adopted as his own private territory. The floor of it was made of polished white and red marble, so that the sunlight pouring in through the windows reflected a reddish glow. He had long ago forgone the ostentatious trappings of his predecessor: where there might once have been a huge gilt throne there were instead a collection of ponderous chairs and a big oak table, around which he and his commanders regularly met. The walls were, like the ceiling, white, but scattered along them were opulent wall-hangings, some of them dating back to long before any historian of the House of Ellon could remember. Embroidered into the hangings were depictions of human beings and animals; some of the animals were unlike anything that anyone living had ever seen. Here there was a crazily askew bright yellow beast with horns that arched backwards from its head to well behind its tail. And here there was a six-legged creature whose eyes stabbed bright white flames at a tribe of hunters, who were quailing away from the intensity of the heat.

Ngur threw himself down on one of the chairs and leant

an elbow on the table. He looked at the bizarre animals shown in the tapestries and realised for the thousandth time that their images threatened one of the basic beliefs of the House of Ellon: that all things in the world had been the same throughout eternity, since the time the Sun had chosen to create Albion. The thought nagged at him, making him feel unsettled: if, in the long ago, things had been different from the way they were today, this implied that they might be different in the future, too. The House of Ellon couldn't rely on retaining power, as a matter of right, forever.

Such notions were, he knew, heretical, and he shouldn't be allowing himself to think them – and certainly he knew that, if he expressed them to any of his commanders or to any of the other aristocrats, he would be signing his own death warrant. But the implications seemed inescapable to him – unless, of course, the distorted animals had been just fantasies born from the embroiderers' minds, or perhaps folk myths current in a less sophisticated age. Yet even these latter hypotheses brought little comfort to him. For one thing, the artists of the House of Ellon were never given to fantasy or imagination: the only pictures they ever created were strictly realistic – or, at least, as realistic as they could be within the limits of the artist's ability. Second, the idea that there had been folk myths in an earlier age which were nowadays unknown involved acknowledging, once again, that there had been change over the millennia. The change implied might be a more subtle one, but it was a change nevertheless.

The future could bring further changes, and one of the possibilities that was immediately obvious was that the House of Ellon might be thrown from its eminence, and all its works destroyed. It was only too possible, he thought gloomily, that he might be the last of all the Ellonian Despots. The Wind seemed to have deserted their cause, and his scouts told him that the peasant army was now close to Ernestrad. His soldiers were showing him scant respect in the wake of his most recent fiasco as their leader. He had guided them confidently for several waking-periods, expecting soon to encounter the peasants, only to be summonded back again to Ernestrad by white-faced messengers. The scouts had discovered he had been misinformed: the peasants were approaching the capital from a quite different direction.

So now here he was, stranded, having initiated a mighty military venture only to discover that it had all been a waste of endeavour. He was puzzled by the enormity of the error. It was as if unknown supernatural forces were somehow conspiring against his every effort. Since becoming Despot he'd done all the right things, yet his military wisdom and expertise seemed to be proving as ineffectual as the ignorant botching that had preceded it.

Ngur seemed to hear a whisper in the air. Alyss . . .

He stared through one of the windows, looking balefully at the sunlight as it played across the hills and fields in the distance; the furthest of them were slowly changing in shape, which meant that at least some things were well with the world. As he watched the light, he recognised that he was – and for a long time had been – involuntarily shedding his religious faith. The Sun, which had appointed itself as the guardian of the House of Ellon, had recently seemed not only to have little interest in the Ellonians' welfare but also little influence on what happened in the world. One particular tenet was that the Sun would guide the Despot wisely, yet it had made no move to avert the death of his predecessor and it had watched impassively as Ngur himself had now, more than once, made military excursions that had resulted in nothing more than his own humiliation.

Was it possible that, despite everything he had been reared to believe, the Sun wasn't a god at all? Might it instead be just a bright light in the sky?

Ngur was an intelligent man. He had the good sense to keep all these ideas to himself. But while he was appalled to find that they were floating around in his mind, in some strange way he welcomed them. If he looked at the world from this new viewpoint – one that was completely different from all that tradition had taught him – he could obtain a quite different perception. He wasn't confident enough to claim to himself that this perception was correct and that the traditional one was wrong – in fact, it seemed to him that to be dogmatic either way would be to commit an intellectual imbecility – but he was grateful to his heresies for the way that they allowed him to have more than one perspective.

Apart from anything else, the ability to see matters from more than a single angle would help him defeat this upstart woman and her ragbag of followers.

He hoped.

The sunlight continued to stroke the comfortably shifting lines of the distant landscape.

There was a hesitant tap at the door of the hall.

'Enter!' said Ngur.

The door swung open.

Resplendent in his full military armour stood a tall blond man of middle age.

'Aropethrana,' said Ngur, getting to his feet and holding out his arms as if to embrace the man he regarded as his most loyal commander.

Aropethrana bowed formally; both of them knew that the formality was a pretence, because they'd often, in times past, got drunk together and then chased the wenches – normally, in Aropethrana's case, with success.

But the commander's face, as he straightened up, didn't break into its usual ready smile.

'Sire . . .' he began.

'Surely we know each other too well, Aropethrana, for you to call me "sire".'

'Ngur,' the commander said, although it was obvious that the name came to his lips with difficulty, 'we must review the state of our army. We must make changes, and we must make them very quickly. You know as well as I do that the men are restless, searching for some kind of immediate leadership; now their officers – yes, even some of my fellows – are beginning to talk about supplanting you in favour of someone else.'

'Who?'

Aropethrana looked embarrassed.

'Me,' he said.

'And you declined?'

'No.'

'You accepted? You . . .'

Ngur was shocked by the betrayal.

'I did neither,' said Aropethrana. 'I let my heart rule my head, Ngur, for the sake of our old friendship . . . and also it was clear to me that, if I refused outright to accept the elevation, I would be discarded in favour of one of the others, who wouldn't share the affection I have for you. Oh, there were many reasons for doing what I did, and saving your skin was only one of them. Another was, if I may be frank, that it would be a bad precedent to establish if Despots could be removed every time the army became dissatisfied: if I accepted the results of the coup, and was appointed Despot myself, how long could *I* rely on having the support of *my* senior officers? Mine might be the next neck to be broken – hmmm? But the most important reason was that I don't *want* to be Despot . . . and I do want you to be, because I think you could be brought to perform the task well. That's why I said to the others that I'd need time to consider their offer, and that's also why I'm here.'

'Come over and sit down,' said Ngur. 'It's clear we have a lot to talk about.'

They sat at opposite sides of the table. The light from the windows made its polished surface gleam as if it were glass.

'These chairs are bloody uncomfortable,' said Aropethrana, smiling for the first time since he'd entered the hall. 'Why don't you get in something upholstered?'

'I've tried,' said Ngur, grateful for the opportunity to spend a little while skirting around the subject, 'but it's difficult to persuade people that I don't want us to have to squirm miserably on huge glittering thrones.'

'Squirming on the throne has little to do with how comfortable the throne is,' Aropethrana observed.

'True.'

They looked at each other, neither knowing where to start.

'Shall we have tea?' said Ngur, again seeking a way to avoid coming to the point.

'I would be glad of tea,' Aropethrana replied, similarly glad to postpone serious discussion.

Ngur found a little golden bell and rang it. Within moments there was a slave at the door. She was nervous, because she had spent a short time as a concubine to the previous Despot and seen many others of her kind executed for little more reason than having knocked at a door incorrectly. She smiled in gratitude when all that Ngur asked of her was to fetch a pot of aromatic tea and two small cups. She backed away from him, holding her hands to her face as her training in the junior aristocracy had obliged her to do.

Ngur was annoyed by the gesture, but pretended not to notice.

'Why are the officers so disenchanted?' he said abruptly.

'You lead an army that's largely destroyed because of a grave error of your judgement,' said Aropethrana, leaning forwards. 'Then you let the same thing happen all over again. And then you take a new army away from Giorran in the wrong direction. These are hardly actions likely to endear you to your troops – those few who survive. What they're looking for is victory – clean, easy, ruthless, but above all rapid victory. You're failing to give them what they should reasonably expect from their Army-Master and Despot.'

'Everything's changed,' said Ngur, pushing his chair back from the table and stretching out his legs in a mimicry of casualness, 'since the time when Lian led his uprising. What the soldiers don't know – because it's something they've never been told – is that Lian was the offspring of a person who came from somewhere outside Albion.'

'That can't be true,' said Aropethrana. He wiped his thighs with his hands.

'Yes, it can be. It has been told to me by somebody whom I trust implicitly. No – it *will* be told to me . . .'

He held his head miserably, wondering why time was playing tricks on him.

'This is something I can't understand . . . I'll be told it, and I know I'll be told it, but . . . how can I know something I haven't yet been told?

'Look, let me tell you what he – no, on second thoughts it was a she – said to me . . . *will* say to me. This man was called Terman, and he mated with a woman called Mina. The product of their mating was a son called Lian. Lian grew to become a leader and took to himself many women, but notably one called Syor, who gave him a child, and that child was called Anya. The same Anya who now leads the rebellion. There's a "somewhere" outside Albion that Terman came from – a place where even the lowest of peasants can recall what happened in the last waking-period and can think about what they plan to do in the next.'

Aropethrana shifted unhappily in his chair.

'That can't be true,' he said. 'There's no other world but Albion.'

He looked directly at Ngur, wondering if his friend were losing his senses.

'Prove it,' said Ngur.

'We're told by the mages that . . .'

'Forget the mages. Use your own mind to prove it.'

Ngur pointed a finger at Aropethrana's chest. 'Prove it,' he repeated.

The tea arrived, and Ngur made a great ceremony of pouring it for both of them. Aropethrana used the time to think. His old friend had clearly been misled either by heretics or by madness. It was impossible for there to be or ever to have been any other world but Albion. The case was simple. Where *were* those other worlds? Aropethrana didn't believe in such ideas as astral planes; as far as he was concerned, there was the here and now – and fixed, firm Ellonian reality.

He lifted his handleless cup to his lips, and smiled respectfully but doubtfully at Ngur. The hot liquid scalded his mouth, but he sipped at it, displaying all due courtesy.

'We're finding ourselves talking heresies, old friend,' he said, wiping his mouth. 'We can talk about such notions later, perhaps over a bottle or two of wine, but it'd seem to me to make more sense for us to think instead of ways in which we can avoid insurrection from the army.'

'Agreed,' said Ngur, looking down onto the darkly shiny surface of his tea. 'The commanders have grievances against me – and I've had more than my fair ration of ill-luck. I can't change luck – no one can – but there's a chance I can change their hostility towards me.'

He took another sip of the sweet-smelling yellow-brown liquid and glanced up questioningly at Aropethrana, who said: 'A chance, yes. But it's only a slender one.'

Ngur continued to stare directly into Aropethrana's eyes, and eventually the commander shifted his gaze, as if he'd suddenly become interested in the details of one of the wall-hangings.

'You have,' Aropethrana said slowly and with a waft of his hand, as if he were discussing nothing more consequential than the state of the weather, 'to defeat the peasants. Not just to defeat their army but to exterminate it altogether, so that not a single peasant warrior remains. It'd be good if you could capture the woman, Anya, and her senior officers alive, so that they could be brought here for ritual execution. You need to make it plain to all of the House of Ellon that you have a complete mastery of Albion, and that anyone who disputes that mastery will be trampled into the soil. The longer that Anya and her horde defy you, the more likely it is that you'll be deposed.'

Ngur swirled his tea.

'Those thoughts – those exact thoughts – have been going through my own mind for a long while, old friend,' he said, 'but it's easier to tell me what I ought to do than to tell me how I should do it.'

Aropethrana smiled at him.

'We were both lazy bastards during our schooling for the militia, weren't we?' he said.

Ngur was baffled, and looked it. The comment was true, but hardly seemed relevant.

Aropethrana saw his confusion and moved quickly to explain.

'When we were given a succession of chores to do, we

both always opted to do the easiest one first, and left the most arduous until the last possible moment. Hmmm?'

'True,' said Ngur. Both of them had tended to prefer sword practice, which was just a game, to scrubbing out the stables.

'When we grew older we learnt to do things the other way around,' said Aropethrana. 'We'd start with the things we didn't want to do – the difficult things – so that we could relax, having got them over with, and take our time over the things we actually enjoyed doing. It was a wise ploy then . . . And it's a lesson that both of us brought into our later life, remembering the stupidities we committed when we were boys. But I think it's a lesson you could do well to unlearn.'

'What do you mean?'

There was no more tea in Ngur's cup.

'Start with something *easy*,' said Aropethrana. 'Send out a patrol and capture just *one* of these peasants – half a dozen would be preferable, but one would be quite enough. The capture would serve as a symbol to remind your troops that you still exercise the ultimate power. What happened to the captive afterwards would be something for you to decide: all that's important in the short term is that one of the peasants be brought here to Giorran in shackles.'

'Would you lead this patrol?' asked Ngur, looking anywhere but at Aropethrana's eyes.

'Friend,' said Aropethrana, 'it'd be a pleasure to serve you. As I say, catching a single peasant shouldn't be too hard. Their army isn't far from Ernestrad, and like ourselves they must have sent out scouts. We can easily find one and bring him back here, so that his very presence reinforces the resolve of our army.'

Ngur poured yet more tea. He looked down through the pale liquid and saw the contours of the inside of the cup distorted by the liquid and by the steam that rose from it.

'You have my permission,' he said, as if it were a matter of no importance.

'The person need not be a peasant warrior?' said Aropethrana.

Ngur was startled.

'What do you mean?'

'We shouldn't have any trouble finding a warrior, of course, but if need be we could simply drag some labourer out of the fields, truss him up in primitive armour and bring him back here – in fact, the more I think about it, the more that seems to be the easiest option. Then we could execute him, and the troops would see that you were acting as their leader.'

'But he'd be an innocent!'

Aropethrana shrugged.

'Nobody's an innocent.'

'No,' said Ngur. 'I can't allow that.'

'Can you allow yourself to fall?' The big man leaned over the table. 'Can you allow this rabble to bring the House of Ellon to its knees? If so, tell me now – and I'll kill you now. Where did you get all these scruples from? You never used to have them. These are bad times, old friend, and in bad times you have to take harsh measures. You have to forget about what happens to one person or another person, and just remember what happens to the world and all the people in it.'

Ngur looked away again. The argument was logical: he couldn't find anything in it with which he could rationally disagree. Not long ago he'd have embraced it eagerly, but he'd changed. Although he'd presided over considerable injustice during the short span he'd spent as Despot, and was aware that he'd done so, he was reluctant to slaughter a human being, even a peasant, simply in order to satisfy the bloodthirstiness of his soldiers.

But, if he didn't . . . ?

He made a sudden decision, and hated himself for it.

'Yes,' he said. 'Go ahead.'

Aropethrana stood up, pushing back his chair with his calves so that the feet of the chair screeched on the stone floor.

'I think you're wise, Ngur,' he said as he turned to leave.

'I hope I am,' said Ngur miserably.

A while later, long after Aropethrana had left him, he

repeated the words to the empty air.

'I hope I am.'

The wind was crisp as Aropethrana's patrol left the great gates of Giorran. A few soldiers cheered the little band of a dozen mounted men, but most of the warriors looked at them sullenly. The rumour had gone out – thanks to the determined efforts of Aropethrana – that the patrol was going, as a result of covertly received information, to capture one of the chief officers of the rebel army, perhaps even Anya herself. The Ellonian soldiers had heard a lot of similar rumours before; the vast majority of the men were becoming sceptical.

Aropethrana himself was full of ebullience. He *liked* the sound of the standard whipcracking above him. He *liked* the feeling of his horse's strong muscles working beneath him as it walked elegantly through the Ellonian camp, picking its way carefully among the guy-ropes. He *liked* the knowledge that, by the end of this waking-period, he and his patrol would be returning with a sacrifice, so that the gloomy expressions would be banished from the soldiers' faces, to be replaced by that curious glow which anticipated triumph and therefore almost always heralded triumph. He'd seen soldiers, before practice bouts with the sword or the club, exercising with long and solemn faces; he'd watched them almost invariably lose the contests. Others of the men had had bright smiles as they'd cut at the air with their weapons, and they'd been the winners . . . always. All that Aropethrana needed to do was to bring that smile of confidence – however unfounded the confidence might be – to the faces of the soldiers of the Ellonia, and he was certain that the impending battle would be won.

Leaving the camp and all its mixed aromas behind, they found themselves at the foot of a scree-covered slope. Some of the horses balked at the prospect of trying to climb it, and so Aropethrana pressed his own steed forwards. The animal obeyed him, making no protest as its hooves sank deeply into the mass of small, softly curved stones. The other horses then followed, even though it was immediately clear that the animals were finding the ascent punishing. The sound of the falling stones was like the rushing of water.

At last they were out of the scree and onto firm ground. The grass was brown and coarse; here and there were straggly shrubs. The hillside was still steep, so that the horses struggled pantingly as they scrambled up it, but the footing was good. Once again Aropethrana urged his own horse onwards and found that the others followed obediently.

At the crest he turned; the rest of his patrol, as they arrived in dribs and drabs over the next few minutes, did likewise.

From this eminence they could see so far that it seemed they were able to look out over the entire world. Everything was in a state of constant flux in the heat haze, yet still they could see chains of high, blue-white mountains punching towards the sky; even the sight of them made Aropethrana feel cold, as he envisaged himself approaching their summits. And far, far away there was a curtain of whiteness that had been hung so high that its top was lost in the sky. That was the edge of the world.

That was where the world stopped.

Aropethrana had never seen it before. He began to think about some of the things that his Despot, Ngur, had earlier muttered. Maybe it was true that there was a world outside this world – a place somewhere beyond the clouds of mist?

He shook his head.

It didn't matter – any of it.

His task was to find a peasant who looked sufficiently like a leader, and then execute him. It would be even better if he could find a female peasant with fair hair, so that then he could claim that she was Anya herself. All he needed was a victim, someone whose death would bring hope to Ngur's troops.

'Excuse me,' said a voice beside him.

He looked around. There was no one to be seen.

'Excuse me,' the voice repeated.

This time Aropethrana looked downwards.

Tapping at the bridle of his horse was a small, flat-chested woman with rather badly close-cropped hair. He was just about to kick her away when he felt the power of her eyes.

'I'm a peasant,' she said, 'and I came here to be taken captive by you. It's extremely impertinent of you not to have taken me captive at once. Get a move on. I've got better things to do, you know, than hang around here for hours on end waiting to be seized, thrown over the back of a horse, taken down to Giorran, tortured and executed. I could be doing something much more interesting, like turning the sun round so that you could see what was on the other side. I think you ought to show a little more consideration towards people you're going to torture to death.'

Aropethrana looked towards the distant hills for a moment, then looked back at the woman.

'You're a peasant?' he said.

'Well, sort of.' The woman moved away and sat down, inspecting one foot and finally pulling a thistle's spike from it. 'I was very close to Lian – no, stop smirking, not in *that* sort of way – and I'm a good friend of Anya's. If you want to take one of us rebels for summary torture and death, I'm probably your best bet. The others are well hidden – even though they're watching you and me at this very moment – and it would take more than your little patrol to tussle with them. I think it'd be best for all concerned if you just seized me now.'

Aropethrana looked at his soldiers.

They looked back at him.

'No rapes, by the way,' said the woman, looking at her fingernails almost inquisitorially, as if one of them might be preparing to annoy her by having grown just a little too long. 'Rape each other, if you wish – I'm not prudish, you understand – but please don't try to rape me. I'd hate it if I had to burst your blood vessels in places inconvenient to describe.

'Now,' she added brightly, 'shall we get on with you taking me as a hostage? The quicker it's over with, the quicker we can all be back in Giorran.'

She got to her feet and wandered over to Aropethrana.

'Get a move on,' she said impatiently. 'Throw me over your saddle. It's the done thing, you know.'

'I don't believe you're a peasant,' he said.

'Yes you do,' said Alyss.

She smiled at him.

He fell into the colour of her eyes, so that for the smallest moment of time there was nothing else.

'You are a peasant,' he said, woodenly.

'I've heard it put more politely,' she said, touching the lobe of one ear just to make sure it was exactly as she wanted it to be, 'but, if you'd like to, you could say that.'

'And you want to be executed?'

'Of course I do. I'm not going to be dragged all the way to Giorran just to sit around doing crochet, am I? My execution's got to be pretty gory, mind you: I won't be satisfied with a straightforward beheading, or anything like that. I want a full-scale ritual disembowelment, and lots of music. A string quartet would be nice.'

Once again Aropethrana and his soldiers looked at each other.

'Seems a bit stupid not to take her up on her offer,' said one of them, 'especially since it'd save us so much time.'

Aropethrana felt himself make a sudden decision.

'I can't guarantee the music,' he said.

Alyss looked resentful, but then her face softened.

'Oh,' she said, 'that's all right. If need be I'll sing while you're disembowelling me. I've got a very good singing voice, you know. It's not quite high enough to be a soprano and I can't quite reach the lowest notes in the contralto range, but it's been widely described as . . . what's the word? . . . ah, yes, "mellifluous". I'm sure I'll be able to think of something dignified to sing while I'm being executed, so that the crowds will be entertained.'

Aropethrana raised his eyes to the sky and wondered if they couldn't find another peasant. Still, this one had admitted being close to Anya, and would presumably continue to do so as she screamed her last. As the soldier had said, it was too good an opportunity to miss.

'All right,' he said eventually.

His soldiers were soon looking at him with contempt. Nothing in the training manuals covered the techniques of hauling people over one's saddle.

'Could you sort of clamber up here?' he finally mumbled.

'But of course,' Alyss said cheerfully. 'I was only waiting for you to ask.'

She jumped up and flopped over the saddle in front of him, dangling her hands and legs loosely.

'Do I look half-dead enough?' she whispered.

'Quite enough,' he sighed.

They turned back towards Giorran, Aropethrana's heart heavier than the body of the woman in front of him.

'Barra 'ap Rteniadoli Me'gli'minter Rehan,' he said to the sentries when they asked him his name, 'although I'd be happier if you could just call me "Rehan".'

The sentries scowled at him. One was short and fat; the other was tall and fat. Both were dressed in the red and green uniform of the Ellonian Army, and both were holding their swords so that the razor-sharp tips pointed directly towards Rehan's heart. In the distance, behind them, reared the walls of Giorran. He stretched his arms out, showing that he was carrying no weapons. In one hand he held his flute, in the other his bodhran.

'I'm a singer,' he explained. 'I've travelled all over Albion, from one shore to the other. People remember my songs while I'm with them, and then later they're forgotten.'

He bowed deeply.

'A singer, at your service.'

'We don't have any need of a singer,' said one of the sentries – the short one.

'Nobody ever thinks they need a singer,' said Rehan, yawning histrionically and making as if to turn away, 'until afterwards.'

'Who are you?' grunted the tall sentry.

'I've told you, I'm Barra 'ap Rteniadoli Me'gli'minter Rehan, perhaps the finest singer ever to have graced this world. Well, let's forget the "perhaps" bit, shall we?'

It was something that Alyss had told him to say.

He smiled at them, hoping that the smile would conceal his abject terror.

'Wouldn't your fine soldiers be cheered by my music?' he said, looking backwards and forwards between the two instruments he was still holding at arm's length. 'I can make the very clouds in the sky dance a light fantastic by playing just a single trill on my flute.'

'We don't want our soldiers dancing no light fantastics,' said the tall sentry. 'What the clouds do is their own business.'

He sniffed disapprovingly.

'Or,' said Rehan, 'I can stir your men to battle by the beating of my drum.'

He glanced significantly at his bodhran.

The sentries looked at each other.

'Seems harmless enough to me,' said the shorter of them.

'He'd better be,' said the taller, his face splitting in a gap-toothed smile, 'or he'll get killed.'

'I like a bit of music,' said the shorter sentry. 'I've found it helps my bowels move regularly.'

Rehan lowered his arms to his sides. They felt weary from having held the weight of his musical instruments.

'May I join your army?' he said to the taller sentry, who was staring dumbfoundedly at his companion.

'Yes. Sure. Go on.'

The man waved Rehan past them.

'Oboe sonatas are the best,' Rehan heard the shorter sentry explain to his companion as he disappeared into the chaotic clutter of the Ellonian camp.

He was assaulted by the smells of burning food and uncovered cesspits. None of the soldiers seemed to pay any attention to him as he wandered down the avenues between their tents; they seemed, rather, to be preoccupied with their own gloominess. Rehan felt almost guilty, because he was by now – having succeeded in talking his way past the sentries – feeling rather light-headed. He had to remind himself not to stop and sound a jig on his flute in order to cheer the soldiers up. That wasn't what Anya had sent him here for: the more dismal-minded the Ellonian soldiers, the happier she'd be with him.

He stepped aside to make way for a group of infantrymen who were striding out purposefully on some mission of their own. To his surprise, the last of them nodded an acknowledgement to him for his courtesy.

Rehan wasn't quite certain where he was going or what he was doing, except for one thing: he knew he was bound to die. All that Anya had instructed him to do was infiltrate the camp the Ellonian military had set up around Giorran: she'd given him no explanation as to why she'd wanted him to do this, except that he was to use his music, in the way that he'd promised he could, to help her overthrow the army of the Despot. But he was accustomed, wherever he went, to find a singer given a ready welcome, and so he had no immediate concern about where his next meal might come from.

Anya couldn't hold off too much longer. The Despot had been sending out scouts to keep a track of their movements – the peasants knew this was the case because they'd caught, interrogated and subsequently killed several of the scouts. The fact that they'd found some meant, inevitably, that there must have been others whom they hadn't detected, who must have escaped back to Ernestrad to report what they'd seen. No one, not even She Who Leads, could guess at how much the House of Ellon might know; but it was impossible for the Despot not to realise that her army was now very close to Ernestrad.

Yet the Despot had shown no signs of trying to strike at them. He'd led his army off, some waking-periods ago, for a seemingly futile expedition into the surrounding country-side – the peasants' scouts had watched from a height as the Ellonia had seemed to mill about purposelessly for the best part of a waking-period before returning dejectedly to Giorran. It was as if the Despot were trying deliberately not to see them. The behaviour of the troops of the House of Ellon was bewildering to the peasants, and was deeply worrying to Anya. She'd expected that by now they'd have met on the field of combat, and that one army or the other would have emerged victorious. This waiting game that the Despot seemed to be playing was tugging at her nerves, making her irritable at the wrong moments. Rehan had been using a fair amount of diplomacy to stop Anya from coming to blows with Reen.

Reen.

Yes, it would have been kind of fate to have allowed Reen to be here with him. *I hope my death isn't too painful . . .*

As he walked from bonfire to bonfire, thankfully ignored, he conjured up Reen's face in his mind, and smiled at it. He saw her grey hair, the point of her chin, and the darkness of her eyes.

What he hadn't expected to see was her spontaneous smile back at him.

He blinked and almost tripped over a log of wood that had been left lying out on the grass.

Reen's here, in a way, said Alyss's voice, *or she very soon will be.*

Barra 'ap Rteniadoli Me'gli'minter Rehan looked all around him, trying not to be too furtive. The voice had sounded as though someone had been whispering close to his ear, yet there had been no one near him.

I'm here as well. They've put me in a dungeon at the very heart of Giorran, and they've told me that I'm going to be crucified. I'm quite excited. I've never been threatened with crucifixion before. I was almost tempted to go through with it, just to find out what it feels like.

That mightn't be one of your best ideas, thought Rehan in reply. *Some of my best friends have been crucified, and they say it's fucking unpleasant.*

He grinned meaninglessly at a corporal who was trying to quench the flames of an over-eager fire.

Don't worry, said Alyss. *I've dismissed the idea.*

A large black dog ran up to Rehan and stood in front of him, its tail erect and its lips drawn back to show its teeth and the pinky-redness of its gums and tongue.

Some of the Ellonian soldiers near to him were watching. They laughed jeeringly.

The dog growled, a low, threatening sound, so that

Rehan retreated a pace or two.

That was the worst thing he could have done. By his movement he'd admitted his fear to the dog, and it prepared to leap, its haunches tight against the ground.

We all have our little foibles, said Alyss.

'Now's not the moment to discuss them,' he said out loud, involuntarily taking another couple of steps backwards.

One of mine is helping out the people I regard as my friends. I can't do it all of the time, because it's only rarely that I'm able to be everywhere simultaneously, but, you know, I do do my best. Like now, for instance.

The dog sprang.

Rehan turned away, trying to shield his face and throat.

And then everything seemed to go into slow motion. The dog was flying casually through the air towards him, its body twisting and its fur creating haphazard patterns that altered as if with difficulty. Rehan was looking at one of the fires the soldiers had lit to cook their meal, and he could see the flames *clicking* lazily from one configuration to the next. It was if he were seeing not the flames but a sequence of a hundred pictures of them painted by an artist who had studied them for a whole waking-period and then set down on paper the images he'd seen. They didn't flicker in the elusive way that real flames flicker. It was almost as if they were hard-edged forms – as if he could have reached out, run the end of his finger along one of them, and cut himself on its sharpness.

I told you I'd try to help you.

Rehan realised that he could ignore the dog. He walked away from the place where it was going to land, feeling the air against his face much hotter than it should have been.

Some of the soldiers were beginning to turn their heads. The movement was like that of the flames of the fire: an unnatural jerking and clicking from one position to another. Rehan tried not to look at them: the sight caused him pain. It seemed as if the bases of their necks were slowly being wrenched away from their shoulders.

He slunk away, wondering how long Alyss would – or

could – maintain this situation.

There was a total silence. He could hear nothing, not even the little liquid noise of the grass beneath his feet. Nevertheless, annoyed at his own illogicality, he found himself trying to move as quietly as he could. He stepped on tiptoes over the motionless form of a soldier who'd been lazing on the ground. He crept away from the place where the dog was still twirling in the air, its spittle a haze around it.

'Thank you,' he muttered.

It's all part of the service. Now I'm afraid I've got to do something really nasty.

Barra 'ap Rteniadoli Me'gli'minter Rehan recoiled from an arbitrary direction.

Not to you, you fool. To the dog.

Only a short while ago the dog had been the beast that Rehan had most loathed in all of creation. Now he found himself wanting to save it from any cruelty that might be inflicted on it.

'Leave the dog alone,' he said.

I won't do anything to the dog myself. What's going to happen to it will be a result of its attack upon you.

'Couldn't you save it from that?'

He was walking away, watching the stillness of the clouds that seemed too timid to approach the sun. In one sense he didn't care too much about a bad-tempered dog that had tried to attack him, but in another he recognised it as a dumb animal of limited acuity. He wanted nothing to do with what would happen.

Rehan was a little distance away when he was suddenly, once more, in the midst of a forest of sounds and smells.

No one around him seemed to register his presence at all. They were all turning to look incredulously upwards.

What they were watching was one of their tents fluttering off into the sky, its canvas flapping like the wings of a huge red and green bird.

Rehan turned to watch as well.

He saw the tent flying away until it was just a distant mote, a spark moving against the brightness of the sky.

But one of the wooden tent-poles had been left behind, spinning high up in the air.

Then it fell with the venomous precision of a javelin.

Blood spurted from the dog's back as it gave one last anguished howl. It tried furiously to twist itself away from the pole that pinned it to the ground, but the struggle could last for no more than a few seconds.

The beast died, blood trickling from its mouth to stain the coarse, trampled grass.

The spitted dog.

It was the symbol of the House of Ellon.

The soldiers were silent.

The omens were poor.

I don't like *killing*, said Alyss's voice inside Rehan's mind, *even when it's only a dog. But it was important that the image was stamped on the Ellonia's minds.*

Rehan looked around him.

Some of the soldiers were still watching the sky, as if the pole hadn't yet fallen.

He was hungry. That was the curiosity: he was in danger of losing his life, once the soldiers gathered the full import of what had happened, but the only thing he could think about was the fact that he was hungry. Rehan was the newcomer; Rehan had been threatened by the dog; the dog had died, impaled by magical means. It couldn't be long before the soldiers connected the event with him. And yet, more than anything he was hungry: his stomach felt to him like a vast, echoing cavern.

He stole some meat from a skewer that had been placed over one of the fires, burning his fingertips as he did so. The meat was so tough and gristly that it hurt his teeth, but he gobbled it down anyway. Almost immediately his digestive system began to grumble.

He moved away rapidly, trying to find somewhere where he'd be less obviously an outsider. The soldiers were shouting at each other, and some of them were fighting. Rehan wasn't wearing Ellonian uniform, and was terrified of his vulnerability for this reason. The fact that he was carrying a flute and a bodhran made him even more conspicuous.

But was conspicuousness necessarily a bad idea? The thought struck him as he was scurrying between two tents, skipping unevenly over their interlaced guy-ropes. If he made himself as conspicuous as possible, might it not be that the Ellonia would regard him as blatantly innocent . . . because no one with a guilty conscience would be so damned stupid?

Rehan sat down in the centre of one of the alleys between the tents. Putting his flute on the ground behind him, he took his bodhran in his left hand and the small drumstick in his right. He worked his fingers for a few seconds, loosening them up until he was satisfied with them. Then he began to tap the ends of the stick softly on the drum, so that the leather hummed warmly at him as if it were asking him to play something on it.

And then it was as if the muscles of his hand took over the control of what he was doing. His knuckles seemed to start dancing, so that the drumstick became a pattern of motion in the air, too fast to be seen any longer as a solid object. Barra 'ap Rteniadoli Me'gli'minter Rehan touched it to the surface of the bodhran once again, and was astonished by the rhythms that emerged. They weren't of his creation – he was sure of it. The drumbeats were producing a tapestry of sound quite unlike anything he'd ever played before. Their pitch varied as he moved the flickering stick backwards and forwards across the taut skin. He became lost in the rhythm, oblivious to anything that was going on around him.

Alyss, in her cell and in Rehan's mind, grinned happily. The large, bald man who was busy torturing her looked puzzled. This wasn't the way things were supposed to happen, he thought confusedly: the little woman should have been screaming by now. He renewed the grip of his pliers on one of her fingernails and pulled with all his might, but the blasted thing *still* wouldn't come out.

The beat of the bodhran spread out through the camp like the expanding circle of ripples from a stone dropped into still water. The sound was not loud, but it seemed to be taken up by the air and passed from one little eddy of wind to the next, so that it swirled into every tent and along every alleyway.

The rhythm had an *unrightness* about it. It insinuated its way into the minds of the soldiers who heard it, so that they could think of little else but attempting to restore the rightness. *This beat here was just a little too late, or perhaps it was too early; and the pitch of that beat was wrong but I'm not sure why it was wrong.* Several of the men drummed their fingers on whatever was nearest to them, trying to bring some sort of sensible order to the patterns of sound, but all they succeeded in doing was worsening their own mental confusion.

It was impossible to think of anything else.

All work stopped.

One of the soldiers lurched against a brazier so that it fell over, spilling its orange-red coals across the floor of a tent. Within moments the canvas was ablaze. The officers who'd been sitting or lying inside the tent were too preoccupied with the bodhran's rhythm to move to save themselves. The soldier who'd tipped the brazier was oblivious to what he'd done, and wandered away, his eyes focused on something infinitely distant.

The torturer was sucking on one of his fingers. During his last excursion with the pliers his hand had slipped, and he'd split his knuckle. He removed the bleeding finger from his mouth for a few moments to curse a surprising number of aspects of life but, most especially, the woman spread out in front of him. To increase his fury, she gave him one of her very sweetest, most sympathetic smiles.

Barra 'ap Rteniadoli Me'gli'minter Rehan's hand seemed to be moving ever faster. He had no control over it any longer, and no wish to have any control. His wrist felt no tiredness. It was as if he'd left Albion to discover himself in some other world – a world where there were no such things as the grass on which he was sitting or the sunlight that was shining down on him, but just the notes from the bodhran stretching out into a foreverness.

Alyss smiled again when the sound reached the cell where she was being tortured.

The big man lost interest in his futile attempts to pull out her fingernails and backed away, his face adopting a meditative expression. He crashed into one of the gloomy stone walls behind him and slowly folded down into a seated position, looking mildly confused but not overly concerned; he had other things on his mind than what was happening to him.

Ratta-ta-tatta-ratta-ratta-tat-TAT-ratta-ratta-ta-ratta-tatta-RATTA-ratta-tatta . . .

There was something so wrong, and yet so right, about the rhythm – but what *was* the something?

Alyss, who was rather pleased with the rhythm she'd created, reached out with her mind and snapped the bonds that had been holding her. She thought for a moment of doing the same to the torturer's neck, but then decided against it: he'd only been doing his job, after all – and, besides, he'd already suffered enough mental torment through having to watch his inability to cause her pain.

She patted him affectionately on his bald pate as she moved to the heavy wooden door.

He didn't look up.

Alyss wasn't sure whether or not she liked Giorran.

Some of the corridors she strolled along were light and airy, with whitewashed walls punctuated by large windows and floors of interestingly streaked marble or brightly polished parquet. Others seemed to have been deserted for decades, if not centuries: windowless and filthy, with spiders' webs dropping from the corners and dust covering their floors, they were filled with a grey light from meagre lamps hung on sconces just a little too high.

Still, she thought, it was none of her business to criticise the way that the aristocrats of the House of Ellon wanted to live.

She was pleased to discover that the hall Ngur was using as his centre of command was one of the lighter ones.

He looked up as she entered.

Aropethrana, beside him, looked up as well, and blanched.

'Who are you?' said Ngur irritatedly.

'She's the peasant,' said Aropethrana before Alyss could speak, 'the one I brought back here for execution. Something's wrong: she's supposed to be being tortured at the moment . . .'

'From the point of view of the House of Ellon,' said Alyss, 'it's not just *something* that's gone wrong but really quite a lot. If you don't believe me, take a look out of the window.'

Ngur immediately leapt to his feet and strode across the room. Aropethrana, scowling at Alyss, moved more slowly as he followed.

The army camp was a shambles.

At least a dozen tents were now in flames. Wherever Ngur and Aropethrana looked they could see soldiers lolling vacantly or stumbling around as if they were drunk, ignoring the carnage around them, their minds clearly filled with something that was utterly divorced from their current military duties.

Aropethrana turned away from the sight.

'*You* did this!' he shouted at Alyss.

'Would you have expected me to have done anything else?' she said.

'I was a fool to bring you here.'

'True.' He drew his sword.

Ngur grabbed him by the arm.

'Wait a moment, old friend,' the Despot said. 'Perhaps she can help us.'

'How?'

The word was snarled so ferociously that the Despot for a while had difficulty in understanding it.

'By dying,' he said eventually. 'You brought her here to be executed.'

'That's right,' said Alyss with a wave of her hand. 'You brought me here to execute me, and so far all I've had is a dose of somewhat ineffectual torture. I honestly don't think that's good enough – do you?'

'Have her executed,' said Ngur dismissively, turning away from her.

'Oh, good!' said Alyss.

Aropethrana looked at her unhappily.

That was when the Wind struck Giorran.

Look at that from another point of view, sings Rehan . . .

You're a soldier, and the military way of life is all you've known since you were an adolescent. You've been drilled under various commanders, some of whom you've respected and some of whom you haven't. You've been trained in arms, and you and your fellows have acted out mock-battles using wooden weapons; sometimes you've been bruised a little – sometimes quite a lot – but you've never been hurt so badly for it to have taken longer than a few waking-periods for the pain to go away. It's a joy to be doing your duty.

Now here you are in a military camp on the plain that lies in front of Giorran, camped with several thousand other soldiers who owe their allegiance to the House of Ellon, and something seems to have gone wrong. You try to concentrate your mind on the fact that soon you will have to battle against the army of the rebels, but all you can think about is the sound that seems to be attacking you from every side. There's no escaping from your own mind, which is filled by the sound. You can't see anything any longer, or feel the touch of anything, because all of your senses are saturated by the rhythm and its *unrightness*.

And then suddenly there's another sound – a sound so loud that it drowns the sound of the drum.

There's something pulling at your uniform, but in your blindness you don't know what it is. You flail out at this invisible attacker, trying to beat it off, but all that happens is that you're wrenched away from the ground. Somehow you know that you're being pulled higher and higher into the air, and all the while you feel your body being pummelled by cold fists, until it becomes a mass of numbness. You know that you're being turned end over end: the dizziness makes bile rise in your throat.

Now that you're so far away from the singer with the

408

bodhran, your vision returns. The fields are just tiny moving squares beneath you. That's when the Wind leaves you.

And you fall.

Fall.

Fall and seem to be falling forever.

Chapter Eight
World

The devastation was spectacular. Bright tongues of fire were racing everywhere around Giorran, moving more quickly than a man could have run. Clouds of blue-grey smoke were hauling themselves into the air, seeming to pull up behind them twisting fragments of smouldering cloth. High above, soldiers were screaming thinly as they discovered themselves tumbling back down towards the ground.

Anya and Reen grinned at each other.

'Alyss is a good friend,' said Reen, suddenly beginning to look guilty.

The two women were on horseback, gazing down from a plateau to which the Wind had led them, watching the destruction of Ernestrad and Giorran. The Wind itself was blowing the flames from the army's camp through the tinder-dry houses of the city, whistling and shrieking down Ernestrad's streets to make the conflagration ever greater. People were stumbling out of their homes, trying to beat away the smoke that was choking them. Some were burning their hands as they tried to put out the fires that had spontaneously appeared among their clothing.

'Alyss is a bad enemy,' said Reen, more quietly this time.

Behind them, hushed, was the army they'd brought here. Some were mounted and others on foot. Anya looked back over her shoulder and saw that her peasants, grouped beyond the cairn, were maintaining a perfect discipline of stillness. It seemed as if they might not need to fight the Ellonia hand to hand after all.

'The Wind's a good friend,' Anya said, 'too.'

'The Wind's a good ally to have,' Reen corrected. 'I don't think it's capable of being a friend. And I don't know if it'll be even our ally for long.'

Her horse moved its forefeet impatiently.

The smoke was becoming so thick that the two of them could hardly see any longer what was going on beneath. Instead, they caught only brief glimpses of a disaster in progress. Men, women and children were being devoured by the hungry flames which spat from the burning tents and from the short, stubbly grass. Some were stripping away their clothing; others were rolling on the ground.

'Our best friend,' said Reen, 'is Barra 'ap Rteniadoli Me'gli'minter Rehan.'

'You say that because he's your lover,' said Anya, her eyes dancing as she watched the mayhem that had come upon Ernestrad.

'No,' muttered Reen, 'that's not my reason at all.'

'Then what is?'

Anya's face, laughing only a moment before, was now serious as she peered at Reen.

'He went there,' said Reen, pointing to the fire, 'knowing that he was going to die – that he was giving his life away for us. To help us. To help *you*. Alyss isn't going to die, and neither is the Wind, but Rehan almost certainly will. For *your* sake. Don't kid yourself, Anya: he loves you in a way that perhaps you'll never be able to understand.'

'He loves *you*,' said Anya, looking perplexed.

'It's different,' Reen said, patting her horse affectionately on the rump. 'He loves me because I love him and cherish him and because, blast it, I'm available; for all he cares we could be brother and sister, except for the fact that we have fun in bed together. You – well, you, as far as Rehan is concerned, are something very different. The kind of love he's had for you is so strong that sometimes it's been hatred, too. He sees you as if . . . how can I describe this? . . . as if you were an impossibly beautiful and untouchable statue.'

'But he *has* touched me,' said Anya.

'No,' said Reen. 'Your bodies have touched each other,

412

but that's all. What Rehan hasn't been able to achieve is the touching of your minds. He's been trying to tell you this since the first time the two of you met, but you chose to ignore him. Now he's dying down there, willingly, because he'd rather do that than live out the rest of his life knowing that he'd never been able to touch your mind.'

'Can we save him?'

Even up here, the heat was becoming unpleasant. The brilliance of the flames was forcing both of them to turn their faces away. The sky was dark, the clouds of smoke dimming the light of the sun.

'Do you want to?'

'Of course I want to. I used to be very fond of him, you know. Also, you're right: he's the only one of the three of them down there who's risking his life in order to help us defeat the House of Ellon. For that alone he should be rescued.'

'Thanks,' said Reen.

She smiled at Anya.

'You and I are going to have a fuck of a big argument if we save his life, you know,' she said.

'No,' said Anya sombrely, 'we're not. You're his lover and you're going to stay his lover.'

'That's not something for you to decide. Rehan is the person who has to make his mind up about that.'

'And me,' said Anya dismissively.

She turned on her horse and gestured urgently for the people behind her to come closer. The harsh breathing of the horses surrounded her as the first few of the warriors rode across the plateau to join her.

Reen recoiled as she saw the killing-light return to Anya's eyes. She'd hoped that it had been banished forever, after the hangings, but now it seemed to have returned with all its original glee. When Anya was in a mood like this, no one was safe.

A few more of the peasant warriors neared them. Most of these were on foot, struggling to pull their swords from their belts. Reen looked at them with her eyes pricking, certain that most of them would be cut down by whatever

413

remained of the army of the House of Ellon. They were enthusiastic to join battle – that much was obvious from the way they flexed their weapons in the air – and yet it was equally plain to Reen, who had fought against the Ellonia before, that these were youngsters who were marching or riding to almost certain death.

It isn't up to me to turn them away . . .

She looked from the plateau, wishing against wish that she could contemplate anything except the sight of death. If anything, the blaze had become worse, and the Wind was pounding down on the Ellonian soldiers as if it were trying to flatten them into the ground. Reen glumly thought it unlikely that they'd be able to save Rehan. She wished that she were doing something else entirely, something loving and soft and slow.

Being in bed with Syor . . .

She hadn't thought of Syor for a time that was too long to be calculated. Rehan was almost young enough to be Reen's son, or Syor's.

Her mind was confused. She felt Marja's hands stroking her body, then Syor's, then Rehan's. All of them were trying to give pleasure to her, to make her purr like a cat stretched out in front of a warm fire.

Marja was dead.

Syor was dead.

Rehan was alive.

'We must save Rehan,' she said to Anya, 'if we possibly can. It's the very least that we owe him.'

Anya moved her lips and incongruous laughter-lines appeared around the edges of her eyes.

'I thought we'd already decided that,' she said. She adjusted the woollen gloves on her hands and twisted her head sharply so that her hair flicked through the air.

Reen's eyes narrowed.

'You're too fucking beautiful by half,' she said, miserably.

'Let's go and fight a battle,' said Anya. 'We can argue about things afterwards.'

She shouted a command and the peasant army began to

descend from the plateau, the horse-riders moving slowly and carefully down through the shale so that the infantry could keep pace. It was a terrifying journey. Scree rattled away from them as they made their way, and the stench of the smoke in their noses became ever stronger. Some of the horses placed their feet wrongly, and they and their riders died, toppling and tumbling away down into the distance beneath. Reen found, within minutes, that her eyes were watering so much that she was barely able to see. Anya, on the other hand, seemed totally unperturbed, as if the whole venture was nothing more than an enjoyable party.

Reen's horse stepped fastidiously over the corpse of a soldier whom the Wind had dropped from the sky. She stopped herself from vomiting by looking away towards the colours that the sun was making through the smoke. The body had fallen with such force, face-downward, that its shoulders were at the same level as the ground.

Reen had seen war before and, despite her efficient practice of its arts, had hated it. Now she was in the vanguard of an army that was – she hoped – going to save the life of Barra 'ap Rteniadoli Me'gli'minter Rehan, but which was also going to take the lives of tens of hundreds of human beings whose sole crime was that they were soldiers in the Ellonian Army. It had probably never occurred to them that they had the choice of being anything else.

She looked to her right. Anya's face still bore that expression of eagerness.

The smoke got thicker the nearer to Giorran they came. Reen wasn't the only one to start coughing. The whole area ahead of them had been razed, so that the vast white edifice of Giorran seemed to be standing in the centre of a burnt desert. Some of the houses of Ernestrad were still standing, but they were only a few. The air was full of the screams of the dying and of the crackling of the thousands of fires that had broken out.

Rehan must – must – *be dead, surely*, thought Reen sadly as their horses became more and more reluctant to go any further into the wasteland.

Eventually they found what was left of him. They were able to identify him because his blackened, scorched arm was still clutching the remains of the bodhran and because, beside the body, there was a long cylinder of cinders lying among the darkening embers.

Reen looked at what was left of her reluctant lover. She'd expected to feel grief but all she felt was an uncontrollable anger and a strange sense of disappointment. The Wind had done this – the Wind and Alyss between them. First she wanted to kill some of the House of Ellon, then after that she'd like to kill – and here she couldn't decide the order of priority – the Wind and Alyss.

She sang to herself the first couple of lines of Rehan's song about the women of Starveling; it was both a dirge and a tribute. Anya looked at her sharply, as if Reen were implicitly criticising her. Reen jumped down from her horse and touched the thing that had been Barra 'ap Rteniadoli Me'gli'minter Rehan.

'Let's go and kill a few Ellonia,' she said, looking up at Anya. She didn't like the rather high-pitched sound of her voice, but right now she seemed unable to change it.

'Let's do just that,' said Anya.

Behind them there was a colossal shout.

The rebel army began to move more and more quickly towards the fortress of Giorran.

The smell of burnt meat seemed to be everywhere.

Reen threw herself up onto her horse, and something caught her eye as she did so. High above the white battlements of Giorran a curlew was circling.

Alyss accepted tea, although she wasn't thirsty: she never was. Through the window she could hear the roar of the advancing army, and she smiled sympathetically through wafts of steam at Ngur and Aropethrana.

'You have few defences left,' she observed calmly, putting the hot cup down deliberately on the polished oak surface of the table. 'Maybe fifty or sixty men-at-arms here in Giorran, plus a few hundred aristocratic nincompoops who'll rush around shrieking hysterically and getting in your way. Your mages will go mad with panic and do their very best to convince everyone else that their supposed magic can repel the attack. That won't be very helpful to you, because your people will relax their efforts, trusting the mages, until everybody's discovered the error through being, not to put too fine a point upon it – um – passed on.'

Ngur smiled, despite himself.

Aropethrana didn't. 'We still have time to kill before the fortress is taken,' he said, glowering.

'Not if I'm going to be able to finish my tea,' she pointed out, looking at him as if he'd just farted. 'It's hot, you know, and it'll be quite some while before I'll be able to drink it. After that, you can carry on with your stuffy old execution, but I really do think it'll be a bit late by then. And don't forget, if it's going to include the stipulated disembowelment – and you promised me that, Aropethrana – you'll have to wait a little while longer even than that, as otherwise your executioner might get his hands scalded.'

Ngur slapped his friend on the shoulder.

'Let her free,' he said.

'Why?'

'Because I ask you to. If we try to execute her, I'm convinced things will go even more drastically wrong than they're already doing. Get one of your men to eject her from Giorran, and then start organising our defences. How many archers do we have?'

'About ten with crossbow and about fifteen with long-bow,' said Aropethrana sullenly.

'Too few, too few,' said Ngur, standing at the window, hands held behind his back, and looking out over the plain of ashes. 'Spread them out around the windows as best you can. Arm the men and women of our much beloved aristocracy with crossbows, too; they may not have been trained in archery, but at least a few of their bolts must, by the law of averages, cause harm to the peasants. Yes, and make sure that everyone has a sword: most of them'll just drop it on their foot but a few of them might be able to waggle it about effectively enough to help us.'

'Can I have a sword, too?' said Alyss.

'Shut up and go away, wench,' said Ngur without turning to look at her or changing his tone of voice. 'Aropethrana, see if some of our people can wrench stones from the battlements – it'd be good to be able to drop them on the bastards beneath.'

'It's discourteous to tell a lady to shut up,' remarked Alyss.

'Then fuck off, instead.'

Little patches of pink came to Alyss's cheekbones.

'I was hoping to arrange things so that you could all live,' she said tartly. 'I'm beginning to change my mind.'

Aropethrana stared at her.

'You were thinking of trying to save us from . . . *that*?' he said, gesturing towards the noise outside the window.

'Pay her no attention, Aropethrana,' said Ngur. 'You've got other more urgent things to do than have petty arguments with this little minx. Try to kill her if it'll make you feel better, but stop attempting a debate with her. Get rid of her any way you want to. Once you've ordered all the things I've asked you to, come back here. There may be other things we can do to help defend ourselves. To be truthful with you, though, old friend, if I were you I wouldn't expect to find yourself on Albion by the end of this waking-period.'

'Neither should I,' said Alyss. 'Shall I show you what could happen to you?'

She put the tips of her two thumbs together and winked at Aropethrana.

Immediately his body was thrown past Ngur's shoulder and directly through the window, so that shards of glass showered everywhere, both inside the room and down over Giorran's wall. About twenty metres away from where Ngur was standing, Aropethrana exploded into a thousand pieces of flesh and a million drops of blood, making a red cloud.

And then Aropethrana was back in the room with them, sitting on one of the chairs, and the window was intact.

Ngur looked at her, his eyes critical.

'You're some kind of a sorceress,' he hissed. His hand moved to the hilt of his sword before he thought better of it. 'You've brought your wizardry into Giorran, and you plan to use it to destroy the House of Ellon.'

Alyss sipped her tea. Aropethrana looked as if he were about to faint.

'That,' she said, 'was not in fact what I'd intended.'

'Yes, yes,' said Ngur with angry sarcasm, 'you ally yourself with the peasants and then you tell me that you want to side with the Ellonia. Is that a likely story, witch?'

'I'm not a witch. I'm not even a sorceress.'

'You're doing a bloody good imitation of one.'

'I'm told I'm rather good at imitations,' she said. She turned to Aropethrana. 'Hurry up and do all those things that Ngur instructed you to do. They won't make a blind bit of difference, of course, but at least you'll feel as if you're doing something constructive. The war's been won, even if you two don't yet realise the inevitability of it. The final stages – the manoeuvres, if you like, which might save your miserable lives – will need to be fought out in this room between myself and Ngur. I don't like to make people feel rejected, but in this instance it would be productive if you just sort of got lost.'

'Execute her!' shouted Aropethrana at Ngur.

'No,' said the Army-Master thoughtfully, 'and, on second thoughts, don't even throw her out of Giorran.'

'You're beginning to see sense,' said Alyss. 'I don't like this tea very much.'

Ngur walked across to sit beside her.

'Frankly,' he said, 'nobody does, but it's all you're getting – all right?'

She looked at the tea fixedly. The surface of the liquid seemed to tremble momentarily, and then the room was filled with the aroma of fragrant herbs.

'That's better,' she said cheerfully. 'Now, where was I? Oh, yes. Aropethrana, could you kindly shove off so that Ngur and I can start talking seriously?'

Ngur waved dismissively at his commander.

'Do as she says.'

His face almost purple with rage, Aropethrana left, slamming the door behind him.

419

'You wish to negotiate with me so that your life may be spared,' said the Despot, leaning forwards over the table.

Alyss laughed directly into his face.

'No,' she said. 'I wish to negotiate with you so that *your* life may be spared. You've seen' – she pointed in the general direction of the window – 'what the Wind on its own can do to your militia. Even a humble singer, Barra 'ap Rteniadoli Me'gli'minter Rehan, was able to strike fear into your army using no more vicious a weapon than a bodhran. Myself, I have my own ways of destroying people, as you must realise, although I hardly ever use them. Now tell me: is it sensible to put up a show of resistance in the face of the forces ranged against you?'

'The singer . . .' Ngur began.

'He's dead until such time as I choose to recreate him. Would you like me to improve *your* tea as well?'

'That'd be kind,' he said distractedly. He looked at the window and saw how thin a sheet of glass defended Giorran from the might of the Wind. 'So what do you want of me?'

'I don't like to see carnage, whoever it is that's being killed.'

'I agree with you.'

'Then why did you allow – no, *command* – your soldiers to kill the peasants?' She looked at him with bright eyes. 'We have things to talk about.'

She twisted her fingers and the yells of the peasant army were suddenly silenced as she slowed time for all but the two of them.

'I was appointed Despot to protect the House of Ellon,' Ngur said defensively.

'The House of Ellon,' she said, leaning back in her chair and stretching her arms out to either side as if just about to yawn, 'is lucky if it's so much as a cottage by now. You've got very few options left to you, you know. Oh, yes, sure, your archers could kill a few peasants, but they couldn't kill several hundred others. Could they?'

'Things are . . . difficult,' he conceded.

'This place' – she waved an arm in a circle, embracing

all of Giorran – 'might be a charnel-house very soon. I hope that it won't be because, as I've said over and over again, the sight of humans being slaughtered depresses me. Not much – but enough. You can't do anything to make Anya's warriors turn away: if you went out of here and tried to speak peace to them, you'd be dead before you'd got half-way through the first syllable. Me, on the other hand, I could persuade them to spare the remainder of the House of Ellon. They know me. They trust me. Better than that, though, is the fact that I can *make* them trust me. If you wanted me to I could make sure that they refrained from massacring you and all that's left of the House of Ellon. I can't spare all of them, I know, but I could save *some*.'

'How?'

'As I said, I have my ways. But I won't use them – in fact, I won't be *able* to use them – unless you start to think afresh about what's going to happen in the future. You see, even *I* have my limitations. I can have the jolliest games with you humans, but I can't *make* you do things unless I can first find some way of making you *want* to do them. In that sense, you – and the rest of the Ellonia and even the peasants you so despise – have more control over the shape of the future than I have: your decisions affect it directly, whereas I, in order to change it, am forced to work through you. Right now, the sum of human decisions entails the imminent annihilation of the House of Ellon – lock, stock and barrel, the few good things along with the bad. Kindly pass me a little more tea.'

Ngur solemnly poured her a fresh cup and then, as an afterthought, poured one for himself. He was initially irritated, then amused, by the fact that, even as he poured the hot liquid, Alyss's looked and smelled so much more appealing than his own.

'Why are you trying to save us?' he said.

'I told you. I don't enjoy the sight of humans being killed unnecessarily.'

He took a gulp of tea, accepting the half-truth.

'But,' she continued, 'things will have to change. The House of Ellon will no longer rule Albion. Anya will become your ruler. I have no certainty that she'll be a more benign ruler than the Ellonian Despots have been, but I think it's likely that she will be. The aristocrats of the House of Ellon may be incarcerated for short or even long periods, but I think it improbable that they'll suffer death by torture. Even you would be spared your life.

'But,' she said, 'all of that can happen only if you surrender to me now. In a few minutes' time it'll be too late, and there'll be nothing I can do to save you.'

Ngur looked as if a great hand had taken his body and deliberately crumpled it.

'But the peasants can't rule,' he said in a low voice, 'they can't remember what's gone before and they can't think of what might happen in the future.'

'Yes, they can. Or, at least, they could.'

'What are you talking about?'

'I've been on many worlds,' Alyss said.

'What worlds?'

'Out there, there are billions in this universe alone. I once tried to count how many there are, but I got bored after a millennium and went off to do something else instead.'

'There's only the one world. Albion.'

'That's not what you believe. Is it?'

Ngur looked grey. He was about to commit open heresy . . . and in the presence of this rebarbative woman.

'No,' he said reluctantly. 'It seems to me that there might be other worlds other than this.'

'Good,' said Alyss, reaching out to pat him on the shoulder, just as a teacher might pat a child who'd answered a question with unexpected precocity.

'Albion,' she said, 'isn't even all of a single world.'

He nodded. He knew what was coming.

'It's just a part of a world. A world that's filled with human beings who look much the same as you do – and who think in the same way, too. But the skies of the rest of the world are studded with stars – bright little points of light which people can see at night. Oh, of course, you don't know what I'm talking about when I use the word "night". Elsewhere in this world, you see, the sun isn't always at the zenith: it rises and sets. During the waking-periods it seems to move slowly across the sky, and during the sleeping-periods you can't see it. The sky is black, like the inside of a dark room, except for the sparks that are the stars. Once upon a time people, even the people of Albion, could see moons as well; the moons looked like the sun, but they were white and shone very little light down upon the world. All of the stars in the sky that the people in the rest of the world can see are suns, like the one that shines down on Albion – some of them are bigger and some of them are smaller. These suns have worlds circling them – more and stranger worlds than you could possibly imagine. And the suns of all of those worlds seem to rise and set, so that there are times of light and times of darkness.'

'You're lying,' he said, without conviction. What she was describing was something totally at odds with everything he'd experienced during his life, yet he couldn't see any reason why she should deliberately lie. He shifted uneasily in his chair, feeling its hardness pressing against his buttocks, and decided that Alyss was almost certainly telling him the truth.

'Of course I am,' she said.

He started. It was almost as if she'd been reading his . . .

'Of course I am,' she repeated. 'It makes pretty dull reading, if I have to be blunt – well, I don't really *have* to be, but it's fun.'

'You tell me about these worlds . . .' he began.

'Yes.'

'And you tell me about a world that surrounds Albion?'

'Yes.'

'Where sometimes the sky is dark?'

'Yes.'

'Why should I believe you?'

'Because,' she said, 'you already do.'

'You know that?'

'Yes. I told you. I've been reading your mind, and I know everything that you've been thinking – or ever *have* thought, for that matter.'

She tapped her fingernails against the rim of her cup and smiled at him.

'But there's another thing of interest to you,' she said, 'about the world beyond Albion – and about all the other worlds I've visited, too. The sentient creatures who're there can remember their dead. They can remember all of the past and they can make sensible predictions about their future. Some of the creatures would look pretty rum to you, but we can call them all "people". One of the best friends I've ever had couldn't breathe out of water, but that didn't stop her being a person. The trouble with the House of Ellon was that, millennia ago, it stopped calling most of those who looked exactly the same as they did by that name: "people". They decided that they were a different type of creature – "peasants". It's curious what that word can do: it acts as a tag when it's applied to human beings, so that it makes them somehow less than human.'

'But the peasants,' he exploded, '*are* less than human!'

'How?'

'They're *mindless*!'

'Are they? Anya is leading an army towards your last fortress, and you call her "mindless"?'

'A sport of nature.'

'No, she's not. She's just what every one of the caste you Ellonia choose to describe as "peasants" could be, if you would allow them to be.'

Alyss caused her cup to be refilled with tea. This time it tasted even better than it had before: it was a rich and heady brew, poignant to the nose and tangy to the tongue. She wondered absently which herbs she'd brought into existence in order to create this blend.

'I don't know what you're talking about,' said Ngur hesitantly.

'No,' she said, 'you don't. The reason that you don't is that the House of Ellon stifled all mention of its crime against the peasants – the evil that it did – millennia ago.'

'What crime?' His voice was harsh.

'They imprisoned the magic in Albion. In the outer world there is magic, and it can be used for good or evil. Magic

– it's hard to describe. It's like an extra layer on top of reality; if you can sense that it's there it feels as if you can just sort of reach up above your head' – she demonstrated – 'and find your fingers wriggling in something like soft toffee. And, if you can do that, you can pull down pieces of magic towards you and make them do things for you.'

She drew her hand down.

Ngur was startled to see that she was holding a butterfly which patrolled her palm inquisitively for a moment or two before fluttering off to a far corner of the ceiling.

'Magic,' she said, 'is like the Wind – because the Wind itself is magic. You can pluck away pieces of it, as if you were calling up breezes, but really there's only one entity of magic. There's another reason it's like the Wind. It has very little conception of right or wrong, and it doesn't care about the fates of individual human beings. If you can touch magic, you can make it work for you in a bored sort of a way. It'll kill your enemies or help your friends as quickly as it can, because it wants you to leave it alone, to get along with its own preoccupations, as soon as possible.'

Ngur nodded, while at the same time listening towards the window in case the din of the rebel army recommenced.

'Your mages in Albion,' said Alyss, 'can no longer reach out and touch the magic that's there.'

'For a long time,' admitted Ngur, 'I've been convinced that they're useless. Worse than useless. Actually, some of them are so much worse than useless that one struggles to find a more apposite word.'

'You're right. But that wasn't always the case. When Albion was still a part of the World, and before the House of Ellon decided that it should be a conquest of theirs rather than a land for them to govern, your mages could do as I do – they could reach out and touch magic. There are still a few people in Albion who can touch magic – the dreamers and the singers – but the mages merely pretend to have powers that they simply haven't understood for centuries. That's because of the way that the House of Ellon used magic to isolate Albion.

'Your ancestors made a deal with magic. It must have

seemed good to them at the time, but in fact it was a rotten deal. They called in magic to keep the sun forever in the sky and to wall off Albion from the outer world. One side effect was that it took away the minds of the peasants until all that was left was enough to let them tend the constantly mutating fields. The mages who achieved this felt content: they'd obeyed the instructions of their rulers in the House of Ellon, and all seemed well – at least for a little while.

'The trouble was that magic was aggrieved by the amount that had been drawn from it, and it took its revenge. It moved itself so . . . high . . . above Albion that no mage could ever reach out and touch it again. Also, when it was far from the people of the House of Ellon, it used its imagination to start altering Albion into a pattern of colour which would be more pleasing to it. But magic is an indecisive entity, Ngur, and it still hasn't made up its mind about the configuration of the land that most appeals to it.'

She took another sip of tea and stared into his gloomy eyes.

'You've seen how I can touch magic,' she said, almost sadly. 'I can speak with it – in fact, in a way, I *am* it, just as, in another sense, it's me. So far magic has stayed well away from the House of Ellon, because of its pique over the agreement that was made all those centuries ago. But times have changed, and magic doesn't feel itself tied to the deal any longer.

'I'd make friends with magic, Ngur. If I were you, I really would.'

The hooves of the horses and the tired feet of the infantry kicked their way slowly through the cinders of the plain. Up ahead, Reen and Anya were still riding side by side, both of them silent, thinking of the man whom they'd both taken to their beds.

As they came closer to Giorran, the outline of the vast white building seemed to shimmer in the air.

Both of them had a curious physical sensation, as if time

426

had passed . . . and yet somehow hadn't. They looked at each other.

Reen smiled, a little sadly. 'Alyss,' she said.

'I wish in some ways,' Anya said in a voice that made it seem as if she were trying to make a gash in the air between them, 'that I had never met Alyss.'

'She's helped to bring us to the outskirts of Giorran. She's probably helped us to victory,' Reen pointed out.

'And in so doing she's taken away so much of *us*. This is a war which we could have won on our own – don't tell me it isn't! – and we'd have been all the prouder for having done so. Instead what's happening is that we're looking at a victory created for us by *things* that aren't a part of us – like Alyss, and the Wind, and Joli, and even Barra 'ap Rteniadoli Me'gli'minter Rehan.'

Reen sneezed. As they moved through the ashes, many of the peasants were sneezing. 'Don't call them "things",' she said eventually, her eyes streaming.

Anya didn't respond. Her mouth tight, she was looking ahead towards Giorran. Here, close to, the fortress seemed impossibly huge, straining up above them until it looked as if it were trying to scrape the few wisps of cloud down out of the sky.

The first of Aropethrana's crossbowmen fired a bolt. It took Anya through the right eye, and she fell slowly away to land in a cushion of ash.

Waving behind her, Reen drew up her own horse and leapt down. She ran to where Anya was lying and felt at her wrists and her chest. There was nothing – not even the slightest hint of a pulse.

Anya was dead.

Reen, still squatting by the girl whom she'd raised from childhood, looked up at the bright face of Giorran, and her own face twisted. Her love for Anya had been very like Rehan's – so powerful that her emotions towards the girl could never be moderate. The House of Ellon – a pampered crowd of the effete – had, in a single waking-period, killed first Barra 'ap Rteniadoli Me'gli'minter Rehan and now Anya. She'd expended her love on very few people during her lifetime. Marja had died in battle, and somehow that seemed fair enough. Syor had killed herself, and Reen still felt the pain of that implicit rejection. But both Rehan and Anya had been killed during this waking-period: their lives were very present in her memory.

In her memory.

She stared down at the head of Anya and saw the bright blood seeping into the ashes.

Reen had no writings, and she had no music. By all rights her memory should have left her already.

She looked at the warriors, who were milling about uncertainly but who seemed very definitely to know where they were and why they were here.

Again Reen squinted up at Giorran.

Alyss.

A second bolt fled from one of the narrow windows, but it twisted away and landed uselessly in the ground.

Alyss could have saved Anya's life, just as she'd saved somebody's life by causing that bolt to curve away through the air. Alyss could have saved the life of Barra 'ap Rteniadoli Me'gli'minter Rehan. Reen no longer felt any particular wrath towards the House of Ellon: they were, of course, tyrants – and very foolish and cruel tyrants. But their callousness was directed against those whom they perceived as potential threats to their welfare. That was more understandable than Alyss's apparent willingness to sacrifice those who regarded themselves as her friends.

Anya – She Who Leads – was dead.

Reen got to her feet, feeling weary. The rebels were being kept alive and fully aware only so long as it suited Alyss that this should be so. She touched the pommel of her sword.

'Stay here!' she shouted at the nearest warrior. 'Tell everyone to stay here!'

Alone, and feeling even smaller than she was, she made her way on foot towards the main entrance of Giorran.

Just outside it, she drew her sword.

They've renamed the place where Giorran once stood, of

course. Now it's called Starveling. And they still sing the song that Barra 'ap Rteniadoli Mẹ'gli'minter Rehan once created:

Seven women rode down through the town of Starveling that night,
Horses' hooves spitting galaxies in the pale moons' empty light.
And their eyes sought out the corners where the shadows grew
As deep and as dark as wine.

Somewhere along the way, though, somebody added a new verse:

The walls screamed out their agonies of age –
Too young for resignation, but much too old for rage.
But the women, with their grey hair flying, still rode on,
Isolated in their own time.

People enjoy embellishing legends. There weren't seven women, however magical that number might have been – only the one, and she was on foot, not on horseback. Later singers were unable to believe that a single woman could have done what she did, and so they took Rehan's song as being an accurate account, and then elaborated on it. The walls didn't scream, and there were then no moons to cast shadows; nor were there nights.

What happened was more prosaic.

Reen, ignoring what had now become a hail of arrows, beat on the great metal doors with the hilt of her sword. Where she was standing, directly in front of Giorran, it was almost impossible for the archers from the windows above to get any clear line on her. To her surprise the doors swung back just enough to allow her to slip through the gap. (Alyss, several floors above, smiled at Ngur.) Inside Reen found four guards, three of whom died with merciful swiftness; the fourth chose foolishly to dash out through the gates and across the burnt plain, where he was seized by the enraged peasant mob and pulled to pieces horribly slowly. The next person Reen met was a mage, who looked confused for an instant as his body fell in half, cut off just above the waist by a single backhand sweep of her sword. Reen found a doorway in the courtyard which led to a flight of stairs. Two young princesses of the House of Ellon who had decided to throw themselves on the mercy of the rebel army lost their heads as Reen ascended. On the next storey an archer who'd been aiming an arrow towards the peasants outside Giorran lost first his arm and then his intestines; an Ellonian soldier who ran to help him was stabbed with brutal force through the throat.

Already Reen's plundered Ellonian uniform was covered in blood, none of it her own. There was a grin on her face, and her eyes were points of sparkling ebony; although she was unaware of it, it was the killing-light she had so often detested seeing on Anya's face.

A fleeing mage was the next: he never saw the blow that whipped through his chest, spilling out the shreds of his lungs over his stomach. Reen found Aropethrana – to her he was just another Ellonian soldier – running along a corridor, and stabbed him in the back with such force that she had to put her foot on his neck in order to be able to pull her sword free. By then he was almost certainly dead; she made sure.

One of the soldiers was prepared to oppose her in her frenzy, and she respected him for that. He was a medium-sized man and seemed to have few skills in weaponry. They faced each other in a badly lit room; he was armed with nothing more than a light sword, barely more than a rapier.

Reen put up her own sword.

'Surrender,' she said, spitting someone's blood off her lips.

'Never!' he shouted.

'You're sure?' she said, incredulous. Without a further thought, she cut him down.

More stairs, more deaths, more blood.

It seemed that wherever she looked she could see nothing but blood. She'd passed through rooms of lightness and rooms of darkness, and now all of their walls had been sprinkled by the sticky sweetness of blood. She herself was bleeding from several superficial wounds, but she felt hardly any pain – except from a cut across her left elbow, which stung so much that it was an effort to divert her attention away from it. The shit who'd given it to her had been rather more ruthlessly killed than the rest.

There was a door guarded by two soldiers with longbows. Before either of the weapons could be raised the guards were dead, blood spreading out across the floor.

Reen threw the door open.

The room was all in white. At its centre, quite calmly, Alyss was drinking tea with a middle-aged man dressed in a cloak made of expensive cloth. Reen could feel the rage swelling up inside her.

'Oh, hello,' said Alyss, waving her towards one of the chairs. 'I was expecting you to turn up about now. I'm sure the Despot will be able to find another cup for you.'

'Anya's dead,' said Reen, hardly able to see through her fury.

'I know,' said Alyss, 'although if need be it might not be a condition that lasts forever. Come *on*, come on over here and sit down with us. Although, if you really want to know, you look as if you could do with a bath.'

'You let her die!'

'Yes.'

'Traitor!' Reen swung her sword.

'No. My loyalty's never been to Anya alone. It has suited me to be "loyal", as you would say, to all of you.'

'You allowed She Who Leads to be killed!'

Alyss gazed at Reen coolly.

'No, I didn't,' she said. 'Have a little think about it over some of this tea.'

Ngur looked backwards and forwards between the two women.

'You can take my surrender as read,' he said softly to Alyss, 'as long as you spare whatever's left of the House of Ellon.'

Alyss's green eyes were still focused on Reen's face.

'Spare them,' she said. 'Spare all of them, including this man here beside me.'

431

'Why?'

Despite herself, Reen moved towards the table.

'Because you're thirsty, and because I ask you to. There's no reason to have any more killing. Ngur, here, opposite me – he agrees, and if the Despot of the House of Ellon can say such a thing, then surely you can say the same? Do sit down. You look very tired standing there, dripping blood all over the place.'

Reen threw her sword away blindly. The blade spat against one of the walls, so that sparks flew. She paid no attention; instead she accepted some plum-coloured tea, and as she tasted the liquid she felt all her wounds healing. She took another mouthful and found that her body was whole again.

'I should have done it long ago,' said Alyss, 'and certainly, if I'd been here long ago, I would have.'

Both Reen and Ngur looked baffled.

Alyss laughed.

'Allowed you to change things, of course,' she said.

Once upon a time, very long ago, there were four people sitting on a hillside. Three of them had discovered what it was like to die, and then – something much more painful – what it was like to regain life. From left to right, as you looked at them, they were called Joli, Anya, Reen and Barra 'ap Rteniadoli Me'gli'minter Rehan. A little way behind them, further up the slope, stood Ngur, who'd once ruled over all of Albion.

What all of them were watching was a curtain of mist.

Somewhere out there was Alyss. From time to time one or other of them thought they could see her – but maybe it was just a bird flying across the moving silvery walls.

Then, starting from the foot, the mist began to clear, until soon all of them could see a huge expanse of choppy water that seemed to stretch out for the entire distance that there could ever possibly be.

Ngur came and sat beside Barra 'ap Rteniadoli Me'gli'minter Rehan. The singer turned slightly and smiled in acknowledgement of the Ellonian's arrival, then looked back out over the ocean.

Now the tapestry of the mist was reaching only halfway down from the sky, and the sun already seemed to be beginning to move slowly, like a somnambulist, away from its eternal position at the zenith. There was a little fishing vessel, far off in the distance. They could feel the magic leaking away from Albion as more and more of the mist disappeared.

Then there was a sky that was so, so much different from anything that any of them had ever seen before. It was grey, a complete cover of cloud from one horizon to the other. Now only a milky glow of light betrayed the position of the sun. It was the most beautiful sky in the world.

In the World.

She Who Leads got to her feet, feeling the stiffness in her old muscles.

Anya grinned up at her.

There were a limitless number of possibilities for the future.

And each of those possibilities was, in its turn, limitless . . .

Reprise

Let's hear it again, sings Rehan. *Let's hear that final stanza once more on behalf of the dead.*

Here are a few facts, friends, that it's very improbable that long ago you'd have liked very much.

You're a peasant, you see – you can imagine that, can't you? – and as such you're not only the lowest of the low, you're a bit lower than that. You're one of those insects that people instinctively tread on. It's not very often that you have a very strong grasp on reality, and when you get it you discover that reality's not something you particularly want to have a strong grasp on, because those are the occasions when the convoys of the Ellonia come through your village to take away everything you have, leaving you with just enough so that you can survive until the next time they come to take away . . .

You get the general picture?

Actually, you wouldn't have if you'd been around then. If you'd had the mental apparatus to get the general picture you'd have been dead long ago, and nobody would have remembered you, not to mention your mental apparatus.

So let's start from the top again.

There's a new waking-period and so you fall out of bed and find yourself something to eat – usually a not very nice something, but at least it'll keep you going until the middle of the waking-period. It might be a few mouthfuls of the grain that the animals would prefer not to eat. Nevertheless, although a tiny part of your body seems to recall having disliked this fodder before, the rest of your body is overjoyed that your hunger is

435

being assuaged. You and your mate, your minds on your stomachs, leave your cottage or shack and those of your children who're too young to work, and you go to the fields. Picture it. There, under the bright blue of the sky, you pick fruit or gather grain until it seems that your back wants to split into tiny splinters; after you've worked a little longer, you slowly head for home, remembering only very approximately where home is – which is hardly surprising, because home is only approximately where it was when you left it. You bring with yourself a tiny proportion of the food that you've gathered – no more than that, because you have no wish to bring down the wrath of the House of Ellon upon your village.

All you can think about as you climb into bed with your mate is your weariness. You can't recall why you're tired: indeed, you don't properly realise that you're tired, because that's the way you always are. Instead you think for a short time until the thinking stops and you're asleep.

It's different when the Ellonia come.

Those are waking-periods which you're likely to remember at least until it's the time for you to sleep, and perhaps even beyond that. They take things away from you and they invade your bodies: usually it's the women who're assaulted, but the Ellonian soldiers are not always averse to the bodies of men. You think of the way that you've watched their invasion of your friends, and for a while the memory is fire in your mind, but then it seems to fade away until it's something you can no longer grasp.

That's the end of your anger.

It's not so much that you've forgotten the event as that you've forgotten your sense of outrage.

Then there's a different waking-period.

There's someone who comes among you who's different from all of the villagers whom you vaguely recognise every time you come across them.

Because this person is here, you find that you remember everything from one waking-period to the next – and to the next after that.

It's not just a matter of the events: you also recall the emotions that you felt when those events were taking place. You discover how much love there is inside you, because you've made love hundreds of times with your mate and, until now, remembered nothing of the love. But there's another thing: your fury at what has been done to you.

So the person who's come among you, and who has the power to give you back your memories and your feelings, is somebody whom you regard as very valuable. The sudden exposure to your emotions is a bit of a shock, and is normally quite painful, but it's as if you'd been surrounded by a suffocating mist all of your life and abruptly it had retreated. Now all the colours of the world are different, almost like someone had taken the time to wash them so they looked cleaner. The brightness and blackness you've never seen before sometimes hurt your eyes, but you find yourself glorying in them.

Your village is host to a small party of other peasants who have the power to open up your memories. In fact, there are only three of them. They explain that they have names, and then they explain to you what names are and then why it is so important for you, too, to have a name. These are particularly difficult concepts for you to understand until they give you a name, and then you look at the bits of your body you can see – your arms and your legs – and you realise that this mess of syllables, your name, describes not just all of that but also you, yourself, the part of you that is capable of understanding what's going on.

As soon as you give permission, a few hundred others of their kind come to your village. They're fine people, and they want you to be their friend, and so of course you agree, because it's only now that the idea of friendship seems to make any sense to you.

Well.

There's no need any longer for warfare, and the reason is that you've all been given a name, and now you're all a part of the World.

The long bitterness and the pain that was always there for all of you – peasants and Ellonia alike – have gone now, thought Alyss, *and their burden on you will ease with time.*

She spiralled higher and higher above the motionless landscape of Albion, a dot against the mother-of-pearl sky.

Live with the love that I have for you, she thought, *and live well with it.*

But all of that, sings Rehan, was in the old days.

A selection of bestsellers from Headline

BURYING THE SHADOW	Storm Constantine	£4.99 □
SCHEHERAZADE'S NIGHT OUT	Craig Shaw Gardner	£4.99 □
WULF	Steve Harris	£4.99 □
EDGE OF VENGEANCE	Jenny Jones	£5.99 □
THE BAD PLACE	Dean Koontz	£5.99 □
HIDEAWAY	Dean Koontz	£5.99 □
BLOOD GAMES	Richard Laymon	£4.99 □
DARK MOUNTAIN	Richard Laymon	£4.99 □
SUMMER OF NIGHT	Dan Simmons	£4.99 □
FALL OF HYPERION	Dan Simmons	£5.99 □
DREAM FINDER	Roger Taylor	£5.99 □
WOLFKING	Bridget Wood	£4.99 □

All Headline books are available at your local bookshop or newsagent, or can be ordered direct from the publisher. Just tick the titles you want and fill in the form below. Prices and availability subject to change without notice.

Headline Book Publishing PLC, Cash Sales Department, Bookpoint, 39 Milton Park, Abingdon, OXON, OX14 4TD, UK. If you have a credit card you may order by telephone — 0235 831700.

Please enclose a cheque or postal order made payable to Bookpoint Ltd to the value of the cover price and allow the following for postage and packing:
UK & BFPO: £1.00 for the first book, 50p for the second book and 30p for each additional book ordered up to a maximum charge of £3.00.
OVERSEAS & EIRE: £2.00 for the first book, £1.00 for the second book and 50p for each additional book.

Name ....

Address ....

....

....

If you would prefer to pay by credit card, please complete:
Please debit my Visa/Access/Diner's Card/American Express (delete as applicable) card no:

Signature ....Expiry Date ......